WATER FIRE FAE
STORIES

WATER FIRE FAE

STORIES

CARRIE VAUGHN

Carrie Vaughn, LLC, Boulder, CO

ALSO BY CARRIE VAUGHN

The Kitty Series
Kitty Saves the World
Low Midnight
Kitty in the Underworld
Kitty Rocks the House
Kitty Steals the Show
Kitty's Big Trouble
Kitty Goes to War
Kitty's House of Horrors
Kitty Raises Hell
Kitty and the Dead Man's Hand
Kitty and the Silver Bullet
Kitty Takes a Holiday
Kitty Goes to Washington
Kitty and The Midnight Hour
Kitty's Greatest Hits (collection)
The Immortal Conquistador (collection)
Kitty's Mix-Tape (collection)
The Cormac and Amelia Case Files (collection)

OTHER BOOKS

Questland
The Wild Dead
Bannerless
Martians Abroad
Dreams of the Golden Age
After the Golden Age
Discord's Apple
Steel
Voices of Dragons
Amaryllis and Other Stories (collection)
Straying from the Path (collection)

Table of Contents

This goes out to the backers of my
WATER FIRE FAE Kickstarter campaign.
Thank you!

THAT GAME WE PLAYED DURING THE WAR

From the moment she left the train station, absolutely everybody stopped to look at Calla. They watched her walk across the plaza and up the steps of the Northward Military Hospital. In her dull gray uniform she was like a storm cloud moving among the khaki of the Gaantish soldiers and officials. The peace between their peoples was holding; seeing her should not have been such a shock. And yet, she might very well have been the first citizen of Enith to walk across this plaza without being a prisoner.

Calla wasn't telepathic, but she could guess what every one of these Gaantish was thinking: What was she doing here? Well, since they *were* telepathic, they'd know the answer to that. They'd wonder all the same, but they'd know. It would be a comfort not to have to explain herself over and over again.

It was also something of a comfort not bothering to hide her fear. Technically, Enith and Gaant were no longer at war. That did not mean these people didn't hate her for the uniform she wore. She didn't think much of their uniforms either, and all the harm soldiers like these had done to her and those she loved. She couldn't hide that, and so let the emotions slide right through her and away. She felt strangely light, entering the hospital lobby, and her smile was wry.

Some said Enith and Gaant were two sides of the same coin; they would never see eye to eye and would always fight over the same spit of land between their two continents. But their differences were simple, one might say: only in their minds.

The war had ended recently enough that the hospital was crowded. Many injured, many recovering. In the lobby, Calla had to pause a moment, the scents and sounds and bustle of the place were so familiar, recalling for her every base or camp where she'd been stationed, all her years as a nurse and then as a field medic. She'd spent the whole war in places like this, and her hands itched for work. Surely someone needed a temperature taken or a dressing changed? No amount of exhaustion had ever quelled that impulse in her.

But she was a visitor here, not a nurse. Tucking her short hair behind her ears, brushing some lint off her jacket, she walked to the reception desk and approached the young woman in a khaki uniform sitting there.

"Hello. I'm here to see one of your patients, Major Valk Larn. I think all my paperwork is in order." Speaking slowly and carefully because she knew her accent in Gaantish was rough, she unfolded said paperwork from its packet: passport, visa, military identification, and travel permissions.

The Gaantish officer stared at her. Her hair under her cap was pulled back in a severe bun; her whole manner was very strict and proper. Her tabs said she was a second lieutenant—just out of training and the war ends, poor thing. Or lucky thing, depending on one's point of view. Calla wondered what the young lieutenant made of the mess of thoughts pouring from her. If she saw the sympathy or only the pity.

"You speak Gaantish," the lieutenant said bluntly.

Calla was used to this reaction. "Yes. I spent a year at the prisoner camp at Ovorton. Couldn't help but learn it, really. It's a long story." She smiled blandly.

Seeing the whole of that long story in an instant, the woman glanced away quickly. She might have been blushing, either from confusion or embarrassment, Calla couldn't tell. Didn't really matter. Whatever it was, she covered it up by examining Calla's papers.

"Technician Calla Belan, why are you here?" The lieutenant sounded amazed.

Calla chuckled. "Really?" She wasn't hiding anything; Valk and her worry for him were at the front of her mind.

The other Gaantish soldiers in the lobby were too polite to stare at the exchange, but they glanced over. If they really focused they could learn everything about her. They were welcome to her history. It *was* interesting.

"What's in your bag?" the lieutenant said.

Some food, a couple of paperbacks for the trip, her chess set in its small pine box. Calla couldn't help but think of it, and the woman saw it all. Calla could only smuggle in contraband if someone had put it there without her knowledge, or if she had forgotten about it.

The lieutenant's brow furrowed. "Chess? That's a game? May I see it?"

It still startled Calla sometimes, the way they just *knew*. "Yes, of course," she said, and opened the flap of her shoulder bag. The lieutenant drew out the box, studied it. Maybe to reassure herself that it didn't pose a threat. The lieutenant could see, through Calla, that it was just a game.

"Am I going to be able to see Major Larn?" With a glance, the lieutenant would know everything he meant to her. Calla waited calmly for her answer.

"Yes. Here. Just a moment." The lieutenant took a card out of her drawer and filled out the information listed on it. The card attached to a clip. "Pin this to your lapel. People will still stop you, but this will explain everything. You shouldn't have trouble. Any more trouble." The young woman was too prim to really smile, but she seemed to be making an effort at kindness. Calla was likely the first real Enithi the young woman had ever met in person. To think, here Calla was, doing her part for the peace effort. That was a nice way of looking at it, and maybe why Valk had asked her to come.

"Go down that corridor," the young woman directed. She consulted a printed roster on a clipboard. "Major Larn is in Ward 6, on the right."

"Thank you." The gratitude was genuine, and the lieutenant would see that along with everything else.

Enithi never lied to the Gaantish. This was a known, proverbial truth. There was no point to it. Through all the decades of war, Enith never sent spies—or, rather, they never told the spies they sent that they were spies. They delivered messages without telling the bearers they were messengers. Their methods of conducting espionage had become so arcane, so complex, that Gaant rarely discovered them. Both sides counted on this one truth: Enithi never bothered lying when confronted with telepaths. The Gaantish had captured thousands of Enithi soldiers, who simply and immediately confessed everything they knew. Enithi were known to be a practical people, without any shame to speak of.

Enith kept any Gaant soldiers it captured sedated, drugged to delirium, to frustrate their telepathy. The nurses who looked after them were chosen for their cheerful dispositions and generally straightforward thoughts. Calla Belan had been one of those nurses. Valk Larn had been one of those prisoners when they first met—only a lieutenant then. It had been a long time ago.

Gaantish soldiers continued staring at her as she walked down the corridor. Some men in bandages waited on benches, probably for checkups in a nearby exam room. Renovations were going on— replacing light fixtures, looked like. In all their eyes, her uniform marked her. She probably shouldn't have worn it but was rather glad she had. Let them know exactly who she was.

On the other hand, she always felt that if the Enithi and Gaantish all took off their uniforms they would look the same: naked.

One of the workmen at the top of a ladder, pliers in hand to wire a new light, choked as she thought this, and glanced at her. A few others were blushing, hiding grins. She smiled. Another blow struck for peace.

Past several more doorways and many more stares, she found Ward 6. She paused a moment to take it in and restore her balance. The wide room held some twenty beds, all of them filled. Most of the patients seemed to be sleeping. She guessed these were serious but stable cases, needing enough attention to stay here but not so much that there was urgency. Patients had bandages at the end of stumps that had been arms or legs, gauze taped over their heads or wrapped around their chests, broken and splinted limbs. A pair of nurses was on hand, moving from bed to bed, adjusting suspended IV bottles, checking dressings. The situation's familiarity was calming.

The nurses looked at her, then glanced at each other, and the loser of that particular silent debate came toward Calla. She waited while the man studied her badge.

"I'm here to see Major Larn," Calla said carefully, politely, no matter that the nurse would already know. By now, Calla was thinking of nothing else.

"Yes," the nurse said, still startled. "He's here."

"He's well?" Calla couldn't help but ask.

"He will be. He—he will be glad to see you, when he wakes up. But you should let him sleep for now." Between Calla and Valk, how much was the nurse seeing that couldn't be put into words?

"Oh, yes, of course. May I wait?"

The nurse nodded and gestured to a stray chair, waiting by the wall for just such a purpose.

"Thank you," Calla said, happy to display her gratitude, though she was afraid this only confused them. They could see that Valk was more important to her than other considerations, even patriotism. They could not see why, because Calla was confused about that herself. Calla fetched the chair and looked for Valk.

And there he was, in the last bed in the row, a curtain partially pulled around him for privacy. He'd been like this the first time she'd seen him, lying on a thin hospital mattress, well-muscled arms at his sides, his face lined with the worries of a dream. More lines now, perhaps, but he was one of those men who was aging into a rather heart-stopping rough handsomeness. At least she thought so. He would laugh at her thought, then wrinkle his brow and ask her if she was thinking true.

An IV fed into his arm, a blanket lay pulled over his stomach, but it didn't completely hide the bandage. He'd had abdominal surgery. Before settling in, she checked the chart hanging on a clipboard at the foot of the bed. She'd never really learned to read Gaantish, but could read medical charts from when she was at Overton and they'd put her to work. Injuries: Internal bleeding, repaired. Shrapnel in the gut. He'd been cleaned and patched up, but a touch of septicemia had set in. He was recovering well, but had been restricted to bed rest in the ward, under observation, because past experience showed that he could not be trusted to rest without close supervision. He was under mild sedation to assist in keeping him still. So yes, this was Valk.

She settled in to wait for him to wake up.

"Calla. Calla. Hey."

She woke at her name, shook dreams and worries away, and opened her eyes to see Valk looking back. He must have been terribly weak—he only turned his head. Didn't even try to sit up.

He was smiling. He said something too quickly and softly for her to catch.

"My Gaantish is rusty, Major." She was surprised at the relief she felt. In her worst imaginings, he didn't recognize her.

"I'll always recognize you," he said, slowly this time. He switched to Enithi, "I said, this is like the first time I saw you, in a chair near my bed."

She felt her own smile dawn. "I wasn't asleep then. I should know better than to fall asleep around you people."

"They tell me the cease-fire is holding. The treaty is done. It must be, if you're here."

"The treaty isn't done but the peace is holding. My diplomatic pass to see you only took a week to process."

"Soon we'll have tourists running back and forth."

"Then what'll they do with us?"

His smile was comforting. It meant the bad old days really were done. If he could hope, anyone could hope. And just like that, his smile thinned, or became thoughtful, or something. She couldn't tell what he was thinking. Never could, and usually it didn't bother her.

She said, "They—people have been very polite to me here."

"Good. Then I will not need to have words with anyone. Calla— thank you for coming. I'd have come to find you, if I'd been able."

"I worried when you told me where you were."

"I have been rather worried myself."

His telegram had said only two things: *I would like to see you*, and *Bring the game if you can*. A very strange message at a very strange time. Strange to anyone except her, anyway. It made perfect sense to her. She had explained it to the visa people and passport department and military attachés like this: *We have a history*. He had been her prisoner, then she had been his, and they had made a promise that if peace ever came they would finish the game they had started. If they finished the game it meant the peace would last.

Calla suspected that none of the Enithi officials who reviewed her request knew what to make of it, but it seemed so weird, and they were so curious, they approved it. On the Gaantish side, Valk was enough of a war hero that they didn't dare deny the request. Out of such happenstances was a peace constructed.

She looked around—there was a bedside table on wheels that could be pulled over for meals and exams and such. Drawing the chess set from her bag, she set it on the table.

"Ah," Valk said. He started to sit up.

"No." She touched his shoulder, keeping him in place with as strong a thought as she could manage. This made him grin. "There's got to be some way to raise the bed."

She'd moved to the front of the bed to start poking around when one of the nurses came running over. "Here, I'll do that," he said quickly.

Calla stepped out of his way with a wry look. Gaantish hospitals didn't have buzzers for nurses. It had driven her rather mad, back in the day. In short order, the man had the bed propped up and Valk resting upright. He seemed more himself, then.

The chess set opened into the game board, painted in black and white alternating squares, and a little tray that slid out held all the pieces, stylized carvings in stained wood. Valk leaned forward, anticipation in his gaze. "I haven't even seen anything like this since we played back at Overton."

Gaant did not have chess. They did not have any games at all that required strategy or bluffing. There was no point. Instead, they played games based on chance—dice rolls and drawn cards—or balance, pulling a single wooden block out of a stack of blocks, for example. And they never cheated.

But Calla had taught Valk chess and developed a system for playing against him. Only someone from Enith would have thought of it. The two countries had approached the war much the same way.

"I'm rusty as well. We'll be on even footing."

Valk laughed. They'd never been on even footing and they both knew it. But they both compensated, so it all worked out.

"I made a note of where the last game left off. Or would you rather start a new one?"

"Let's finish the last." He might have said it because she was thinking it, too.

She arranged the pieces the way they had been, and reminded herself how the game had gone so far. There was a lot to recall. She didn't remember some of the details, but given the rules and given the pieces, she only had so many choices of what to do next. She considered them all.

"It was your move, I think," she said.

He studied her rather than the board. The Gaantish didn't have to see someone to see their thoughts—a blind Gaant was still telepathic. But looking was polite, as in any conversation. And it was intimidating, in an interrogation. This idea that they could see *through* you. Enithi soldiers told stories about how when a Gaantish person read your mind, it hurt. That they could inflict pain. This wasn't true. Gaant encouraged the stories anyway, along with the ones about how any one of them could see the thoughts of every person in the world, when they couldn't see much past the walls of a given room.

Valk was going to decide, by seeing her thoughts, what move he ought to make, what move she hoped he would, based on her knowledge and experience. He would try to deduce for himself the best choice. And then he would know, almost as soon as she did herself, how she would counter. She kept her expression still, as if that mattered. He moved a piece, and she saw her thoughts reflected back at her—it was just what she would have done, if the board had been reversed.

Next came her turn, and it was no good staring at the board, analyzing the rooks and pawns and playing out future moves in her mind. All such planning would betray her here. So, almost without looking, almost without thought, she reached, put her hand on a piece—any piece, it hardly mattered—and moved it. A bishop this time, and she only moved one square, and yet it was as if a bit of chaos had descended on the board and disrupted everything. No sane chess player would have made that move, and she herself had to pause and consider what she'd done, what new lines of play existed, and how she could possibly go forward from here.

But, and this was the point, the telepathic Valk had not been expecting what she'd just done.

Playing at random was no way to play chess, and she was sure her old teachers were turning in their graves. Unless, she would explain to them, you're playing with a Gaantish commander. Then the joy in the game became watching him squirm.

"I am glad you are enjoying this," Valk said.

"I am. Are you?"

"I am," he said, looking at her. "This gives me hope."

She had traveled here because she had nothing left. Because she was unhappy. Because her whole life had been spent in this uniform, for all the pain it had brought her, so what did she do now? She hadn't had an answer until Valk sent that telegram.

And now he was frowning. She'd been able to keep up a good front before this.

"We are all of us wounded," he said softly.

"It's your move."

He chose his piece, a pawn, a completely different move than the one she'd been thinking of, which made her next choices more interesting. This time, she took the correct one, the one she'd do if she'd been playing seriously.

"This isn't serious?" he asked.

"I'm never serious." Which he'd know was a lie, but he smiled anyway.

She'd taught him to play when she was his prisoner, but he asked to learn because of what he'd seen when he was her prisoner. She'd had a game running in the prison ward with one of the other nurses. They'd slip in plays between their rounds, in odd down moments, to clear their minds and pass the time. This job wasn't real nursing, when all they had to do was administer medications, make sure no one had allergies or bad reactions to the drugs, and keep their patients muzzy-headed. Their board had been set up in Valk's ward that day. Calla had been grinning because her opponent was about to lose, and he was studying the board with furrowed brow and deep concentration, looking for a way out.

A voice had said, "Hey. Hey. You." He might have been speaking either Enithi or Gaantish. Hard to tell with so few words. Their handsome prisoner was waking up, calling for their attention. Because it wasn't her turn, Calla had been the one to jump up and get her kit. They'd had trouble getting the dosage right on Valk; he had a high tolerance for the stuff. But they couldn't have him reading minds, so she made a mark on his chart and injected more into his IV lead.

"No," he'd protested, watching the syringe with a helpless panic. "No, please, I just want to talk—" He spoke very good Enithi.

"I'm sorry," she said, and she really was. "We've got to keep you under. It's better, really. I know you understand."

And he did, or at least he'd see what she understood, that it wasn't just about keeping information from him. It also kept the Gaantish prisoners safe, when otherwise they'd be outnumbered and battered by hostile thoughts. He still looked very unhappy as he sank back against the bed and his eyelids shut inexorably. As if something fragile had slipped out of his hand.

"Poor things," Calla said, brushing a bit of lint off the man's forehead.

"You're very weird, Cal," her chess partner said, finally making his move. "They're Gaantish. You pity them?"

"I just think it must be hard, being so far from home in a place like this."

She found out later that Valk hadn't quite been asleep through all that.

Valk made his next move and winced, just as a nurse came over with a hypodermic syringe and vial on a tray, sensing his pain before he even knew it was there.

"No," Valk said, putting up a hand before the nurse could set the tray down.

"You're in pain; this will help you rest," he said.

"But Technician Belan is here."

"Y-yes sir." The man went away without administering the sedative.

So much conversation didn't need to be spoken when the participants could read each other's minds. They would only say aloud the conclusion they had come to, or the polite niceties that opened and closed conversations. The rest was silent. Back at Ovorton it had often left her reeling, when she was meant to be working with a patient and two nearby doctors came to a decision, only ten percent of which had been spoken out loud, and they stared at her like she was some idiot child when she didn't understand. She had learned to take delight in saying out loud, forcefully, "You have to tell me what you want me to do." They'd often be frustrated with her, but it served them right. They could always send her back to the prisoner barracks. But they didn't; they didn't have enough nurses as it was. She had accepted an offer to trade the freedom of the rest of her unit for her skills—send the others home in a prisoner swap and she would work as a nurse for the Gaantish infirmary. They trusted her in the position because they would always know if she meant ill. Staying had been harder than she expected.

The nurse lingered near the game. It made Calla just a little bit nervous, like those days at the camp, surrounded by telepaths, and she the only person who hadn't brought a spear to the war.

"This is a very complicated game," the nurse observed, and that made Calla smile. That was why Valk told her he wanted to learn—it was very complicated. The thoughts people thought while playing it were methodical, yet rich.

"It is," Valk said.

"May I watch?" the nurse asked.

Valk looked to Calla to answer, and she said, "Yes, you may."

Enithi troops told awful stories about what it must be like in Gaantish prisoner camps. There'd be no privacy, no secrets. The guards would know everything about your fears and weaknesses, they could design tortures to your exact specifications, they could bribe you with the one thing that would make you break. No worse fate than being captured by Gaant and put in one of their camps.

In fact, it worked the other way around. The camps were nightmares for the guards, who spent all day surrounded by a thousand minds who were terrified, furious, hurt, lonely, angry, and depressed.

As a matter of etiquette, Gaantish people learned—the way that small children learned not to take off their pants and run around naked just anywhere—to guard their thoughts. To keep them close. To keep them calm, so they didn't disrupt those around them. If they often seemed expressionless or unemotional, this was actually politeness, as Calla learned.

To the Gaantish, Enithi prisoners were very, very loud. The guards working the camps got hazard pay. They didn't, in fact, torture their prisoners at all. First, they didn't need to. Second, they wouldn't have been able to stand it.

When her unit had been captured, processed, and sent to the camp, she had been astonished because Lieutenant Valk Larn—now Captain Larn—had been one of the officers in charge. Her shock of recognition caused every telepath in the room to stop and look at her. They would have turned back to their work soon enough—that she and Valk had encountered each other before was coincidental but maybe not remarkable. What made them continue staring: Calla revealed affection for Valk. Not outwardly, so much. She stood with the rest of her unit, stripped down to shirts and trousers, wrists hobbled, hungry and sleep-deprived. No, outwardly she'd been amazed, seeing her former patient upright and in uniform, steely and commanding as any recruitment poster. Her expression looked shocked enough that her sergeant at her side had dared to whisper, "Cal, are you okay?"

The Gaantish never asked each other how they were doing. She'd learned that back in the ward, looking after Valk. During his brief lucid moments she'd ask him how he was feeling, and he'd stare at her like she was playing a joke on him.

The emotion of affection was plain to those who could see it—everyone in a Gaantish uniform. And she was, under all that week's pain and discomfort and unhappiness and uncertainty, almost happy to see him. She was the kind of nurse who had a favorite patient, even in a prison hospital.

He couldn't *not* see her, not with every Gaantish soldier staring at her, then looking at him to see his reaction. She couldn't hide her astonishment; she didn't want to and didn't try. She did realize this likely made the meeting harder for him than it did for her—whatever he thought of her, his staff would all see it. She didn't know what he thought of her.

He merely nodded and waved the group on to continue processing, and they were washed down, given lumpy brown jumpsuits and assigned quarters. Later, she suspected he'd been the one to arrange the deal that won the rest of her unit's freedom.

Calla had always thought it strange that people asked if prisoners were treated "well." "Were you treated well?" *No*, she thought. The doors were locked. The guards all had guns. Did it matter if they had food and blankets, a roof? The food was strange, the blankets leftover from what the army used. Instead she answered, "We were not treated badly." They were treated appropriately. War necessitated prisoners, since the alternative was slaughtering everyone on both sides, which both sides agreed was not ideal. You treated prisoners appropriately so that your own people would be treated appropriately in turn. That meant different things.

She was treated appropriately, which made it odd the day, only a week or so into her captivity, that Valk had her brought to his office alone. It wasn't so odd that the guards hesitated or looked at either of them strangely. But she had been afraid. Helpless, afraid, everything. They left the binders around her wrists. All she could do was stand there before his desk and wonder if he was the kind of man who enjoyed hurting his prisoners, who enjoyed minds in pain. She wouldn't have thought so, but she'd only ever known him when he was asleep and the brief waking moments when he seemed so lost and confused she couldn't help but pity him, so what did she know?

"I won't hurt you," he said, after a long moment when he simply watched her, and she tried to hide her shaking. "You can believe me." He asked her to sit. She remained standing, as he must have known she would.

"You were one of the nurses at the hospital. I remember you."

"Not many remember their stays there."

"I remember you. You were kind."

She couldn't not be. It was why she'd become a nurse. She didn't have to say anything.

"You were playing a game. I remember—two people. A board. You enjoyed it very much. You had the most interesting thoughts."

She didn't have to think long to remember. Those afternoon games with Elio had been a good time. "Chess. It was chess."

"Can you teach me to play?"

"Sir, I'd lose every single time. I'm not sure you'd enjoy the game. Not much challenge."

"Nevertheless, I would like to learn it."

This presented a dilemma. Could it be interpreted as cooperating with the enemy? More than she already was? He couldn't force her. On the other hand, was this an opportunity? But for what? She was a medic, not a spy. Not that Enith even had spies. Valk gave her plenty of time to think this over, waiting patiently, not revealing if her mental arguments and counterarguments amused or irritated him.

"I don't have a board or pieces."

"What would you need to make them?"

She told him she would have to think about it, which would have been hilarious if she hadn't been so tired and confused. The guards took her back to her cell, where she talked to the ranking Enithi officer prisoner about it. "Might not be a bad thing to have a friend here," he advised.

"But he'll know I'm faking it!" she answered.

"So?" he'd said, and he was right. Calla was what she was and it wouldn't do any good to think differently. She asked for a square of cardboard and a black marker and did up a board, and drew rudimentary pieces on other little squares of cardboard. She'd rather have cut them out but didn't bother asking for scissors, and no one offered, so that was that. It was the ugliest chess set that had ever existed.

Valk learned very quickly because she already knew the rules and all she had to do was think them and he learned. The strategy of it was rather more difficult to teach. He'd get this screwed-up look of concentration, and she might have understood a little bit of what attracted him to the game: There was a lot to think about, and Valk liked the challenge of so much thought coming out of one person. And yes, he always knew what moves she was planning. Which was when she started playing at random. If she could surprise herself, she could surprise him. Then she agreed to the deal to get her people released, she worked in their hospital, they played chess, and she got sick.

She could not learn to marshal her thoughts and emotions the way these people learned to as children. She tried, as a matter of survival, and only managed to stop feeling anything at all.

The diagnosis was depression—Gaant's mental health people were very good. She, who had been so generally high-spirited for most of her life, had had no idea what was happening or how to cope and had grown very ill indeed, until it wasn't that she didn't want to play chess against Valk. She *couldn't*. She couldn't keep her mind on the game, couldn't recognize the pieces by looking at them, couldn't even think of how they moved. One day, walking in a haze between one ward and another at the hospital, she sank to the floor and stayed there. Valk was summoned. He held her hand and tried to see into her, to see what was wrong.

She didn't remember thinking anything at the time. Only seeing the image of her hand in his and not understanding it.

He arranged for her to be part of another prisoner swap, and she went home. Before the transfer he took her aside and spoke softly. "I forget that this is all opaque to you, that you don't know most of what's going on around you. So, since I didn't say it before: Thank you."

"For what?" she'd replied. He'd looked at her blankly, because he didn't seem to know himself. Not enough to be able to explain it, and she couldn't see.

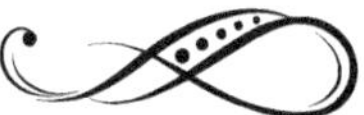

Others came to watch the game—drawn, Calla presumed, by the tangle of thoughts she and Valk were producing. He was getting frustrated. She was playing with the giddy abandon of the six-year-old she had been when her mother taught her the game. And now the whole room shared her fond memories, and the fact that her mother had died in one of the famines that wracked Enith when food production had been disrupted by the war. Ten years ago now. Everyone on both sides had stories like that. *Let us share our stories*, she thought.

"You won't win, playing like that," one of the observing doctors said. After half an hour of watching they probably all understood the rules completely and could play themselves. They'd have no idea how the game was really supposed to be played, however. She wasn't playing properly *at all*, which was rather a lot of fun.

"No, but I may not lose," she said.

"I'm still not sure what the point of this game is," said a nurse, her confusion plain.

"This game, right now? The point is to annoy Major Larn," Calla said. This got a chuckle from them—those who'd been looking after him knew him well. Valk, however, smiled at her. She had not spoken the truth, precisely. Everyone else was too polite to say anything.

"The point," Valk said, addressing the nurse, "is to fight little wars without hurting anyone."

And there was silence then, because yes, they all had stories.

He made his next move and took his hand away. Her gaze lit, her heart opening. Even the way she played with him, all messy and at random, a moment like this could still happen, where the board opened up as if by magic and her way was clear. Because it was her turn it didn't matter if he knew what she was thinking, because he couldn't do anything about it. She moved the rook, and his king was cornered.

"Check."

It wasn't mate. He could still get out of it. But he really was backed into a corner, because his next moves and hers would all lead back to check, and they could chase each other around the board, and it would be splendid. Neither could have planned for this.

He threw up his hands and settled back against his pillow. "I'm exhausted. You've exhausted me." She laughed a gleeful, satisfied laugh.

The observers looked on. "This is how you won," one of them said, amazed. He wasn't talking about the game.

"No," Calla said. "This is how we failed to lose."

"I learned the difference from her," Valk said, and was that a bit of pride in his tone? She might never know for certain.

Calla started resetting the board for the next game, not even realizing that meant she was having a good time. The nurse interrupted her.

"Technician Belan, the major really must rest now," he said kindly, recognizing Calla's eagerness when she herself didn't.

"Oh. Of course."

"I promise I'll rest in just a moment," Valk said. He was speaking to the doctors and attendants, who'd expressed a concern she couldn't see. They drifted away because he wanted them to.

That left them studying each other; he who could see everything, and she who could only muddle through, being herself, proudly and unabashedly.

She asked, abruptly, "Do you still have that old cardboard set I made?"

"No. When Ovorton closed, I lost track of it. Probably got swept away with the trash."

"Good," she said. "It was very ugly."

"I miss it," Valk said.

"You shouldn't. I'm glad it's all over. So glad."

That dark place that she barely remembered opened up, and she started crying. She had thought to pretend that none of it ever happened, and so carried around this blackness that no one could see, and it would have swallowed her up if Valk hadn't sent that telegram. She got that message and knew it was all true, knew it had all happened, and he would be able to see her.

She scrubbed tears from her face and didn't try to hide any of this.

"I wasn't sure how much you remembered," Valk said softly.

"I wasn't sure either," she said, laughing now. Laughing and crying. The darkness shrank.

"Are you sorry you came?"

"Oh, no. It's just…" She put her hand in his and tried to explain. Discovered she couldn't speak. She had no words. And it didn't matter.

THE GIRL WHO LOVED SHONEN KNIFE

I only want one thing in the whole world: for my band, Flying Jelly Attack, the world's greatest Shonen Knife cover band, to play at Cherry Blossom High School's Spring Dance. Two things stand in my way:

1) Lizard Blood, a Lolita death metal band, our bitter rivals

2) The end of the world

Lizard Blood isn't a real band. They only care about going viral and how many hits they get on UltraPluz. They never really learned to play their instruments. Instead, they use synthesizers plugged into programmable neuromuscular implants, upload whatever song they want to play, and play it—or "play" it, rather. They even have their implants synched so they play together—not that that really matters when it's death metal.

Lizard Blood's fake lead singer and fake lead guitarist, Yuki Niamori, is very rich—or at least her family is— and she can have anything she wants. What she wants is to be lead singer of a Lolita death metal band that will play at Cherry Blossom High School's Spring Dance.

She must be stopped.

As for the end of the world, I'm not really paying attention. It's got something to do with cyber attacks on big banks draining all the money out of their systems—not transferring it, not stealing it, just deleting it as if it never existed. The banks are shutting down and the government can't stop it. Experts are saying to change your online passwords and stuff, but that doesn't help because the hackers fix the system so it doesn't need passwords at all. Change your passwords and biometric logins all you want, doesn't matter. The hackers still delete everything you have.

It's not like I have much money anyway, since I spend everything on guitar strings and upgrading my amps. And we still have to go to school, even though half the teachers haven't shown up all week and the other half are threatening to strike if they don't get paid soon. Our parents are making us go because they think it's safe—Cherry Blossom High School's security guards are still here when the actual police have fled the city. It's all very complicated, but I'm working too hard to get the chord progression right on "Brown Mushrooms" to notice. If we don't get to play at the Spring Dance, nothing else will matter.

The big audition for who gets to play at the Spring Dance is in three days. Only two bands have signed up: Flying Jelly Attack and Lizard Blood. Attrition—we scared everybody off. Yuki possibly made threats—at least, she's made them to us.

Miki, my bass player, says our best course of action is to avoid Yuki and her girls entirely. Ru, my drummer, goes into a murderous rage whenever we even mention Yuki or Lizard Blood. She's prone to murderous rages, where all her hair stands on end and her eyes go wide and she bares her teeth like some kind of demon. Miki and I both have to hold her back to keep her from doing damage. It's this kind of thing that makes her a great drummer.

Trouble is, we can't avoid our enemy entirely when our enemy seems bent on searching us out.

There we are, just hanging out between classes—or these days, just hanging out until we find out whether we'll even be *having* classes. Miki, hair in a ponytail and her wire-rimmed glasses slipping down her nose, hunches over her deck doing something online—because she's *always* doing something online when she isn't playing—while Ru and I discuss what we should wear to the audition. Modern art mini-dresses or jeans and leather jackets? Cute or vintage rebellious? Whatever would make us the most different from Lizard Blood, is my opinion. Ripped jeans and anger.

"I don't really care, you pick," Ru says. When she isn't angry, her hair lies flat in a pixie cut. Really, I don't even know why I'm asking her—she doesn't have any fashion sense at all. Me or Miki pick out all her clothes. If we didn't have school uniforms she might not wear anything at all.

"I just want you to pick one, skirt or jeans?"

"Kit, look!" Ru points down the hallway, and I swear the lights dim and a mysterious wind begins howling past us. Even Miki looks up from her deck.

Lizard Blood appears, standing together, glaring a challenge at us: Yuki, with Azumi and Hana flanking her like acolytes. Between all of them, their poofed-out skirts fill the corridor. They have dyed their hair three different shades of pink: hot, bubblegum, and rose.

We get to our feet and it's like an Old West standoff.

"Hello, Yuki," I say. "What are you doing here? Shouldn't you be *practicing?*"

"You can't win," Yuki says. Her arms are at her sides, her hands in fists. She's wearing a black and white striped tea dress trimmed in lace and a little derby hat the size of an apple. She is above school uniforms, as she has often informed us. Just think, if she spent as much time practicing guitar as she did dressing, she could actually learn to play. "Why don't you give up?"

"We'll let the judges decide." I cross my arms. I'm not afraid of her. "It's only fair."

"I'm trying to save you the humiliation of losing."

"That's very kind of you, I'm sure."

She studies a manicured, black-painted nail. "I don't know why I bother. You're too stupid to listen to *anyone*."

At that, Ru roars and launches herself as a mad battering ram at the trio across from us. Miki and I grab her just in time, hooking our arms across her body and holding fast.

Predictably, Yuki laughs. Her henchthings start in a second later, and stop a second after she does. Throwing a last glare at us, they turn on their high-heeled patent-leather Mary Janes and march away.

"I hate her *so much!*" Ru hisses, slumping in our arms out of exhaustion.

"Our best revenge is to win the audition and play at the dance," I say. "We'll practice tonight, right after school."

"I may be late," Miki says, her expression scrunched up in apology. "I have ... a *thing*."

"A thing? What *thing?*"

"Just. It's. I'll explain later."

She turns and runs, bumping up against a boy standing at the end of the corridor. It's like he just appeared. He glances briefly at Miki, then stares at us, and I wonder how long he's been standing there. Did he see the whole confrontation with Lizard Blood?

This guy, he's *cute*. He's in a pale suit with a blue shirt and a thin tie. The jacket sleeves are rolled up and his hands are in his pockets. His dark hair flops perfectly over his forehead, framing his very mysterious gray eyes.

"Who is *that?*"

"I think it's the new boy," Ru says. "Just transferred in."

I can't look away, but I have nothing to say to him. Then, with a final dismissive glance, he turns and is gone.

Seriously, this is not the time to be distracted by such things as new boys at school.

I try to find out everything I can about the New Guy, but it's not a lot. He transferred in from New Tokyo Polytechnic, but I don't know anyone from there I could ask for gossip. He's taking a normal roster of classes, but rarely speaks. Even though he's collected a gaggle of girls and a few boys following him wherever he goes, he ignores his admirers completely.

"I bet he's a secret agent," Ru says. "He's spying."

"On what?"

"I don't know. Just on something."

What can there possibly be to spy on at Cherry Blossom High School?

"Or an undercover cop, like in the movies. He's going to make a drug bust and set the whole school in an uproar."

"As long as he waits to do it after the Spring Dance."

The guy stands in the doorway of the lunch room and just ... watches. I'm not thinking it's drugs because with the city falling apart and the police on strike, would they really send someone to bust drugs at a high school? This has to be bigger than that, which means he's a government agent. There's an international spy ring made up of teachers. Or a secret cavern under the school with a breeding den of giant monsters.

"I bet the school is home to a secret laboratory creating superheroes," I say, and Miki and Ru just stare at me. I keep going. "You know, like some of our fellow students may in fact be superheroes in disguise, with strange mental and physical powers. There's a secret high-tech gymnasium under the real gymnasium where they do their training."

Miki says, "If there are secret superheroes, why don't they do something to save the city?"

That is a very good question.

Finally, school ends and we can get to work.

Despite saying she would be late, Miki's already at our practice space in a second music room behind the school auditorium's stage. She's finally put her deck away. Ru and I hurry to get our instruments and tune up. We have the space for an hour and have to make the most of it.

We've spent months working on our set: "Twist Barbie," "It's a New Find," "Banana Chips," and of course our signature "Flying Jelly Attack." This is for a dance—we have to get people dancing first thing or we're doomed. But Shonen Knife makes it easy to dance. Their music is all about dancing and being happy. How can we not win the audition, when Lizard Blood is all about death and fashion? Of course, times being what they are, maybe people are in the mood for death.

We practice and I start to feel better.

Besides the dancing and expressing happiness, another reason I started a Shonen Knife cover band is that the lyrics are pretty easy to learn.

"Naaaa na na na naaaaa na na na naaaa na na naaaa na na naaa—"

This is music in its very purest form, I think.

Everything's coming together, we're rocking, and I start to think maybe we should back off, save our strength to ensure that we don't peak before the audition. But then Miki biffs a chord. I'm about to yell, but she's staring at the door. We all look.

And there he is, studying us with this little frown and a narrowed gaze, like he's on some kind of treasure hunt. The New Guy, in his perfectly starched suit and his very cool manner. Is he following us around? What does he want with us?

"Hey!" I yell. "This is a private rehearsal, can't you read the sign?" I'd taped a handwritten sign to the outside of the door to discourage gawkers.

He glances at the sign, then back at us, and his lips press into a thin, uninterpretable line. Why doesn't he *say* something? Then I have a terrible thought: Is he spying for Lizard Blood, so they can learn our strategy for winning the audition?

Before I can yell at him again, he walks away. Only one thing to do: I unsling my guitar, gently set it down, and charge after him.

"Kit, wait!" Miki yells, as Ru shouts, "That's not a good idea!"

"I have to do something," I shout back. "He can't just lurk in doorways and get away with it!"

Miki turns panicked. "But he could be dangerous!"

He's far too handsome to be dangerous. Mysterious yes, but not dangerous. At least not a bad dangerous. Heroic dangerous, maybe. He looks like a hero.

"*Hey!*" I yell, and what do you know, he actually turns around.

"What?" he asks. His voice is soft but somehow compelling, — authoritative and full of secrets. The voice totally goes with that suit.

"I want to know what you're doing here! You're not really a student, are you?"

His gaze is appraising. Smoldering, and appraising. He has better eyelashes than I do.

Finally, with a curt, dismissive nod he says, "It's best you don't know. Don't pay any attention to me. Go back to your friends." He walks on, turning the corner ahead.

When I chase him around the corner, he's gone.

Disaster.

Principal Jono is trying to cancel the band auditions for the Spring Dance. I argue with him, explaining that the auditions are a necessary distraction from the current tragic events and that hearing us perform would raise morale among the students.

"But Kit," he says sadly. He's a large, balding man with a thin comb-over and drooping face. "I don't think we'll be able to even hold the Spring Dance. Band auditions seem just a little ... pointless right now."

I declare, "What lesson are you teaching us with that kind of attitude? Are you saying we should give up? Are you telling us that perseverance in the face of adversity is not a good quality to have? Of course not! We must show that we are better than the evil that lurks in the rest of the world! Cherry Blossom High School and the Spring Dance will not be defeated!"

He relents, but I think only to make me go away.

Another reason I started a Shonen Knife cover band is the clothes. Basically, we can wear whatever we want, as long as we match. We can wear surf T-shirts or white tunics or leather jackets or bell-bottoms or miniskirts. And no matter what, we're *cute,* spreading brightly colored happiness wherever we go. Lizard Blood, with their fancy corsets and big crinolines and little bitty hats and velvet boots and too much makeup—it's like a uniform with them. Baby-doll fascists. It's sad, really.

I would spy on Lizard Blood—do they plan on playing a lot of screechy thrash or are they actually going to go with a set list that people can dance to? Because if they expect to win the audition they have to play stuff that people can dance to. Unless Yuki has paid off all the judges. This is an angle I haven't considered, and it leaves me thoughtful, because even with all the banks shut down, her family is so rich that she still has money. She keeps telling everyone she still has money, anyway.

If she's paying off judges, what can I do to compete? Nothing. Unless I can somehow expose her bribery plot. Maybe, just maybe, the New Guy is here to investigate Yuki. That would be helpful.

After the banks lost all their money, a bunch of people started looting grocery stores and things because pretty soon they wouldn't be able to buy anything. Some people tried to keep going to work and pretending everything was normal, convinced that their money would return and they'd get paid and the police would arrest all the looters and everything would be fine.

But then the water stopped. The hackers broke into the computer systems handling the city's water treatment and distribution plants and deleted the software. Water flowing through pipes stopped. No more showers, no more drinking. The hoarding of bottled water began. People fled, and the streets and trains out of the city became impassible.

Everyone says it will only be a matter of time before the hackers destroy the power grid as well. I don't think they'll go that far since they need the power grid and computer networks functional in order to do all that hacking in the first place. Nevertheless, just in case, I acquire a gas-powered electric generator for our instruments. Even if the city goes completely dark, we will still be able to audition for the Spring Dance. If I'm truly lucky, Lizard Blood will not have an electric generator, but since Yuki is rich I'm not counting on it. She has everything. If we're going to defeat her, we need to rely on our immense talent, the fact that we are good guys, and the sheer uplifting power of the music of Shonen Knife.

The dance will be in the gymnasium, the biggest room in the school, with polished wood floors, a high ceiling, and one wall full of windows looking over the city's downtown skyscrapers and monorail tracks. The monorail isn't running anymore because the hackers corrupted the system's software. A couple of trains crashed before the authorities shut it down.

Miki and Ru come with me to scout out the area where we'll be playing for auditions tomorrow. Well, Ru and I scout, and Miki sits in a corner and works on her deck: headphones on, eyes on screen like there's nothing else in the world. It's weird.

"What are you doing on your deck all day? You can't possibly have that much homework." The teachers who still bother showing up have stopped assigning homework in favor of teaching us survival techniques like starting fires, collecting dew for drinking water, and spinning wool into yarn. Who knew they're all survivalists? It's almost comforting.

"Nothing. Never mind. It's a secret."

Like that isn't suspicious.

And then when I turn around—there he is again. New Guy. Watching us from yet another doorway. *Staring*, like some creep. A very handsome creep in a nice suit, but still.

I'm about to yell, but he slips away as if he hadn't been there at all. Miki and Ru also look after him.

"That's it," I mutter.

"You said it," Ru mutters with me. Her hair starts to get messy, which means she's about to rage out.

"Don't worry. We'll find out what this is all about. I have an idea."

Here's how we set a trap for New Guy. First, we schedule another impromptu practice. Technically, we don't have the practice room reserved, but since no one else at the school is playing any music and most classes have been canceled, no one stops us. The trick is, we have to catch him as soon as he shows up. No delay, no time for him to figure out anything's wrong. Just boom, captured, and then we can shine a bright light on him and demand that he spill the beans.

But Miki isn't there. We get to the practice room at the right time, have our ropes and a flashlight and everything ready to go, and she's not there. How are we going to fool New Guy into thinking this is a legitimate practice if Miki isn't here?

"This isn't going to work." Ru looks despondent.

"No, it will. The plan doesn't change."

We wait in ambush, standing on either side of the doorway, each of us holding a can of Silly String. I plug my phone into speakers and play a concert bootleg of "Redd Kross." Maybe it won't fool him—maybe he'll know it's actually Shonen Knife on a recording and not us—but I'm willing to take that risk.

We hold our breaths and wait, wait... At our other practice, this was about the time New Guy appeared in the doorway. Sure enough, listening hard past the beat and the bass line, I hear footsteps, a careful approach of expensive loafers. Ru and I exchange a glance.

New Guy peeks in, looking confused for a moment when he doesn't see anyone. That's when we attack.

Silly String is a really good weapon because it's totally shocking and totally nonlethal. We cover him in instant rubbery spaghetti. Futilely, he puts up his hands to fend off the swarm of plastic, but it's no good—he's covered. When he stumbles back, trying to turn and get a good look at his attackers, he trips over the rope we slung across the floor. He goes down with a crash and lies prone. We stand over him, empty cans held out like guns. Ru is growling.

"What are you *doing?*" he exclaims, picking Silly String from his face, blinking at us. His thin frown might be curled into a snarl.

"Why are you following us?" I demand. "What do you want with us? Are you spying on us for Yuki? Are you working for Lizard Blood?"

"What are you talking about?" he says with admirable calm, given that he's lying on the floor covered in yellow, orange, green, and blue Silly String. He starts to sit up. The plastic bits come off him in one giant sheet.

"Don't move!" Ru shouts. Her eyes are red and her teeth are bared like a wolf's. If she could grow fangs, she would. He doesn't move.

"It's all right," I say to her, lowering my now-empty cans of string. "I think he's safe."

He regards us both. "Where is your friend? Your bass player."

My heart gives a little jump knowing that he pays attention enough to know who plays what instrument and that he knows the difference between a bass and a guitar. Not everyone does.

"She's out. Why do you care?"

He looks at us so calmly, speaks so evenly, you'd never know he'd just been attacked with Silly String. "Because it's true. I am spying on you."

"What?!" Ru yells, and I have to grab her arm before she starts clawing at him.

"Why?" I say. "Who are you working for?"

"May I ask you a question?"

He totally isn't a student. He's not even trying to pass for one anymore, not that he ever did. He stands, scraping off the rest of the string. "Do you know what your friend Miki does on her deck all day?"

Ru and I look at each other. I say, "Homework, I think."

New Guy is very serious now. "We've traced the cyber attacks on the national banks and water system to this school. We believe one of the students here at Cherry Blossom is the hacker."

"You ... you don't think it's Miki, do you? It can't possibly be Miki!"

"Why not?"

"Because she's a good guy! Because she knows all about Shonen Knife! Because I trust her!"

He presses those skeptical lips together. I almost cry.

"If you trust her, then help me clear her. Find out what she's doing with her deck. But don't tell her I'm investigating her."

"We can't spy on our friend!" Ru says. But of course, we can. We have to, and New Guy knows it.

"If you'll excuse me." He adjusts the cuffs of his jacket and leaves the room like nothing happened.

Half an hour later, Miki shows up with her bass. And her deck. Ru and I haven't had the heart to start playing without her.

"Sorry I'm late, I got held up. They're rationing water now, you know that? I'm trying to find a way to sneak bottles out of the kitchen— hey, what's wrong?"

I stare, stricken. Miki, dear sweet Miki, hacking the city infrastructure to destroy it? I don't believe it, not for a minute.

"We're depressed," Ru says, which is true enough.

"You can't be depressed, auditions are tomorrow! We have to practice!" Miki says.

I feel grim. "I think we've practiced as much as we possibly can."

"You mean—"

I nod. "We're ready. It's time to face Lizard Blood."

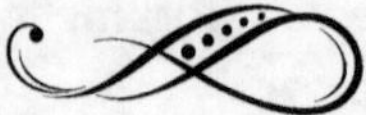

This is it. The most important day of my life. Will I be allowed to spread the message of true pop rock throughout the universe, or will I be defeated? I feel sick to my stomach.

We decide on wearing A-line tunics and pants in primary colors to better channel Shonen Knife, and to separate ourselves from the frilly bleakness of Lizard Blood. Sure enough, they show up in black and white with double the crinolines and corsets and curly purple wigs and giant eyelashes dashed with glitter. They carry their instruments proudly, and their neural implants gleam along their arms and foreheads. Like they think they can't lose.

All we have are calluses on our fingers.

Everyone's there. At least, everyone who is left is there: Principal Jono and the remaining survivalist teachers, clipboards in hand and pencils raised, ready to judge our worthiness to play at the Spring Dance. A crowd of students gathers in the back of the gym, thrumming with eagerness. This is going to be the fight of the century.

The stage waits, bare.

I hate this, waiting, my guitar slung over my shoulder, plinking the strings. They make weak little ringing sounds, since the instrument's not plugged in yet. It's the same sound my heart will make if it breaks, if we lose. Ru holds her fists over her eyes, like she can't even watch, her drumsticks sticking out of them like antennae.

But even right before the audition, Miki sits on the floor, working on her deck.

I glare at her. "What are you doing? You're always on your deck. I'm worried about you."

"What? Oh—it's secret. But you'll like it. I promise."

Off to the side, New Guy watches us closely. What if he's right? What if Miki is behind the destruction of the city?

What would Shonen Knife do? They would trust each other, and they would play. That's all we can do.

Principal Jono will flip a coin to see who goes first. He announces: "Flying Jelly Attack is heads, Lizard Blood is tails. Whichever side lands up will get to choose whether they go first or last."

Yuki and I stand on either side of Principal Jono, seething. Soon, it will all be over. The coin spins, glinting in the light coming in through the windows. It seems to spin forever before falling like a bullet into Principal Jono's hand. He slaps it on the back of his other hand, looks at us both, and finally reveals the outcome.

"Heads!"

I should have thought more about what would be best: play first and get it over with, play last to leave the final impression with the judges, play first to show how great we are at warming up a crowd, play last so we could respond to Lizard Blood's strategy—

Miki taps me on the shoulder. "Let Lizard Blood play first."

She seems very confident, hiding something behind her big brown eyes and glasses. Okay, then. Shonen Knife trusts each other, so I trust her.

"Lizard Blood will go first," I say and step aside.

It takes them a stupidly long amount of time to set up because they have to plug in their instruments, warm up their neural implants, synch all their systems, and I figure this will be a black mark against them because the longer they take the more restless everyone gets. But I know them, and I've heard them, and once they start playing, they'll cast some kind of weird headbanger spell that will overpower the crowd with a wall of death metal. They'll burn out everyone's hearing before we even get onstage.

But then something happens. Something *amazing*.

Yuki starts to strum a chord—that is, her uploaded programming directs her arm to play a chord. And nothing happens. Her hand goes limp and splats over the frets, and her other hand tangles in the strings instead of strumming. Azumi does a little better, getting her bass to play a couple of chords, but they're *bad* chords, out of tune and wavering. The drumsticks fall clean out of Hana's hands. When she scrambles to pick them up, she falls off her stool.

It's like they're not in control of their own bodies. It's like something has gone wrong with their neural implant programming.

I look at Miki, who nods with satisfaction. "That's what I've been doing with my deck—hacking the implant software Lizard Blood uses to play their instruments. It was tough because they had massive protections on their system. Military-grade firewalls. Best money can buy—you know Yuki. But I got through, you know?"

I stare at her with really big eyes. "You. Are. A. *Genius.*"

She's my new hero. I could kiss her, but I have to go back to watching Yuki and Lizard Blood fumble around, trying to figure out what to do with their instruments without the software to guide them.

New Guy arrives in time to hear the explanation. "Ah. That clarifies much," he says. "That only leaves one suspect in the bank-hacking case. Thank you, girls."

"What?" I blink at him.

He approaches the stage and draws a badge from his pocket. Yuki and the others finally go still.

"I am Detective Fukaya, and you, Yuki Niamori, are under arrest for destroying the city through the cybernetic network."

Well, who expected *that*?

Yuki should deny it, but she doesn't. She throws down her guitar and clenches her fists. Even Azumi and Hana look surprised, so they must not know anything about it.

At the edge of the stage, Yuki looks over us all, green eyes filled with rage.

"You think this is just an act!" she shouts. "You never respected me because you think all this is fake!" She gives her frilly skirt a tug. "It's not an act! It's *anarchy!* Yes, I destroyed the city's banking and water infrastructure! I want everything to *burn!*" She throws horns with both hands and screams, "ANARCHY!"

I have to admit, I finally sort of respect Yuki a little bit because she seems very honest about her mission.

She jumps off the stage and shoves Detective Fukaya aside. He's so surprised he doesn't go after her right away—I mean, who expects Yuki to do anything that smacks of effort? So she runs and we all think she's going to get away, but then Ru trips her. Just sticks out her foot, and Yuki goes sailing, purple curls flying and tiny hat spinning off toward the ceiling. It's great. Detective Fukaya arrests Yuki. Azumi cries while Hana leads her away, arm around her shoulders to comfort her. And that's that.

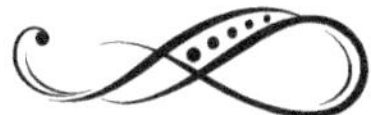

It turned out Miki had such a hard time hacking Lizard Blood's system because all of Yuki's neural interfaces and military-grade firewalls were a cover for her high-level hacking activities. Lizard Blood really was a fake band. Who knew?

So, that's how Flying Jelly Attack triumphed and won the chance to play at the Cherry Blossom High School Spring Dance. We auditioned with our signature song, "Flying Jelly Attack," and we sounded triumphant. That just goes to show that Rock and Roll Will Never Die.

Unfortunately, by the time of the Spring Dance the power had indeed gone out all over the city. But that doesn't matter because we have the generator, and we insist that the Spring Dance go on as planned for the sake of good morale. We decorate the gym and fill it with students. It seems like a miracle that everybody comes, but I know I'm right: times like these, everybody just wants to dance.

So we play for them. Outside the windows, far away in the city, mobs riot at bank headquarters and government buildings for not doing more to stop the economic collapse. A couple of skyscrapers are on fire and helicopters buzz around them, recording footage for the news. The city really is falling apart, but I don't care, because my dream has come true: my band is playing at the Spring Dance. The Cherry Blossom High School gym is the safest place in the city. Hundreds of students surge screaming at the stage, and me and my girls have our instruments plugged into amps, ready to go. I look at Miki and Ru, meet their gazes, and they nod back at me. Their hands are poised to begin. Nothing else matters.

I turn to the microphone and call, "One two three four—!"

THE MIND IS ITS OWN PLACE

Professional fingers pried open Mitchell's left eyelid, and white light blinded him. The process repeated on the right. He winced and turned his head to escape. The grip released him.

"Lieutenant Greenau?"

He lay on a bunk in an infirmary. It wasn't the *Francis Drake's* infirmary. The smell was wrong; the background hum of the vessel was wrong. This place sounded softer, more distant. Larger. With effort, he shifted an arm. His head hurt. He felt like he'd been asleep for days.

"Lieutenant Greenau? Mitchell?" The figure at the side of his bed gave him something to focus on. A middle-aged man in a white tunic, with a narrow face and a receding hairline, frowned at him. "How are you feeling?"

"Groggy." He struggled for awareness.

"You were sedated."

"Can you give me something to clear it up?"

"I'd rather not put anything else into your system just yet."

He wished he didn't have to ask: "Where am I?"

"You're at Law Station, Lieutenant."

Law Station was a Military Division forward operating base and shipyard. It would have taken the *Drake* days to get here, and he didn't remember the trip. Law also housed an extensive medical facility.

Softly, as if afraid of upsetting a fragile piece of equipment, he asked, "Why am I here?"

"What do you remember?"

He'd arrived on the bridge for his shift. He'd checked in with Captain Scott. Then he assumed he'd taken his place at the navigator station. He must have done his job as he had a hundred times before. He checked in with the captain, the duty log scanned his thumbprint—

"I was on the *Francis Drake*. On the bridge. I said good morning to the captain. Then—I don't remember." He kneaded the sheet draped over him, cramping his fingers. He was wearing a patient gown, not his uniform.

"That's all right." The doctor smiled, but the expression was shallow, artificial, a forced attempt at bedside manner. "I'm Doctor Dalton, one of the supervising physicians here. If you need anything, a pager is at the side of the bunk."

"Doctor—" Mitchell forced himself up, rolling to his side and leaning hard on his elbow. The effort left him gasping. "What happened?"

Dalton's manner was implacable, as if he'd had this conversation before, with other patients, over many years. "This is the neurophysiology ward. Are you familiar with what we do here?"

His heart pounded; his tongue was dry. "Yes."

"You were brought here because you have OSDS."

Among themselves, in private, the navigators called it Mand Dementia. The condition was degenerative and incurable. It was one of the risks of the job. An acceptable risk.

"But I feel fine. I don't feel—" Except for the sedation—why had he needed to be sedated? "I don't feel sick. I'm not—" *I'm not crazy.*

"I know, Lieutenant. I'm sorry."

Mitchell slumped back against the mattress.

He kept a close count of the time. It seemed important, to prove he wasn't sick. Everything he did had to be normal and healthy. He wasn't sick, and the doctor was wrong.

Halfway through his first waking day cycle, he heard voices coming from the office next to the infirmary. Doctor Dalton was one, and he brightened to hear the other: Captain Crea Scott.

Dalton said, "He didn't exhibit any symptoms before?"

Scott answered, her normally brash voice hushed and brittle: "He didn't. I know what to look for. He was fine at the start of the shift, and an hour later he was screaming about flying monkeys to starboard—"

Mitchell lay very still.

"He hasn't exhibited any symptoms since he's been here. He also doesn't remember anything that happened. We won't know the extent of the damage until we run tests."

"Could there be a mistake? Could it be something else?"

"I reviewed the log myself, Captain."

"May I see him?"

"That should be all right."

Mitchell lay with his back to the door and didn't see them enter. He waited to turn when Scott said, "Lieutenant Greenau?"

Scott stood a few feet away from the bed, her petite frame tense, her arms crossed. Her face was drawn; she looked ten years older than the last time he'd seen her—when?

He sat up and smiled, relieved. Like she was going to rescue him or something. "Captain Scott. It's good to see you."

She didn't return the smile. "How are you feeling, Lieutenant?"

"Still groggy from the sedative. But I'm okay. I feel fine." He glanced at Doctor Dalton to make sure he heard.

"That's good."

"Captain, I don't understand why I'm here."

"That's okay. Just rest. Don't worry about it." After putting a hand on his arm, she bowed her head and turned away.

"I did something, didn't I? What did I do?"

Scott didn't turn around. Her voice was painfully steady. "Just take care of yourself, Mitchell. Don't worry."

Dalton followed Scott out of the room, and Mitchell heard his captain say, "He'll be safe here?"

"Yes. As safe as we can make him."

Then Scott said, her voice low and angry, "Make sure he never remembers what happened."

A door slid open, then closed again, and the captain was gone.

He pressed his thumb to the duty log, he said good morning to the captain, he went to his station—

He only knew that much because it was the routine, what he'd done over and over for years. Was he remembering some other time, or *that* time?

Compared to his quarters aboard the *Drake*, the room he was given here was spacious, an eight by eight square with a bed, desk, computer console, and private washroom. For the whole of his adult life, Mitchell had slept in closets, with a narrow bunk and a cupboard for his belongings. He'd shared washrooms with other junior officers. Who needed more? Who ever spent time in their rooms? He'd always been so busy.

The door to the room locked from the outside. He couldn't leave without escort. Orderlies brought meals and returned to take away the trays. Mitchell counted two of them, Baz and Jared, working in shifts. They were polite. Mitchell said thank you, and they smiled at him. He had a change of clothing—pale blue hospital-issue jumpsuits—every day. He could read or watch entertainments at the console to pass the time, when he wasn't in therapy.

That first night he didn't sleep, but lay back on his cot and stared at a bubbled security monitor in the ceiling, wondering if this was a test.

The second doctor he encountered had an unflappably optimistic professional demeanor, and Mitchell distrusted her for no good reason except that nobody was that genuinely enthusiastic about anything. In spite of himself, Mitchell shook her hand after Baz escorted him to her lab.

Her space was a bit more inviting than other areas of the hospital. Handheld terminals lay strewn across the desk among forgotten drink bottles and writing implements. A sweater hung over the back of a chair. Photos shone from wall displays: image after image of human brains, parts color-coded and labeled.

A dark-skinned woman with short hair and an eager smile, she came around the desk. "Lieutenant Greenau? I'm Doctor Ava Keesey. I'll be starting your therapy today." She offered her hand.

"Not Doctor Dalton?"

"I've requested your case. I hope that's all right?"

He didn't know what his choices were to be able to make one, so he said nothing.

"Have a seat right over here, Lieutenant." She guided him to a reclining chair surrounded by unidentifiable equipment. Gingerly, he climbed in; its cushions molded under him, supporting his body. The chair tipped back until he was horizontal.

"Any questions before we start?"

"Is the *Drake* still in dock?"

"I don't know. I can check for you."

Her smile was fake; he didn't think she would check.

"What happened? Why was I brought here?"

"It's better if you remember on your own, rather than construct false memories based on anything I tell you. If you can please keep your head back, I'd like to start the scan." Her cool hand on his forehead eased him back against the headrest. "You've been through a cortical mapping session before, yes?"

"Yes." Every navigator had one done at the start of their career. A baseline.

"Then you know all about this. Just relax."

Machinery closed over his crown, sensors pressing against his scalp, tickling the fuzz of his hair. He looked straight up to off-white ceiling.

"Can you hear me?" she said.

"Yes."

"I'd like you to move your left thumb. And again. Left index. And again. Left middle. And again."

And so it went, through the range of motor skills, then across the range of sensory input. Keesey played music and noises, offered him tastes, put sandpaper and cotton into his hands, recording the results with straightforward efficiency.

"Now I'm going to show you some colors, each one for a few seconds. Pay attention, please."

A screen swung into view over the chair and flashed to life, displaying solid blue, then green, then yellow.

He went to the navigator station, slid into his chair and belted in. Ready for the jump in three, two—the monitor showed a swirl of color. The wrong colors, circling like predators—

Orange, red, purple. Mitchell blinked. Solid squares appeared in sequence on the screen. Harmless.

"What is two plus two, Lieutenant?"

"Four."

"Two times two?"

"Four."

"Four times four?"

"Sixteen."

"Sixteen squared?"

"Two hundred fifty-six."

Yellow, orange, red.

"Thank you."

The wrong colors. They were the wrong colors.

Keesey moved away, her footsteps clicking on the hard floor of the lab. He remained locked in the chair, unable to turn his head.

"Can I sit up?"

"In a minute, Lieutenant."

He wished he could see what she was doing. He heard clicks, movements, maybe fingers tapping on a keypad, or machinery shifting into place. All the sounds were inexplicable.

Mitchell waited a painful, silent minute before saying, "Doctor?"

"Patience, Lieutenant. I want to get a little more data." Did her voice sound stressed? Uncertain?

She went through the entire sequence again, generating a second cortical map. Finally, she released him from the equipment.

"What's wrong?" he said, sitting up.

Her smile didn't seem any different than the one she gave him at the start of the session. "How much do you know about OSDS?"

Occupational Synaptic Dysfunction Syndrome. It was the bogeyman, the monster in the dark. The price they paid for crossing the void. Some people said M-drive propulsion violated the laws of physics, and the Universe took the cost of that somewhere else: in the minds of the navigators who plotted courses through the unreal. Their minds became…nonlinear.

"It affects the neural organization of the brain," he said.

Keesey said, "It develops when some neurotransmitters don't reach adjacent neurons, but instead stimulate neurons in distant parts of the brain. Reducing the stimulation our patients receive can prevent the damage from getting worse by keeping faulty connections from developing. That means sheltering patients, perhaps more than seems reasonable. I'll have some instructions for you once I've had a chance to study the scans."

"You made two maps. Is that normal?"

"Just confirming the data, Lieutenant."

She hadn't believed what she saw the first time.

"But I don't feel sick." If he were really well, he wouldn't have to keep saying it.

"And we want to keep you that way."

She escorted him back to his quarters herself. He would never be allowed to just wander, would he? He was curious about every door, every branch in the corridor. Every place he couldn't go. And where was the *Drake* now?

They'd almost reached his quarters when a scream rang out and echoed along the walls. The corridor curved to match the curve of the station; the scream came from ahead, just out of sight.

Keesey's practiced demeanor slipped. "Stay here." She gripped his arm and pushed him against the wall, as if she could stick him there.

When she trotted ahead, Mitchell followed her, to where Baz was half-helping, half-dragging a thirty-year-old man in a hospital jumpsuit through an open door. Mitchell couldn't tell if they were trying to enter or leave what must have been the man's quarters. Baz held the man's shoulders, as if he were simply guiding him, but he stumbled, his legs buckling as if he couldn't support himself. Disheveled brown hair hung around his shoulders, he held his hands over his ears, and his face was twisted in an anguished cry. He screamed again.

Keesey knelt by the patient and tried to take hold of his face.

"Morgan, look at me. Morgan! Focus!"

The man, Morgan, squeezed his eyes shut and shook his head.

Keesey said, "Baz, I can't look after him now. Take him to the infirmary and I'll be there in a minute." She pulled something out of her pocket—a patch—and slapped it on Morgan's wrist. His struggles subsided; his moans continued.

The orderly nodded and lifted his burden, guiding Morgan along the corridor, past Mitchell, stopping every few steps as the man doubled over, then raising him up and continuing.

Keesey quickly took Mitchell's arm and steered him back to his own room—just a couple of doors down from Morgan's. She keyed it open with her wrist band and urged him inside. He was being put away in a box.

"What's wrong with him?" Mitchell asked.

"Get some rest, Mitchell. We'll talk later about your treatment."

"But—"

"He has OSDS, Mitchell."

He sat at his tiny desk and pretended it was the *Drake's* navigator station, the self-contained compartment located through a hatch at the fore of the equipment-laden bridge. Here, isolated from the bustle at the heart of the ship, he monitored the calculations that allowed the M-drive to fling the ship from one point to another across folded space. It was a mind-boggling journey, possible through a complex quirk of physics, comprehensible through advanced mathematics. Nevertheless, Mitchell was a romantic, and he could imagine the journey—not an instantaneous manipulation of space-time, but a race across the galaxy, stars flying past in a Dopplered rainbow of colors, the gas of nebulae swirling in his wake. The stuff of children's adventure stories.

If this were the chair in his station, the computer console would have been here, the screen here, the proximity monitor here, the holo-maps there. Where had they been going? Had the blank space in his memory happened before or after they'd jumped? He would have located departure and arrival matrices, he would have generated equations describing those endpoints in real space, converted the holography…

He thought some part of the process would jog his memory. He calculated a dozen iterations of the same equation, variations in the matrices, imagined the graph they would plot, imagined traveling along that shape. The Universe and all its paths could be described this way.

The path made a swirl of colors—gases inflamed by cosmic

radiation, distant starlight—and the colors made him nervous. They never had before.

The computer had to be connected to Law Station's network. The *Drake* had docked here, so the station database would have some record of it. The *Drake's* logs might even have been uploaded.

From this terminal he was only supposed to have access to entertainments, but with a little hunting, he found that the library's reading material included the station's daily news feed, which listed a record of dockings by interstellar ships. Mitchell found the records from a couple weeks before and worked forward.

A week ago, the *M.D.S. Francis Drake* had docked for temporary repairs. It was scheduled to continue to the MilDiv Sol shipyards for more extensive repairs. That hadn't been on their schedule; the *Drake* had years of operation left before it needed an overhaul. Unless something had happened. And something *had* happened, or Mitchell wouldn't be here. The logs, he had to find the logs—

The screen went blank, the computer shut down. Its power had been cut off. Standard procedure for any terminal being used for unauthorized access.

He stared at his hands, flattened on the surface of the desk. They weren't even shaking.

"Lieutenant, I'd really appreciate it if you not work on any math." Keesey said.

He had started physical therapy—work on a treadmill, standard weightlifting. It was very boring, but the doctors watched him closely. Maybe in case he started singing when he only meant to move his leg.

He stopped walking. The treadmill powered down. "What?"

"You have books to read, vids to watch. You should avoid mathematics problems."

He laughed. Navigational math lived in his brain like his own heartbeat; he didn't even think of it.

Keesey explained: "The mathematics involved in navigation instigated your injury. I don't want you making it worse."

"Doctor, what was wrong with my cortical map?"

She consulted her handheld, donned her pleasant demeanor. "I think you might benefit from some social time. Meet some of the other patients so you can realize you're not alone here."

He knew he wasn't alone. He'd seen Morgan.

The common room where stabilized patients were allowed to socialize was carpeted, comfortable, and round. It gave an impression of nest-like safety. There were no corners to cower in. A few upholstered chairs occupied one side, some tables the other. The lighting was soft. An orderly stood watch inside the doorway.

Three people wearing hospital jumpsuits sat in the room, all apart from each other. Only one, a shorthaired woman curled up in one of the easy chairs, reading a handheld, looked up when Mitchell and Keesey appeared in the doorway.

The other two, a man and a woman, sat at different tables. The woman's eyes were closed, and she nodded in time to some tune all her own. The man held a stylus and bent over a handheld datapad, which he marked now and then. There was something odd about him, something small and shrunken. Maybe because he wore a helmet shielding him down to his ears. Mitchell expected him to start banging his head against the table at any moment.

Mitchell whispered to Keesey, "What's the point of socializing if no one talks to each other?"

"Have a little patience." She gestured to the man and woman at the tables. "Communication is difficult for Jaspar and Sonia, so they've isolated themselves. That doesn't mean they shouldn't spend time in proximity with others. But here—this is Dora."

No ranks, no surnames. Their old lives had been thoroughly erased here. He wanted his uniform back.

She led him to the side of the room where the woman watched them expectantly. "Dora? I'd like you to meet our new resident. This is Mitchell."

"Hello, Mitchell." Dora, head propped on her hand, smiled up at him.

Mitchell gave a mental sigh of relief. She sounded normal. Friendly, even. Not prone to screaming.

Keesey said, "Baz will come fetch you in half an hour." She left them alone.

Dora gestured at the chair next to hers. "Sit. You look uncomfortable."

"I am uncomfortable. I don't think I belong here."

"Because you're not crazy. Because you're not like them." She nodded at the others.

"I'm not. I'm not."

Dora smiled a thin, cat-like smile. "What made them send you here?"

"I don't remember."

She tapped her nose and grinned wider.

"So why are you here?" he asked.

She gave a demure tilt to her head. "It was a conspiracy. Captain didn't like me. Some of the crew didn't agree with the decision to lock me up. They'll come back for me, break me out of here."

And to think she acted so normal.

"Ah," she said. "You're giving me a look like now you think I'm crazy, too."

"They break you out. Then what? You become pirates?"

"Hm, that sounds like fun. Didn't you dream of that when you were a kid? Being a pirate, blazing across space having all sorts of adventures."

"I was going to save innocent starships from the bad pirates. Kids never dream about being bad pirates; it's always good pirates."

"There are no good pirates."

Mitchell gestured toward Jaspar and Sonia. "Do you know anything about them?"

Dora sat back in her chair. "Jaspar doesn't do anything but work puzzles—for six year olds. Sonia will talk to you, but she won't make any sense. Go try it."

He half-expected this to be some sort of initiation—humiliate the new kid by making him try to find something that wasn't there. But he crossed the room to Sonia anyway. She was pretty, if ragged. In her thirties, like all of them were, because that was when Mand Dementia tended to strike.

"Hello," he said, sitting in the chair across from her.

She looked up. Her eyes were swollen, shadowed, tired. Her light-colored hair needed brushing.

"I'm Mitchell. I'm new, so I thought I'd introduce myself."

She sat very still, in contrast to her previous nodding.

"Dora says you'll talk."

"Glass. Concerto for Violin," she said in a hesitating voice.

Mitchell blinked, startled. "What does that mean?"

Her eyes glistened. There was a spark of something there, a flicker. Understanding. Sentience. Something that wasn't insane. Like she was staring through the bars of a cage.

"Chopin. Opus 28, Prelude Number 6."

Composers. Music. She was speaking pieces of music like they meant something. He stared at her, wishing he could understand, and it was like staring into his own future.

"Chopin. Opus 28, Prelude Number 6," she called after him when he turned to leave. Her gaze pleaded, but he didn't understand what she wanted. Except maybe out of here, like him.

He tried talking to Jaspar next, but the man turned his back on him, filling Mitchell's sight with the off-white mound of his helmet—that was protecting what, exactly?

He returned to Dora, who explained, "She was a musician. The dementia cross-wired music and language. Keesey thinks there's some correlation between the mood or situation and what song she says. You know, 'Ride of the Valkyries' means 'pissed off.' I think it's a smokescreen and she's just hiding from everyone."

"She looks like she's listening to something."

"The music in her mind. The doctors won't let her listen to actual music. They're afraid it'll 'reinforce faulty neural pathways,'" she said. She did a pretty good impression of Dalton's flat tone. "I knew her, before. She associated every step of navigating to different songs. She said the sound of an M-drive powering up matched the opening measures of the overture to 'The Marriage of Figaro.' Then it all went to hell, I guess."

If someone locked you in a room full of crazy people, was there any chance that you *weren't* crazy?

She said softly, "You know, everyone here commits suicide sooner or later. The whole place is a futile attempt to keep us from killing ourselves. But everyone manages it. They can't help us. This isn't a hospital, it's a hospice."

Quietly he said, "How do you stand it?"

She spread her hand over the handheld in her lap. "I'm looking at this as a chance to catch up on my reading."

"Lieutenant? It's time to leave." Baz stood at his shoulder. Mitchell hadn't been aware of his approach. Meekly, he let the orderly guide him away.

Back in his room, he listened to the piece of music Sonia had named, the Chopin. A sad piano melody wafted gently from his terminal, like a ghost. He wondered what it meant to her.

Dora was wrong: This was not a place where navigators killed themselves. Keesey was wrong: he was not ill. He kept trying to remember what happened on the *Drake*. The thing Scott didn't want him to remember, that the doctors didn't want him to think about.

He'd signed in, said good morning to the captain, went to his station. *We have an hour until we need to jump, Lieutenant.* The first step to initiating a jump was identifying the arrival matrix and locking in coordinates. The next step: convert the holography of local space from manifold to loop representation, another computerized operation that nonetheless required monitoring.

Ultimately the navigator, the human element, confirmed the optimum departure matrix generated by the navigation system, or chose an alternate. Then the M-drive would push the ship through it to emerge across interstellar space at the desired arrival matrix. At some level, even if only intuitively, he had to understand the mathematics that connected the two ends of the ship's journey.

By remembering routine, he forced himself through his breakdown, moment by moment.

He confirmed the departure matrix—and it was wrong. The colors swirled around it like light bursting to its death, and the space through which the ship should have been traveling was a mouth waiting to devour them. It wasn't a departure matrix but a black hole. The colors were wrong, the math was wrong, the computer was broken—

"Mitchell! Look at me."

Keesey leaned over him. Her cool hand touched his cheek. His skin was clammy, and his heart was racing. He couldn't control his breathing; air rasped roughly through his throat. He was on the floor of his quarters; some alarm must have summoned the doctor.

"What is it, Mitchell? What happened?" Her concern was professional, unemotional.

"I-I think I remembered something."

"Can you describe it?"

He had to speak very carefully. He didn't want to say the wrong thing. He had to say the thing that would explain all this away. "I saw colors. They were wrong."

He winced and turned his head, or tried to, but Keesey held him in place. Baz stood behind her. A vent fan hummed somewhere.

"Make your mind a blank, Mitchell. Let the images fall away until you see nothing."

He obeyed her psychiatrist's calm, and the colors faded. Baz came closer with a bottle and urged him to drink. Mitchell was obedient. The rehydrating fluid somehow made him feel weaker. He shouldn't need all this attention, this treatment. He wasn't sick.

"There was something wrong with the computer," he tried to tell them. That would explain everything.

Keesey wrote on a handheld as she spoke. "Your cortical map shows a faulty connection within your visual cortex. You can't trust your eyes, Mitchell. I know this is going to be hard, but I'd like you to limit your visual stimulation over the next couple of days. I can give you a blindfold if you'd like."

Blindfold? Like taking away Sonia's music.

"What are you writing down?" he asked. Maybe he shouldn't be looking. Is this what she meant by visual stimulation?

"Some exercises we'll try at your next session. We need to stabilize the dysfunctional area of the visual cortex. Please, rest your eyes if you can."

If they could reduce his world to a tiny, thoughtless box, then nothing at all could damage him. They could blindfold him. But he was still going to try and remember.

"I overheard Dalton and Keesey talking about you," Dora told him. He was sitting in his usual chair with his eyes closed. It didn't help. *If he could just figure out what was wrong with the computer…*

She continued, "You've got the piss scared out of Dalton. He seems to think you should be locked up and tied down full time. You must have done something spectacular. On the other hand, Keesey thinks you're the key to the holy grail that's going to save us all."

Dora was wrong—this wasn't a hospice, this was a laboratory. A hundred years of interstellar travel and they hadn't figured out how to prevent or treat Mand Dementia. That was why they were here; they were data points.

"I don't know why either of them should think that."

"Let me ask you a question. What is Mand navigation? Is it the math, or is it the mind of the navigator? See, the math alone isn't enough. Otherwise the computers could do it all. But no—they need *us* to process it. Not just anyone can be a navigator. A navigator has to understand what the computer is doing when it crunches those numbers. All those aptitude tests—they're measuring us, making sure we have the right kind of brain. We're the key. So why does the Trade Guild have this place?"

She leaned over the arm of her chair and lowered her voice to a bare whisper. "The Guild doesn't put us here because we're crazy. They put us here because they're afraid of us. It's not that we're sick. It's that they can't control us. We're too powerful, and this hospital, this so-called disease, all the sedatives, it's the only way they can keep us under control."

Powerful? He was a navigator. Part of a crew. He wouldn't do anything to hurt anyone. "We're not that special—"

"Mitchell, what do we do?"

"We review the M-drive navigation system, confirming departure and arrival matrices—"

"Do we confirm them? Or do we create them?"

He stared at her. He had to squint against the light, and the colors seemed wrong.

Her eyes grew even wider. "What if some of us have learned to manipulate the process without M-drives, without starships? What would that make us?"

His voice was small. "Powerful."

"It drives some of us crazy." She nodded at Jaspar and Sonia at their same places at the table, absorbed in their same tasks. "But some of us are the next step in evolution. It's not God that makes the Universe, it's math. Know the math, and you are God."

Mitchell found Baz and asked to be escorted back to his room. He flinched, though, when Sonia walked smoothly to intercept him before he reached the door.

She touched Mitchell's arm. "Prokofiev. *Prokofiev.*"

He could only stare and wish to understand. Bowing her head, she stepped aside and him them pass.

"What did that mean?" Mitchell asked Baz.

"It doesn't mean anything."

They passed far enough along the curve of the station that the common room door was out of sight when a buzzer sounded, and Baz brought his wrist comm to his face. "Yeah?"

A desperate voice—Mitchell thought it belonged to the other orderly—replied. "Morgan knocked out Dalton and sealed himself in the decompression chamber."

Baz ran, shouting, "Damn! Damn, damn—"

Running after him, Mitchell's slippers skidded a little on the floor. This was what rebellion looked like in the Mand Dementia ward; he wanted to see it. Baz rounded a corner, flashed his wrist band to open the door, and Mitchell followed him into the infirmary.

Jared pounded on the control panel of the decompression chamber and called Morgan's name over and over. Baz joined him, pushing at the chamber's sliding door as if he could open it with brute force. Impossible, of course, with the difference in air pressure. Mitchell had stopped in the doorway; Keesey pushed him aside.

"Oh no," she breathed, her voice thick with despair.

Jared said, "He locked up the controls and pumped out all the air. I couldn't do anything. I tried, but I couldn't stop him, I couldn't."

Keesey's face was twisted into an expression that might have been a comforting smile, or suppressed grief. She rested her forehead against the window. "Where is Doctor Dalton? Is he all right?"

Jared pointed back to where Dalton was sitting on the floor holding a cold compress to his head.

Mitchell's feet were leaden as he moved toward the chamber door. He'd come this far. He had to see.

The chamber was a gray room, large enough for a stretcher. Morgan lay on the floor, curled in fetal position, naked. His hospital jumpsuit was tangled around his feet. The half-light that entered the chamber through the window cast weird shadows over him. His skin looked silver, painted with the dark splotches of burst blood vessels. His brown hair, haloed around his bent head, looked silver. He was hugging himself, as if this was what he'd wanted.

"Why?" Mitchell asked, his hand on the door, like he could reach through, reach him.

Keesey said, "The air against his skin was screaming. He felt the air and heard it as screaming. He was trying to get away from the screaming."

"I don't understand," he said. All people had to do to kill themselves in space was let the air out. It was so easy.

"Good," Keesey said.

"What is *he* doing here?" Dalton said from across the room, pointing at Mitchell.

Keesey went over to him and commenced a hushed conversation, but at the last exchange Dalton's voice carried.

"It's cruel giving them hope, Ava!"

"Hush!" she hissed back.

Baz stayed with Mitchell, who stared through the window at the man lying curled in the gray shadows.

Morgan turned his head. His eyes opened and met Mitchell's gaze. He blinked, and movement trembled along his arm.

"He isn't dead." Mitchell pressed both fists to the door and lurched forward until his nose touched the window. "He moved, he's alive!"

Baz looked. "He hasn't moved."

"He did!"

Morgan brushed his hand along his cheek, tugging open his mouth, which was dark, bottomless and dark, like a black hole.

"Open the door! He's alive!"

Baz took hold of his shoulders and pinned him to the wall next to the hyperbaric chamber. Keesey stood in front of him. Mitchell hadn't seen her approach.

"Mitchell, what did you see? Tell me what you saw."

"There isn't time, we have to save him, we have to—"

"It's too late, Mitchell." She held his cheeks in her hands. "Tell me what you saw."

He wanted to pull away from them, their oppressive touches. He wanted to put space between them, because he didn't trust them. But Baz held him firmly against the wall, and Keesey immobilized his face so he couldn't look away. His throat tightened, and a primitive voice inside him tried to whimper.

"What did you see?"

He swallowed to clear his throat. "He turned his face. He looked at me. I saw his eyes, there was life in them."

"Baz, are his eyes open?"

"No, Doctor."

"Mitchell, think about it. Does that seem possible? There's no air in that chamber."

Logic said no. Common sense said no. He swallowed again, this time to quell a growing nausea. He saw what he saw. She was asking him to deny the truth of his own observation. He said, "The M-drive isn't supposed to be possible. But it is."

Keesey held one of his arms, Baz held the other. Their grips were tight, he couldn't get away from them. If he could just get to Morgan, he'd show them. He lurched, writhed, strained to escape. Keesey pinned his upper arm between her arm and body, pulled up his sleeve, and slapped a patch on his wrist. Immediately a flush like warm syrup flowed up his arm, to his heart, to his head. His knees buckled. She and Baz lowered him to the floor.

A Keesey-shaped shadow knelt by him. She brushed her hand over his face, touching his eyes, closing his eyelids for him, and the world was dark. "Go to sleep, Mitchell. Just go to sleep."

Mitchell worked to move his lips, to say something, to scream, to curse them. To curse them for being right.

...an hour later he was screaming about flying monkeys to starboard...

Space could be described in terms of numbers and colors. Hydrogen burned orange, helium glowed red. But when the colors were wrong, he—

He couldn't remember.

He awoke in his quarters, his cell, lying on the bed. When he sat up, his belly lurched sickeningly, and he lay back down. He had seen a dead man move, and it hadn't been real.

At least, they *told* him it hadn't been real.

A navigator told the captain what departure matrices to use. They were invisible, regions in space identified only by the navigator. The captain trusted him to know the way. Captain Scott had always trusted him. He was used to being trusted. He was used to seeing what others couldn't. To doubt this, to doubt that he could see what others couldn't—he could never trust himself again.

Morgan had been trying to tell him something. That last look he had given him, those wide-open eyes. If Morgan had wanted to kill himself, there were easier ways.

He wondered what was under Jaspar's helmet. How had he tried to kill himself?

But what if Morgan hadn't been trying to kill himself? He'd gone to that specific place, like it was one end of a set of coordinates of a journey he'd plotted. That was the matrix he'd found; he'd needed to launch himself from there to get to the place he really wanted to be— away from here. The jump hadn't worked. That happened sometimes.

Morgan had tried traveling without a ship, and he'd sent Mitchell a message. Looked in his eyes and told him, *it almost worked.* They could see what no one else could.

The door opened and Keesey appeared, smiling and happy, as if nothing bad happened, ever. She had the attitude of a doctor about to give a child an injection.

"Hello, Mitchell. How do you feel?" She'd been watching for the moment he woke, he was sure.

"Numb," he said flatly.

"The sedative's still wearing off."

"What difference does it make?"

He didn't know what was worse—being treated like a sullen teenager or discovering that he was acting like one. He didn't have any dignity left.

She continued. "I'd like to help you figure out what's going on inside your head. The kind of things a cortical map can't tell us."

He turned his head toward the wall and shut his eyes because tears threatened to fill them. He was trapped on so many levels he'd lost count. On the station, in the ward, within his own mind.

"Nobody will ever let me on a ship again. And I don't know why. I just want to go back to the *Drake*."

After a moment of thoughtful silence, she asked a question that sounded genuine, and not like a scientist fishing for answers. "If you hadn't become a navigator, what would you be?"

He'd joined Trade Guild and applied for shipboard duty because he loved space. He'd become an M-drive navigator because he could, he had the aptitude, and the Trade Guild had gladly taken him and assigned him to MilDiv. Being a navigator had seemed as close as a human being could ever get to the stars. The math was the language he used to understand space.

"Maybe mathematics. Cosmology."

"The theoretical side of M-drive navigation."

"I suppose."

He'd always visualized his journeys through space. They happened quickly, leaping over real space, but he always imagined stars, gases, nebulae soaring past him in a blaze of color.

Keesey said, "I've observed—in a completely unscientific fashion, mind you—that there are two kinds of navigators. There are those who are tested, identified as having the proper aptitude, and recruited. For them, it's a job, like any other. Then there are those who love the work, who couldn't think of doing anything else. They live for the distances between the stars. I've observed that everyone who ends up in this ward falls into the latter group."

So, those who loved navigation would eventually be destroyed by it.

One glimpse of the *Drake*. To say goodbye, to have one more chance to try and remember. If he could see the *Drake* again, he might remember. If he could see anything besides these corridors, the lab, the walls of his tiny room. A longing overcame him, a physical pain settling in his gut. He refused to wipe away tears, because if he brought his hands to his face Keesey would know he was crying.

Careful to steady his voice, he said, "I'd like to see outside. The station has to have an observation area near the docking ports. I want to see a ship again. Any ship."

Spoken aloud, the desire sounded vague and childish.

"I'm not sure that's feasible. The sensory input might trigger another episode."

How many patients had she watched kill themselves, and still she smiled. Such blind dedication was its own insanity, but Keesey wasn't the one locked in a cell.

"Then when can I leave my quarters? I'd like to go to the common room."

"So you can talk to Dora some more? I know what she says, what she thinks. She's paranoid, in a clinical sense."

He tried sitting up again and managed to keep his stomach on an even keel. He stared at the gray rubberized floor instead of Doctor Keesey and her pitying, patronizing face.

"Dora says that all the patients here commit suicide."

"Dora says a lot of things."

I'm going to die soon. Being here, that was the only conclusion Mitchell could draw.

"She says Dalton thinks I should be locked up. Why would he think that?"

"I think you shouldn't listen to everything Dora says."

He looked up, glaring. "I don't have anyone else to talk to."

"I'm sorry, Mitchell, but we need to stabilize your neural—"

She didn't need to do anything. It was all about him, his brain; he was the one who had to live with it. He'd lost his rank somewhere. Wasn't Lieutenant anymore, just Mitchell.

"Doctor, I need to know what happened on the *Francis Drake*."

"I'm sorry, but I don't think you should." She paused a moment, her mouth open in mid-sentence. Then changed her mind. "We haven't been able to do much about controlling OSDS, much less curing it. The physicists who understand the M-drive don't know anything about physiology, and the doctors don't know anything about the M-drive. Sometimes I think we're just waiting for the genius who's an expert in both to come along and tell us what we've been doing wrong."

Mitchell took a deep breath, ignoring the pressure of the headache that threatened to build whenever he tried to think too hard, to dig in those places in his mind. His own body was telling him to leave it alone.

"The colors were wrong. I remember looking at the monitor, and the colors were wrong." Something was wrong with the departure matrix. He'd chosen a course correction, an alternative that would avoid the wrongness he was sure was there. He'd announced the course correction, he'd entered the course correction—

Frowning, he touched his temple and shook his head. It was gone, what happened next was gone from his mind, and the pressure was building.

Keesey gripped his wrists. Startled, he flinched back.

"Mitchell," she said, her voice stern. "Stop. Stop trying to remember. The more you do, the more you'll exacerbate the problem. That's where the damage started, with those memories. So just—just stop."

She let him go and went to his desk computer, typed in a few commands. Music started, something slow and classical.

"I've disabled the screen on your computer. You only have audio output now. I'd like you to just listen for a while. All right?"

Who was he to argue? He didn't say anything, didn't even nod or shake his head. She wasn't giving him a choice; no need for him to respond.

She left, and the door shut and locked.

M-drives pushed ships between coordinates in space dozens of light years apart. Dora insisted some navigators—the elite ones, the crazy ones—could create jump points themselves. Mitchell had never heard of such a thing. Wouldn't someone have tried it by now?

Maybe they had and ended up here. Sedated in a featureless room, like him.

Everything that could be done could be described by mathematics. Sometimes the equations took years to discover, and M-drive mechanics were only a hundred years old. What if the technology could be scaled down to the size of an individual human body? It was a nice idea to think about, so Mitchell did.

The room could be described in terms of dimension and volume. His chair, his position on it, his distance to the door, graphed and defined.

If a memory could be delineated by the laws and structures of mathematics, then the equations defining it could be discovered, reconstructed, remembered. And he could escape from this.

The point on the middle of the plane of the door had a set of coordinates in space, identifiable along a standard set of recognized coordinates. Or he could define his own system, with that point on the door as zero-zero-zero. Any location Mitchell could wish to find himself, from any place on Law Station to, say, the bridge of the *Drake*, had another concrete set of coordinates. He had only to identify those coordinates, describe those coordinates. In those terms the entire Universe was finite, concrete, describable. In the end, those numbers defined what one could know, what one could manipulate.

That was all navigation was, identifying two points and traveling the most likely route between them. The math, the ships, the drive, were only tools that enabled people to travel more easily. But what if, what if… What if they'd been missing something all along?

He put his hand flat against the door that would not open for him. Given this point in space had a finite value, and some other point in space also had a finite value, and an equation could be found describing a relationship between them, and the path between them could be collapsed, the distance between them could be made into nothing. He could step through the door.

He'd done this a hundred times, sitting in the navigator station of the *Drake*. He knew the process so well, his training had ingrained it in him so thoroughly, it was part of his mind, second nature, as unconscious as dreaming.

Captain Scott said, "Greenau, do you have our heading?"

"Yes, sir. Transferred to your monitor."

And the matrix was there. He could touch it. He could put his fingers inside it, work it open wider, stretch it open, and he could climb through and out, away from here. He dug with his fingers to make the area wider, to make a doorway. He should have listened to Dora. People would be able to travel across the galaxy with a thought. No more ships, no more danger. When he stepped through the door, he'd find Keesey and show her she was wrong, that there was more happening here than a neurophysiological disorder. Humanity was on the cusp of learning something it couldn't yet control. The navigators who were patients here were only the first pioneers, sacrificed for the pursuit of knowledge. Mitchell felt proud to be in their company.

Only a little more, and the point would be wide enough for him to climb through.

"Lieutenant!"

The sound was a shockwave rattling his ears.

"Lieutenant Greenau! Mitchell!" Baz appeared out of nowhere. No—he'd opened the door, and he shoved Mitchell back, grabbing his hands.

Mitchell tried to explain. "No, it's all right. I know what I'm doing. It's all in the mathematics."

"Mitchell, focus on me. Focus."

That was what Keesey had said to Morgan. Mitchell looked at Baz, the clean-shaven face lined with worry. Mitchell's gaze furrowed with confusion.

"Mitchell, look at your hands."

He did, as Baz lifted them to hold before him.

They were bleeding, the fingertips shredded, bits of torn flesh dripping red. Mitchell lurched, trying to get away from the vision, but they were his own hands, and they followed him.

He fell against the wall, breathing hard, his arms rigid before him.

Baz touched the door controls. The door shut, revealing a red stain, blood smeared across the metal from the point through which Mitchell had been trying to escape. He'd rubbed his hands raw and bleeding against the door. Where he'd seen a jump matrix, there'd been nothing.

So what had there been when he directed the *Drake* to those coordinates, the ones he'd been so sure were safe?

"Come on, Mitchell. Come on, buddy." Baz manhandled him off the floor, got him to stand, and walked him, puppet-like, to the infirmary. He murmured condescending encouragements. Mitchell heard them only distantly. He kept staring at his hands, which were the wrong color.

This time when he woke up, he was restrained. His hands, still stiff and sore from treatment, rested at his sides. He couldn't move his legs. He lurched up anyway, thinking he must have been imagining it, that he couldn't really be tied to the bed. He got his shoulders off the padding, then had to stop, because no matter how much he pulled and strained, he couldn't move any farther.

He rattled his hands to make the bindings rub and squinted against the searing light that lanced pain through his mind. His whole head throbbed.

"Please," he said, clearing a hoarseness from his throat. "Turn the lights down, please. They're too bright."

"The lights aren't on, Mitchell," said Doctor Keesey's voice, but he couldn't see her, couldn't even tell where she was. She might have been close by and whispering. He winced. He knew he was in the infirmary. It smelled like the infirmary. He didn't know anything else.

"I don't understand." The rich tone of despair in his own voice startled him. The voice came from another place, far from here, a place he hadn't yet arrived.

Someone touched his arm, and he let out a startled yelp, because he hadn't heard anyone approach the bed, but someone must have. Another dose of sedative warmed his blood, soothed his muscles, and he fell asleep gratefully.

Another voice woke him, this one speaking very close by.

"I don't have much time, Mitchell. But I wanted to talk to you. You did it, didn't you?"

He opened his eyes and was more relieved than he could have imagined to see the beds, supply cupboards, and equipment of the infirmary around him, gray and lurking in the dimmed to near-nothing light.

Dora was leaning on the bed, speaking close to his ear.

"Dora." His mouth was sticky, his throat dry. His wrinkled jumpsuit scratched against his skin, his scalp itched, and he suspected he smelled ripe. He felt like an invalid, too sick for the luxury of a shower.

"Easy." She rested a hand tenderly on his arm. "Mitchell. You have to tell me how you did it."

"Did what?"

"Saved Morgan. You saw him—the orderlies were talking about it. You saw his soul pass on. That was what you saw, wasn't it? He jumped to the next phase, and you saw it, and you're getting ready to follow him. I want to know how you did it."

Mitchell stared at her, meeting her wild-eyed gaze. Her fingers clenched on his jumpsuit, like she expected him to help her somehow, even though he was the one strapped to the bed. One of her hands had a fresh white bandage wrapped around it.

"You aren't supposed to be here, are you?"

"I cut my hand. I did it so they'd bring me here." She displayed the bandage. "I had to talk to you. You have to tell me what you saw."

"I don't know what I saw, Dora. I don't know." His visual cortex was damaged…

"But you do. You're special. You are, Dalton says so. Tell me about Morgan. Tell me."

Baz or one of the doctors must have been in the next room, distracted while Dora stole in to speak with him. Dora's urgency must have meant she didn't have much time until they discovered her and returned her to her quarters. Which meant Mitchell didn't have much time, either.

He had to learn the truth.

"Dora, untie me. Undo the straps, please. Then I'll tell you."

Nodding slowly, she touched the straps, studied them a moment, then moved to a control panel at the head of the bed. She tapped a couple of keys, and the tension on the straps released. He could move his feet, and by wriggling his hands he freed his wrists.

Dora held his hand and pressed something flat into the palm.

"I took Baz's wrist band. He didn't notice. You're going to follow Morgan, aren't you?"

"Maybe, maybe—"

"Dora!" Keesey called, reprimanding, from across the room. "Dora, I asked you to wait in the chair."

Mitchell wrapped his hands around the loose straps and hoped the doctor didn't examine him too closely. Dora didn't move, until Keesey called again.

"Dora."

Slowly, Dora stepped away, her gaze still on him, not wavering, until she reached the doorway where Keesey was waiting. The doctor was a shadow, indistinct in the room's dimness, but he recognized her shape, her posture.

"Mitchell?" she said. "Are you all right?"

He swallowed back a laugh. "Not really."

"I know this is difficult." She sounded sympathetic, but it was the sympathy of a person who didn't really know what she was sympathizing with. "I'll come back to talk with you in a little while, all right?"

"Sure."

When she was gone, he slid off the bed to his feet, and his head swam and vision wavered. He was still tired and woozy; whether from the remnants of the sedative or his rebellious senses, he didn't know. He was ill. He could admit that now. It only meant he had to be a little more careful. He slipped Baz's band around his wrist.

The corridor was empty. He reached the first bulkhead door. He showed the wrist band to the scanner.

The door slipped open, an escape portal, and a weight lifted from his mind. Free. He could run if he wanted.

You're going to follow Morgan.

If he could only see space again, see ships traveling against the backdrop of stars, he'd remember, and everything would be all right. He'd remember and tell them what really happened.

He passed the common room. Only Jaspar was inside, which was too bad. If Sonia had been there, he might have asked her if she wanted to go with him. It didn't matter what she replied; the words that came out of her mouth didn't matter, as long as she went with him.

Still working on impulse, he crossed the room and took hold of the man's helmet. Jaspar looked up at him. If he had looked at all confused or scared, Mitchell would have left him alone. But the man looked resigned. So Mitchell took off the helmet. His stomach spasmed with shock.

Jaspar was missing about a third of his skull, a great bite taken out of the right side, from his temple to the top of his ear and disappearing around to the back. A jagged edge of bone showed under his skin, which stretched to cover the remains of his head, dipping like a sinkhole into a concave space where the right half of his brain should have been. Looking at him from the left side, one might never guess he had anything wrong with him. From the front, he was a ruin.

Mitchell carefully set the helmet back in place. It protected whatever was left.

"What happened to you?" Mitchell breathed. Jaspar looked back and couldn't say.

Everyone here commits suicide.

Whatever Jaspar had done hadn't been successful. Mitchell turned and ran.

He coded open the next bulkhead door and left the ward. He could tell by the smell, which turned industrial instead of antiseptic. The corridor branched ahead, and Mitchell guessed which one would lead him to the center of the station, to the docking area. Other people he encountered struck him as strange-looking, as if he were traveling in a foreign country. He took calming breaths and tried not to look out of place. He knew the formulae that could take him from one end of the galaxy to the other. There ought to be formulae, equations, to do anything. He should find a way to turn invisible, so no one would see him. Visibility was all a matter of light and color. Space was color, the color of numbers. He could make himself transparent.

The corridor he followed now was straight, not curved, indicating he was walking along one of the spokes, toward the center of the cylindrical station. The gravity should be lessening. Mitchell stretched, lengthening his stride, to see if he could fly yet.

He keyed himself through two more bulkhead doors. Other corridors branched off to different levels, other departments, other wards. Mitchell's heart lurched at the sight of blue MilDiv uniforms. He almost stopped to study the faces of those who wore them to see if

Captain Scott was among them, if he recognized any of his crewmates. But that was unlikely. Surely the *Drake* had left the station by now.

Mitchell's steps developed spring, but he wasn't yet weightless. Ahead, the corridor opened into a wider thoroughfare, large enough for mechanized carts to travel. Equipment lockers lined the walls, vacuum suit closets in place between airlock doors. He could just go through the airlock and fly away. He could follow Morgan into an airless world.

He turned right and looked for an observation area.

"Mitchell! Mitchell, stop!" Both Keesey and Dalton appeared at the intersection of the corridor.

Mitchell ran.

"Stop him! Somebody stop him!"

He hunched his shoulders and kept on, grimly staring ahead, anticipating obstacles. Station personnel stared after him, shocked, or looked back at Keesey and Dalton pounding after him. Ahead, the corridor bulged outward. In most station designs, this meant there was some kind of work area, often with view ports that would let him see the ships in the dockyards. He was almost there. He just needed a glimpse of a ship's running lights in space.

Somebody tackled him. A man half a head taller wearing a MilDiv uniform enclosed him in a bear-hug and slammed him against the far wall. Mitchell's head rang with the impact. He couldn't hope to escape. He tried anyway, bucking and thrashing against his captor.

"Mitchell, look at me! Look at me!" Sweaty hands pressed against his cheeks. He shook his head, trying to break free of their grasp. "Mitchell!" Keesey shouted, pleading.

You're going to follow Morgan.

He begged, "Let me look! I just want to look! I'm not going to kill myself, I'm not going to do anything! I haven't done anything! Let me go!"

Multiple grips pinned his arms to the wall now. Others had come to help, he didn't know how many. The more he struggled, the harder they held him. When he felt his sleeve being pushed up, he knew it meant somebody wielded a sedative patch.

Mitchell screamed in defiance; his voice echoing in the steel corridor startled him.

"Mitchell!" Keesey managed to make herself heard over his noise. He clamped his mouth shut.

In the sudden quiet, the scene paused for a moment. Dalton held the patch ready, but hadn't yet pressed it against his arm.

Softly, Mitchell said, "Let me look. Just let me look outside one more time. Please. Please trust me. Please."

This was his last chance at life.

He saw his desperation clearly reflected back at him in Keesey's gaze. He thought he knew: She wanted to cure all her patients, and she kept failing. In him she was failing again.

He whispered, "You've never tried giving us what we want. What can it hurt? I'm already dead. Let me look."

Dalton released him first. Then Keesey said, "Let him go."

It had taken two others beside the doctors to restrain him. They all stepped back, tense, even Keesey, like he was a wild animal and they couldn't predict what he'd do next. He moved deliberately, brushing his sleeves back into place. He would give them no cause to capture him like an animal and drag him back to the cage. Keeping a shoulder to the wall, he moved toward the observation area. The others followed, forming a half-circle around him, penning him in.

At last he rounded the corner, entered the darkened observation area, and his knees almost buckled. He leaned against the wall, and his eyes stung with tears.

The windows looked out over the edge of the dockyards where Law Station opened into space. A trio of ships were in dock and a scattering of light from the hull of the station—traffic guides, lights shone out of other view ports. The rest of the view looked into the black and the points of light of distant stars.

The Universe opened before him. This was seeing home after a long, impossible journey.

He put his face close to the window and cupped his hands around his eyes to cut out reflections.

Ships, bulging lengths of steel, drifted in the open. The blisters of modular sections—decks, sensory apparatus, weaponry, docking space—made their silhouettes uneven, monstrous, confusing. The shapes distracted the eye, which looked for the streamlined profile of something that might swim through water but only found these accreted, unartistic objects. Yet they moved so gracefully. The eye could not judge their scale against the backdrop of shadow and gray steel. He was watching a scene impossibly distant. Yet the lights threatened to swallow him.

One of the ships was a Research Division cruiser, probably returned from a frontier mission for a refit. The other two were MilDiv. The far one—his heart fluttered, because it was a courier class, a sleek, minimalist ship built for speed, blockade running and dodging firing lines. The *Francis Drake* was a courier. They were the prettiest ships in the fleet. It might even be—hard to tell from here.

His brow furrowed, he pulled away from the window. "Is that the *Drake* in dock?"

"Yes," Keesey said.

"She should be long gone by now." He turned back to the window, rubbed his sleeve over it when his breath fogged it.

"Look again."

He watched for a long time, as long as he needed. The ship was locked into long-term docking, not simply linked by umbilical and airlock tubes like the other ships. She'd been damaged, a hole blasted into her starboard side as if a great monster had taken a bite out of her. Lights moved around her like fluttering insects: repair drones, suited workers on maneuvering platforms. A search light happened to run over the name written in bold cursive: *M.D.S. Franc—*. The remaining letters were charred.

The ship looked a little like Jaspar's skull.

His mind formed the question, *what happened*, but he did not speak the words. A neural pathway that had been ruptured rebuilt itself when offered the proper bridge.

He pressed his hand to the window.

He put his thumb on the duty roster scanner inside the hatchway to the bridge.

"Good morning, Captain."

Captain Crea Scott spared a glance over her shoulder. "Lieutenant. We have an hour until we need to jump. That enough time?"

"Yes, sir. The arrival matrix data's on the console?"

"Ready and waiting."

After two years together on the *Francise Drake* their routine was well-practiced. He passed along the bridge's upper walkway, paying only cursory attention to the displays and consoles which monitored the ship's systems, nodding to the crewmates who looked up from their work, and arrived at the hatchway leading down to the navigator station.

M-drive navigation was a one-person booth isolated from the rest of the bridge. He settled into the couch, belted in, and activated the console. Monitors, scanners, processors lit up, casting a cool glow and humming comfortably. It was his own realm—quiet, secure, and powerful. Here, he controlled the equipment that could propel the ship light-years across space.

He clipped his comm piece over his ear and called up the navigation data, destination and optimum window of arrival. With the ease of habit, he started the process which would identify the departure matrix for the most efficient jump to the designated arrival matrix.

Departure matrices flashed on the holographic display in unfamiliar hues. He frowned, reviewed the data, then cleared the equations. He had time; he'd simply run the calculations over again.

If he weren't entirely clear on which matrix they left from and where they were arriving, the ship would break apart as it tried to make the crossing. An anomaly in the possible departure matrices made him pause. If he wasn't certain about a matrix, he rejected it.

He'd never failed to find a departure matrix before. The Universe was massive and diverse; a solution could always be found. But this time they were all mouths, ready to swallow him, spitting out the wrong colors. The numbers cycled and showed him a void.

Except one. There it was, the solution. The matrix that would carry them safely away from this hole in space. He entered it, and the numbers flashed red.

Captain Scott said over the comm, "Greenau, do you have our heading?"

"Yes, sir. Departure matrix data transferred."

A silence answered him. The workings of the ship hummed and murmured.

"Greenau, send those coordinates again, please."

He did, with a touch of frustration.

"We can't follow that heading, Lieutenant. Those coordinates are inside the hull of the ship."

Of course not, the M-drive would push the ship into itself, making for one hell of an explosion. But Mitchell couldn't ignore the numbers.

"It's the only one, Captain." All the other colors were wrong.

"Mitchell, are you all right?"

"There aren't any other matrices. The space here is wrong. The colors are wrong."

"Oh my God—"

They didn't know it, they couldn't see what he saw. He had to save them.

He'd fought as every crewmember on the bridge tried to stop him because he thought he was saving them. That he could see something no one else could see. It never occurred to him that he'd gone mad. They'd seen it instantly—everyone knew what could happen to navigators, they all knew the symptoms. Still, he'd managed to get to the helm and punch in the drive protocol with the faulty departure matrix still entered—

They should have killed him before letting him get that far. They stopped short because he was theirs.

Parts of three levels ripped open instantly, spilling the ship's guts to the void. Captain Scott managed to cut all the ship's power, deactivating the drive before the ship was destroyed completely. The ship's medics sedated Mitchell. The accident had killed twenty people, a third of the crew. Through sheer, stubborn heroism, Scott and the remaining crew patched up the ship and managed to fly to Law, the closest outpost. There, Lieutenant Mitchell Greenau could be deposited with people who might be able to explain what had gone wrong with his mind.

Head bowed, Mitchell knelt on the floor below the window as Doctor Keesey explained.

"The dysfunction usually develops gradually. The patient experiences memory loss, synesthesia, schizophrenia, dystonia, ataxia—any number of neurological anomalies. The captain of the ship will take a navigator off duty at the first signs. A sudden, catastrophic episode like yours is very rare."

Who had died? He wanted to ask, but he doubted Keesey would know. Twenty names was too many to remember. But Mitchell would have to learn someday who among his friends and colleagues he had killed.

"You saw the right numbers, like you always saw," Keesey said. "But your mind showed you something else."

"Captain Scott didn't want me to know what happened."

"Because she knew it wasn't your fault. It's a terrible memory. I'm sorry."

A memory that, for all he had struggled to reclaim it, now felt pristine, nestled in the center of his mind.

Mitchell felt calm now. Dalton stood nearby and Keesey knelt beside him; both were watchful, like they expected him to break, or burst, or something, with the knowledge he had found.

Keesey finally said, "Mitchell, how do you feel?"

He despised that question.

He chuckled a little. "I'm sorry. I'm so sorry—"

"Mitchell—"

He could look up, and even at this awkward angle he could see lights on the opposite curve of the station, the blackness of the shadows. The beauty was an ache in his gut. That he could still feel that beauty startled him. "Don't isolate us from what makes us happy. We kill ourselves trying to get back to it."

"Are you ready to come back to the ward?"

He climbed to his feet, using the wall as a prop. He looked out the window again to the stark vastness of even this little corner of space. "Just another minute, Doctor."

They waited for him.

When Mitchell finally returned to the common room, Dora wasn't there. She'd made an escape attempt and had been sedated.

Jaspar was at his usual table, working his word puzzles on his handheld. Mitchell found what had happened to him: he'd tried to close his head in a bulkhead door. No one knew why. The trauma team got to him quickly and he'd survived, somehow. People were resilient.

Sonia was also present, humming, her eyes closed. Mitchell sat across from her.

He placed a player with earpieces in front of her. She stopped humming. She looked at him, her gaze narrowed and confused.

"It's yours."

Her hands trembling, she reached for the headphones. They skittered away from her fingertips the first time, but she caught them, slapping her hand to the table. Then she hooked on the earpieces.

Mitchell had gotten Keesey to give him the records of Sonia's musical vocabulary, all the pieces of music she'd been known to speak of. He convinced the doctors to let her have the player.

She touched the play key. Her face tightened, an expression of anxious disbelief. Then tears slipped down her cheeks. Mitchell heard the music, a faint buzzing through the earpieces, and his fists clenched nervously. He thought she would smile. He wanted her to smile.

Then she did smile, though she still didn't relax, and Mitchell realized that she was concentrating on the music with every muscle she had. She met his gaze, and he thought she looked happy.

DEAD POETS

I say someone in another time will remember us.

—Sappho, trans. Diane J. Rayor

The study of literature is the process of continually falling in love with dead people.

A sentence can do it. A well-turned phrase. Nearly all we have of Sappho are well-turned phrases, and she has survived more than twenty five hundred years on that. I tell my students, you will fall in love with these dead people, copying their poems in your notebooks, memorizing them because you can't help it. You will tell yourself you love the poems, not the poets. But you will love the poets, too.

Even though so many of them were difficult people. Opinionated, prone to locking themselves in rooms, drinking too much, and betraying their long-suffering lovers. We forgive them because of the words. But no matter how much we peel back those words, looking for the people who created them, they're all we have. And it's so easy to fall in love with someone who can't respond, whose difficulties you never have to confront. They can't reject you. They can't cheat on you or hurt you.

You can love an idea of someone to the core of your heart, seal that idea in amber, sink it in a well of longing, and never suffer any consequences. You will get tenure for the dispassionate papers you write and congratulate yourself that at least you were able to turn that love into a career. You understand that your love is for an image, a construct, and that is fine. You tell yourself you're satisfied with that.

I sneak into the archeology department lab after hours, and using my credentials I'm able to steal a small package. No, not steal. Borrow. I'm only borrowing it.

Safe at home, door locked, curtains drawn, I open the box, pull away the packing material, and reveal the artifact. It is an ancient kylix: a wide, shallow drinking cup with a sturdy foot and two slender handles. It's in extraordinarily good condition, an example of black-figure pottery, red terracotta with gleaming black images of elegant figures: a woman sitting in a curving chair, her tunic draped in folds. She is holding a lyre. Her expression is intent.

I had examined the cup earlier, at the request of an archeologist who made some speculation and wanted an unofficial opinion. Just to give my thoughts on the matter. There is no way of knowing for certain. Ancient poets didn't write their names on the bottom of their mugs so they wouldn't get lost in the dishwasher in the department break room. But yes, Sappho would have owned a cup very like this.

I need both hands to hold it. Drinking from it would mimic the motion of drinking from my cupped hands. It is approximately twenty-six hundred years old, and was excavated on the island of Lesbos. I want to believe with all my heart that this cup belonged to Sappho.

This is the point where that irrational love makes one just a little bit crazy. Where one's imagination goes a bit sideways. Where frivolous self-indulgence has made me break a pile of university rules, to bring this cup home.

At a specialty wine dealer I find a Vin Santo, a sweet white wine, from Santorini, the closest I can get to a wine that comes from Lesbos. They're both islands, at least. The grapes that made this wine could not possibly have grown on vines that were alive when Sappho was. It's as close as I can get. I can pretend she would have drunk a wine much like this. I have a clay oil lamp—a modern reproduction, but cast from an ancient example. She might have written at night by the flame of a lamp just like this. Too bad I'm in Boston and not Greece.

The sweet tang of the wine rises up and tickles my nose. The weight of the cup is steadying. The glow from the lantern is warm, flickering, casting shadows on the clutter of books and the cheap drapes closed over the window. I can almost imagine a more atmospheric setting: the courtyard of a villa at night, the texture of a tiled wall.

I put my lips on this two-thousand-six-hundred-year-old piece of pottery and imagine that her lips once touched the rim of this same cup, like a kiss. A sting on the tongue, as the sweet wine hits it.

It's a silly idea, reaching across the centuries to try to touch someone beyond her words. Thrilling, nevertheless. A striking image to share. I'll have to write it down, get a poem or two of my own out of my frivolity.

The light changes. My eyes are closed, but even so I can sense the surge from buttery yellow to bright red. My heart yearns into my throat, the room grows hot, like a sun has come to life in it. The floor opens up and seems to turn into a door and—

I open my eyes. I'm standing in a stone room that smells musty. Through a narrow window I can see an overcast sky, fading at dusk. Embers burn in a small fireplace. I shiver, maybe from the cold.

Why am I disappointed that this is not a Greek island? I should be on a sunny Greek island, looking down from a vantage on the edge of a cliff with view of a distant trireme plying blue Aegean waters. On the warm air drift the gentle notes from a lyre, which I follow to a marble courtyard, where poets have gathered and where she—

I have no reason to expect such a thing. To expect anything but feeling silly, and maybe aghast that I have poured wine into a priceless artifact. But somehow I'm standing in a chilled stone room that might be part of a castle, and there is a man, age thirty or so, lying on a cot in the corner. He seems dramatic, flung back, arm draped over his face. He's wearing a loose linen shirt, an unlaced doublet, rumpled breeches, and is stocking-footed.

My academic brain tells me his clothes are from 16th-century England. Given the scant furnishings in the irregularly shaped room, I think he might be a prisoner. A high-ranking prisoner, entitled to a cot and a fireplace, a table and a jug of something with a cup to drink from, but not much else. The window looks over the castle yard, a river beyond. . .

Oh. I know where I am.

I have loved many poets in my time. You don't subject yourself to a PhD in literature without being in love with words, and who made them.

This is ridiculous. I'm furious that I'm here in the Tower of London and not on a beautiful Greek island. I drank Vin Santo from an ancient kylix, not sack from a pewter cup a mere five centuries old.

The cup is still in my hands, the taste of wine still on my tongue. I set it down on the nearby rickety table before I drop it, because my hands are shaking. I rub them together.

Sir Thomas Wyatt still has not moved his arm or apparently noticed the strange woman standing in his cell.

I have to say something. I have to, but my stomach is churning. I know his words, the lines I fell in love with, but I don't know him. I have a lot of questions, but the questions I have when I read his poems sound silly now.

"Um. Hello?"

He starts, flinching back on the cot, pressing his back to the wall.

I'm not sure what he sees when he looks at me. A flushed woman in her thirties in what must seem like very strange clothes to him, striped yoga pants and an oversized sweater, my brown hair pulled back with a ragged headband. His eyes are wide, gleaming.

"A ghost has come to torment me," he says. His voice is…pleasant. A little rough, but clearly from exhaustion and stress. He has a light tenor that probably sounds lovely when he sings. Many of his poems would have been sung, lyrics written to entertain the ladies of court, accompanied by the lute. My knees go a little weak, thinking of him singing.

Sappho's poems were meant to be sung as well, and I suddenly wonder about my attraction to poets who also sang.

It's madness. It's all madness.

"No, I'm not—" But I don't know how to explain, and maybe it's best if he thinks I'm a ghost. "Um. Hi."

This man wrote the first sonnets in English. Within the formal structures English Renaissance poetry he poured a mountain of emotion. He inserted his own biography into his work, barely dressed in metaphor. If I could ask him anything, say anything—

"What are you?" He shifts to the edge of the cot. His hands clench as if reaching for a sword or knife.

"I don't know what I am," I say. "I think I'm having a dream."

He studies me. "If this is your dream then what am I?"

He is tragic. He is a painting. He is unpeeled from the formality of the era's portraiture, the polished, glowing images with their details of embroidered doublets and gold lace trim. Those serious faces, filled with inscrutable mystery. Or simply the images of people who are bored with sitting for an artist. If they had known how those portraits would live after them, they might have been more interested.

His beard is ragged, but he seems to have one of those faces that gains an alluring edge when it loses its polish. His dark hair is swept back, a little greasy. A man who has been lying in bed, despairing, for days.

I shake my head a little, wincing, as the history comes back to me, the date and context, along with a sinking feeling. "What day is it? The date?"

"The darkest," he says and moves to the window, leaning against the stone to look out.

He was imprisoned in the Tower because he was one of the men suspected of being Anne Boleyn's lovers. The lore is that he watched her execution from his cell. He wrote a poem about it. *"These bloody days have broken my heart…"*

"Is it true?" I asked. One of the questions anyone would ask him. He makes a disgusted sigh, and I realize I should have specified. Not *that* question, if he really was one of Anne's lovers. The other one. "Did you see it happen? Some people say you did, and some say you couldn't have, but it's such a good story—"

"It has only just happened, not these few hours past, and there are stories?"

It's been almost five hundred years, I don't say.

"Why should they even speak of me? I am nothing here." He slumps, his gaze still out that window. Riveted by the view, it seems.

"You write about it," I say. "Everyone wants to hear stories of unrequited love, of tragedy. Of irony." Because if Anne had chosen Wyatt, she wouldn't have died here, like this. "It appeals to the sense of the dramatic, to think you watched from your cell."

He chuckles. "To write about it I will have to survive it. That seems unlikely now."

"But you will," I say. "Maybe that's why I'm here. To tell you that you'll survive." A vision. An omen. His dream, not my own. He was imprisoned in the Tower twice and escaped with his life both times. He is charmed.

I'd sit but there isn't an extra chair. His interrogators, Thomas Cromwell and the rest, must have brought their own when they came to speak to him.

He says, "I cannot remember what it was like to be in love with her. All I see now is the blood. "

Ink stains his fingers, though there's no paper or anything to write with in the room. I know from his words, all the words of his I've read, that nothing I say will comfort him. I think of all the well-turned sentences this man wrote, that I loved. *I am not he such eloquence to boast to make the crow singing as the swan...*

He glances over. "Everyone loves her, at first. That is her talent. She sweeps her gaze up your body and looks away before she can possibly have the measure of you. It makes you wish to cry after her, wait, look again, see me. Please see me. You want her to look because you want to see her eyes again. Those gem-like eyes. As deep as a mine that is sure to collapse and bury you. But why do I tell you this, you cannot understand what it is to look upon a woman and feel pain."

No one knows what Sappho looked like. If I had a time machine… it's a silly question, a party game. If you had a time machine, where would you go? If I drink from that cup again, maybe I can get to the Greek island this time and learn what Sappho looked like.

"Every man loves her," he says again. "She captures them. And then she leaves them, but still they love her. Even as they hate and curse her, still, they love. But when she captured the king, we were all lost. Fitting, that it took a king to devour her."

This is a man who has spent his life using words, arranging them, making pictures with them, lining them up until they did just what he wished. He did this in a culture that valued the masterful use of words. He takes the skill for granted.

"You don't believe women can love at all, do you?" I ask.

"Of course not," he said. "Women are cold and feel no passion. They torture men because they must, it is their nature. They are driven by devils to ruin us."

Nothing he has said surprises me. It's all right there in his work, the words he wrote. He saw himself as a man brought low by women who mocked his pain.

He turns his back on them and so never sees the longing in their eyes.

"*I say nothing, my tongue broken, a delicate fire runs under my skin, my eyes see nothing, my ears roar...*"

"Yes, just so. Who wrote that? Whose words are those?"

"Sappho. A woman."

"Ahh." He breathes this out, a sigh. "I suppose, then, you want me to reconsider."

"You've had your heart broken, I get it. So have I. We all have."

"And do you write poetry about it?"

"I might," I confess. "Some. It's not any good. And don't tell me it's because women can't write poetry."

"You could perhaps recite for me—"

"No! Just…no." I don't want an impromptu critique from Thomas Wyatt. I might never recover. Not to mention having to explain postmodernism. "It would probably be better if I tried to write about something other than love."

"All poetry is about love," he says. "It can be about court or a journey or a war or God and it is still about love, when passion drives the words. It isn't only women who've broken my heart." He leans against the wall of the Tower, where he has been imprisoned by the councilors of Henry VIII, whom he has served loyally. So many loyal servants died here.

"You keep looking at the window," he says. "Come, and I will tell you what I saw." He shifts aside, to make room. I can't resist, not when I've come so far, and move beside him to see.

There is just enough light to reveal the scene. The wall of the keep encloses the green; on the outer wall beyond the green a guard stands watch.

On the green, the scaffold is still in place, the raised platform allowing all to see the deed. There was no block—Anne Boleyn had been executed by sword. The swordsman would have stood to the side. Where would her head have fallen? Would it have tumbled back? Did anyone worry that it might fly out into the crowd? I don't know anything about these things. There were dozens of eyewitness accounts of the moment. It's said that the coffin they used was too small and so they had to nestle her head by her feet when they carried her away.

I suppose I could ask.

"There is still blood on the dirt," he says. "Do you see it?"

The stretch of gravel before the platform is pale, and if I squint I can see one or two dark spots on the edge. They might just be shadows. It's too dark to see color.

He is at my back. He puts his hands on my shoulders to shift my angle, to see just what he sees. To picture the exact scene. The yard would have been filled with people. I try to imagine the sounds of it.

"Was the crowd silent or did they murmur? Did they cry out?"

"They were quiet. No one has ever executed a queen before. They were thinking of history, but, you see, I loved her. She was never mine, but I did." His breath touches my hair. His hands are still on my shoulders, just resting. How long has it been since he had any human contact?

"They hated her, because of how she made the world turn around her. She would not have fallen so hard, otherwise. She was brave. She did not weep nor beg. But I hoped. . .I hoped she might look this way, just once."

What else is there to say? "I'm sorry for your loss."

"It is a crime, to mourn the death of a traitor. No one will wear black for her." Wyatt's doublet is black.

I laugh a little. "They'd have to catch me before they could punish me."

He chuckles. His smile is bright, bringing a glint to his eyes. The old portraits never show anyone smiling, so that it's easy to think they never did. His smile changes him. *A delicate fire under my skin…*

He says, "When you go back to whatever spirit realm sent you, might I go with you?"

When I turn, just a shift of my shoulders, he is right there. His face near mine, hands still touching me. His lips part as if to say more, to tell yet again how much and how tragically he loved her. Yes, yes, I want to say, we all know, he can't shut up about it.

He kisses me.

And I let him. My hands grip his arms, his fingers stroke my neck and then tangle in my hair. Does he even see me or is he still looking out the window?

I kiss him back, arms closing around him as he presses me to the wall.

"I don't even know how I got here," I say.

His gaze lights on the kylix, sitting on the table across the room.

It is 1536. I'm trying to remember the dates, the timelines. Renaissance England is my hobby, not the focus of my research. I teach a survey class every other year. I'm trying to remember: what year is it that Wyatt first translates Petrarch from Italian, and introduces the sonnet into English? Is it after 1536?

He can't go, he has too much left to do, and I don't know if he understands that. He still thinks he's about to die.

There's a knock at the door. Supper, maybe. I don't know how meals work in the Tower. Wyatt flinches back; my eyes go wide. The door is about to open, and so I scramble away from him—

"Wait," he says, reaching. "What is your name—"

But I have already lifted the cup with both hands and drunk down the rest of the wine.

They flee from me that sometime did me seek
With naked foot stalking in my chamber...
It was no dream: I lay broad waking.
But all is turned thorough my gentleness
Into a strange fashion of forsaking...

Wyatt never wrote about ghosts. Not literally, not overtly. Still, all his writing looks different to me now.

Or maybe it's my imagination and it never happened at all. A bad batch of wine.

In my apartment, no time has passed. I'm standing right where I was, with an empty ancient cup in my hands. I'm appalled that I might have done damage to this artifact by pouring actual wine into it, but I'll have to worry about that later. Immediately, I set it down and grab a spiral notebook and pen. I want to remember every moment, every detail, the feel of his beard on my cheek, the sooty smell of the fireplace. The faint light on the green, the longing in his voice when he said he could see the blood there. He was looking for a point of connection, no matter how faint.

I write it all. The great tangled mess of it. There is a struggle, trying to manage the words. Some embarrassment, this falling in love with dead poets. There is confusion: I've fallen in love with a dozen other poets, why not send me to another? To Emily Dickinson, to demystify nearly everything about her. To Frank O'Hara, who never would have loved me back but wouldn't it be nice to just have coffee with him? Why did I meet Wyatt when I wanted to meet Sappho?

Maybe Wyatt needed to hear someone tell him he would live. Maybe this was about him and not me.

I write it all down because it's no hardship to do it. Paper and pen are right there, and the lamp is still burning. In the morning I will pack away Sappho's kylix and return it to the archeology lab before anyone knows it's gone.

"Um. Hi."

My pen smears across the page as I'm startled by the voice. Gasping, I turn in my chair to look behind me.

"Oh! It's you! It's really you!" An intruder stands there, a woman. I hadn't heard her come in, I could have sworn the door never opened. Was I so wrapped up in the work that I wouldn't have noticed? Possible.

I stammer out, "What are you—"

Then I notice. She is holding a clay cup. A Greek kylix. There is a shining drop of wine still on the edge.

WE TAKE CARE OF EVERYTHING

Part I: The Department of Talent Resources

Sara knew from experience that she made more in tips playing covers than she did playing her own songs. Fran, who owned the Muskrat Tavern, couldn't pay her up front, so all she had were tips. After a couple of hours of Dolly Parton standards and maybe a whacked-out acoustic Journey cover, she could walk out with enough for a couple weeks of groceries.

She needed more, of course.

Fran always apologized at the end of the night, when Sara cleaned out the tip jar and tried not to count it right there. "Wish I could do you better. You're good, honey. Ever think about heading to New York? Or maybe L.A.?"

Along with everyone else who had a guitar and a decent voice and dreams of making it big? Or even making it small? She'd settle for making it small. Sara needed money she didn't have to get to New York or L.A.

"Maybe next time *American Idol* has auditions," Fran suggested. She meant well.

"*American Idol* got cancelled again, Fran."

"Well. Maybe it'll start back up. Here's some for your GoFundMe." Fran slipped her a five-dollar bill. A fraction of what her prescriptions cost.

"Thanks." Sara grabbed her cane, shifted her guitar case over her shoulder, got herself balanced right, and limped out to the bus stop. Then climbed onto the bus, taking too long while the driver glared, impatient. The front three rows were taken so she had to maneuver halfway down the bus for a seat. No one moved to offer her an easier space to get to. When she finally sat, her cane jammed in awkwardly with her, she breathed shallowly against the pain, squeezed her leg as if she could stop the nerves from sending their wretched torturing signals.

And then had to reverse the whole process when the bus arrived at her stop. This all would have been easier with painkillers, but she was saving them to take before bed, so she could sleep.

When Sara finally got home, she almost didn't check her GoFundMe page. It was a battle: did her need to know outweigh the disappointment she would feel when the amount wasn't any higher than when she checked four hours ago? When that green line hadn't grown any longer? Was she ready for another round of tweets asking for help from people who weren't any better off than she was? Could she figure out a way to make her story more compelling, to make the page go viral? Get a celebrity endorsement? She'd already posted videos of her playing and suspected that was too corny to get any traction. Posting x-rays of her shattered leg had apparently just grossed people out.

The car had clipped her coming around the corner. The driver at least stopped to check on her, but he didn't have insurance and it didn't matter what the lawyer did; there wasn't any money there. Now she had to pay doctors *and* the lawyer. With her leg jacked up she couldn't wait tables anymore, and she couldn't stand to sing for more than a half hour at a time, even if she could get enough singing gigs to pay the bills. She kept playing at Muskrat Tavern because there she could sit on a stool the whole evening. She supposed this was her fault for not having a decent job, richer friends, a better family. She'd almost clawed herself out of the rotten life she'd been born into. The accident had thrown her into a different rotten life. If only that green line on the GoFundMe page would creep up, just a little. If only she didn't have to beg for every dollar. Maybe she shouldn't have expected miracles, not when so many people needed miracles, and bigger ones than she did. She was just trying to get PT and painkillers. Not like she was trying to save her life with insulin or a kidney transplant. Not like she had a ticking clock on her need. But there it was, she needed so little and even that was too much.

The thermostat in her studio apartment stayed at sixty to try to save on heat, and she wore three sweaters, a hat, and gloves. She'd gotten rid of the rug and coffee table because they'd proved hazardous, moving on her unsteady legs. Her laptop stayed by her bed, and she'd taken to keeping a kettle of water and packages of instant soup nearby so on bad days, she wouldn't have to maneuver to the kitchen. It was only a few paces away, but some days, even that distance was insurmountable.

At least she still *had* an apartment, but for how much longer? She couldn't imagine being on the street with a knee that didn't work. She was sinking further into the hole. She couldn't even see sunlight anymore.

The need to know how much she didn't have won out, and she checked the page, and sure enough that green bar hadn't moved. But a private message alert interrupted her, flinging a text box in the middle of her screen before she could ignore it.

A single line: *I will pay $100 to your GoFundMe if you'll Skype with me for ten minutes.*

Sara's heart jumped. Reflexively, her hand reached out to click a reply, yes yes, of course yes. The next moment, the reasons why she shouldn't say yes flooded in. This was weird. Creepy. Skeezy. What was she going to have to do, during those ten minutes?

A hundred dollars.

She replied, Okay. The next message, a Skype request, arrived instantly—the sender had been waiting. Ten minutes? All she had was time. She accepted the request, expecting a million things. A blank screen, a skeevy neckbeard in bondage gear. Of course this was going to be some pervert. But no—the face that appeared on her screen belonged to a nice middle-aged white woman in a business suit. Thin-rimmed glasses. Perfectly highlighted, honey-colored hair. You couldn't help but trust a woman who looked like this, even when you knew you shouldn't. The wall behind her was beige, with nondescript office shelves to one side, arranged with a perfectly neutral combination of books and objects d'art.

Propped up in bed, Sara was a mess and refused to show video on her end of the call.

"Sara. Hello." The voice was sugar. "I'm Miranda."

"Um. Hi."

"I've been following your story. I'm so sorry for the difficulties you've faced."

"Thanks." Sara sounded defeated. A lot of people told her how sorry they were.

"I want to help."

"I can always use some extra donations—"

The woman, Miranda, closed her eyes, shook her head. "I don't mean a few dollars that might buy a few pills. I mean *help*. Long term help that will get you back on your feet. You'll never have to worry again."

Any offer that sounded too good to be true probably was. Sara needed help, she couldn't deny that. But that need—her desperation—made her vulnerable.

"I don't understand," she said, to buy time and to fish for the catch.

"I can give you a job."

"I can't work. I mean—I *want* to work, but…I have trouble standing for more than half an hour or so. There isn't much I can do." She could sing and play guitar. She could wait tables—if she could get her knee fixed. She didn't have the training for a desk job.

"My organization needs many different kinds of people, with many skills. You don't have to make any decisions now. With your permission I'd like to send you some literature about PanCorp and what we do. What our expectations are. What I'd most like to get across to you now is this: we take care of our people, Sara. We don't let anyone fall through the cracks. I've been following your story because I think—I know— you're a good person. And I think you're a good fit for PanCorp."

It was a sales pitch. It wasn't even trying to sound like something other than a sales pitch.

Miranda continued. "As I said, you don't need to say anything right now. Read over the prospectus. Message me with any questions you have, any at all. Or never talk to me again. It's up to you. As I promised, I'll make a donation to your GoFundMe account as a sign of good faith. You don't have to do anything you don't want to, ever. How does that sound?"

"I'd like to read things over. I… I can't really decide anything right now."

"I understand." She was so calm, not making any demands. "I look forward to hearing from you, Sara."

The call cut off.

Quickly, Sara closed the app and switched to the browser window, the one that always showed her GoFundMe page. She refreshed it.

A hundred dollar donation from Miranda at PanCorp. Just like that. The accompanying message said, *So nice to talk to you.* As if the woman actually meant it.

Sara started crying. She didn't mean to, the money was a fraction of what she needed, but that jump, that much more green than she'd had before—the feeling washed through her system like a drug. Maybe she'd be okay. Maybe she'd stop plunging down the endless hole. Maybe she could even climb back out of it.

Imagine, not having to worry anymore.

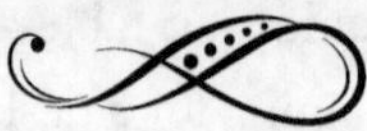

Sara read over the brochures Miranda emailed her and had flashbacks to every Scentsy party invite she'd ever gotten through Facebook. This was multi-level marketing. This had to be a scam. She'd sign up and all she'd have to do was sign up another hundred people and she'd be rich. Back to begging all over again.

Then she read it again.

A lot of PanCorp's business model seemed to be monetizing various online outlets through ad clicks and pageviews. From what she could gather, what they wanted her to do was generate content and promote it online. They made it sound like it wasn't any different than what she already did on social media. She couldn't find any statistics on how many people they already had working for them and what the company's revenues looked like. She'd never heard of PanCorp, but they appeared to be behind a lot of apps and platforms she knew.

Miranda waited three days before Skyping back to ask if Sara had any questions. Sara decided to just come out and ask the big one.

"I'm not really sure how you make money—how I can do anything that's going to make you money. It seems like there are already so many people doing online marketing already—"

The woman nodded like she understood, like she heard this argument every day. "PanCorp is different than other large online media conglomerates. We're looking to centralize the entire experience, and solidify the loyalty of our client base through outreach rather than relying on a more distributed approach."

Sara had no idea what any of that meant.

Miranda continued, "The important part of our model is our commitment to taking care of our talent pool."

"Talent" was what they called their employees, according to the brochure. Like a peppy chain restaurant that called its wait staff "associates," as if that somehow elevated the work.

"We have immediate access to our producers, to better deploy our income strategies," Miranda said. "How's your leg feeling, Sara?"

"It's not great," Sara confessed. The pain of shattered bone only partly healed stabbed up her thigh; just mentioning it seemed to make it worse. If she did the exercises, it got better. But to do the exercises she needed to manage the pain, and she needed medication for that. The cycle went round and round.

"Did you get to the part about our health plan? If you sign our comprehensive talent agreement, you'll have access to complete health coverage. You won't need your GoFundMe anymore."

Sara ducked her gaze to hide the tears welling in her eyes.

"I know you mistrust the very idea because you've never heard it before—but PanCorp takes care of its people, because people who are cared for are more productive. It's that simple. Our talent is our real asset. PanCorp understands that."

Still Sara hesitated, because Miranda was right—she didn't trust.

"I'll tell you what, why don't we start a trial period? Just a month, and you can see how you like it before considering the comprehensive agreement. You won't have the health plan—not yet—but you'll earn credit on your profile."

"What would I need to do for a trial period?" But she was thinking: *a health plan.* She could get her leg *fixed* and not just managed. Have a life and not this stumbling existence.

Miranda said, "You sing, don't you? Why don't you make a video. Post it, see what happens."

"Really? You'd be okay with me doing that?" It's the kind of thing she was doing anyway, and if she could actually make money at it… None of her videos had hit big enough to reach any kind of threshold that would start generating income.

Sara only wondered for a second how Miranda knew about her singing. She'd put it all online, hadn't she? She'd wanted people to know about it. A couple of links on social media and Miranda would know everything about Sara and exactly what would win her over. Sara should have hung up right there, knowing she was being steered into something—but then she thought about that green line on the GoFundMe page.

"If the clip goes viral, who knows? That's what PanCorp wants to encourage—experimentation. Try it and see." Her smile was kind, encouraging. Like that of a supportive mother, not a salesperson.

Sara chuckled. "I can't just make something go viral. If I could, my GoFundMe would have paid out ten times over."

"Leave that to PanCorp. All you have to do is make the video, submit it under our trial-basis talent agreement, and we'll handle the rest."

In the end, Sara thought, *What do I have to lose?* The answer was: nothing. Literally nothing.

The process of becoming a PanCorp employee—the talent— turned out to be pretty complicated, even on a trial basis. Sara carefully read over the twenty-page agreement, because she couldn't afford a lawyer to read it over for her and didn't know anyone who could help with that, even though she sort of suspected she really ought to have someone official read it.

In the end, she decided it was okay because of the clause that said she could leave PanCorp any time she wanted, for any reason. She'd have to leave what she earned behind, but that sounded fair. It also sounded abstract since she hadn't earned anything yet. But if she could leave whenever she wanted, how bad could it be? She'd had ex-boyfriends who weren't that forgiving.

She signed the agreement online while Miranda looked on from a chat window, beaming. Sara assumed she got some kind of bonus for each new person she signed up, even on a trial basis. Miranda gave her a login to PanCorp's talent portal—she'd upload her video there. PanCorp distribution would give her exposure, and ideally an audience that she'd never had access to before. The more hits, the more she'd earn.

Sara thought long and hard about what she should record for this trial video. She imagined it being an audition for a big record label, her big break, her chance for the musical career she'd always wanted. She'd find her best original song, put her heart into it…

But no, this was different. This wasn't a record company; this was about popularity. This was more like playing for tips at Muskrat's. So she picked her most popular cover, the one that always got people cheering, her soulful acoustic version of Journey's "Separate Ways."

She dressed in something of a caricature of herself, a down-on-her-luck hipster chick with long tousled hair, nose ring, lacy camisole. Made a corner of her apartment look homey instead of cold. Did it all in one take and sent the video off to the PanCorp portal before she lost her nerve. Then she logged out of all her social media, shut down her phone, and crawled into bed, wondering what the hell she'd done.

What Sara really wanted the next morning was a bottle of wine, but she was trying to be good and not spend her money on non-essentials. Since she didn't have wine, she turned her phone back on. She had to know.

Her account at PanCorp's talent portal had dozens of notifications. Hundreds of message requests. Link after link, all of them comments on her video. It hadn't even been a whole day yet, and thousands of people had watched the video on dozens of sites, and the numbers kept scrolling up.

Nothing like this had ever happened to her.

She sent a message to Miranda, who called back just a minute later. "Sara, how are you?"

"I'm…I'm confused. What *happened*?"

"That video you posted was just lovely, and a lot of other people thought so too."

"What does this translate to in, like, actual money?"

"Well, if you check the PanCorp portal, you'll see what your credits are and what they're worth."

Not money. That was the catch. Sara's heart sank, and Miranda must have sensed the disappointment because her smile turned sweet. "Just check your profile, Sara. You'll see what it translates to. Call me back anytime. I'll answer all your questions."

Hands shaking, feeling stupid, still not sure what any of this meant, Sara clicked through to the page on her talent portal account.

Her profile had one thousand, four hundred eighteen credits. The number was going up. Maybe not *quickly*, but a couple credits every minute. Every time her video was shared. She had no idea if that was a lot, or if it was worth anything at all besides a number on a screen.

She clicked over to the "Redeem" link, which opened a menu. Options included "Shopping," "Travel," and "Fun." Also "Essentials," "Home," and "Health." This looked like some rewards plan, where you cashed in points for stuff. A whole, vast catalog that seemed to cover every imaginable category. She clicked the "Travel" link and scrolled through dozens of thumbnails of pretty scenery and beautiful people lying on beaches, all of which was out of her reach, she was sure. This kind of thing wasn't for people like her, and this whole credits deal was a cruel joke. But then she focused, actually started reading. And saw that one thousand credits would buy her a train ticket to New York. She could afford that. She had enough.

Holding her breath, she searched through the "Essentials" category. And "Health." With her credits she could get three months worth of groceries, delivered to her apartment. A couple of sessions of PT, and the pain relievers she'd need to get through her exercises.

Anything she wanted, anything she needed, she could get through the portal. New clothes. A new guitar. Concert tickets. Music and movie subscriptions. Earn enough, she could lease an apartment at PanCorp's new housing development. That listed as cheaper than the rent on the rathole she was living in now. The development had its own gym and grocery store. It had a clinic, and they were working on getting a university extension where residents could finish degrees or work on new ones.

We take care of our people, Sara.

She would never have to worry about anything ever again.

"I'm so happy you're joining us, Sara. You won't regret it."

Sara went in person to PanCorp's offices, the corner of a downtown high rise, to sign the full Talent Agreement. Miranda sent a car for her, so Sara didn't have to navigate the buses. She was being so nice. The place was stylish, displaying wealth in its simplicity, spring green accents against off-white floor and walls, video artwork imbedded in the walls. Created by PanCorp talent, no doubt. The place smelled faintly of gardenias.

Ushering her to a seat across the desk, Miranda winced in sympathy at Sara carefully maneuvering as she sat, arranging her leg and cane in a way that was obviously painful.

"We'll get you healthy again just as soon as we can." She was just as kind and motherly as the image she projected online. She wasn't too tall, wasn't too thin, and her smile never wavered. "Since we discussed everything already, all we need to do here is sign."

Miranda handed over a tablet, and Sara signed before she could chicken out. Focus on the health care, on getting the leg fixed. On never needing to check that green line again.

"You won't regret this. You'll see. We take care of everything." Miranda pressed an intercom button, and a young woman entered the office through a side door. "And here's your Key," she said, beaming. Sara wondered, how many credits was she getting for signing someone up for the full contract?

The Key was a watch-like device that strapped to Sara's wrist. The young technician was polite, professional, asking Sara to hold out her arm, pressing the device to it and adjusting the strap. "Is that comfortable?" she asked, and Sara had her tweak it a little. Then the technician secured it, bolting it in place.

As per the terms of the contract, Sara couldn't take it off, now. Not without help.

"It's powered by your body's nervous system. Isn't that neat?" Miranda said.

Sara could ask to have it taken off any time, she assured herself. It was right there in the contract. She could leave, anytime.

Miranda typed on her tablet, submitting the contract Sara had just signed. The screen on her Key lit up, a friendly "welcome" message over top the spring-green PanCorp logo. A moment later, a second message replaced the welcome message: A thousand credits had just been deposited in her account. Sara's eyes widened, and she looked back at Miranda.

"That's just for signing up," Miranda said. "I imagine you'll be excited to get to work? You'll get some messages about new opportunities very soon."

"Thank you," Sara breathed.

"No, Sara. Thank *you*."

The message Miranda promised was waiting for her when she got home. It contained a list of tasks. They were simple, meaningless even. Upvote links and posts made through the PanCorp talent portal. Each upvote would get a credit in her account. Supportive comments: five credits. She spent twenty minutes just cruising sites and clicking and commenting, racking up credits. Ten. Twenty. Thirty. Her portal Key chimed each time she completed a task, and her credit count increased.

She took a break to make some tea and use the bathroom. When she returned to her screen, a new message appeared, with a kind of vibrating frame around it, anxiety-inducing. *It has been ten minutes since you completed a task. Choose another task in the next five minutes for a ten-credit bonus!*

The portal sent a new list to her, with some of the same tasks and some new ones as well. Ones she could complete for ten credits, twenty credits. As expected, these weren't as simple as clicking on links and upvoting and commenting. Downvote links and posts from rival companies. Report links and posts from rival companies as spam.

Not as simple at all. Sara hesitated. Drank her tea. How could it be harder to dislike something than like it? The PanCorp portal even offered her lots of links to choose from, already selected. She didn't have to go hunting for them. Upvoting the company's own stuff seemed fine, but didn't this—downvoting the competition—seem like…cheating? An icon with a countdown clock flashed in the corner of her screen. In two minutes, she'd lose the bonus.

She hunted for posts she didn't like anyway and downvoted them for the credits. She'd never downvoted anything in her life. It had always seemed a little like bullying. But she did it, and the countdown clock icon turned into fireworks and a big smiling star, which seemed a bit childish but felt good all the same, and her Key chimed with more credits. And a new message:

Complete three tasks in the next hour for a ten-credit bonus!

She could keep this up all night and be *rich*.

Her Key pinged with a new task list. *Choose a new task in the next five minutes for a ten-credit bonus!* And this one was *fifty* credits—what did she have to do for that?

Sign this petition to be submitted to state government to relax residential zoning codes to allow PanCorp to build additional Comprehensive Communities in your area!

She had to think about this one, while the clock ticked down to four minutes, then three. Then she signed it, because she wanted those credits, and she decided that nothing ever happened with those online petitions anyway.

Her Key flashed hearts and stars, a surge of celebration that filled her with the kind of simple joy she usually only got from singing. She was a success, she had done well, she would be taken care of.

She called Fran at the Muskrat Tavern and cancelled her next gig. Her time would be better spent with PanCorp.

Her credits ticked up, and up, and up.

Part 2: Keep Your Streak Going!

On the tiny stage at PanCorp Meridian Tower's Karaoke Heaven, Sara belted out Journey's "Separate Ways," accompanied by raucous cheers from the drunk crowd. She'd done this song before—she didn't need to follow the words on the screen—and so was able to make it a real performance and not just a party trick. Besides, this song had made her famous. Well, internet famous. For a day or two. That first video she'd done still made the rounds now and then, even six years later. Some people in the audience remembered, so for them this was almost like seeing a movie star at the coffee shop.

And it was *fun*. She gripped the mic and *danced*. On *pain-free* legs. She never would have been able to do this six years ago when she was playing for tips at dive bars, propped up on a stool because she couldn't stand for long on her smashed leg. But PanCorp made good on its promise to take care of everything—including her health expenses, and the knee replacement was holding up great. These days, she felt great, and she put it all into the performance. She could always get the crowd going at Karaoke Heaven. Next song, she'd take requests.

She finished the song, arms straight up, head tipped back triumphantly as the last guitar riff faded, and she basked in the adulation. Place had never been louder than it was right this minute, and it was all for her.

As she left the stage, her audience still clapped, patted her arms, reached for her and she clasped their hands in return, like she was some kind of real rockstar. She was sweaty, flushed, and grinning like a mad thing. She glanced at her Key—the creds were pouring in, a flurry of animated gold stars, everyone in the place tipping her a cred or two or more if the spirit moved them. On a good night she'd walk out with a hundred creds, a tangible symbol of the goodwill of her peers and neighbors. That little thrill was still there, watching as the number ticked up, accompanied by animated sparkles.

That had maybe been the best part about moving into Meridian

Tower, getting in on the We're All Friends Support Program. If someone did her a favor, or was just nice to her, she could drop them a cred or two directly. Everyone here worked so hard to be nice to each other, to help each other, and it meant so much when you could show—or receive—thanks directly.

Her Key flashed a message: *You are sixth on Meridian Tower's We're All Friends leader board! Your neighbors love you!*

Flushing happily, she started planning what she could do to move up by the end of the month, when the ranks were tallied. Those in the top five slots were awarded prizes.

She reached the bar, and a guy sidled up beside her. She'd seen him around. He lived upstairs from her and they'd run into each other now and then at the third level gym. He was a regular at Karaoke Heaven but never got up to sing. Maybe six foot, average build, not ripped but no slouch, either. Sandy-colored hair swept back, a fashionable level of stubble just shy of a beard. Bright dark eyes. Yeah, she'd noticed him. He wore a plain T-shirt and jeans. Nice and simple.

"Hi," he said, and she smiled back. "Can I buy you a drink?"

It was clearly a line—Karaoke Heaven had an open bar, one of the perks of being at Meridian. But she chuckled because the line made his intentions clear. "Gin and tonic."

"Oh? I figured you'd either be red wine, or scotch on the rocks."

She shrugged. "Sometimes I am. It all depends."

"You like keeping people on their toes?"

"No, in fact I'm very predictable. I'm here every Thursday night and I'm betting you knew that already."

His smile flickered, just for a second. A hint of honesty and not the come-on. "Maybe I did."

He also asked for a gin and tonic. The drinks arrived.

"Cheers," he said, and they clinked glasses. His name was Tom. She took him back to her apartment.

It just made sense. By providing housing, PanCorp's Talent could live in a prime location with all the amenities for a fraction of what they'd pay on their own, never mind the savings in transportation. By centralizing everything from utilities to food costs, PanCorp saved money, and all members benefited. They all lived better, but it only worked if they all supported the system. Sara could go outside for food, clothes. Convert her creds to currency, do it all on her own and still work for PanCorp. But why would she? Everything was cheaper here. Easier. She barely had to do anything at all.

Sara didn't have a window—apartments with windows cost more creds than she had. She was saving up for a trip to London, and, besides, she didn't need a window. She had the video screen on the wall set for sunrise, and the light would fade up as if coming through lacey curtains. Almost as good as the real thing.

As the room got light, she rubbed her eyes, and snuggled up against Tom's warmth. He woke up just enough to put his arm around her. She'd had a good night with him and would have to figure out how to maybe have another. Hoped he'd be into that, and that he wasn't just prowling Meridian's bars and clubs for a different girl every night.

She'd looked him up on the directory—his profile wasn't that prominent, he didn't have a huge amount of cred, but he didn't have any downvotes either, so that was something. She wasn't quite ready to give up the fraught dating life within Meridian's limited options for PanCorp's matchmaking service. Not yet, at least. She liked Tom. She couldn't decide if she should tell him that straight out, or play it cool out of fear she might chase him away.

"Hey, you okay?" He brushed a strand of hair over her ear.

"Yeah," she murmured, pressing her face to his shoulder. "Thinking about making coffee but that would mean getting up."

"Hm, don't get up yet." Happily, she pressed her body to his, enjoying the feel of skin against skin.

She did get up though, a few minutes later, when her Key chimed an alert. A message flashed on the screen, accompanied by a gentle chime. The usual wake up call.

Good morning, Sara! Here's today's task catalog!

Pushing back the covers, she grabbed her tablet on the nightstand and scrolled.

"What're you doing?" Tom murmured, burrowing into the bed's warmth.

"Task catalog's up. The good stuff gets taken early so I like to check first thing. You can log on from here if you want to."

You have a thirty-eight-day streak on the following tasks. Keep your streak going! Five-credit bonus!

His complaining moan suggested that no, he didn't want to. He asked, "Why did I think you were career track?"

"I don't know. Did you check my profile?" Everyone checked each others' profiles. He only chuckled.

Career track meant locking yourself into one task, aiming for management, or even entering the PanCorp organizational structure. Gunning for the job of someone like Miranda, who'd been Sara's recruiter. Miranda had advanced to a VP position in the Department of Talent Resources, so Sara didn't talk to her much anymore. Her case file had been handed off to another talent manager. Sara didn't have too many problems that needed managing.

She said, "I like to leave time for side projects, making videos and things." It had been a year or so since she'd had a video go viral, but she still had enough subscribers on her channel to make keeping it up worthwhile. And there was always karaoke, and creds from We're All Friends. Maybe she ought to start recording some of her karaoke performances. Or writing new words to old songs, something with enough novelty to get attention…

"I think I'll just take the day off," he said, freeing a hand from the sheets to rub her thigh. "Come on, want to spend the day in bed with me?"

Lock in tasks before 9 a.m. for a five-cred bonus!

Tom's offer was tempting. But not even looking at the day's task list was a five-credit penalty. Might not mean much for one day, but it added up over time.

Today's Urgent Tasks! Ten-cred bonuses! Custodial Rotation. Sweeping floors and cleaning bathrooms in public areas. Food Service in various capacities. Yeah, those almost always came up urgent. Unappealing, but worth more cred. If she wanted to get to London sooner, maybe she ought to take on a couple of those tasks over the next week or so.

She clicked on the task labeled Network Engagement—promoting PanCorp online—because of that thirty-eight-day streak and because she wouldn't have to leave the apartment. She could spend part of the day in bed with Tom, then earn some cred. She highlighted the task, held her breath a moment to see if the request went through or if someone had snatched the job out from under her, and sighed when the message came back with a victory chime and a burst of friendly animated fireworks. She had ten hours to complete the listed task. She felt like she'd already gotten something done today.

Meanwhile, Tom was pulling her back into bed. She'd only need to spend a couple of hours on the task, and that could wait.

Her Key chimed the countdown clock: *You have nine hours and fifty minutes to complete your assigned daily task!*

They were kissing gently, still waking up and warming up, Sara only a little distracted by the countdown clock on her Key. Then her Key pinged an alert. Not a serious buzzing that would mean she'd done something wrong, but still urgent. A friendly sort of even-toned hum that meant, *you really want to look at this.* Confused, she shifted to get her arm free of Tom's shoulder and looked at the wristband. Alerts came through to announce time-sensitive tasks, when PanCorp needed a lot of people right this minute, like to sign a petition—last week it had been a petition to state government for a minimum wage exemption for special circumstances, and they'd paid a hundred credits for it—or when there was some kind of building maintenance issue. This was probably it, because Tom's Key pinged half a second later, which meant they were both staring at their wrists together.

Text flashed at her in an urgent font, with the feeling of a sale that would be over in seconds, a deal that she couldn't possible turn down: Get pregnant. Have a baby, file a PanCorp Talent Agreement on the baby's behalf, and earn thirty-thousand credits. Each.

Tom's portal flashed the same message. Directed at both of them together. Combined, sixty-thousand credits could get an apartment with a window, an extra bedroom. And the trip to London she'd been saving for.

They looked at each other. Sara's heart was racing. She hadn't really thought about having a baby—she wanted to find the right guy first, then she figured the baby would take care of itself. But this—well, she wasn't getting any younger. And Tom had a way about him, a wry turn to his smile, hinting that he was usually in a good mood and always ready to cheer people up. Maybe PanCorp saw something in the two of them, maybe it knew something. Did anyone ever get so clear a sign?

She didn't know him well enough to be able to tell what he was thinking, but thought she imagined the same calculations playing over his expression—shock, then thoughtfulness. Then eagerness. Thirty thousand credits each.

Without a word, they fell into frenzied lovemaking.

Years passed, and things were fine. PanCorp took care of everything, and everything was fine.

Twenty years passed.

You have one hour and fifteen minutes to complete your daily assigned tasks!

Failure to complete your assigned tasks: fifty credit penalty!

Keep your streak going!

Sometimes Sara wished she could shut off the Key. Well, no she didn't, not really. She needed it. But sometimes it was really hard to ignore it, and right now she really needed to focus on what was in front of her.

Her daughter Emily had asked to meet her away from their apartment, at a café on one of the promenade levels. This meant she was trying to avoid a confrontation, a fight, which meant she had something awful to say that would upset Sara. Sara thought she knew what it was, but avoided even considering it. It simply didn't bear dwelling on.

Her Key pinged a message: *Your heart rate shows some distress. Please breathe calmly for one minute. Five-credit penalty for ignoring this message.*

Sara stopped right there in the hallway and tried to bring her heart rate down so the Key wouldn't buzz again. Didn't know if she succeeded, but stopping must have been enough because her Key didn't signal a penalty.

Down twenty floors to the atrium she reached the promenade café—the one that cost five credits just to walk in the door. Which meant Emily had something *really* awful to say. Of course, the way she'd been spending her credits lately… But no, that couldn't be it. Emily was doing just fine. She was simply going to tell Sara what school she'd decided on and wanted to give her the news someplace nice. This was going to be a celebration.

She tried to breathe calmly so her Key wouldn't notice her pounding heart.

Meridian's nicer levels were markedly different from the levels where Sara lived, where she spent most her time. The lighting was softer, the floor had patterned carpet instead of tile. The orchids and flowering shrubs were real, carefully tended in carved planter boxes. The wrought-iron bistro tables and chairs gave the place the air of French café. The music on the PA was classical. The hissing of the espresso machines was muted. Sara relaxed just being here. Breathed a little deeper, moved a little slower, even though she worried she looked out of place here—she was dressed neatly enough in a colorful skirt, shirt, and sandals. She might be pushing fifty but she still looked put together. Her clothes, her hair, pulled back in a pony tail—they looked neat. They just didn't look *expensive.* She usually didn't regret it, but… If she worked harder, if she'd gone career track, say, she could have this all the time, instead of just for special occasions. She could still, she supposed. She had time. She had nothing but time.

Have water instead of coffee—five cred bonus!

Her blood sugar, cholesterol, and stress levels had been way up at her last checkup. She wouldn't have gone for a checkup at all, but missing an annual physical was a hundred cred penalty. *People who are cared for are more productive,* Miranda had said. PanCorp was trying to steer her toward better choices. They took care of everything.

But she'd really love to have a coffee right now. Actually, she'd really love a glass of wine. But no, if she wanted the creds she should have water. That wouldn't be too hard.

Sara scanned the tables, and there she was, her beautiful daughter. Nineteen years old, her hair pinned up to the back of her head in artful disarray. She wore a too-big T-shirt and too-tight jeans, sandals, lots of bracelets and big earrings. She looked way too young, impossibly young and bright and fragile. Sara's heart ached with the sight of her, and what she didn't want to admit was coming.

"Hey kiddo," she said, joining her. Emily stood up to hug her, and Sara kept forgetting that her daughter was two inches taller than she was. It surprised her every time. "Want me to get—"

Emily already had two drinks set on the table—real ceramic mugs at this place. "Latte, right?" she said.

"Oh honey, I could have gotten it, it's no trouble." She was going to get water. Five cred bonus. Her Key seemed to hum a disappointed note.

"I wanted to. It's fine." Her smile was thin, anxious. Sara settled into her seat and sipped her latte. She imagined that despite the nice surroundings, the coffee tasted just the same as it did on any other level. But gosh, it just felt so much nicer here. Five creds worth of nice.

Emily sipped her own coffee. Didn't say anything, just watched her mother across the table.

"Is everything okay?" Sara asked, and regretted it. She hadn't meant to ask that. If Emily had something terrible to say, let her say it. Somehow in the last couple of years, she'd lost the ability to make small talk with her daughter. How is school, how are your friends, do you want to see a movie—all seemed too vacuous.

You have one hour to complete your daily assigned tasks! Penalty: fifty creds!

Emily's smile tightened and she glanced away which meant that no, things were not okay. "Have you seen Dad lately?" she asked, instead of telling Sara what was wrong.

Sara played along. "Not for a while. Maybe a year or so ago?" She and Tom had lasted longer than most people would have expected. The rush of the huge bonus they got for making Emily lasted years. They'd have had a couple more kids, one right after the other, but the offer never came again. In fact, right after Emily was born they'd gotten a reminder: They would need to provide for additional children out of their own store of creds, and would they like to hear about convenient birth control options? The penalty for not taking advantage of these options was steep. So there was only Emily. She was enough. "He wasn't doing very well, I'm afraid."

"They took a kidney from him."

Sara nodded. Yes, she knew that. He'd accumulated a lot of penalties, for lots of reasons that had seemed understandable at the time. Too many days of not checking the task list, taking too much and giving too little. The child bonus ran out, and eventually he hadn't been able to pay for his half of their upgraded apartment. That had been the start of their arguments. Did they pool their credits, did she take on the responsibility for him not working as much as he could, did she turn into the kind of person who nagged her partner for not being who she wanted him to be?

He'd surprised her by moving out before the crisis got that far, into one of Meridian's minimal efficiency units. There'd never even been a question of Emily living with him in a place like that, so Sara had kept custody of their daughter. Tom had never really had enough to help out with her, once he ran through the bonus. But Sara hadn't needed his help. She was proud of that. Emily was smart, beautiful, and had paid for herself a couple times over, with her education bonus creds. Would continue to do so.

"Yes, I heard," Sara said. "I'm sure he's doing better now."

"They'll take part of his liver next."

His liver wasn't worth much, Sara guessed. She lowered her gaze.

Emily was insistent. "He hasn't returned my messages. I need to talk to him. I mean, after I talk to you. I need to tell him."

"About school? You've decided?" Sara straightened, compulsively gripping the latte.

Emily shook her head. "No, Mom—"

Your heart rate shows some distress…

"The medical program is so good. Have you thought any more about that? You used to want to be a doctor. A surgeon. You've got the profile for it." Between her excellent grades and her maintaining such a high profile score, PanCorp counted Emily as an asset on their ledgers. She would make the company money rather than cost them. PanCorp would never take a kidney from her. And if Emily went to medical school, Sara, as primary caregiver, would get a ten thousand credit bonus. PanCorp would get a doctor, and Emily would be taken care of for the rest of her life. That was all Sara wanted, for Emily to be cared for. To not have to face what she'd been through at Emily's age, not knowing if she could make rent, scraping pennies together for every meal.

"No, Mom." Emily's Key remained quiet, unconcerned about her heart rate. Despite everything, she was calm.

Sara was making this more difficult, not less. She wasn't trying to be difficult. She was just…postponing. When clearly all Emily wanted to do was get the words out.

"Mom, I'm leaving."

And there it was, a stone dropping through her gut. Sara had expected this. For years now, if she were honest. She just hadn't wanted to admit it. Still didn't. "What do you mean? You talked about going career track at a different tower when a spot comes open, right? Well, that's fine…I'll miss you, but—"

"I'm leaving PanCorp."

Tears welled in Sara's eyes, and she was mortified. She was stronger than this, she could handle this. "But why? I… I don't understand."

But she did. Maybe she did. The look in Emily's gaze was determined. "I just want something different."

"You'll lose everything." All the cred she'd already built up, all the opportunity—not to mention all the cred Sara would get for being her mother. Was there a penalty for having one's child leave PanCorp? How much would she be penalized, if Emily left? "It's a risk."

"But a good one. And you…you could come with me."

Of course she could, yes, she would follow Emily anywhere. Weirdly, just then, her knee twinged. The old injury, the one she hadn't been able to get medical care for until she signed on with PanCorp. It ached as a reminder. She had twenty-five years of equity built up. If she had any hope of retiring, any hope of holding on to what she'd earned—she couldn't leave.

"Emily, please think about this. This is just a whim. What if you change your mind?"

" No, I've thought enough, I really want to do this—"

"You're nineteen, how can you possibly know what you want to do!"

"I know exactly what I want to do. I'm not a kid anymore—"

Both their Keys pinged. Only Sara looked at hers.

We're All Friends here! Arguments are unproductive. A crying emoticon filled the screen. *Penalty for not ending current argument: ten creds. Hug it out in the next thirty seconds for a ten cred bonus!*

Sara marveled that Emily never once looked at her wrist. How could she possibly resist?

Emily glared, and Sara looked pleadingly back at her. Ten creds. "Emily, I love you, I just want what's best for you."

"It wants us to hug it out, doesn't it?"

Sara nodded, feeling desperate. Emily didn't move.

The timer counted down. Twenty seconds. Sara's heart rate was spiking, making sure the Key knew the argument was still ongoing.

"Emily, please," Sara murmured, her voice taut. Ten seconds, nine…

Sighing, her daughter came around the table and hugged her. Their Keys chimed the bonus,. Such a lovely, calming sound. She leaned in to her daughter's embrace; she'd never held Emily so tightly. If she could just hold on tight enough—

"I'm still leaving," Emily said, pulling free.

Sara bit her lip and looked away, because at nineteen she'd known exactly what she'd wanted to do and spent years playing guitar and singing in bars…until she gave up. She'd given up. "Do you know what happens if you leave and decide to come back? You'll be working off the penalty for, for decades."

"I guess I'll just have to make good on the outside."

"Emily. You don't understand what it's like out there, how hard it is. How one little thing can set you back—"

"As opposed to the million little things that set Dad back?"

"Emily. Please. Don't go."

"You can always come visit. We could go out for coffee or something."

"It'd cost me a hundred creds to get coffee at an outside shop." That shouldn't matter. It was just creds. But the words just fell out of her mouth. Everything was about creds. The conversion rate between PanCorp creds and outside currency fluctuated—right now, it was steep. She was lucky she'd managed that trip to London when the rate was good.

You have fifty minutes to complete your daily assigned tasks! Penalty: fifty creds! The message was flashing yellow now. Sara kept looking at her Key. Emily never stopped looking at Sara.

"There's something else. Some friends and I, we've been doing some research." She glanced around, a quick scan. Maybe she was looking for someone, or someone was waiting for her. Whatever crazy person had talked her into this; surely Emily hadn't come up with this idea on her own. Sara almost craned her neck over her shoulder to see what it was, but Emily touched her hand, drawing her attention. Focusing her. "Here, let me show you." She set a sticky note on the table. Kept her hand on it.

"Honey, you could just message—"

Emily shook her head. Brow furrowed, Sara went to pick up the note, but Emily shook her head. Her hands were cupped around it, hiding it from any cameras. Sara leaned in to read:

PanCorp manipulates viral posts, inflates view counts, uses as leverage. Sara Barrows, acoustic "Separate Ways," 80% of upvotes fake/manipulated.

The date listed with the information was…well, it was a long time ago. The note was handwritten. These people—whoever they were—weren't leaving a trail. Sara had to read it over and over, and it still didn't make sense. She wouldn't *let* it make sense.

"Em, where did you get this?"

She drew the note back and tore it in half. Then again, again, and again. The scraps of paper went into her latte. The ink smeared and bled away.

All those clicks, all the upvotes…all the other PanCorp drones doing it for credits, just like she was—

Sara swallowed thickly. "I don't know what this means, Emily. What are you trying to say?"

"They tricked you, Mom. They lured you in under false pretenses. They promised you things—"

"They fixed my leg. You don't understand what it was like, how bad it was."

"Mom—"

"And where did you even get that information? Can you trust it? Who are these friends of yours? These so-called friends?"

"You don't have to stay here," Emily said, and she sounded so sure. But she didn't understand. She just *didn't.*

Sara wadded up a napkin—cloth, here—and brushed it across her eyes. She had always promised herself she would be supportive of Emily no matter what she wanted to do, if she wanted to be a doctor, or go career track, or peddle viral cover videos—

"I'll send you a note when I get settled. We can talk about it then."

All messages from outside the PanCorp network were screened. Didn't Emily understand? She wouldn't just be leaving, she'd be cut off. From everything.

"Mom, if you need anything, anything at all, call me, please." Emily squeezed both her hands, then turned and walked out of the café.

Sara should have been the one saying that. Mothers were supposed to be the ones to take on that responsibility.

She sat for a long time, until her Key told her she would be charged another five creds if she wanted to stay.

You have ten minutes to complete your daily assigned tasks! Penalty: fifty creds! Complete your tasks NOW or be penalized!

The words flashed red. The Key buzzed ominously against her wrist. This time, it didn't care that her heart was racing and she was crying.

Just this once, she took the penalty. She could make it up tomorrow.

Part 3: You Have Been Crowdfunded

Four women in their sixties, gray in their hair and fatalistic worry lines in their brows, gathered for drinks at the sixth floor atrium bar of PanCorp Meridian Tower. Every week, they paid ten creds each to get a recreation period scheduled at the same time for this; years ago they'd decided that the tradition was worth the expense.

The friendships seemed harried sometimes, maintained through messages and occasional outings when they could get the time and credits together. But once a week, this face-to-face moment became a touchstone. They could reassure each other that they were all still here, alive, and doing okay.

Sara looked forward to the weekly respite like a sailor heading into port. Sit down, splurge on a couple of martinis, and remind herself that she wasn't alone.

Today, they were poring over their tablet screens. Billie had sent them a set of brochures, and had raised a difficult question. She'd had a cancer scare, and decided it was time to talk about cashing out.

When she turned sixty, Sara had started getting notices from PanCorp, pictures of elegant gray-haired women holding filled wine glasses and gazing over ocean vistas. *When it's time to rest,* the headers said. At first, the notices came a couple times a year and she ignored them. Over the last year, they'd increased to once a month, and Sara had started thinking. Maybe it was time to think about retiring.

"What do you think of Sunset Vista?" Billie asked the others. She was a tall wily woman with curly dark hair and expressive hands. Sheila, brown skinned, short cropped hair, regarded her screen skeptically, her gaze narrowed. Rita the redhead, who would have looked great in cocktail dresses but always wore jeans and T-shirts. And Sara. She'd had lots of friends come and go over her years in Meridian, but the four of them had managed to stick together. They'd found each other because all four of them had a kid who'd left PanCorp. They never talked about it, what their children were doing now, how they were managing to survive on the outside.

If they were managing to survive.

"I can't afford that," Sara said. She'd need fifty thousand more creds in her profile for Sunset Vista. Billie was career track, so her account was beefier than the rest of theirs, who were task track. They usually didn't discuss it.

"Sunset Meadows?"

"Maybe…" Vista was seaside. Meadows wasn't right on the beach, but it was close. A shuttle ride away, the brochure said. For a hundred thousand creds Sara could buy her retirement there, have all her needs taken care of for the rest of her life, however long that might be. She was sixty-five—retirement age on the outside. Maybe it was time.

She could keep working odds and ends to buffer her profile, maybe. Her videos still brought in a few creds from views and upvotes. She sometimes joked that pretty soon she'd get to an age where having a white-haired old lady belting out Journey's "Separate Ways" on an antique guitar would be enough to go viral for sheer novelty factor. "See the grandma rock out!"

She wondered if she was a grandmother. Every day, she wondered where Emily was and what she was doing. Keeping in touch hadn't been as easy as Emily had said it would be when she left. Messages sent outside the PanCorp network cost creds. Messages incoming cost more. To go meet Emily for coffee, Sara would have to convert her PanCorp creds to outside currency. Which…wasn't so straightforward. And then Emily just sort of disappeared. Stopped messaging completely. Sara tried not to assume the worst. Emily was busy—of course she'd be busy on the outside, scrambling to try pay her own rent, health care, everything. Even now, Sara remembered what that was like, not having PanCorp taking care of everything. She tried not to be terrified for her daughter.

"Sunset Springs is more my speed," joked Rita, showing them the simplest brochure of the lot, a sprawling set of apartment complexes in the largest of PanCorp's assisted living communities. Amenities included a roof and meals in a community dining room. "A Comfortable Place," the tagline read. Well, they weren't wrong. It wasn't a cardboard box.

"Why do they all say 'sunset?' That's a little morbid," Sheila observed.

They fell silent a moment.

There were rumors. There were always rumors, and Sara hadn't paid much attention to this one over the years, but the topic of it was becoming more relevant. More worrisome. The rumor: that there *were* no PanCorp Sunset properties. You'd sign up, empty your account in exchange for never having to worry…and there'd be no retirement. Only a sudden accident and a brief hospital stay and the sad news sent out to friends and family that you were gone.

Sara didn't believe it. It was easy to lose track of people. Just because people didn't respond to messages didn't mean … Well it didn't mean anything. *She* didn't respond to messages, often enough.

"Whatever we do, we all sign up together," Billie said decisively. "So we can be in the same place. Keep track of each other."

"Right," they answered, determined.

They tricked you, Mom, Emily had told her. They lured you in and tricked you. How could Emily have known such a thing? Sara had done her best to ignore her daughter's warning.

Her Key chimed, along with everyone else's around the table, a flurry of soft, gentle tones. Like a reminder to take a pill.

The message read: *Sunset Group Discounts. Sign up with your partners and friends, share a suite, and get a discount on full-term retirement packages! This offer expires in twenty-four hours.*

It was a big enough discount they could definitely all move into Meadows together. Sara almost hit the "accept" button right there. Rita's hand was hovering over her Key. They looked at each other over the little bistro table. Sara's ears were still ringing with the friendly chime, the rush in her skull telling her to hurry.

"Let's think about it," Billie said. "We'll get back together in the morning over coffee and talk about it. We can push the button then. Okay?"

They agreed. Twenty-four hours. Sara's heart wouldn't stop racing until then.

After drinks, Sara made some calls. Or tried to, but the live voice calls confused people. Nobody made calls anymore, everything was done by message. But she needed to get answers *now*, before she and the others made their decision about Sunset Meadows.

Finally, she got through to a service rep, and was so surprised she almost forgot what she wanted. Her question was flustered. "Hi, yes, is this Talent Resources?"

"Yes, my name is Ruth, do you have a challenge I can help you with today?"

"Maybe. I'm trying to find Miranda Lawrence, she was a senior Vice President of Talent Resources until she retired about ten years ago. I just... she was my recruiter back in the day, and I just wanted to check in on her. See how she's doing."

"Do you know what community she retired to?"

"I'm afraid I don't."

Sara expected that Miranda had retired to Sunset Vista, but other possibilities existed. PanCorp's most elite members could retire to a lake village in Italy, and there was also a retirement cruise ship that traveled the world. Sara couldn't even think about affording a spot on the Sunset Atlantis. Her account would need millions of credits. Tens of millions. It didn't seem possible. But Miranda had been a VP. Maybe she'd managed it.

"It looks like Miranda Lawrence has her privacy settings set at a level that doesn't allow me to give out her contact information to anyone not on her list. Are you on her list?"

During her first couple of years at PanCorp, Sara had talked to Miranda almost every day. Miranda had called to see how she was settling in, to ask if she needed anything. She'd always tipped a few credits every time Sara posted a new video, back when she was still posting videos.

"I'm pretty sure I am," Sara said blithely, not sure at all. "Can you check?"

"What I can do is forward a message to her profile for you."

Sara could do that herself. "Can you maybe tell me then when the last time her profile was active? When she last logged on?" If she was like most PanCorp members, she'd be logged on right now. She'd never log off.

"I'm afraid her privacy settings don't let me access that information—"

"There's got to be some way to just check, I just need a yes or no—"

"That's against the rules, I can't—"

"Can I speak to your manager?" The words of doom. In most PanCorp departments, a request to speak to a manager meant a fifty-cred penalty on the worker's account. Ruth started crying.

"No, please, it's not my fault, the manager will tell you the same thing, I can't—"

"Ruth. I just need to know that she's alive," Sara burst. "Is Miranda alive?"

Ruth cried harder. "I don't know, the system won't tell me; I don't have authorization to look at the account, it's all locked down!"

Now Sara felt bad. Sighing, she marshaled her patience and tried to sound gentle. "Ruth, do you work this task a lot or did you just happen to pick this for today thinking it would be easy?"

"It's fine! Everything's fine! If you give me a five-star rating on your satisfaction survey I get an extra three creds on my account. Can you do that for me? Please?"

"Are you sure you can't find anything about how Miranda is doing?"

"I can send a message. That's all I can do. Send a message and then hopefully she'll reply?" Ruth was in a panic now. If Sara filed a complaint, Ruth might even get her work cred for the day wiped out.

"All right, send the message, that's fine."

"Okay, I'm doing it right now, thank you. Thank you!"

Sara gave her five stars on her satisfaction survey. She remembered what it was like to be young and desperate.

Sara sent out a flurry of messages of her own, not trusting that

Ruth's would actually get through. From the main PanCorp help line to various profile search functions, she tried them all, and hoped that Miranda would receive her message. And respond, that yes, she'd retired, and was happy and taken care of, because PanCorp took care of everything. That was what Miranda had said when she recruited her. That was what everyone in PanCorp said.

She really hoped Miranda would message back. Even a brief hand wave or reply chime. Some notice that Sara's message had been received. She didn't need to talk to Miranda. She just wanted to *know*.

Sara spent the rest of the evening reading and replying to messages between her and her friends, debating the merits of cashing out now to buy into retirement, or sticking it out for a few years to see if they could pad their profiles a little more. But they had no guarantee the discount offer would ever come again. None of them had ever seen such a thing before, and the timer was counting down. PanCorp knew what they wanted—to retire together—and was giving them a way to make that happen. To give them what they desired—or at least, something close enough to it to be acceptable. They'd be stupid not to take the offer.

"I need more booze for this," Rita had messaged. Billie was insistent: She wasn't sure she had all that much time left, and she didn't want to spend that time scrambling for creds.

That would be nice. Not checking for tasks every single day. Not jumping every time her Key dinged. Well, she'd probably always jump at every little chime. That never went away, not in all the time she'd been with PanCorp.

They agreed to sleep on it and meet first thing in the morning. Or, try to sleep, rather. Sara hadn't been this torn up all those decades ago when she was trying to decide to sign the PanCorp contract in the first place. Her stomach was practically bubbling. She tried to remember: What had she expected, back then? Miranda had found her, promised to get her out of the hole—continually getting deeper—she was in.

That was what Sara had been thinking: safety. She hadn't thought much farther than that. At the time, she wasn't entirely sure she'd live to see thirty. Or live past thirty, anyway. Adulthood had still seemed abstract. So, she'd signed up for PanCorp because she wanted to be safe. And she had been. Safe, comfortable. And this was the same. Nothing had changed. She just wanted to be safe.

Maybe she should have left with Emily. Left behind all her creds, her Key, the chiming alerts, the gold stars. But that decision was far behind her now. Not much was left ahead of her—Billie was probably right about that.

Sara suspected they would all say yes.

Next morning, Sara was up at seven. Only a few hours left on the retirement offer. The countdown clock had turned yellow. That was okay, the four of them had their coffee date scheduled, they could all press the button together. Make it a ritual. She didn't even check the day's task list first thing like she usually did. She'd do that later, so she wouldn't get any deductions for not trying. Even if it meant getting stuck with something like scrubbing toilets in the gym. It'd only be for a day, she told herself. And the bonuses always went up for tasks still left at the end of the day.

Then a message came in. Not the bright chime of good news, but the hushed hum of something neutral and non-critical. Sara glanced at her Key, saw the word *Miranda*, and hurriedly read on.

The message was an auto-response: *We're sorry, the PanCorp member you are trying to reach is deceased. Our sympathies. Please contact Talent Resources if you have any questions.*

Sara had a million questions, but none of the answers would help. What did it mean? It was a coincidence. It didn't mean anything. What was she going to tell the others? She couldn't tell them. It was too late. They would decide the rest of their lives in one push of a button. But it wasn't like they were really making a decision. *They tricked you, Mom.*

The thought nearly made her throw up. Never mind, it would be fine, it would all be fine. And like Billie said, whatever happened at least they'd all be together.

She was about to leave her apartment when the power went out.

Sometimes the building's power flickered, but their Keys always stayed online and would chime soothing messages that everything was fine, no need to worry, and ring the happy sound of bonus creds depositing. That noise always made people feel better and offered comfort. Usually, a power outage meant some kind of maintenance work, and it never stayed off for more than a few hours.

This one lasted all day.

The elevators weren't working. Sara would need to walk ten floors to keep her date with Billie and the others, and she wasn't sure she was up for it. She tried to message them, but with the power out her tablet wasn't responding. Her Key worked just fine, though, and the retirement offer was ticking down and she didn't know what the others were doing, if they would accept the offer and therefore so should she. She didn't know what to do.

Surely this couldn't go on too much longer. She sat on the bed in her apartment, hands clenched together, waiting for the power to come back on.

Then the bolt on her Key popped open. She didn't even know it could do that. The band slipped off her wrist. She'd only ever had it off a few times over the years for upgrades. This…it was like her hand falling off.

"No no no—" She grabbed at the band, pressed it back to her wrist, fiddled with the bolt, trying to find how it had failed. Her hands were shaking, and she hoped she'd get it back on before the penalties racked up. But the Key stayed off, and stayed dead.

This can't be happening.

She fled outside to the darkened corridor, now filling with people, all the residents of this floor wild with shock, gripping dead Keys. A woman a few doors down was crying, clutching her Key in trembling hands.

"Yours, too?"

"Is it all of them?"

"What's going on?"

"Does anyone know what's happening?"

Sara thought it might be time to take the stairs down to the lobby to see what was happening, but then thought of the hundreds of other people in the building having the same idea and reconsidered.

"We shouldn't panic," Sara said. "There's got to be a reason for this." PanCorp would send a message, some reassuring bell would chime. But her Key was dead, it wasn't telling her anything. She had no way to communicate. This entire building was about to go mad.

"What's happening?!" someone at the end of the hall screamed. The sobbing woman got louder.

"Everybody just calm down!" someone else shouted in a way that wasn't at all calm. Nobody's Key told them to breathe deeply for one minute, for a five-cred bonus.

"You calm down, you didn't just lose a two-hundred credit gig—"

Sara went back in her apartment to get away from the noise. Sat on the bed, hands over her ears. There had to be a reason for this, PanCorp would explain it, they took care of everything.

Her Key remained dead in her hands. She expected it to beep, warning her about her racing heart, urging her to take a deep breath— but it was dead, the Key was everything and it was gone— She gasped a sob, looked around the room which suddenly seemed very small.

Her guitar was leaning up in the corner. She still had it, though she didn't play nearly as much as she used to. Through everything, the worst part of her life until now, she'd had that guitar, she'd been able to play. And now… She couldn't do anything else, but she could play.

Wiping a bit of dust off the body, she took the guitar and sat down in the hall, right outside her door, and tuned it, plucking and tightening strings until they no longer sounded sour.

She strummed, let the chords fall, let her fingers find what song they wanted to play, old pop hits converted to mournful acoustic echoes. Her stomach settled, her breathing slowed. She'd shoved the dead Key in her pocket so she wouldn't have to look at it anymore. It didn't make a sound.

Everyone had left their apartments. The hallway had filled with panicked, shouting people. The door to the stairwell stood open, and a bottleneck had formed, people shoving both in and out. More crying. Still, Sara played.

Around her, in her little stretch of hall, a calm settled. A couple of people turned to her, listening quietly. Then a couple more, until the calm rippled out. In the unlit shadows, the unnatural silence—no one's Keys were doing anything—people gathered, sat on the floor or leaned up against the wall, and listened.

She didn't notice at first; she'd been playing with her eyes half closed. When she looked up and saw she had an audience, her voice caught. But she kept on. She created an island of calm.

After the sixth song Sara paused to stretch her fingers, and soft applause followed. She smiled at that; it sounded good. Maybe not as good as the chiming of creds pouring in. But still—nice to hear, like the old days at Muskrat Tavern when she could forget about her worries for a little while.

A woman—the one who'd been crying? Sara wasn't sure—spoke. "I wish—I've seen you play before, and I always sent you a couple of credits. Tip jar, yeah? I would do it now, but—" She held up her broken Key.

"I'm playing just to play. It's okay," Sara said. The music was to calm herself. That so many others stopped to listen was a bonus. Well, it was nice to do something for the greater good, even if she wasn't going to get a chime for it.

An alarm rang out from the monitors in every room. Not an endorphin-flushing chime, but a spine-rattling alarm. The lights came on at half strength—power returned. A man laughed, a few people cheered weakly. Everyone fled back to their rooms. Maybe there was news.

Sara rushed to her wallscreen, which had lit up with a friendly blue shade. Not the PanCorp logo. Indistinct ambient music played while a message pulsed, *Please stand by, please stand by*. Biting her lip, Sara waited. Her Key was still dead; she still couldn't get it attached back on her wrist.

Then, text. Which was odd. Messages never came in walls of text like this—only in heart-stopping, thrilling bursts and phrases. Whoever posted this must have realized that most people would stare at the text, confused, unable to even get their eyes to focus on the strangeness of it, because a feminine voice read it aloud, slowly and kindly. She sounded like a kindergarten teacher.

"For Immediate Release: PanCorp U.S., PanCorp International, its holding company and all subsidiaries, have been purchased for an undisclosed sum by Grassroots, LLC a not-for-profit employee-owned partnership. The purchase includes all assets, intellectual property, and talent contracts. Please await further instructions during this time of transition."

Sara still wasn't sure what this meant, even when the soothing voice repeated the press release. PanCorp was so big, so pervasive—how could anyone possibly come along and just *buy* it?

Talent contracts.

She'd just been sold. And bought. The realization settled on her like a pallet of bricks. She was going to be sick. What did she do? What would happen to her creds? All her work... belonged to someone else now. It always had.

A light flashed in the bottom of the screen: New Personal Message.

Maybe this had all been mistake. Maybe this would explain everything. Scrambling, Sara grabbed the keypad and clicked on the message.

Hi Mom. Come have coffee? We need to talk. I'm in the atrium café right now.

Emily was here, right now? Emily, after all this time... Oh, this wasn't a good time. Sara couldn't get her brain back on track. Her entire life was potentially falling apart, and *now* Emily wanted to talk? But she was here—was she really here? That, Sara could focus on. If Emily wanted to come back, she'd help her eat the penalties, she'd put off her retirement, they'd scrimp in the most minimal economy unit PanCorp offered—

Except there was no PanCorp anymore.

Still gripping her dead Key, Sara raced to the elevator, which she was relieved to see was working again. She moved down the corridor with such purpose, people called after her, asking what was happening, like she must know something they didn't. But she didn't know, so she ignored them and sighed with relief when the elevator door closed and she was finally alone. But it moved far too slowly.

Her Key didn't chime to tell her she was being charged twenty creds for stepping into the fancy café. Sara stopped for a moment, stared at the dead device that she still gripped compulsively. Decided to worry about it later.

The espresso maker was quiet. The café was empty. With all the Keys dead, no one had credits to spend. The baristas had fled.

Sara flashed on the moment fifteen years ago, when Emily asked her to come for coffee at this same café—it had been upgraded and redecorated a couple of times since, and now the bistro tables were fake-chrome and the Berber carpet was salmon pink. But there was Emily, looking so grown up, waiting patiently, her hands gripping a steaming cup. A second cup waited in front of her. They were in to-go cups. She'd brought them in from outside, as if she'd known she wouldn't be able to buy coffee here.

She glanced up. "Mom?"

"Emily? Oh, Emily!" Sara opened her arms, Emily stood, and they hugged hard, desperately. If her daughter was here things couldn't be so bad. Whatever was happening could just go ahead and happen.

Emily asked, "Are you okay?"

"I don't know," Sara sighed. "The weirdest thing just happened, we got a press release over the monitor—"

"PanCorp got bought out. Yes, I know." She was grinning like she had something to do with it. Because she had something to do with it. "I'm a partner in Grassroots, LLC."

Might as well have said aliens had landed. "I don't understand."

Emily urged her to sit, and they sipped their coffee. Sara had too many things she wanted to ask, so she stayed quiet, uncertain. Emily… looked like a partner in an LLC, wearing fashionable gray slacks and a silk T-shirt under a tailored, short-cropped jacket. Her short hair had frosted highlights, her earrings simple gold studs. She looked so put together. When had she become so put together? Her smile was sly, her gaze confident.

"What happened?" Sara finally burst.

"We bought out PanCorp. Millions of us. A few bucks here and there, whatever people could put in, from all over the world—and it was enough. Some of us got degrees—mine's in forensic accounting—so we could help set it all up. Hostile takeover of one of the biggest companies in the world. Then we distributed the shares. PanCorp is now employee-owned."

"I…I don't understand."

Emily didn't seem surprised at her bafflement, and answered calmly. "Your profile, your creds—it's real money now, and you can take it with you. If you want to leave, I mean."

Sara had existed within such a narrow bracket of possibility for so long, she didn't know what she wanted. She focused on her daughter, on the reality sitting in front of her.

"But you're okay?" she asked, reaching to touch Emily's hand. "I've been so worried about you, wondering what you've been doing, and…"

"Mom, I'm fine. I've been busy—this has been a really big project. But it's been worth it."

"But…how?"

"How does anyone do anything? A dollar at a time, I think. So. What would you like to do now? Where would you like to go…or, if you'd rather stay—" She bit her lip, and the little girl Sara had raised flashed through.

If she could do anything, anything at all, unconstrained—

Around this time, an alert ought to be chiming. A promise of bonus creds if she would choose this thing rather than that. A penalty if she chose wrong. No—a penalty if she chose something PanCorp didn't like. She could always say no, every step of the way that brought her here she could have said no.

Why hadn't she?

And where was the chime and the message telling her the right way to go?

"I don't know what to do, Emily. You have to tell me what to do."

Emily's eyes shone, but she quickly wiped them dry. "I have a place with an extra room. Near the beach. How about we go and drink some wine and play a little guitar? Do you still have your guitar? It won't cost you anything to walk out of the building, not anymore."

The Key was still dead. It didn't buzz, it didn't tell her she was late, that she was about to be penalized. It didn't tell her if this was a good idea or bad. Sara didn't know what she had.

She didn't know anything.

Well, she knew she had a daughter again.

"Yes," Sara said, smiling. "I still have my guitar."

THE OUTLAWS OF BARNSDALE

It was some comfort that Lady Isabelle, the Baroness of Helmsley Castle, despised Mary for her own self, and not for anyone she might be related to. Here, it did not matter at all that she was Robin Hood's daughter.

"Where are you going, Mary?"

Not Lady Mary, not daughter-in-law, not anything but her name barked out like a curse. She had not yet got used to remembering she needed to go out by the kitchen if she wanted to avoid the lady of the castle. Lady Isabelle had just a glimpse of her coming down the stairs, and that was enough. Tucking her basket under her arm, Mary put on a neutral smile and entered the hall where the ladies worked at sewing and spinning.

"The weather is so nice, I thought I would work outside for a little while." The sun had broken out on a beautiful Yorkshire autumn. Hints of a misty, dreary winter to come had made themselves known, and Mary wanted to be outside as much as she could before the cold settled in.

"Nonsense, you'll catch a chill. Come here by the hearth like a proper lady."

At home, at Locksley Manor, Mary's mother—Lady Marian of song and legend—would take them outside to work in the open air, to bring food and drink those working throughout the manor's lands, and to watch the light over Sherwood Forest.

Mary had very quickly learned not to say, "Back home at Locksley manor, we did this or that," to Lady Isabelle. It would bring on a lecture. She was at Helmsley Castle now, wife to the baron's heir. Best act like it. Here, they were *proper*, nothing like those wild folk of Sherwood.

For a moment, Mary considered simply walking out. She wanted to sit outside, she ought to be able to sit outside; there was nothing wrong with sitting outside. But she would certainly hear about it later if she did. For now, she didn't want to argue, so she came to the benches by the hearth where Lady Isabelle, her daughter Katherine, and other women of the castle did their handwork.

The light wasn't good here. Helmsley was a great square Norman tower, all stone and few windows. They bent over their work, squinting. The light was better outside, the air healthier, not smoky and closed-in.

No one spoke. No one laughed. Lady Isabelle watched over them, glaring. Proper women were silent, she would tell them. William's mother hadn't seemed particularly ancient when Mary first met her, when William brought her home after their wedding. Mary was determined to be good-natured, to like everyone she met, to embrace her new home as she had embraced her husband. But Isabelle had looked her up and down like she was livestock, and frowned. The implication was that she seemed to think that William could have done better. Married higher, richer. She had not been consulted in the matter of choosing a wife for William, and she would express her displeasure. You see, Lady Isabelle was a daughter of the King of Scotland. Born out of wedlock, mind you, but Mary didn't judge. Lady Isabelle did enough of that for all of them.

The frown deepened and it made the woman look dreary. If only

Lady Isabelle could let Mary alone. She'd won this round, could she not end it there?

"You go out far too much, Mary," Lady Isabelle began.

Lady Mary, she amended silently. Her neutral smile turned to a grimace.

"It isn't proper for ladies to go out where they can be seen by anyone. I have seen you take off your veil when you walk along the woods. You are married to my son, who will be Baron of Helmsley, you must think of him and his reputation and conduct yourself better."

End it now, please, Mary thought. Just stop.

"You certainly shouldn't be using a bow. I have seen you practicing, even though you sneak out like a bandit to avoid me. What are you thinking? However did your mother raise you so poorly?"

Her mother. Lady Marian of Sherwood. For God's sake.

Stitch. Just keep sewing. Mary could pretend that she hadn't heard a word of it, though her breath was boiling to a scream.

"Well?" the lady of the castle asked, demanding a response. "You are very quiet. Which is proper. But I need you to tell me that you understand me."

She didn't need to tell the woman anything.

"Mary. What can you possibly be thinking?"

Mary studied the mending in her hand, a small tear in one of William's tunics. She said carefully, "I am wondering if it is possible to stab a person with a needle so many times that they die of it. I think it is. But I would need to be very patient."

A small giggle burst from one of the younger ladies, quickly stifled. Stares, from everyone else. Lady Isabelle's deep frown grew fierce.

"You are wild, ungrateful, unworthy—" Lady Isabelle's propriety would not allow her to add anything harsher, but she was clearly thinking it. Meanwhile, Mary put the mending in her basket and stood.

"My lady, you hurl so many insults at me they lose all their meaning."

She walked out, all the way out, to the grassy slope at the back of the castle, where a bench overlooked the stables. Setting the basket on the ground she sat there, looked up at the sky and let the sun warm her face. In another hour the sun would move behind the tower, and cast the spot in shadow.

God forbid the castle ever withstand a siege that would cause her to be locked up with this woman for weeks on end. She would flee back to Sherwood first, through armies if she had to.

On the field near the stables, Sir William de Ros was working with a young horse, assisted by a couple of his stablemen. The horse was newly broken and had only been under saddle a couple of times, but William rode him now and the animal seemed calm. Eager, even. This—training horses—was William's passion and talent. He was getting a reputation and already had a list of requests for his horses. The mounts he trained were steady and reliable. The trick was that he loved them. Mary loved watching him just like this, putting a hand on the brown neck, soothing the animal when something startled him.

William saw her and waved. She waved back. She was lucky to have him, she knew this. She could survive this, with him.

He dismounted, handed the young horse off to Bert, and came up the slope to meet her. Her smile broke wide and genuine.

"Come out to enjoy the weather?" he asked.

"Yes. And your mother finally drove me out."

With a sigh, he sat beside her. "She doesn't hate you, you know. Not really."

"No. I'm just not what she imagines I ought to be." And she never would be. No one would be.

He took her hand, and his grip was warm, calloused, solid. "Someday you will be mistress of this place and can do whatever you like."

"That is why she dislikes me," Mary said. "I am her usurper."

He sat with her in silence a moment, looking out at the fields, the horses, the blue sky and sun that would vanish behind winter clouds in a matter of weeks. "Daisy and Violet need exercising. Would you like to go riding with me? Just an hour or two in the woods."

"I would like that very much."

He stood and held his hand to her. She took it, he drew her to her feet, then pulled her close, a hand on her backside to hold her pressed against him, and kissed her deeply, not caring who might see. He seemed to regard her with great satisfaction, as if possessing her pleased him. As if she were a fine new horse—but William loved his horses, and that was something. He delighted in her. She drank in his delight, a fire to warm her in the Yorkshire chill. She laughed and kissed him again.

She wasn't sure yet if this was love. But she could not be near him without her body flushing, and she enjoyed the feeling. Enjoyed *him*.

Hand in hand, they went to the stables to get the horses ready.

The forest of Barnsdale lay on this side of the narrow road that ran from the castle to the village, and from there to the road that led eventually to York. It was smaller than Sherwood but no less ancient, and the shapes of oak and alder, stands of holly and hawthorn, were familiar and comforting. It wasn't Sherwood—somehow, despite having the same trees growing from the same English soil, it smelled different. The light had a grayer quality, and the earth felt harder. If Mary tried to describe this difference she wouldn't make any sense. In a word, this was not home.

Still, a knot of nerves left her shoulders when she entered Barnsdale's shadow. These woods were willing to be her friend, if she gave them a chance.

Mary rode Daisy, a reliable palfrey she'd met the same night she first met William. Violet was a young mare, still a little skittish. She would stiffen her neck at every noise, and pin her ears back if she thought Daisy came too close. William whispered calming words, and the mare settled. William himself glanced frequently at Mary, as if she too might be skittish. She was sure to smile back at him, to reassure him. Yes, she was well, riding with him was pleasant. The dappled sunlight was lovely, and the horses' hoof clops were comforting.

William took them on a wide, well-trod path used by travelers skirting around the village to go on straight to York. They'd go on until they reached a small bridge that passed over a stream, then turn around and ride back to the castle by dinner. Mary would smell of horse and sunshine, Lady Isabelle would be appalled, and she did not care. Daisy hardly needed any attention, and Mary tipped back her head to soak up sunlight, and admire the shape of branches overhead.

She blinked, startled. One branch of a tall elm stretched right over the road, and something about it looked off. Her tensed muscles caused Daisy to miss a step. Mary's hands tightened on the reins.

Lengths of ivy hung down from the branch—straight down. They weren't anchored to the bark; they'd been torn up, which meant someone had put them there. Now she could see it—the ivy was woven together.

This was an old style of trap. She knew all the stories.

"William," she commanded. "Turn back, now." Already, she had Daisy wheeled around.

She did not know if he would listen to a loud, commanding shout in a woman's voice. She had never tried to command him; she had been so careful before now, so compliant. Suddenly, he seemed a stranger. She had been naked with him and still didn't know him.

He glanced sharply, brow furrowed. Daisy danced on stiff legs as Mary waited to see what he would do, and Violet shuddered. Mary's cry seemed to have confused him, but the horses' anxiety decided his course, and at last he followed Mary, turning his mount back way they'd come.

But before he could spur Violet to a run, the woven net of ivy fell on him. He shouldered it out of the way, but it struck the young mare's flank, and she reared. He was ready for it—almost. He wasn't thrown, but he lost his seat, kicked away from the saddle, landing on his feet and shoving away the mess of ivy.

Shocked into panic, poor Violet galloped for home, and who could blame her? Daisy danced in place, distraught and blowing nervous breaths, desperate to follow her companion but waiting for a cue from Mary. And Mary did not know what to do, whether to stay or go.

William drew his sword in a heartbeat when three men emerged from the woods alongside the path, arrows nocked in bows, shutting the door of the trap. A grizzled, middle-aged man appeared beside Mary, reaching for the reins. If she was going to flee she needed to do it now. In a panic she looked at William, who stood ready in the middle of the road, but he was outnumbered, and the sword did no good against arrows. She couldn't leave him alone.

Pushing, she slid off Daisy's back and slapped the mare's hindquarters. With a kick Daisy broke away from her would-be captor and galloped away, kicking up divots.

The grizzled outlaw turned on Mary, glaring. "What'd you go and do that for?"

"They'll run straight for home," Mary said, catching her breath. "Help will be along shortly, I think."

William threw her an annoyed glare, which she couldn't read. Did she do right? Wrong? What should she have done?

"Put the sword down, m'lord."

A fifth man, arrogant-looking, stepped on to the road, a green cap on his head, leather vest over his tunic. His hair was brown, his beard trimmed. Very neat, for an outlaw.

William didn't put his sword down. He studied each of the five bandits, calculating, as if he really thought he might defeat them all with the right strategy. But the chief of the outlaws, the well-dressed one, gave a signal, and one of the arrows turned to aim at Mary.

"Put it down," the command came again.

William carefully set his weapon on the ground. Showing his empty hands, he straightened.

"Oh, really," Mary muttered. They wouldn't shoot her. They didn't dare. What she ought to do was challenge the outlaws to an archery contest, right now. Right out of the stories. They would be so taken aback, they'd agree out of sheer surprise, and then wouldn't they be shocked when—

Before she could make her challenge, the neatly dressed man started in on an expansive speech. "I am very pleased to announce that you, my lord and my lady, have the great honor to be waylaid by Robin Hood himself." He put his hands on his hips.

Mary of Locksley laughed. Her hand clapped over her mouth, but she couldn't stop. The outlaws stared at her, nonplussed.

"This isn't supposed to be funny!" one of the younger men said. "Why's she laughing at us?" The grizzled man hissed at him to be quiet.

"You are not Robin Hood," she finally managed to gasp.

He'd been thrown out of whatever performance he had planned. His tone turned almost petulant. "Who are you to say I am not!"

William opened his mouth to speak, but Mary gave a little wave of her hand by her skirt. *No, wait.* She hoped he would not speak. That he would trust her.

Who was she, indeed? And what could she say that would convince them? Other than point out that she had recognized the trap.

The grizzled man beside her, studying her with a sneer, and the well-dressed one with crow's feet at his eyes—they were close to her father's age. Maybe just a bit younger. The three archers were quite a bit younger, and they seemed wide-eyed and uncertain, as if they had never done anything like this before. The two elder certainly had. The neat one made a good show of being Robin Hood. He might have copied his manner, his habits of waylaying travelers. Or there might be more to him. She made a guess. A gamble. Gave William one last glance to implore him to be silent, then focused on the chief.

She was not frightened. She had faced down more dangerous men than this.

"You are not Robin Hood, but I think I know your true name, if you'll let me tell the story." She did not wait for permission, not from the likes of him. "When good King Richard pardoned Robin Hood and made him Baron of Locksley, he pardoned all his folk as well, and they followed Robin and Marian to a lawful life. That is, all but seven did. Seven went their own ways, took their own paths."

The two older men had grown very still. Listening close, the archers lowered their bows and let out the tension in the strings. Mary had their attention well in hand.

"George the Bald and Judith married, and went together to Lincoln, where they became fletchers and bowyers and sold arrows to the king himself, as well as all the foresters around. They live there to this day, with their son and daughter." When Mary and her brother and sister were children, they traveled to Lincoln's great fair to visit them. George had given her a set of arrows for her wedding. "Eli of Chester spent another year in the greenwood before he heard the voice of God call to him. He walked all the way to Shrewsbury on bare feet to pledge himself to the abbey there and became Brother Silvius. He is considered a most holy man, blessed with a healing touch."

The grizzled man beside her barked a laugh. "Eli a holy man! Are you joking?"

Mary had them. She had guessed right.

"Weyland also stayed in the greenwood for a time. One winter, he grew sick. Will Scarlet found him shivering in a hut, but not in time. They bundled him up and brought him to the manor, but it was too late."

Mary had been a little girl when Robin's foresters had brought their old friend Weyland in from the cold. She had watched from the corner of the hall as they settled him on a pallet by the hearth, where he died.

This time, the grizzled man stumbled as if she'd pushed him. "Weyland is dead?"

Robin, Marian, Will, Much, all their friends, told stories about their time in Sherwood, about the ones who'd died, who'd gone away. Mary grew up hearing about them. She knew them all.

"Little John stayed in the wood, watching over the manor in secret for years. He finally came to live in the manor with Robin and the rest just a few years ago, after saving the lives of Robin and Marian's children."

"Children," the neat one murmured.

136

"That leaves two. Two men who once followed Robin Hood in Sherwood but did not follow him to a lawful life. So taken were they with King Richard, they joined his army and went to fight for him in France. After Richard's death, they went on to fight in the Crusades, as Lord Robin heard it. But he never heard from them again and he assumed they'd died. They were the youngest of the six—they'd be about your age now, I think. If I am right, that is, and you are Tom and Gerald." She nodded to the neat man and grizzled man in turn.

The grizzled man was crying silently, a few tears tracked down his cheeks. The neat man had paled, and his lips trembled. His hands opened and closed, as if he wanted a weapon.

"Who are you, that you know these things?" he said finally, his voice hoarse. "You are too young, you could not have been there—"

When she glanced at William this time, he was smiling thinly. Just the hint of a curl to his lips. She gave him a quick smile in return before speaking to the man she believed was Tom of Sherwood.

"I am Mary of Locksley," she said. "Eldest child of Robin of Locksley and the Lady Marian. So I know very well you are not Robin Hood."

Gerald fell to his knees. "I see it now, Tom. Don't you see it? She looks like Marian."

Part of her braid lay over her shoulder, visible from beneath her veil. She had her mother's chestnut hair, and Marian's round face. She was not so much older than Marian had been when these men knew her.

Tom rubbed his face. "My God," he murmured, shaking his head. "My God!"

William spoke at last, wryly. "Of all the travelers you could have waylaid, you picked the one person in all of Yorkshire able to spot your trap and say your true names. Well done."

"We're cursed, Tom," Gerald said, tiredly, as if the fact did not surprise him.

"Yes, it would appear so."

The young ones were looking at her, awestruck. "You really know

Robin Hood?" one of them asked breathlessly. Tom threw him a hard glare.

"Oh yes," she said. "My whole life. He taught me to shoot, and if you'll loan me your bow—"

The young man took a step as if he really was about to march forward and hand her his bow and arrow, but Tom growled admonishingly. "For God's sake, don't embarrass me, lads."

"But Tom, what do we do?" another of the young ones said. Mary wondered if Tom had convinced them he really was Robin Hood, to recruit them to this ill-conceived scheme. Outlawry must seem like a fine adventure if you believed the stories.

Tom rubbed the back of his neck, wincing, as if reminding himself that outlawry was not so grand an adventure after all. His small band waited for his reply, but he seemed at a loss.

"You should go see him," Mary said.

Tom looked at her sidelong. "Go back to Sherwood? Go to Locksley?"

"He talks about you. Even now he wonders what happened to you. He would be so pleased to know you are well. Him, Marian, Will, Much, Little John—all of them are there."

"Tom, I want to go home," Gerald said bleakly. He got to his feet slowly, as if his joints suffered for his hard years of fighting. He tilted his head at Mary. "Eli's really a monk at Shrewsbury?"

"He is. Keeps the garden there."

"Huh. How 'bout that?"

Tom frowned. "Rob'll never forgive us for walking on out him."

"He already has," Mary said. "Tell him I sent you."

The man chuckled. "Fate has spoken indeed. My lady." He bowed, and she recognized the dramatic sweep of his arm, the ostentatious flip of his hand. He'd learned that from her father.

William retrieved his sword and returned it to his scabbard. Gave the would-be outlaws a stern look, and then ignored them to offer his arm to Mary. "My lady, we have a long walk ahead of us."

138

"We do, my lord." She took his arm and let him guide her to the start of that walk. Over her shoulder she implored, "Go to him. Please."

Tom, Gerald, and their young apprentices stared tiredly after. Maybe they would find their way back to Sherwood. She hoped they would, and leave Barnsdale in peace.

She and William walked in silence for some time. Even after they had left the outlaws behind and were alone, William didn't speak. His arm felt stiff under hers, even when she drew closer to him.

Finally, she ventured, "You seem unhappy." It was fairly obvious. She had only to discover if he was unhappy with the situation in general—or unhappy with her in particular.

"You should have run," he said sternly. "You should stayed on Daisy and run."

"I couldn't leave you behind."

He stopped and turned to face her. "It's not your place to rescue me! What kind of knight am I, who cannot protect my own wife?" He sighed, looking past her shoulder to the nearby trees. He was ashamed, she realized. He was unhappy with himself. Did he really think he could have defeated all five of them alone? Not doing so was no failing. The situation had called for wits, not weapons.

She took his arm and clasped his hand. "Did you ever hear the story about the time the Sheriff of Nottingham finally caught Robin Hood?"

"Is that the one where the noose is all but around Robin Hood's neck when the people of the yard rose up, and all his men were there to rescue him?"

"That was my mother's plan," Mary told him. "Lady Marian stayed at the castle to gather information. To spy. She knew exactly how the hanging was meant to proceed, and where everyone needed to be for the rescue. So you must understand, in my family it's tradition for women to rescue their husbands. It would be such a nuisance to watch them die and have to find another."

They had begun to walk again, a slow stroll back to Helmsley

Castle, the better to enjoy the autumn weather. She worried that nothing she could say would set him at ease. But then he set his arm over her shoulders and pulled her close.

"You are saying, then, that you do not wish for a different husband?"

"I do not." She put her arm around his middle.

"Well then. I am glad."

"Good."

"Now, how long do you suppose it will be before the horses find Bert and he sends help?"

"Hm, not too soon I hope. It's a fine day for a walk."

"And it'll be that much longer before we have to talk to my mother."

She smiled at him. "You understand me well, my lord."

THE HUNTSMAN AND THE BEAST

One day, long ago, a fierce storm scattered the royal hunting party. The prince, his best huntsman, twelve of his great lords and all their attendants, men and dogs and horses charged every which way, vanishing down one path and another until the prince and his best huntsman, whose name was Jack, were left alone, on foot, at the gates of a strange castle.

"I didn't know there was a castle here," the prince said, leaning close to be heard over the noise of the storm, holding his arm up against the rain. "You'd think I'd know about a castle here."

The maps showed this region as a wide, unbroken stretch of forest. Jack looked again, because he always looked again, and saw that several windows had broken glass and boards nailed across them from the inside. Nearby, he thought a gardening stake jutted from the ivy, but when he tugged at it, he lifted out a spear. Something terrible had happened here.

Thunder rocked the earth, and the rain came down in sheets, then turned to hail.

"I see no lights, sire," Jack said, studying the windows, scanning the grounds for any signs of life. He found none.

"We would do well to wait out the storm inside," the prince said.

Jack wasn't sure, but didn't see that they had a choice. He put his shoulder to the bars of the gate, shoved hard, and with a wrenching of rusted iron, it opened.

Ahead, at the end of a leaf-strewn walkway, was a wall of gray stone with windows and turrets, sloping slate roofs, spikes, and rails that might once have been gilded. The gravel walk led to ornate carved doors under a stone archway. On either side, dragon-shaped sconces held broken lanterns. All around them must have once been gardens, but the hedges had turned to towering thickets, the lawns had become meadows, and seas of ivy had overwhelmed the flowerbeds. This seemed another part of the forest.

They approached the wide set of steps that led to double wooden doors. There was a great iron knocker shaped like a rose on a vine, twisted into a circle. Jack let it fall three times, and the sound echoed, on and on.

The door opened, just a crack. Beyond the door was darkness. Jack couldn't tell what waited inside. Maybe this was a ruin, abandoned. The perfect shelter, with nothing to worry about.

The prince sighed. Rain dripped off his hood; his cheeks were pink with cold. "We're soaking wet, Jack. Let's go in."

Sword in hand, Jack pushed open the door and led the way.

Inside was exactly what he expected to find in an abandoned castle: a wide, tiled hall covered in dust. A musty smell, damp and stale. Vermin had likely built nests in the furniture. A wide, curving stairway climbed to the next floor. Cobwebs draped the stone banister.

The ceiling climbed high. Carved archways on either side led to even grander halls. At its best, this place should have been splendid.

"There's no one here," the prince said. He shook out his cloak, dripping pools of water on the tile.

Jack wasn't sure. He trusted the prickling at the back of his neck that told him something wasn't right.

"There should be beautiful girls in fine gowns coming down that staircase to greet me."

"Of course, sire." Jack agreed; there should be music here. Dancing. At the very least a doorman to welcome them. Servants with mulled wine. He drew out the flask of brandy he kept in his doublet and offered it to the prince, who sipped and handed it back, still looking at a crumbling painted ceiling, at carved wood chairs lined against the wall.

In the next hall they found a fireplace, the centerpiece of what must have been a sitting room. A velvet settee had rotted through or been eaten by mice. A handful of wooden chairs were still intact, and Jack drew a pair of them near the fireplace. As chance had it there were logs piled here, very dry, and soon he had a fire roaring. He spread out their cloaks and found some dried meat in his pouch to make an unsatisfactory meal.

"Well, this is an adventure," the prince said, resting his boots close to the fire, leaning back in his chair, and looking around while he gnawed.

"The storm is already breaking up," Jack said, scrubbing at a grimy window to look out. "I think."

"It's near dark. We'll have to stay the night."

"Yes, sire." Jack by himself would have traveled the woods at night. But the prince was probably right. They were likely safer here than going out after dark. And at least they'd be dry when they set out in the morning.

Jack planned to stay in the hall by the fire. Catch what sleep they could, eat what little they carried, and leave as soon as light came through those grimy windows. But the prince wanted to explore.

"It's astonishing!" he said, dusting off a candleholder on a table, cleaning off the still-extant wick, and lighting it with a brand from the fire. He carried it to the next room. Dutifully, Jack followed. They went like this, room to room, through much of the castle. When the prince started up the grand staircase, Jack protested.

"Sire, I'm not sure we can trust how solid the footing is, it might not be safe—"

"I want to see!"

They explored the next floor, its parlors and libraries, dusty windows and haunted stillness. Dozens of paintings decorated walls, and in the scant candlelight Jack studied the faces for clues of what this place might have been. Stern men in military attire, gracious women in gowns of every fashion from the last fifty years. Whole families, sons and daughters looking placid, painted. His own family had had paintings like this, before they were sold off.

Then, in the farthest room, they found an armory. A whole training salle with a good wood floor, a couple of mirrors, and racks of weapons of every kind.

"Oh," the prince breathed, eyes round with wonder. "It's *beautiful.*"

Whoever had gathered this collection had a good eye and presumably great skill with arms. But now it was all abandoned, shrouded. The prince, as one might expect, went to a display of swords, rapiers arranged on a gilded rack, pride of place, and passed his hand across the hilts, brushing each one. "These rival the blades in the royal armory. These . . . my God, they're too beautiful to leave sitting here in the dark, we must take as many as we can with us—"

Of course he picked out the richest, the one with the inlaid swept hilt, the silk and gold wire-wrapped grip and the faceted jewel set in the pommel, the one that glowed, even covered with dust. He wrapped his hand around it, drew it from the rack, ignoring the trail of dust it left in the air as he swept it in one arc, then another.

"That was my father's sword," a deep voice growled from the shadows.

Jack had the presence of mind to set down his candle before drawing his sword. The voice came from the hallway behind them, and he put himself between the shadow and his prince. The prince dropped the beautiful rapier, which clattered on the parquet.

The beast emerged. It was a great clawed thing, covered in fur and rags, grinning around yellowed fangs, terrible to behold. The prince shouted a curse.

"Why do you trespass?" the creature demanded in a voice more like a bear's grunt, thick and grating. "This is my castle. You are not welcome here."

"We knocked!" the prince shouted. "We knocked at the door!"

"I don't care!" it roared, a sound to rival the thunder outside.

Jack shouted at the prince to run, to get to the stairs and flee outside, the storm be damned, they should never have come here. But the beast was too fast. Somehow, that immense form crossed the floor in just a pair of strides and backhanded Jack, knocking away his sword and spilling him on to the floor. Head ringing, Jack got himself back between his prince and the creature. The beast roared. Jack pressed hands to his ears and winced, and the creature took that chance to knock Jack over again. He bounced and lay still, the breath knocked out of him.

"Stay down," it muttered at him and went again for the one who had handled the sacred blade.

The prince cried out; the beast took him by the throat, swung him, pinned him to the wall. Jack struggled against his own shocked nerves—then he saw the prince had drawn a knife. A little thing, he must have had it tucked into his belt or a pocket of his doublet, but if he could get it into the beast's eye or throat, it would be enough.

But the beast wasn't just a monster, it was a warrior. It grabbed the prince's hand and twisted until the knife fell. The prince cried out; the beast held him immobile and brought its fierce brown eyes, its gaping mouth, close to him. Jack would never get to them in time.

The beast said, "I was only going to throw you out. But now…I will keep you. You will serve me to the end of your days in payment for this trespass."

Heart racing, Jack stumbled forward, reaching. He dropped his own weapon and said, "No! He only held the sword because he saw how beautiful it was. How precious. He only admired it—"

"He was going to steal my treasures," the beast snarled at him. "You both were."

Jack closed his eyes, took a deep breath. Tried again. "I'm sorry. We're sorry. Please let him go."

"No," it said, decisive.

Jack said, "Then take me. I will serve. Let him go and take me instead, please." The beast hesitated, and that told Jack he might have a chance. "I swear to you I will stay in his place, but you must let him go free."

"You…swear?" the beast said.

"I do," Jack answered, trying to sound brave. The beast glared at him, studying him. Judging him. Deciding if it could trust his word.

It let the prince go. Dropped him to the floor.

"Go," the beast barked at the prince, who stumbled toward the door.

"Jack—" the prince called.

"It's all right. It's fine. But you—you must go. Please."

The prince fled, and Jack sighed with relief.

He and the beast stared at one another for a good long time. He opened his mouth to say something, he wasn't sure what—ask a question, like what was going to happen to him, or maybe if the beast had a name—when the beast sprang. So quickly, so powerfully, he didn't have time to draw breath before it caught him up, grabbing him around the middle, slinging him over its shoulder and running, charging through the castle to…somewhere. Jack couldn't tell.

The trip lasted minutes, through halls and rooms, down a set of stairs, and then another. The beast's claws clacked on tile, tore on carpets. The halls grew small—the noise closed in on them, the air grew mustier. Then, finally, the beast threw him down. He hit stone and rolled. A door slammed shut. The beast growled under its breath and retreated.

Jack sat up and took stock. He was bruised and banged up, but otherwise unhurt. He now sat in a dark room with a bare floor and stone walls, no more than two strides in any direction. Some light came in through a narrow slit in the door. A simple cot lay against the back wall, a chamber pot sat underneath. Both as dusty and disused as anything else in the castle.

It wasn't a dungeon. Likely, this was a servant's quarters. Well then, he could cope with that. He'd have to, for the foreseeable future. For form's sake he tried the door, and yes, it was locked from the outside. He kicked it, which didn't do anything, and smacked the stone wall, just to hear the noise.

Well. At least he was alive.

The storm broke; the sun rose. The light coming in through the slot in the door changed, however slightly. The smell of damp fur still lingered. What Jack was thinking, lying back on the cot that he'd dusted off as well as he could: that beautiful rapier was made for human hands, and the beast had said the sword belonged to its father.

Sooner than he liked, the sound of monstrous breathing filled the hall outside, and the door's lock clicked. The door cracked open, a tin plate scraped on the floor. A tin cup followed it, and the door slammed shut again.

He stared for a long time, uncertain as to what he'd seen. The plate contained half a roast chicken and a small turnip. The mug held water. Well, at least he was being fed. Like a pet. He ate because he was hungry, because he might as well. The chicken was burnt, tough, and overdone. After eating, he paced the room. Pressed his face to the slot in the door, but only saw the opposite wall.

Toward evening, the great claws clacked on stone and the lock clicked again. When the door opened, Jack called out, "Wait! I want to talk to you! Please!"

As before, the honest *please* seemed to make the beast hesitate.

"Just for a moment," Jack added.

The door opened, stayed opened. The beast appeared, holding a plate that seemed small nested in its great claws. It had been a day since Jack had first seen it, and it was no less fierce and horrifying. In the light, it was almost worse. The black horns of a goat spiraled above its ears. Its shoulders were almost too large to fit through the door, and coarse, matted hair in all shades of brown covered its body. It wore clothing, or what had once been clothing.

"I just need to know if my prince…if you let him go, if he was able to leave safely."

The beast said, "I made sure he fled back to the forest. He has gone away."

"Then he is safe."

A fang showed underneath a furred lip. "Is anyone, out in the world?"

"Is that why you stay locked up in a castle?"

It snarled at him and went away, leaving behind another half a chicken, overdone. At least Jack would not starve here.

A lot of time for thinking, locked up in a room. Jack thought hard about what he'd seen, that good look he'd gotten of the beast, filling the doorway, the tiny plate in its hands. It would have to return, to collect the plates and bones, to bring more food. Jack would thank it for the food, he decided.

In the morning, the beast came again, the door opened a little wider this time, maybe.

"Good morning," Jack said. "Thank you. For feeding me, I mean."

The beast grunted. "Did you think I would not?"

"I'm not sure what to think."

"Here." It set the plate on the floor. Another half a chicken.

Jack said, "There's nothing else to eat?"

"Do you want it or not?"

"I do. Yes. Thank you. But."

"But what?"

He looked, confirmed what he thought he'd seen the day before. A jeweled ring was fitted on one clawed hand. Rings of silver glinted in its furred ears. The cloth hanging from the beast's middle used to be a skirt. Two skirts, lashed together to make one large. The bits of shirt it wore still had a length of lace around the collar. A hint of embroidery. He could see little else with all the fur, and he was suddenly unwilling to look closer, at the beast's shape underneath all the fur.

"You're a woman," he said.

Her eyes widened, and he knew he was right. He hadn't been entirely sure. It, she, slouched a moment. As if he had made some kind of accusation. Then, challenging, she lifted her chin, met his gaze and bared her fangs. Before he could say another word, she slammed and locked the door, and left.

Jack made note of the fact that learning the beast was female made him immediately sympathetic to her. No matter that she had tossed him and the prince around like they were nothing, that she was three times his size. She was now someone to be rescued. He knew he should mistrust this feeling. But the story lurking behind this place felt bigger than ever. He had to get out of this room. He must speak carefully.

The next meal came. He was standing there, waiting for her when the door opened. He'd thought about kneeling, then decided she might think he was mocking her. He didn't know what she might think, but he must persuade her to let him out.

"What?" she grunted.

Something human lingered in her eyes, but right now he could only see the beast. He swallowed the dryness from his mouth.

"You said you wanted to keep me to serve you. But you lock me up. Let me out, let me do something here. Like…well. I can cook." He nodded at the half a burned chicken on the plate.

The monstrous face shifted, as if she pressed her lips together doubtfully. "You'll kill me in my sleep and flee."

"I never will, I promise."

"How can I believe you?"

"Try it? You see…I think…I believe, that you don't want to kill me. You didn't want to kill either of us, or you would have. Without thinking, you could have snapped our necks. But you didn't."

They gazed at one another. His fear lessened, just a little.

"You can cook?" she asked.

"Yes, I can." He sounded braver than he felt.

"There's food in the kitchen," she said, and left the door open.

There wasn't *much* food in the kitchen. A sack of flour, another of lentils, a barrel of those sad turnips. But there was a spectacular garden just outside, closed in by a low wall. Lettuce, onions, peas and beans, all manner of herbs, and even an apple tree. He discovered a flock of feral chickens still dutifully producing eggs. Near as he could figure, the beast had lived by butchering chickens and sticking them in a pot in the oven.

He wasn't the best cook, but he could keep a hunting party alive in the field with not very much on hand. He took off his doublet, rolled up the sleeves of his linen shirt, and got to work. First, he cleaned. Cleared dust and grime from pots and pans, swept mouse nests from the pantry, scrubbed the stove, and washed the window to let in more light. The place began to smell of soap instead of rot. Only then did he start bringing in food from the garden. Onions and rosemary, a scoop of lentils. He used the bones of the most recent butchered chicken to make a broth.

The beast stood close by, watching him, scrutinizing everything he did. Waiting for him to break his promise. She was a wall of fur and power lurking in the doorway. He only glanced at her. Didn't stare, lest she take offense. He couldn't make out her expression in any case, under the horns and teeth and hair.

As the pot simmered on the stove, the place filled with the warm scent of lentil soup. Made the kitchen smell like home.

"Why do you do this?" the beast asked.

"I like to be useful." He couldn't tell if she approved. Really, he thought he was doing this for himself, so he wouldn't have to eat another burned hen.

"You are a gentleman. I can tell by the way you speak and carry yourself."

His smile was wry. "My father was a gentleman. He had five sons, I am the youngest, and there was nothing left for me. I could be as frustrated and dissolute as my brothers, or I could make my way in the world. As I said, I like to be useful."

"And how does a gentleman—or a gentleman's son—learn how to cook?"

"When his family, however fine its pedigree, is so poor they cannot hire someone to cook for them. My mother was very good at making do. There were no daughters, so I was the one who helped her."

"You say she *was*."

"Yes. She's gone."

"I'm sorry." The beast sounded sad. He was surprised he could tell.

Grief for his mother was an old familiar ache, and he tucked it away. "For my part, I think she was worn out."

"Five of you, you said."

"Yes." He had not thought of his family in a long time. The prince kept him very busy, and he was grateful for the work and the friendship, such as it was. He was glad not to think of his family.

"I was youngest of four," she said.

"So you know how it is—never a word in edgewise, the brunt of everyone's teasing."

"I miss them, my three brothers."

"Then I'm sorry," he said. He couldn't say he missed his, so he didn't. He gave the soup a last stir. "Well then, what do you think?"

She sighed, a rasping breath. "I haven't smelled anything so good in years. But…I don't…I'm…not sure I can." She held out her hands, her thick beast's paws with wretched curling claws. They were terrible hands, capable of ripping apart a chicken perhaps, but not much else. Such hands could never hold a spoon. He looked around the kitchen. There must be a solution. He wouldn't let so much soup go to waste.

He found a wide wooden serving bowl. It wasn't fine, it was the sort of thing used to bring bread to servants. But he thought two large clawed hands might be able to hold it.

"Try this," he said, and she did. She could grip it in her palms, bring it to her mouth, and drink.

They shared a meal together at the heavy wooden table in the kitchen, him eating with a spoon, her sipping carefully. The smell of roses came in from the garden. This was almost nice. But he kept looking out at the low wall. It wouldn't take much to climb over it, to escape. Except that he had promised not to. He didn't have much: a dead mother, a penniless father, and four ne'er-do-well brothers. But he had his word, and he kept it. For now, at least. Later would take care of itself.

He made small talk of how he would try to bake bread tomorrow, maybe do some weeding in the garden to see what other treasures he could discover. Start stealing eggs from the chickens to make more interesting fare. She sipped soup and watched him.

Finally, when the sun was setting, and he lit candles around the room, he turned to her. "I must ask," Jack said. "That is, may I ask—how did this happen? When we first came I saw spears and arrows caught in the ground. There are broken windows, scorch marks on some of the walls outside. This place was abandoned, except for you. Why?"

She growled, shook her head so that all her fur rippled, and raced out of the room.

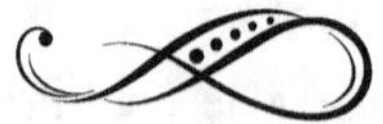

Jack spent the next few days working in the kitchen garden, salvaging squash vines and tying up lengths of peas, pruning shrubs that hadn't been touched in years and seemed to burst to life with the attention. He did indeed bake bread, make pot pies and stews, roast squash and salted peas. They ate very well, though the beast said little.

She watched him. He could feel it.

In the middle of the kitchen garden, a spring bubbled up through the rocks and had been tamed in a stone pool. After working, he'd wash up here. The first time he did so, he pulled his shirt over his head, dropped it to his side, flexed his aching shoulders, and he couldn't say how he knew. Whether he'd sensed an intake of breath at the edge of hearing, if he felt the weight of a gaze. If he looked, he knew he wouldn't be able to see her. She'd be hiding at one of the windows. She'd see him looking back, and she'd flee.

He could be bothered. He could go back to the tiny room and stay there, behave as the prisoner he was. Or he could wash up in fresh water, in a fine garden.

So he turned his back to the windows and kept on. Scrubbed arms and shoulders, dunked his head to rinse out his thick brown tangle of hair before tying it back in a tail. Sat for a moment, enjoying the warmth of the sun. Not thinking about anything else at all.

"I had a thought," Jack said after supper one evening, producing the tools he'd found in a garden shed. "That might make things easier for you."

"Easier how?" she said.

He held up a long, coarse rasp, a set of farrier's clippers. "To make your claws more manageable. If you like."

"I might not be as fierce without them."

He chuckled. "Oh, I wouldn't worry about that."

She crossed her arms, curling her hands into fists, hiding them away. He admitted he was disappointed—he only wanted to help.

"I meant no offense," he said. "I've kept my word, I haven't tried to escape. Will you not trust me?"

"Why should I trust anyone? Men like you with bright banners and shining swords, the stink of righteousness all over you. Men like you destroyed my family and home, trapped me here. You wanted to kill me when you first saw me. Why should I trust?"

"Because…" He had nothing to say; he couldn't explain. Yes, he had wanted to kill her, he couldn't deny that. He had been defending his prince.

She sat back. "So why aren't you trying to escape? Don't you hate me for keeping you prisoner?"

"This isn't so bad."

"It's because I'm a woman. Somehow, past all the fur and fangs, that matters to you. It upsets you, to see a woman brought to such a state." When her lips curled this time, it might have been a smile.

Softly he answered, "It does."

"It shouldn't."

But it did. He said, "If you were male, we'd be enemies. There'd be no question. I wouldn't need to know your story at all."

"But I am not male."

"And that makes this is a tragedy. Doesn't it?" This felt like a trap; the back of his neck itched.

"And if I were a *man* turned into a beast, and you were a woman—"

He swallowed. "I suppose I'd be terrified."

She lunged, all her sharp fangs bared. "And aren't you terrified now?" she roared, slamming her untrimmed claws on either side of his face.

He choked back a scream, pressed himself against the wall, face turned away, eyes squeezed shut, waiting for her to rip out his throat. Her hot breath blew over him. Cringing, he held his own breath. Worse than his sudden terror was his shame at his own terror.

"I fought to defend my castle. When my family was gone, there was only me, and I *fought*. Though I am cursed for it, I will fight, and I will not be tamed!"

With a last snarl, she lunged away, fled.

He slumped to the floor, beside the tools that he'd dropped.

He had a nightmare about those claws sweeping past his hair, so close to his neck. Waking, gasping, he thought of the beast, and his throat closed on a scream. This response was primal, that of a rabbit facing a hound.

He would not be a rabbit here.

The next day he made roast chicken, real roast chicken with crispy basted skin and juicy meat, and brought it to the hall with the fireplace. He'd kept a fire going in it most days since he'd gained some little freedom in the castle. Sitting on the floor, picking absently at the food and watching the flames, ignoring the world outside the walls and the eyes watching him within, he felt almost comfortable.

A great shadow filled a doorway. He couldn't help it; he scrambled to his feet and backed away. His heart pounded loud; he was sure she could hear it and know he was afraid. And he should be afraid of her, she was a beast. He swallowed back that scream, forced himself to calm. She kept the claws hidden.

"Smells good," she said finally, glancing at the platter of food he'd brought out. "Better than I ever made."

"Have some," he said carefully. "Please."

When she approached, he kept his distance. Marked the path to the doorway where he could flee, if he needed to.

She ate, taking great care, holding a piece of chicken between her fingers and bringing it to her mouth, avoiding her claws as delicately as she could, which was not very. She dripped grease on her fur, and only made it worse when she tried to wipe it away. Jack resisted bringing her a handkerchief.

"You want to know what happened to me," she said, after a time, long enough that Jack had added extra logs to the fire.

"If you want to tell me."

She took a deep breath and told him a story of a rebel baron who coveted her family's castle and land. At first, this man had merely asked her father for her hand in marriage. He—and she—refused him. This angered the baron beyond reason, and he called forth a troop of brigands and cutthroats to wage war, to take their home—and her—by force. Her family fought back. They were good fighters, skilled and well armed—Jack had seen the armory for himself. So the rebel lord hired a magician to trick them. One by one he drew out her father and each of her brothers and murdered them. The invading force thought then the castle was theirs. But she and her mother kept fighting. And fighting. Somehow, with rigged traps and buckets of burning oil and a hundred other strategies, they kept the invaders at bay. Until her mother was killed, and she was alone. But still she fought, as best she could.

"And then I put an arrow through the baron's eye. Did it from the roof. The shot of a lifetime. I had my revenge, and I thought it was over."

Jack had been rapt, and now his heart sank. "But the magician cursed you."

"He said that I will be the beast I so clearly am at heart until I find a man who can tame me, and submit to his will."

The lurch in his gut on hearing this was the same he felt when his father told him there was nothing left, he would have no inheritance, he would have nothing but what his brothers could do for him. And they could do nothing.

"That isn't fair," he said.

"No," she said. "And even so, after everything, I will *not* be tamed. I…I fought too hard."

"There must be something…some other magician who could break the spell—"

"And who would listen to a beast? Who would not run screaming from me? Or they would only show the pity that I see now in your eyes."

He looked away. The fire crackled. There seemed to be nothing left to say.

"Do you have any brandy?" Jack asked. "I have a flask in my coat, but it's almost out."

She shook her head. "There's only the bottle of wine my father was saving to celebrate our victory. I will not touch it. Not yet."

"Of course."

More silence, with only the sparking, snapping fire to disturb them. It was actually a cheerful sound, offering a sense of home and warmth. Indeed, looking around, the parlor seemed almost normal. Except for the great beast, sitting back with her clawed hands wrapped around her knees. But even she had become familiar.

"I'm sorry I'm so melancholy," the beast said suddenly.

"If anyone has cause for it, it's you," he said.

"I imagine at your home you're surrounded all the time by friends, by the prince's court and all its good cheer."

Jack chuckled. "Would it surprise you that I'm rather enjoying the peace and quiet here?"

"Yes," she said bluntly.

"Well. Perhaps there is a bit of trying make the best of things." He smiled, meaning it to be a joke. But she sighed, and even with the strange monstrousness of her face, he could see the sadness. He shouldn't have said such a thing.

Carefully, aware of her shape and size, that such a creature wasn't meant for an elegant parlor, she climbed to her feet. "It's late. I'll leave you alone. Let you have a restful evening." Once on her feet, she was nimble, fast, and she left, almost before he realized what was happening.

"Beast, wait!" he called after her, but she kept going.

He only now realized that he didn't know her name.

He knew very little about her, in fact. Where she slept in the castle. What her life had been like before this curse had befallen her. What this place must have looked like in happier days. His heart broke thinking that she kept him prisoner—that she had wanted a prisoner at all—so she would have someone to talk to.

He didn't believe she'd do anything to him if he tried to leave. So why didn't he? He told himself he could be useful here. At least clean up a bit more of the castle before he fled. He'd done the kitchen, the kitchen garden, the servants' quarters, the main parlor. Part of the dining room, most of the foyer. While exploring the second floor, he came again upon the marvelous practice hall. Where this all started, where he had offered himself in place of the prince.

Even stepping softly, his boots echoed. He could track exactly where they had been, where they had tried to fight the beast—they'd left marks in the dust across the floor and on hilts and staves where their hands had brushed. The beautiful sword that the prince had dropped had been replaced on the rack.

She had gotten in the habit of coming to the kitchen to watch him cook, and to talk. He was afraid that she might not do so that evening, after what he had said. He made sure the stew that day was particularly savory and filled the hallway with a rich smell, to draw her in. And she came, lurking in the doorway as she always did.

"Good afternoon," he said, trying to sound bright. She huddled in on herself, but that was normal. "I have a question for you."

"What is it?" she grumbled.

He tasted the stew, added a bit of salt. "May I clean the armory? That lovely practice salle upstairs, I mean." He cringed inwardly at his awkwardness. Of course she knew what he meant, what else would he be talking about?

She scowled. "Why? So you can use my weapons against me?"

"Because it pains me to see such a fine place so neglected."

"What was I supposed to do? What can I do?" Again, she held up her large hands, her awful claws, showing the difficulty of doing anything but fight with them.

"I'm not blaming you. I want to help."

"Because you feel sorry for me."

"Yes," he had to admit. "I do."

"I could kill you."

"Then why don't you?"

"Because…because I like talking to you." She ducked her fierce head and ran, disappearing down the corridor and away.

He sighed and tossed the spoon into the pot. "Would you stop running away!" he shouted after her, then wished he hadn't. The stew was ready to eat, but she likely would not emerge again. He didn't mean to keep chasing her off. Maybe it would be better if he didn't speak at all.

The next day, he brought brooms, rags, and buckets of soapy water to the armory and got to work. The task was hard, mindless, and satisfying. Washing mirrors and windows—they immediately let in so much more light, everything looked less dingy for it. He wiped down each weapon individually, every spear, crossbow, and sword. Exactly the kind of work he did as huntsman for the prince.

"Oh, I had forgotten how lovely this place could be."

The beast's grumbling voice spoke from the far doorway. She entered, looking around her with wonder at gleaming spear tips reflected in the mirrors, at rows of swords and a shelf of helms, all dust free. She paused by a rug where he had made a pile of various pieces.

"Those had a bit of rust on them," he explained. "So I set them aside for polishing."

"It's wonderful. Thank you."

"My pleasure, truly," he said. He set down the dust cloth he'd been using, picked up a rapier from a nearby rack. It was simpler than the one with the twisting gold hilt the prince had so admired, the beast's father's sword. This one had a simple bell guard with a stamped design of vines around the edge, a leather grip, a good blade just exactly right for his reach. Felt good in his hands. This was much more his style.

"That was my eldest brother's," the beast said with a sigh.

"I'm sorry." He started to put it back.

Quickly the beast said, "It can be yours, if you like it."

Jack kept hold of the grip, and now it felt a little like he held hands with a ghost.

"I like it very much. Thank you."

"I think he would like you, my brother."

He smiled. "I'm glad." He extended his sword arm, looked down the blade, ran it through a couple of practice parries, and yes, it sang. Light enough to feel part of his arm, but strong enough to press forward in a fight. He looked at the beast, his lips pursed. "You were cursed for bearing arms. Are you any good?" He saluted with the rapier.

"I was. But I can't hold a sword like that anymore. Though I can hold a spear."

"Oh?" He set the sword back in its place.

Another rack held practice spears, with softer wood and padded tips instead of steel. He looked at her, judged her height, guessed her preferences, and chose one he thought would suit. Tossed it to her from a dozen paces away. She caught it easily, finishing the arc of its fall before gripping it with both hands and coming to ready. Even with her bulk, the movement had grace. He had no doubt of her skill. He donned a grin and chose a spear for himself.

"Let's try our paces, then."

She stepped around to keep him at the center of a circle, just out of her range. "Are you certain? Can you take it?"

"Yes, I need the practice. I've been getting soft, lazing around and eating all your chickens."

"That flock needed to be culled anyway." Snarling, she lunged. The directness of the attack startled him; he thought he had been ready for it. Apparently not. Dodging back, he got his spear in the way for an awkward parry, then danced sideways and tried for his own attack, stabbing at her chest. She ducked, dashed back. They went back to circling one another. Jack's heart pounded—he really was out of practice.

He stepped in, feinted low, thrusting the spear to the edge of his reach, then swept up and over her weapon as she took the bait. Stabbed for her shoulder, but she ducked and pivoted out of the way with astonishing agility. Then she drove him back, striking and stabbing, and while he managed to block each attack, he couldn't gain solid enough ground to counter her blows. He held the end of the spear and swung, just to get some space for himself, but the move was so broad she easily retreated.

Little comfort, when she planted the end of the spear and leaned on it to rest, catching her breath. He was doing the same.

"You're good," he said.

"I know," she said slyly. "That's how I got into this mess."

He laughed. "Again!"

They sparred, laughing and teasing, pulling their blows so that when they struck the padded ends only tapped. Still, he'd have bruises. But they'd be satisfying bruises earned from work. She was better than him, at least with a spear. Even with her size and bulk she had precision, placing the tip exactly where she intended, blocking with conviction. He had no doubt she could handle a rapier just as well. If she had the hands for it.

In an attack of desperation, he let out a cry and charged, leading with his spear. He intended to thrust near her feet, to tangle up her legs as he ran alongside. Make her at least stumble if not fall, and thereby get some kind of upper hand. But even here, she was ready, springing out of his way and shoving her weight into him. She was a wall, implacable, and he crashed to the floor, his weapon bouncing away.

Taking advantage, she moved in, placed the tip of her spear hovering an inch or two above his neck. He'd have been quite dead if they'd been fighting in earnest. Chuckling, he lay back and accepted his fate.

She looked down her spear at him and sounded worried. "You're not hurt, are you?"

Only his pride. He wiped sweat off his cheek. "I'll recover. And you have won. I think I'm finished."

He moved her spear aside, and she let him. Taking hold of it, he used it to steady himself as he got up off the floor, climbing the spear shaft hand over hand, until one of his hands landed on hers. He was tired, unthinking. He didn't even notice, until they were both staring at their hands together. And hers felt like a hand. He could sense the strength, muscle and tendon clenched under the fur. She was gripping the shaft hard, as if she wanted to snap it, and gazed back at him, wide-eyed and fearful. What was she afraid of? Of scaring him off? Of simple human touch? But it wasn't that simple, was it?

He drew his hand away, noticing how warm hers had been now that he wasn't touching it. No longer able to stand the look in her eyes, he glanced away, tried to smile again.

"I don't know how your terrible magician ever thought anyone could tame you," he murmured.

She barked a laugh, looked away, her teeth still bared. The fangs appeared wicked, but he'd long since trusted she would not use those teeth to hurt him.

"Tell me, Jack," she said. "Must one be tamed before she can be loved?"

He opened his mouth, determined to say something, to answer her—the question did not seem rhetorical, she *needed* an answer. But he didn't know what to say, and he waited too long. She hugged the spear to her, ducked her monstrous face away and muttered, "I'm sorry," before racing away, her clawed feet clicking on the wooden floor.

Weakly this time, almost under his breath, he said, "Stop…stop running away, dammit."

The beast didn't appear at all the next day, no matter how much he looked for her. He wondered how a creature of that size could hide at all. He wanted to apologize, but was sure that an apology would insult her. He was rarely at such a loss about what to do.

Climbing several flights of stairs to a dusty storage room filled with wooden crates, broken chairs, rolled-up rugs and dozens of other artifacts, then climbing narrow stone steps to a trapdoor, Jack made his way to the roof. There, he found the spot where the beast had been when she fired the arrow that killed the marauding baron who destroyed her family. She was right, it was the shot of a lifetime, a hundred yards out past the gardens to where attackers had held their line.

It looked peaceful now. Ivy had grown to mask all evidence of battle. In a few more years, the whole forest would swamp the place and no one would ever know there'd been a castle here.

The woods surrounding the castle were vast—it was why the prince had wanted to hunt here, in the most wild and challenging place anyone knew. The prince had dozens of parks ideal for hunting, but those weren't enough, and Jack obliged, however much trouble it caused, however many more guards it required and dangers he needed to plan for. Somewhere far beyond the vast green carpet of trees, to those far-off hills many miles away, lay civilization, and another castle, a great edifice in good repair, the center of a kingdom. Jack found he didn't miss it much at all.

Then he looked again. Something large and wide moved through the forest, and he was afraid he knew what. He went down the steps to the library where he'd seen a spyglass. He carried it back to the roof, looked through it, and saw an army. Still dozens of miles away, but the smoke from their campfires was visible, dark columns reaching up.

And still he could not find the beast. He went through the castle calling for her, cringing at the way his voice echoed, how he disturbed the peace.

The next evening, the movement, the campfires and their columns of smoke were closer. Jack knew an army approached, and he was sure he knew why.

"What do you look at?"

Startled, he turned from the window. The beast was at the doorway. His anxious demand of where she'd been and what she'd been doing stopped at his lips. So did all the apologies he wanted to give.

Instead, he offered the spyglass. "Do you want to see?"

"Not sure I can." She held up her hands, too large for the delicate instrument.

"Never mind. You can probably see from here." He stepped aside, giving her room at the window. "The prince is coming with an army. To rescue me." He snorted.

"To take the castle," the beast countered, and Jack nodded.

"Yes, probably."

"I will fight. I will defend my castle as I always have."

She said this without a hint of doubt, her determination clear. Admirable. But this wasn't a marauder's band. This was an *army*. He wanted to say a dozen things at once. You can't, please don't, and let me help. He began making plans. For all its ominous appearance, surrounded by its unkempt garden, the place wasn't very defensible. But they could board up windows and doors, add spikes to the outer wall. They might have time to make some kind of palisade—

None of it would work.

"Let me go," he said.

Her furred face pursed, eyes narrowing, a first show of anger. But then she looked away. "You wish to flee. I understand."

"No! No, that isn't it at all. That army belongs to the prince. Let me go talk to him. He'll listen to me; I can persuade him to leave off. To leave you alone."

She stayed hunched in, a great beast huddled on the floor. He flattered himself that he could read at least some of her expressions. She remained sad. Unconvinced.

"Will you let me go do this thing? Do you trust me?"

She flinched at the word. Looking out the window, she said, "You will not return."

Oh. Yes, she would think that.

"I promise I will return." He did not know how to sound any more earnest. "I would not leave you here alone. I *must* return, to tell you that the prince listened to me and will turn back. Or…I will return to help you defend your home."

"Jack," she said. "Are you really so honorable?"

"Let me prove it."

"Very well."

He prepared. The prince's army would be here within a day. If only he had a horse he could race to them; as it was, he would have to meet them halfway. The prince would need a lot of convincing—he was likely very excited at the idea of a siege. Jack would have to flatter him.

Before he left, he looked for the beast. In the armory, in the kitchen garden, in her usual parlor. Finally he found her at the front door. She had brought a stack of spears with her, and was sharpening their tips with a stone.

"I was looking for you," he said.

"I was waiting for you." She set aside her work.

"I'll go as quick as I can and be back before you know it."

"You promise?"

His heart broke a little, again. For everything she had been through. For the cruelty, the impossibility of it all. He reached out, took her hand, quickly, before she could flinch away. It dwarfed his own. She could crush his bones in her grip. But her hand lay lightly in his. Almost trembling. Even under the fur, the muscles, and those fierce claws, he could feel a scrap of humanness. The way the fingers flexed as if to curl around his, then pulled back.

"My lady, I promise you I will return. On my honor."

He bowed over her hand as a gentleman would, pressed his lips to the back of it, then let go. She drew the hand to her chest. Her eyes were wet.

"Goodbye, Jack."

He left the castle.

"Halt! You there, halt!"

Outriders caught him by the end of the day. They were two ordinary cavalrymen, their blue coats clean and crisp, their hats just so, their swords polished, their horses fit.

Jack stopped and raised his hands. "I must speak with the prince! It's urgent!"

"Who do you think you are?"

Jack studied them, then sighed. "Peter, you know exactly who I am. Please, take me to see him at once, I beg you."

The shorter of the two stared a moment, and his eyes went round. "Jack? Jack! We thought you were dead! We're marching to avenge you!"

Not even a rescue. Well then. "As you can see, I am quite well, and you're all making a terrible mistake. I must speak with His Highness, please!"

"Yes! This way!"

They reached the front of the army, the prince and his officers lined up, rows of silk banners lined up behind them, the spears of the guards glittering in the sun. The warhorses were grand, white and black, with arched necks and polished hooves.

Behind this company came foot soldiers and archers, the wagons and horses following them, filling the woods with the noise of their existence, an undercurrent of thunder and aggression.

The prince led the company. His helmet was tied to his saddle, so his black hair flowed, and his noble face looked out with the pride of a conqueror. He'd had new armor made for this expedition, polished steel with gold trim, etched all over with his family's sigils. He'd probably had a portrait painted before he left.

"Jack!" The prince slid off his horse and strode up to grip Jack's arms. "You're all right! You escaped!"

"I am well, sire. But I must speak with you. You cannot make war against the castle. I beg you to turn back."

The smile fell from the prince's handsome face. "What are you saying?"

"You mean to attack the castle. Please, don't do it."

The prince chuckled, uncertain. "My dear Jack. I was coming to avenge you. And kill the beast, of course."

"Oh no, sire, you can't! Please, there's a story, dark and terrible. The beast isn't what we first thought. She means no harm, really, her story is tragic—"

"She? Her?" The prince took a step back. "No, I do see what has happened here. The beast has put a spell on you."

Yes, Jack thought. But not like that. And then: I am already dead to him.

"This is a trick," the prince said. "The beast has sent you to trick me. Guards!"

Jack ran, or tried to. While he ducked out of the first guard's lunging grip, slipped past the second, kicked the third's legs out from under him, ten more were waiting beyond, and twenty more after that, and they caught Jack up by his arms and legs, hauled him away, tied him up, and threw him in the back of the surgeon's wagon. The prince's own physician tried to examine him, but even with his hands and feet bound, Jack was able to kick him and drive him off.

They declared him mad and continued on, marching on the lonely castle.

He tried to make the calculations—how fast was the army moving, how quickly would it reach the castle, and how much danger was the beast in. But he was so full of rage he couldn't think. More than all other thoughts, he couldn't stand that the beast would believe that he had broken his promise. That he had betrayed her. Somehow, he had to escape.

He ripped skin off his hands doing it, and nearly pulled his arms out of their sockets, but he managed to loosen the bonds on his wrists. Somehow, by force of will and more struggle than he thought possible, he freed himself. Slipped out the back of the supply wagon using all the stealth that hunting and tracking had ever taught him. He even stole a horse. He'd never done anything so rash in his life. He raced, and that was when the soldiers saw him, drawn by pounding hoofbeats and the rush of motion. Jack heard the calls for him to stop, even heard an arrow or two pass close.

And then, the sounds of horses thundered after him. In later days, he would remember this race as a blur, shrouded in the awareness that he was pushing the horse too hard, praying that the poor creature didn't stumble, that the way would remain clear, and that somehow he could make all this right. Most certainly too big a task, and so the trees, the sky, the state of the path ahead and all the signs he would normally track while on a hunt fell clean away from him. He only knew of the castle ahead, and the army behind.

Then, finally, he arrived at the familiar ivy-shrouded gates, the hulking stone walls. He made a sort of leaping dismount and slapped the horse's hindquarters, yelling for it to go back home, and the horse obliged, launching back down the path.

Meanwhile, they didn't have much time. Or any time.

He rushed through the overgrown garden, up to the front door. It was locked.

Maybe even barricaded. More, there were crossbows resting at some of the windows. She needed help, he needed to get inside. If she would have him. If she hadn't decided that he'd betrayed her. The thought sent him into a panic.

He slammed the doorknocker a dozen times, pounded with his fist. "Beast! It's Jack! The army's coming, I couldn't stop them."

If she never spoke to him again, he couldn't blame her.

Then the door opened, and he just pulled back before pounding on air. They stood staring at each other until she slouched with relief, disappointment, something he couldn't say.

"You came back," she said with a sigh.

"I said I would."

"Yes, but . . ."

"I know."

"Oh Jack, your arms." She reached for his hands, the shredded rope burns on his wrists, red and scabbed over with dried blood, and then drew back. "I'll get bandages—"

"Never mind about that. The prince didn't believe me. I had to escape, to warn you."

She nodded solemnly, as if she had expected this. "What are we to do?"

"I don't know."

"But you came back."

"To stand with you, yes."

"Well then. We'll do our best."

They couldn't win. Not against a whole army, they both knew that. If only Jack could think of some trick, just the right words to keep the prince away from their door. If the prince could meet her without him immediately wanting to kill her—

She was speaking. "I've laid out every crossbow and bolt I could find. If we start firing before they reach the outer wall, they might hesitate. There's a bottleneck at the gate we can use, and I have spears for the ones who come in through the door—"

"No," he said, looking out across the garden. If they had time to build palisades, ditches, traps, maybe then. If they had gunpowder and catapults. But they only had themselves. "Do you trust me?"

Her hands clenched; her expression changed, the fur along her jaw shifting. "I do. Yes."

"I want to try one more time to talk to him. The longer I can keep him talking…well. I have to try. Go inside, find a hiding place—that servant's room where you kept me that first day. Stay there, stay quiet."

She bristled, hair rising across her shoulders. "I will not hide, I'm not a coward—"

"Of course you aren't! You have never stopped fighting, and I love you for it. But if I can convince the prince that you're already gone…" He shrugged, an admission that this might not work. "I don't know. It's all I can think of."

They heard the sound of hoofbeats, of barking dogs. Soldiers shouting at one another. The army had arrived.

"Go, please!" he begged her.

She nodded, turning to vanish down the hall.

He watched her go, wishing he could do more, wishing he had a little magic himself. But he was just a huntsman. Jack found one of the spears, closed the door, and stood before it like a guard.

The great and glittering royal army halted in the yard before the steps. They regarded him for a time. Sizing him up, Jack thought. Finally, the prince dismounted.

"Jack!" the prince exclaimed, approaching.

"Sire," Jack said cautiously, wondering how far he would actually go to keep the prince on this side of the door.

"Jack. Why did you run?"

"You took me prisoner."

"For your own good. You clearly weren't in your right mind."

"What about now?"

The prince regarded the scene, his lips pursed. "You seem to be trying to protect an entire castle alone, with only a spear. I say you're still a bit off."

Jack quirked a smile. "Even so. I can't let you enter, sire."

"Why not?"

He stretched his spine a little straighter. "I promised to protect this castle for its mistress."

"Its *mistress*? What about the beast?"

"Well, sire, I've been trying to explain, there's been a spell cast on this place—"

"Yes, the one that's so badly affected you—"

"No, that isn't it! This castle belongs to a lady, a noble lady, and her family was killed—"

"By that horrid beast, yes, of course."

"No, sire!" How could he be explaining this so badly? If he wasn't careful he'd use his spear to bash the prince over the head. And a hundred arrows would fly into him in the next breath.

"Then tell me what is happening here!" the prince demanded.

At that moment the door behind Jack opened. A woman came out. *A woman.*

She was disheveled, tired-looking, with a round face and deep frown. Shadows under her eyes, stark against her ivory skin. Her long tangle of light-brown curls hadn't been brushed in ages and bunched around her shoulders. She held a wool cloak tight around her, like it was armor. With her hand on the edge of the door, she looked around, blinking at everything, as if she had just woken from a long sleep.

It was her. It was the beast—transformed. Somehow. Jack stared in awe. They all did.

"What is this?" she asked. Her voice was a clear, strong alto. More human, more musical than the beast's, but unmistakably the beast's. The same cadence, the same underlying certainty of someone who always spoke her mind.

Jack renewed his grip on the spear. "My lady, an army has come. I was just trying to learn their purpose."

"My lady," the prince breathed, with a polite nod of his head. She bowed a little in response, but only a little.

"Sire, you see what I've been trying to tell you?" Jack said, his heart racing.

The prince said, "Yes, of course. The castle belongs to this good lady. Clearly the beast has been holding her prisoner. My lady—Jack rescued you. And of course you fell in love with him. Have I got it straight?"

"Close enough, I suppose," she said, looking at Jack, her expression showing stark wonder.

"You know he's only the fifth son of a minor lord," the prince stated.

Still looking at Jack she said, "I imagine that's what makes this a fairy tale."

The prince said, "Did you kill the beast, Jack? May we see its carcass?"

She flinched at this.

"Jack?" the prince repeated.

Somehow he brought himself back to the moment, the door, and the prince. "Ah—alas, no, sire. I merely wounded it. It fled, deep into the forest. I could not give chase, I needed to stay behind…with her."

"Of course! See that the lady is protected, of course! Lucky girl," he said, winking. "Well then. We'll go after the beast and hunt it down. We will avenge you, my lady. Which way did it go?"

"That way. I think," she said. Both Jack and the beast pointed vaguely off to the north.

"Very well then." The prince turned to his company and called in an admirably martial manner, "We ride! Let us hunt!" A great cheer went up, and after a ponderous few moments getting themselves turned around to march back out of the gardens, the army departed.

Quiet fell, enough stillness that they heard birdsong. They were alone, and without thinking they turned to one another.

"What happened?" he asked wonderingly. The question felt abrupt, as if he jostled the universe.

"I don't know." She sounded just as baffled. "I went inside, as you told me to. And, I stopped. Something stopped me. There was light, a thunderclap. And then…and then…I had my hands back. Hands, Jack. Look at them!"

In fact, he had dropped the spear some time back and was holding both hers in his own, making it a simple thing to raise them and study them. Fine hands, with long fingers, slender and strong, with calluses. Perfectly normal fingernails, if a bit rough. The ring she'd worn had slipped off, and he wondered if it had belonged to her father, as well.

He thought a moment, trying to solve a puzzle that he wasn't happy about. To tame her would be to break her, which would break him. "I would never think to command you, to ask you to submit—"

"I trusted you. Maybe that was better."

His smile broke. "Yes."

She looked back, toward where the army had left. "Are you ever going to tell him what really—"

"No, God no."

She laughed, and put her hand, her perfect human hand, on his cheek, and he leaned into the touch.

"You . . . you're taller than I thought you'd be."

"While you are exactly right," he said.

She brushed his cheek, his jaw, making him far too aware that he hadn't shaved in several days, and he almost apologized, then he didn't. He wanted to catch her up in his arms, but he was still so busy studying her face, the lips pressed anxiously together in a familiar expression, the slope of her cheekbones, her brown eyes and the fall of her hair over her shoulders.

"I don't know how to speak to you," she said finally, as if she too needed time to believe. And then she smiled. Her eyes lit.

Part of him would always expect to turn and find the beast standing there when he heard that voice. But her…she was already familiar. "I think…I think I would like to make you dinner. A proper dinner, with cutlery and goblets and everything."

"How daring."

"That is. I mean. If I can stay," he asked hopefully. Everything he did with her would be with hope.

"Jack. I could not possibly manage a castle like this on my own. You saw how it was. Defend, yes. But not manage. Not really."

"Generally, in my experience, fine people like you hire someone. Bring someone on to help with a job like this."

"Like a fifth son who wants to be useful?"

"Just so. Well, my lady. What would you like to do first?"

She kissed him. Lightly, hesitating, as if she was still judging her own strength and distance, she drew close and put her lips on his, and he waited, still as any hunter. When a rare beast draws close, best to be still, lest she flee. She drew away, and he paused long, to remember the warmth of her touch.

She held his hands tightly and said, "And next, I would like to open that bottle of wine."

THE BURNING GIRL

I was told I must swear fealty to William the Bastard. He had taken England, made himself king, fealty was required. But I did not swear and none could make me. He could kill me, or rather order his men to kill me. But he would not, because he wanted to use me.

I was never loyal to King William. All my oaths I swore to Sir Gilbert.

Gilbert—he was fiercely, stupidly loyal to William, so it amounted to the same thing, but never mind. William used Gilbert as he used us all, for what we could do; for the curses we carried. The difference was William owed Gilbert. Gilbert was politic and knew how to ask for favors, such that William granting them seemed like generosity and not indebtedness. And Gilbert used those favors to protect the rest of us. I saw it from the first.

Other chronicles have written much about those times, when England ceased to be what it had been. The great apocalypse. I will not tell that history over again. Instead I will begin at my place in the tale, the moment I first saw Gilbert.

Mother Ursula brought me to the yard in front of the abbey. She stood apart, just out of arm's reach. She did not want me touching her.

Three Norman warriors stood waiting. They might have been knights, even. I could not tell such things, but they carried swords and those domed helmets. Their belted tunics were worn, stained with mud and miles. I stopped just outside the door and stared at them. The nuns and novices had gathered in the yard to gape.

"You must come forward, Joan. Come!" Ursula jerked her hand as if she were calling a dog to be punished.

One of the knights stood a little ahead of the others. His hood was thrown back. He was clean-shaven, young. Not even crow's feet at his eyes. He had a serious set to his mouth, as if he bore more responsibility than he expected or wanted.

Mother Ursula ruled the abbey of St. Edith, but she bowed her head to this young man, deferential. He spoke to her in Latin. I recognized two words: *puella incendiara*. The burning girl.

At a gesture from Ursula, one of the nuns ran back to the hall and returned with an unlit candle, one of the big beeswax ones used to light the chapel sanctuary. I knew what this meant: these knights had demanded a demonstration. At the sight of that candle, I nearly cried. I did not understand, did not want to understand, but I knew what was happening.

Ursula held the candle to me. "You must show Sir Gilbert what you are."

"Mother Abbess, you said that I must never—"

"That doesn't matter."

"But you said that I would be damned—"

"Joan! If you do not do this for Sir Gilbert, the Norman army will destroy the abbey and all of us with it. Please."

Mother Ursula did not have to beg for anything, particularly not from a low-born novice placed here out of charity and fear. A scrawny, awkward novice, coifed and shrouded in threadbare gray and carrying the Devil's spark. But she begged now.

I held the candle before me where the Normans could see it. Its weight was potential; the wick beckoned. Already the spark rose up under my skin. Mother Ursula could not put a candle in my hand and expect I would do nothing.

I touched the wick. The candle lit, a tongue of fire flaring and settling.

"Mon Dieu." This was whispered by the wiry, chestnut-haired man standing to Sir Gilbert's right. The nuns made the sign of the cross.

Sir Gilbert smiled.

Her voice was taut with fear even as she sighed with relief. "Joan, you will go with these knights."

I swallowed back my racing heart. "I cannot go with them, I cannot go alone with these men—"

Gilbert raised a hand and spoke softly to the knight on his left, who was tall and somber. This one pulled back a hood—and revealed braided hair, a beardless jaw, and a woman's eyes. Then he spoke to me in thick and simple English. "You go with Ann. No harm to you."

Ursula's voice was stretched. "You must go with them, child. Or they will destroy us."

Gilbert gazed on stonily. Yes, he would destroy the abbey.

I was being sold to Normans.

Mother Ursula had never been kind to me. I lived here alone in a stone cell, apart from all the others. No one ever came near me. I was cursed and damned already, whether I stayed with the English or went with the Normans.

No harm, this man said. I should not believe him, but I wanted to.

I blew out the candle, set it on the ground, and went to stand before Sir Gilbert. I came up to his shoulder; he seemed to fill the yard all by himself. Gilbert and Ursula exchanged more words in Latin. Then he spoke in Norman-French to the knight on his right, who nodded and ran. No, he did not run; he flew, racing away almost faster than the eye could see, leaving a burst of dust in his wake. A wondrous power. The Devil's touch.

I was not the only damned one here.

Gilbert said in his thick English, "Felix tells army to pass by. No harm. My banner on your door. The abbey, safe." Ursula's shoulders slouched and a tear slipped down her cheek.

How was it that my small life should buy so much? Mother Ursula ought to be grateful, but she did not look at me. Never looked on me again. None of them did, all the nuns and novices. They seemed so cold, and none of them offered to say farewell. They sent me to the enemy with no remorse.

I had nothing to bring with me but my clothes.

There were three horses tied up outside the abbey's low wall. I could not ride, I did not want to ride… But the woman, Ann, was already atop the big gray, and she reached down to me.

No one had ever been willing to touch my hand, not since I came to St. Edith's. But she reached to me, took my hand, and pulled. Somehow, I landed in the saddle behind her. As soon as the horse started moving I was sure I would fall off. The big, rolling, jostling movements rattled my head and shook my spine. I wrapped my arms around Ann's middle and prayed to the God that Mother Ursula had always said would not listen to me.

Felix came running back within the hour, meeting us on the road. At the abbey, we had thought the army was much farther away, several days' travel at least, but this man had crossed the distance easily. The horses flinched at the rushing of air and dust that accompanied his skidding stop. He reported to Gilbert, then got up on the third horse, because even someone who could run so fast grew tired.

We went south and met the harrowing.

The last Saxon lords in the north had rebelled, rebelled again, defended poor King Harold's would-be heir fleeing to Scotland, and finally William the Bastard had enough and sent his army to raze the land.

To the south and east, farmland and villages burned. We choked on the smoke that filled the sky. Hundreds fled. Whole families with all they owned on their backs or loaded on handcarts filled roads and fields; a river of people stumbled along, staring ahead with blank haunted expressions, the weeping long finished. Even the children were silent. They moved with no destination in mind, just trying to get away, away. We had been safe in the abbey, except there had not been enough to eat. That would get worse. With the farms burned, soon no one would have enough to eat.

On their big warhorses, Gilbert's company, so plainly the enemy, cut right through the fleeing crowds. Folk scattered and were left stumbling, as in the eddy of a stream, staring in confusion and consternation. Sometimes, confusion turned to helpless fury and hurled curses. Sometimes, one of them hefted a pitchfork or ax they'd managed to rescue from their burning homes and charged.

They never came within an arm's length of Gilbert's horses. Somehow, they seemed to trip and fall back, or it would be as if they met a wall and stood with unnatural stillness, arms upraised, helplessly cursing. And so Gilbert's company trotted on fearlessly through a sea of its enemies.

I stared back at these people who had Saxon features like me, not like these tall, fair Norman warriors. My people, dispossessed of everything, burned out by the Conqueror's army and fleeing their lands. On horseback, I floated above them, borne away by some fate outside my control. I could fall, I thought. Slide off the back of the horse and run… Or I would break against the hard ground and be finished. I stayed put.

Ann called to Gilbert, who answered. Felix laughed. I understood nothing. Only that these people had gone to a lot of trouble to get me, and they must need me for some reason. I could not even ask them why.

At sunset, we stopped at a camp some ways off the road, by some trees near the bend in a stream. A trio of tents were pitched around a rock-ringed fire with a pot set up over it. The smell of cooking stew displaced the smoke. My belly spoke; I hadn't thought I was hungry. I was also dusty, thirsty, exhausted, morose. Gilbert's company had dared not stop among the refugees. Even a knight could be brought down by an angry crowd.

But now, at last, we stopped. Gilbert dismounted, then Felix, who took the reins and led off the horses. From Ann's horse I looked down at the ground and wondered how I was going to get there. I could not simply swing my leg over the way they could. I tried, and tumbled. But Gilbert caught me and set me upright. Ann dismounted much more elegantly and gave me a wry look. As if I were a chore she'd rather not face.

I stood planted, uncertain, staring at the three who were already here.

Sitting with legs crossed was a man with brown skin, dressed in the wool and leather of a warrior. He wore his dark hair in a tail down his back, and a crow perched on his shoulder. Gilbert called him Ibrahim.

Next was a beautiful woman with cinnamon hair in a long thick braid, wearing a green belted tunic. Her mouth was full and smiling. She studied me closely, so much so that I looked away. For the last five years I had only seen women cloistered and veiled, somber and judgmental. They might have smiled and laughed, but they never did so around me. Rather, they furtively escorted me from my cell to chapel and the garden to work and back, avoiding my touch. As if they might burn just being near me. This woman's openness was disconcerting.

The third was a monk of middle years, wearing a thick dark habit, his tonsure well trimmed, a wooden cross around his neck. He rose and came forward, arms wide, and he and Gilbert clapped each other on the shoulders.

The monk looked past Gilbert to me. "Is this all you found?"

I brightened. He spoke English.

"It is," Gilbert answered, and the monk sighed with what seemed to be sadness.

"I had hoped…never mind. You are welcome, child. I am Brother Edwin."

I tried to say my name, but my mouth stuck.

"She is Joan," Gilbert said. "Is shy."

The beautiful woman said something quickly and handed a cup to Gilbert. He passed it on to me. "Isabelle asks…thirsty?"

It was water. I drank it all down and blinked back, at a loss. Gilbert said a word—French for water. I nearly started crying, then. I had not asked to be brought here among strangers. But I did not want to go back. I didn't belong anywhere.

"Rest here," he said, and I folded right there, on the ground by the fire, blinking back tears. I pulled off my veil and coif, baring my head. My cut hair stuck out all over like a nest.

Felix glanced at me and said something merry. There were chuckles. Gilbert replied curtly, and they subsided. Listening to speech I did not understand made me so very tired. Even my mind became stiff and sore.

The monk, Edwin, said kindly, "You will have to learn French quickly so you will know when they're teasing you. They like to tease."

"What did he say?"

"That you look like a kitten thrown in a pond and pulled back out again."

"Rescued."

"Yes."

Isabelle began scooping stew from a pot into bowls, passing them around. The brown man, Ibrahim, took a piece and offered it to the crow on his shoulder, who snapped it up with a clacking bill. The talk went on around me and might as well have been birdsong. A noise in the air.

Brother Edwin sat nearby, but not too close. Like the nuns at St. Edith. "Have you taken vows, child?"

"I'm not a child. I'm fifteen."

"All right. Have you taken vows?"

I thought of what would happen if I said yes, or if I said no, and how my answer might change my fate. I could not guess, so I told the truth. "I'm only a novice. I don't think Mother Ursula would ever let me take vows. She says I am damned."

He frowned. "You know you are not. You have only the sins that any of us have."

"How do you know?"

"I believe God made us as we are for a reason."

Us. We. What could he do? What power had damned him? I shivered. "God made us, not the Devil?"

"No, not the Devil," he said firmly, crossing himself.

Gilbert studied me. He did not seem to believe I was made by the Devil, either. But he was Norman, what did he know?

"You, safe here," Gilbert said. So confident in this declaration. "Belong here."

"No one is safe! Your army is burning everything. Everyone will starve—"

Gilbert glanced at Edwin, who translated. Gilbert's smile went crooked.

"I send you back? So they burn you, for what you do?" He broke a stick and threw it in the fire. It seemed to make him angry, that Saxons burned those cursed by the Devil. The Normans did not.

I stared at the stew in my bowl. I should eat. It smelled good and I was hungry. "They already tried. They put me in the fire, but…"

I reached into the fire, and the flames parted around my hand. A warm touch, a caress. I picked up the stick Gilbert had thrown in. Drew it out and held it in my palm, watching buttery flames melt harmlessly across my skin. Dropped it back and brushed off the ash. "They put me in the fire and I did not burn." I had lived in a cell at St. Edith's ever since, praying for salvation.

They all stared at me, and yes, there was the fear. Even from them.

Just a bit, mixed up with awe and wonder. Except for Gilbert, whose expression softened to kindness.

The beautiful woman, Isabelle, asked something. Probably, "What did she say?" Edwin answered, and she put her hand over her mouth in horror. Such pity in her eyes. The others, they looked away. Ibrahim said something harsh that was clearly a curse.

"Child. You should eat, please." Edwin nodded at my bowl. I only managed a few bites. My eyes stung and everything felt awful. After dark, Isabelle, who seemed very much to want to do something, anything, put a blanket over my shoulders. I flinched at first. She persisted, and so I hugged the cloth close without looking up. Curled up on my side, I stared at the fire that was like a comforting touch, a warmth brushing my cheeks, and fell asleep.

I awoke inside one of the tents. I'd been moved and hadn't known it. The blanket was tucked up around me. I was alone. Calm, and… safe. A muted light painted the canvas, and the soft patter of raindrops fell against it. This promised to be a wet, chilled morning.

A cry of frustration sounded outside, along with a bit of laughter.

The rain stopped.

Scratching my bristly head, I pulled the blanket around me and looked out. The clouds parted as I watched, thick gray breaking up into a golden morning haze. Isabelle stood, arms stretched, a gentle wind flicking the loose strands of hair around her cheeks when no wind touched the nearby trees. She smiled up at the sky, and the clouds moved away with the gestures of her hand.

Isabelle commanded the weather. I was astonished.

Edwin saw me watching. "Wouldn't want to pack up a wet camp, would we?"

I supposed we would not.

A small cart pulled by a mule had been drawn up. Tents were folded, cooking pots settled. A bundle of spears was visible under a length of canvas. Ann and Ibrahim were saddling horses.

Gilbert wore a simple tunic this morning but did not have on his belt and sword. "Ah! Good morning, Joan. You are well?"

I scratched my hair again and shrugged. I did not know if I was well. Isabelle beamed and quickly brought over a dish of porridge. She fussed. She seemed so happy to have a thing smaller and more delicate than she was to care for. I gaped at her a bit.

"Where are we going?" I asked.

"We wait. For message," Gilbert said. "Then we know."

"You go looking for others like me?"

He paused, his hand resting on the side of the cart. "There are no others."

Brother Edwin had started dismantling the tent behind me, pulling down poles and folding fabric, all by himself with little effort, it seemed. He said, "Have you never met anyone else who had a power? A mirabile?"

Latin. A wonder. A miracle. I shook my head.

He took a knife out of his belt, a small and slender utensil for eating. Holding it in both hands, he bent the blade. Folded it on itself as if it were tallow, with no effort at all. He offered it to me, and I could not help but try to bend it back, but it was steel. Gilbert said something in grouchy French.

Edwin took the knife back and tried to straighten it, but a kink remained, a swerve in the metal. "He says I ruin a lot of knives. He's right."

Meanwhile, Ann knelt near the fire, took off a glove, put a bare hand on the ground—which split open. A small crevice appeared and traveled toward the remaining embers, swallowing them up. With a crunch and puff of dust, the crevice closed back up again, and the fire was out. All clear. She didn't even glance over to see what I thought. This was just what she did: opened the earth to put out fires.

I was beginning to be frightened again. More frightened. Each of them…could they all work wonders? It was too much.

"What do you do?" I asked Gilbert, who was watching me.

"Never mind," he said. His smile flickered like a flame and vanished.

"He's shy, too," Edwin said. "One thing our Gilbert does is collect people like us. Good of him, I think. Better than being burned." Spoken like a man who had avoided being burned, and not the way I had.

A shadow passed over us—a crow, circling. A second crow; the first was still perched on Ibrahim's shoulder. He reached up, and the bird tilted its wings and descended, swooping in on a rustle of feathers and coming to land on his gloved hand. He bent his head to the bird's, murmuring. Speaking to it. That was his miracle.

Gilbert asked him a question, and Ibrahim answered. Edwin's expression turned serious.

"The king has summoned us," Edwin said. "Well, Joan. You will soon meet William of Normandy himself."

William the Bastard. William the Conqueror, who had destroyed the England that had been, and whom Gilbert served.

What was to become of me?

I did not want to meet William of Normandy.

I also did not want to flee alone into a countryside being razed. Gilbert and his company fed me, at least.

I did not want to learn French, but I could not help it, the way one could not help but learn a bit of Latin listening to prayers. Especially when Brother Edwin was a good teacher, saying a thing in English and then again in French, all lined up, until the sounds became words and not noise. I tried, but I spoke badly. On my tongue, French words sounded like a goat bleated them, not watery and elegant the way Isabelle said them. But she lit up and praised me excessively whenever I repeated her, so it was hard to refuse.

Even though my shorn hair made me look like a wet kitten, I left the veil off. I was not a nun, I did not want to be a nun, but that left me a raggedy-haired, gaunt-faced girl, a thing to be pitied. But I was in the sun, at least. Out of the cell. If not free then at least not caged.

I did not want a lot of things. As for what I *did* want—how could I tell? I had never been allowed to want anything, and I did not know where to start.

William's army was camped a short march away from York, which was still held by Saxon earls and their Danish mercenaries. The others rode, but Edwin walked with the cart, leading the mule, and I walked beside him. We soon encountered the first of the Norman camps. Hundreds of soldiers went helmeted and armored. Wary, they had posted guards, and Gilbert called to them. His banner, a black arrow on gold, hung from a spear tied upright in the cart, marked him.

The soldiers, Gilbert's fellow Normans, did not smile at him. Did not banter. They watched him and the rest of us coolly and kept a good distance from us. Gilbert's own company became somber, traveling among the army. Ibrahim's crows flew off and stayed away. Gilbert seemed not to notice that William's soldiers did not like him. That they looked at him the way the nuns of St. Edith's looked at me.

Nervously, I wondered if I would know it when we came to the king. If I would recognize him from all the rest of the army. I shouldn't have worried. The king's own encampment was large and spread out. Many guards, many camp fires. A muddy road had been worn into the field leading up to it.

Edwin glanced at me and said to Gilbert, "Perhaps we should make camp and rest awhile before going to see the king." As if resting would make this any easier. We were all muddy to our knees and smelled of smoke and ash.

"No," Gilbert said. He would not delay; he would report to his lord immediately.

Gilbert's odd company left the horses and cart with stablemen outside the royal encampment and continued on. Ibrahim and Isabelle hung back; Ann stood apart, glowering. Felix bounced on his feet a little as if he would rather run away. Edwin stood near Gilbert, his chin up. They put me between them, like a prisoner.

Gilbert said, "His Grace the king…will want to see your fire. You show him? Please?"

"I could do nothing. He'll think you made a mistake and that I have no use at all."

He tilted his head, an agreement. "I cannot force. And, how you say…I might still send you back. To the abbey. You want this? To go back?"

"No. Oh, no." Even after just a few days in the air, I could not go back.

Brother Edwin said, "Joan, I believe there is…some joy in using this miracle God has granted us." Gilbert nodded as if to say, yes, that was what he wanted to say.

He added, choosing each word. "If it comes from God or the Devil…is in its use. Do you help or harm? How do you say…" A string of French. I recognized the word for candle, and light.

"Have you ever done anything but light candles, he asks," Edwin said patiently.

I had taken bits of straw from my bed and scattered them across my cell, then burned them up one by one to see how far I could throw my sparks, and how quickly. I could never do more without being discovered. Without burning down my own room, which wouldn't have hurt me but would have lost me my home. I did not know how much I could do with my spark.

Gilbert nodded, understanding. "I want torches," he said. "Bonfires. Beacons. To see…what is possible." His tone was mischievous.

"What is your…miracle? I still don't know."

He merely raised a brow and shrugged.

We waited in the yard before the grandest tent, and the king emerged, pushing back a flap.

He was fair-haired, full bearded, broad shouldered. Arms made strong from wielding weapons. He moved with a sureness that obstacles would fall before him. His glare instantly found Gilbert, and he strode forward, unafraid. Conqueror, unconcerned that he was also Bastard. His clothing was rough and sturdy, stained with sweat, his boots scuffed. Not at all dressed like a king, but he did not need to be.

I shrank back and hid behind Edwin, but the king saw me, studied me.

Gilbert bowed low and spoke deferentially. William put his hand on Gilbert's shoulder and raised him up. These two were close. I was fairly certain William said, "What have you found for me, Gilbert?"

Both Gilbert and Edwin stepped aside, revealing me. I met the king's gaze. He frowned skeptically. They spoke so quickly that I could not hope to understand.

Then Gilbert turned to me. "He asks to see fire."

William's army burned the villages and fields of the north with mundane fire, brands and torches they must light themselves. If William ordered me to take part in the burning, I would refuse. Surely Gilbert knew I must refuse.

"A small thing," Gilbert said. "Please." He said the please in French.

I looked around the camp and all the soldiers staring back at me. None of them knew what I would do. I could burn the tent. I could burn everything. Well, no, I could not. I could start a flame that would be easily put out. I could start a dozen and cause an uproar. And I would be killed in the next moment. I could not be burned, but an arrow through my heart…

Gilbert's expression was eager, his eyes alight. I could set fire to the tent and he might not even mind, because at least he could see what I could do. He nodded as if to say, go on, it's all right.

It was all right.

Gilbert wanted bonfires. I wanted them too, I decided. A candle would not impress the king. I could do more than impress him. I could make him afraid.

Some ways behind the royal tent was a line of picketed horses and a cart full of sheaves of hay. Sheaves of hay were much like a candle, only larger. A spark flared in my palm, and between one thought and the next, a thread of smoke rose up from the top of the pile. Tongues of flame danced along a dozen stalks of hay, which burst into flames until the whole cart was engulfed.

Horses squealed and spooked, men cried out. Some ran away, others ran forward with buckets of water, but the fire burned very hot, and the hay and cart were quickly consumed and fell to ash, with only a few embers and stray flames remaining.

William crossed himself. Gilbert laughed, a big, triumphant sound. That of a boy showing off some great feat.

He was not afraid of me. He…was not afraid.

After that, William took Gilbert aside, near his great tent, to speak with him. His somber knights and lords stood intently at his back. Ignoring the flurry of panic as his soldiers put out the fire and calmed the horses, William made urgent gestures and seemed to be pleading with Gilbert, who shook his head.

The rest of us clustered together, a wide space around us. Any who passed us did so with wary, sidelong glances and often crossed themselves. It was tiresome. Edwin attempted a comforting smile. I was not comforted. A crow flew in and perched on Ibrahim's shoulder. It squawked and muttered, anxiously kneading its claws on his tunic. As worried as the rest of us. He finally whispered to it and it flew off.

Their voices became shouts, in angry French. I recognized a few words. Gilbert saying now and then, *But…if you please…sir…* and the king replying, *You must. You will. I command it.* Gilbert gestured. The king stood implacably. Gilbert pleaded. The king touched his shoulder in a way that would have seemed like camaraderie, if Gilbert's head hadn't bowed the moment William turned away.

Felix cursed. Isabelle covered her face with her hands. Ibrahim and Ann merely frowned fatalistically.

"What are they saying?" I asked. "They speak too fast. What did they say?"

Edwin's lips worked, uncertain, but finally he explained, "The king wants us to take York."

The great walled northern city. The stronghold of the last Saxon lords of England.

I said, "He wants you to *help* take York…"

"No." Edwin smiled weakly. "This task he has given to Gilbert's company alone."

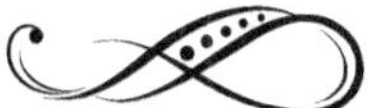

The awful and astonishing truth of it was that Gilbert's company might just be able to do it. Six people to break a siege and end any further opposition to William's rule.

Without a word, Sir Gilbert led his company back to the horses and cart and brought them to camp apart from William's army. I could not tell if he wished for them to be alone or if the rest of the army did not want them too close. Gilbert served the king, but he was not part of the king's army, not really.

"Can you do the honor?" Edwin asked me, putting together fuel and kindling for the cook fire.

"You will forget how to light fires yourself." I knelt and put my hand on the wood, breathed out, and felt flames rise up. Useful flames, contained, after a whole life of being told never to do such things.

Gilbert finally broke his silence when food was set to cooking. He spoke in French, but his tone was that of a man making plans. I understood some of it. Words like *walls* and *river* and *fall*. Gilbert said *rain* and *wind* while looking at Isabelle, and *watch* while looking at Ibrahim. *Break the gate* while looking at Edwin, who nodded somberly and did not seem to mind that he made war against his own people.

Because they weren't really his people. His own people were here, with Gilbert.

I could imagine it. How Ann could undermine the walls, how Edwin's strength could tear a gate off its hinges, how Felix could knock weapons out of the defenders' hands and be gone before they knew he'd been there, and how Isabelle could bring torrential rains and fog. Ibrahim's birds could watch from high above and carry messages to Gilbert about the city's weaknesses and where to strike next. Gilbert himself…I did not know what he could do. After they broke open the walls and routed the defenders, William's army would come to occupy the city. Simple, yes?

Gilbert did not look at me. He did not make me part of the plan. Even though…I could make so much destruction, if I wanted.

"What about me?" I asked finally.

"You stay with Ibrahim and Isabelle," Gilbert said. Ibrahim's sword would protect us while his birds scouted. Then he chuckled a little. "William, he thinks your fire makes us, how you say…invincible. But I will not ask you to fight against your people."

Gilbert was not asking me to burn the city. I could. I had not seen York, but I had heard of its walls of stone, its stone churches and abbeys. However, the houses within would be wood and thatch, and I could send fire to them, too much fire for the people to put out, and Isabelle could send wind to fan the flames, and Ann build up earthworks and dig moats so that no one could escape—

It was too easy to think about. I did not want to burn the city. Gilbert did not ask, so that I would not have to say no. I hugged my legs to my chest and stayed quiet.

After some back and forth the plan was settled. We would set out in the morning, in secret. Gilbert urged his company to sleep. He touched my shoulder and smiled kindly before going off to his tent.

If I was going to run away, this would have been the night to do it. I could even make my way to York and warn the defenders. . . And then what? They could not defend against what was coming. And if they learned what I was, they would not be kind.

"You are uncertain," Edwin said to me. In English. Strange, to suddenly understand every word in a sentence after feeling slow and stupid.

"I don't know what to do," I said.

"Gilbert thinks it isn't fair to ask you to be part of this. You are so young, and your talents still untried."

"I need to practice first, he thinks."

"You need to learn your own mind, first."

He and Gilbert seemed so different on the one hand, a monk and a warrior, age and youth. But they also, strangely, seemed to journey the same path.

"How did you learn yours?" I asked.

"I am called by God. My abbey…turned me out. Gilbert was there waiting. Saxon or Norman, I believe God's message to me was clear. This is a good man and I do not regret following him."

"Even if it means making war against Saxons?"

He chuckled a little. "I am from the south. Some would say the men of the north are barely my countrymen, their Danish blood is so thick and their manners so rude. But…I think we can take the city more quickly and more cleanly than William's army, and I believe that would please God."

"But how do you know?"

"Goodness, child. I don't. I can't. I pray a lot. But you know you are safer here, with us, than anywhere else in England right now, yes?"

I believed that, yes.

Gilbert led us cross-county on a route Felix and Ibrahim scouted to avoid burning fields and fleeing refugees. We left the camp and horses behind, traveling light. I got to see what it meant to live as a warrior in the world.

We crossed one of the rivers and found a small rise from which to view the city. The famous walls were a gray haze in the distance, so that the city seemed like a lurking creature. Ibrahim's birds flew over and returned to tell him what they saw.

Gilbert altered the plan. Edwin would go first, approach the gate, tell them what was about to befall them, and ask for surrender.

"They'll kill him! Even if he is a monk!" I said, in English. But I had understood enough of the French to be able to respond. Gilbert raised a brow at me, to acknowledge.

"Not with sword or arrow they won't," Edwin said, wearing a wry half smile. "What gives me my strength makes me so that weapons cannot harm me. I'll be fine." He could have been the greatest warrior in all the world. But he was a monk.

So he went to the city, and no one was worried at all.

He returned at dusk. The defenders had laughed, and he did not seem surprised.

"Tomorrow," Gilbert said, and urged us all to get some sleep.

I could not sleep. We did not have a fire, to keep Saxon scouts from finding us. Our camp was in a small glen, but if I walked just a few paces up the hill, I could see the nighttime city, alight with the glow of torches. Soldiers on the wall were just visible, walking back and forth, blocking the light when they did. The orange light of flames, misted with smoke.

Too far to send the spark under my skin, but I imagined I could still feel the fires calling to me.

Ann was pretending to sleep. Isabelle was not; I could see her eyes gleaming in starlight as she lay, staring up. Ibrahim and Felix set a watch, though Gilbert had said it was not needed. Owls would tell Ibrahim if danger came close. Edwin had propped himself up against a tree and seemed to sleep, but I was sure he also was pretending. I sat hugging my knees, too afraid of what would happen if I closed my eyes.

Gilbert came and sat near me. He seemed so calm. He had probably been in battles before. "You…not tired?"

I was very tired. The world was tiring, and French was a muddle in my head, and I would never forget the smell of burning villages as long as I lived.

"Why do…this?" I asked.

"Do what?" he said wearily, and I thought, aha, he does feel the weight of this.

I could not think of how to say it in French, so I mixed up the words. But he understood me. "Fight William's battles for him."

"I swear to serve. Fealty," he said, lip curled, as if the English word for it felt strange.

"But why?"

"To be a knight…is to serve."

"And win lands and favor," Edwin put in archly from his spot by his tree. So no, he did not sleep.

"Then you do it for the reward?"

Gilbert scowled. "You ask many questions."

I sagged. "Because I don't understand anything. Brother Edwin, why do you follow Gilbert and wage war against your own people?"

"We talked about this already. You should sleep." He snugged more firmly against the tree and still did not sleep.

"Why does Isabelle follow you?"

She blinked bright brown eyes at Gilbert. "What does she say?"

That was French. I understood it. I had asked that exact question myself so often. The language was seeping into me.

"She asks why you follow me," Gilbert said, and I understood that too.

"Gilbert is a good man," she said, and continued with words I did not know.

Gilbert explained, "She say…she had nothing, before. Was lost. And…this is her family now."

"And the others? Would they all say the same?"

"Do not know," he said, picking at grass. "I do not know why. Why me, why…this. I do not know. But I *do* know—we are safer together than apart. We stay together, we are safe."

How could he say he felt safe, how any of them could be safe, when he would lead them against the walled city in the morning?

Gilbert looked at me and spoke English. "You not trust me."

"No. I don't know. I don't know what I should think."

He chuckled. "Then…know what you want? If you could choose."

I thought a moment. I didn't know what was possible to want. I was such a child. "To grow out my hair," I said finally, scratching my head, the nest that was still too short to brush out but getting too long to leave alone.

"Done. No one will make you cut your hair."

He could declare it, just like that. "To see the ocean. I have never seen the ocean."

"When this over? We see ocean."

I considered. "And I would like a great hall with a hundred servants."

He laughed. "I also like that." And his smile fell. "Sleep, Joan. Sleep now." He pulled a blanket over his shoulders and moved a little ways off. He closed his eyes but didn't sleep any more than the rest of us.

In the morning, Edwin set aside his monastic robes and wore a warrior's garb like the others. He, Ann, Felix, and Gilbert gathered to approach the city. Even knowing what they were, I still did not believe they could do anything against the walls and all the soldiers there.

They left Ibrahim, Isabelle, and me behind.

Gilbert gave instructions. I understood only a few words—signal, crows, and storm—but I did not have to ask what would happen. Ibrahim clasped his hand and nodded. A dozen crows perched in trees around us, cawing and muttering. He signaled to them, and they took to the air in a flurry of black wings. One stayed behind, taking up a post on his shoulder.

"Be safe, sir," Isabelle said, and stood on her toes to kiss Gilbert's cheek. Then she put her arm over my shoulder. "We watch. It is well." She said more, but that was all I understood.

We stayed sheltered by a stand of alders. I had nothing to do but watch.

For the next few hours, we watched the city, which remained unchanging to my eyes. Whatever was happening, I could not see it. I had never seen a battle and could not guess what one looked like. The plain outside the city was hazy with a winter chill.

Ibrahim shaded his eyes suddenly. "There," he said.

The haze shifted. A puff of dust rose, as when we shook out rugs and blankets in the abbey yard. Then, part of the wall that ran along the river seemed to fold. A crack broke the stone, and the whole thing fell inward, as if pushed by giant hands. The low rumbling sound of breaking stone reached us a moment later. The falling structure must have crushed a dozen men.

"Ann," Ibrahim said with a smile, and it took me a moment to recognize he'd said the name and not some other word. The next thing that happened: a crow cried out as it flapped overhead. "Now, Isabelle."

She stepped forward and raised her arms.

The wind came up so fiercely it brought a mass of dust that scoured the top of the remaining length of wall. I almost believed I could hear shouting, screams of men falling. It was my imagination, though, because the storm roared; I could hear nothing else. Isabelle stood serenely. The ends of her hair tossed a little; her skirt rippled. Her hand was upraised as if she greeted approaching travelers. She donned a small satisfied smile. There is some pleasure in being useful. Using what we could do instead of hiding away.

She was so kind and cheerful she could not be a tool of the Devil, but then this was exactly the sort of deception the Devil would offer, wasn't it? So fair, so powerful.

What more Gilbert's company did, we could not see from here. Ibrahim watched for crows that would return to tell him how things progressed. But the crows didn't speak first. A chorus of chattering erupted, a dozen or more songbirds in the trees around us.

"Down!" Ibrahim shouted, grabbing my arm and pulling me to the ground. Isabelle dropped, and arrows flew over us, thudding into tree trunks. Ibrahim reached for her. She took his hand, and we lay still a moment, hiding, holding our breaths for what came next. The birds still screamed warnings; this wasn't over.

Ibrahim tilted his head, looked, and cursed. I saw it, then. The arrows had traveled in the wrong direction; they did not come from the city but from the south. From the direction of the Norman camp. Soldiers—wearing domed helmets, dressed in Norman tabards—appeared soon after, a pair with swords and a pair with bows, trotting toward the copse.

"But why?" I exclaimed.

Ibrahim stood and drew his sword. "You two, run. Find Gilbert. Run!"

Isabelle got to her feet, clenching her fists at her side. "No, I won't—"

Ibrahim tried to argue. "Isabelle!"

She joined her hands together and slammed them down as if swinging an ax.

Such wind. A terrible, ear-shattering, scouring wind rose up from nowhere and blasted through the trees. Ibrahim put his arm up to protect his face and sheltered behind her. The soldiers—they tried to keep their feet. They tried to press forward toward their quarry. The bow was ripped out of an archer's hand. Another stumbled and tried to crawl forward on hands and knees.

Ibrahim hissed at me, "Joan, you run. Find Gilbert." His crows could not fly in this storm.

More soldiers came up behind the first. They circled 'round. I did not know if Isabelle would be able to stop them all. Ibrahim would defend her with his sword, as much as he could—

"Run!" he said.

I ran, hoping the archers would not see me and take aim, my breath catching in my throat with every step. The wind fell away the moment I left the trees. Isabelle aimed her power like a spear.

Another group of Norman soldiers advanced up the river, swords drawn. They had waited until the city fell, until Gilbert's company had done their work…and now, the army had no more use for such dangerous tools. Gilbert had said I would be safe…

Where was Gilbert? How could I find him? I glanced overhead, looking for crows, and saw none. Not until I came upon a dead one in the field, with an arrow through it. They were killing Ibrahim's crows.

What could I burn? I had nothing to burn.

A burst of wind passed by. This one was brief, stopping abruptly as Felix skidded in a cloud of dust. "Joan!"

I cried. The tears just came out. "I must find Gilbert, where is Gilbert—" My jumble of English and French was incomprehensible, even to me, and Felix just stared. I asked, "Gilbert?"

"Soldiers hunt us," he said, or I thought he said. "Gilbert is there, west. He tells me to warn—"

"Ibrahim and Isabelle!" I pointed back the way I had come. "They fight, they need help!"

He looked up the hill to our shelter, consternation twisting his features. The trees no longer bent in a fierce wind, and I did not know what that meant. What had happened to Isabelle?

Felix shuffled his feet, seeming torn between running back to Gilbert or helping Ibrahim and Isabelle. "Go help them," I said.

"But you…" He spoke quickly, of course he did, though I only understood a few words. *How will you be safe?*

He barely knew me. None of them did. Why should they look after me?

I could not explain further than I already had. The spark was building under my skin. "Them, help them!" I said and pushed him.

He vanished in wind and dust. I kept on toward the city.

Up ahead, near the break in the walls, I saw the signs of what must have been battle. The chaos I had looked for earlier. Dust and shouting, soldiers falling. All of it centered on one figure. I approached as if invisible, my gray robe part of the dust around me. As I watched, details resolved.

And I swear on my knees before the Blessed Virgin that Sir Gilbert was holding off an army all by himself, with no weapon.

He reached out his arm as if to stay *stop*—and they stopped.

Soldiers fell back as if they had crashed headlong into a wall and then were dragged through the dirt away from him. He did not need a sword when his attackers could not get within thirty paces of him. He kept them away by will alone. This was his power: to move a thing without touching it. He kept a space around him, knocking down his assailants, over and over. He could have crushed them all, snapped their necks with a thought. But he was trying not to kill his fellow Normans. My God, why try to keep them alive when they meant to murder him?

At first they came at him in a melee, charging from all sides as if each raced to be the one to reach him first, to strike the killing blow, though none of them could. Then some commander shouted, and they organized. In clusters of three or four men, they circled 'round him. Gilbert turned this way and that, trying to keep them all in view, the group in front of him, the one to the side, the one behind. This one attacked from the rear, and Gilbert spun, slashed his hand in a shoving gesture, and the men fell back as before. But as he turned around, the second group struck, and as he flung them back the third group moved, and so he did not have time between one attack and the next to gather his defense.

He was growing weary. The power seemed like it came from air, as if made of spirit, but it took strength and effort to use, and he could not do this forever.

The plain outside the walls was littered with the remains of the old siege and past battles. Broken wagons, shattered barrels, half-burned timbers. The planks of the nearby wooden gate. The clothing of the men who attacked. Their bodies.

They did not see me approach because they were not looking for me. Why should they notice a scrawny girl with a nest for hair, in a place like this? The spark rose up from my bones, along my skin. It crackled across my palms, between my fingers. I sent it out.

A broken wagon exploded into a bonfire. The scraps of wood around it caught next, then the dried grasses around that. A path of fire grew up around me. So much fire. I shaped a wall of it between

Gilbert and his attackers. Between them and me. For a moment, the fire wavered, reaching toward me, hesitating as if it resisted me. Who could ever tell fire what to do?

Me. The flames cowered from me, and I commanded Hell to give way.

I pushed it, as Gilbert had pushed back his attackers. I swept my arms out, as Isabelle did when she steered the winds, and sent it on two different paths, breaking like a river around a stone. Flames made a ring around Gilbert, then spread away from him, sparks jumping to spear shafts, to tunics, to beards. Men screamed and fled.

In the middle of it all Gilbert crouched, arms over his head. Sheltering, waiting for death to take him.

I ran to him through the wall of flame. He saw me, and understanding shone in his eyes. I thought he might command me to stop, to quell the flames, but he did not.

The fire began to die out on its own, when there was nothing left to burn. The roaring faded to a crackle, the oven to a mere throat-closing heat. But the noise of devouring flames and the screams of its victims seemed to linger for a long time, as if the sounds stuck in the air like a summer haze and could not settle.

The stench was awful. I had never smelled air like this, after fire had burned so much.

Gilbert unbowed himself and straightened. Across the length of just a few paces, we looked at each other. I could not move. I rubbed soot-scratched eyes and realized I'd been crying. Tears, stung by the smoke.

He crossed the space, put his arm around my shoulders and kissed the top of my head. The touch…calmed me. We were alive.

"You should not be here," he said. "You should be safe, elsewhere."

"But they attacked. Ibrahim told me to run—"

He held my shoulders and looked at me. "Ibrahim? Isabelle?"

"I don't know," I said, crying.

He swore roughly, using words I had not yet learned. He surveyed the field of battle, all the scorched bodies and the last of the soldiers still fleeing. I expected him to chide me for killing them, but he did not. His eyes had gone hooded, dark. As if he were looking upon another battlefield in the past.

I made a guess. "There was a moment when your power saved William, wasn't there? And so he owes you everything. What did you do for him?"

Gilbert wiped a hand down his exhausted face, smearing soot across his skin. "Did you hear…how King Harold died? *Exactly* how?"

Stories came to us at the abbey three years ago about the arrival of the invaders, Harold's flight to stand against them, and the battle. "There was an arrow…"

He spoke in English, perhaps wanting to make sure I understood.

"I made the arrow fly. Guided it." He made a gesture in the air, following a wobbly flight. "Where it might…inspire awe and terror. I send the arrow…straight into Harold's eye. So that people tell stories of it. So that they fear William forever." He shook his head, said a phrase in French. Saw me uncomprehending and tried again. "William knights me…there on the field at Hastings. I was seventeen. So yes, he owes me…much. Too much, some think. They think to remove me. Forget the debt. The north beaten, they think. . .no longer need me. Us. *Merde.*"

I could guess what that word meant.

"You think…King William ordered his men to kill you here?"

"Him. His vassals. Anyone who thinks…William gives too much favor to such as us. I will learn why."

Scorched Norman helmets lay scattered around us. Huddled shapes that were burned bodies if I looked too closely, so I looked away. This was what Mother Ursula and the others had always been afraid of, that I could burn them all if I chose. I looked at my hands. They tingled with the spark that still lingered there, and the soot and ash smelled like power.

And still, Gilbert did not fear me.

Gilbert sighed. "Come, we go find others." He patted my shoulder and scanned the sky, looking for crows. "There." He pointed to a black speck wheeling against the high clouds and waved. This meant Ibrahim must still be alive, and that made me glad. The speck turned sharply and flew off toward the river.

We met Ann and Edwin on the way. He was carrying her, in all her armor, as if she were light as a child. She had an arrow stuck in her right shoulder, and a river of blood matted her tunic.

"Ann!" Gilbert cried in anguish and rushed to them.

"I'm fine," she muttered, but her breaths came shallow and she was limp in Edwin's grasp.

"She will be if I can get water and bandages to take this out," Edwin said.

"You should not move her!"

"Soldiers were coming," Edwin said, his expression like stone. "I thought it best we move."

"Yes. Up the river to the trees, come." Gilbert patted his shoulder, murmured words I couldn't make out, and Ann smiled.

Edwin blinked at me as if startled. "Joan, child, what are you doing here? You were supposed to stay safe with—"

"We were attacked," I said. "They found us in the trees."

"Oh dear God." His face drew long and he suddenly looked old. "Ibrahim, Isabelle—"

"Talk later, come," Gilbert said. He'd drawn his sword. We traveled up river, slower than Gilbert liked because of Ann.

There came a whoosh of air, a now familiar puff of dust, and Felix suddenly stood nearby. "I've found you! Thank God!" His eyes were wide, shining.

"Felix! The others—"

"They are alive. They'll be along soon. Ann, oh God—"

"I'm *fine*," she muttered, scowling. Felix looked as if he might cry.

We reached the first stand of trees along the river and could go no farther. Edwin set Ann down; she groaned. Felix knelt beside her and helped Edwin cut away her tunic. I looked away.

Felix said, "That's a Norman arrow in her. Gilbert, what happened?"

Gilbert was keeping watch across the plain. There were soldiers moving toward the city; none were coming here. He spoke quickly, tiredly. I caught a bit: *the king,* and *we are too dangerous.*

None of them seemed surprised by what he said. They might have expected this for a long time. Since Hastings, even. His enemies had waited until the city was taken, the northern rebellion crushed, the last hard job done, before breaking William's best tool.

Edwin explained to me in English, so I understood better: "Gilbert's enemies could make it look like we died in battle. The king might question it, or might not."

"What if it's the king who ordered it?" I said.

Gilbert looked sharply at me. "I not believe it. I go speak with him." Standing, he brushed the dust off.

Edwin said. "You cannot. You dare not."

He spoke French slowly, because he was tired, not for my benefit. "Take care of Ann. Have Ibrahim send a crow to me when he finds you. If I am not back by nightfall, go to Scotland. Seek shelter there."

"Gilbert—"

He sighed. "I am sorry. I am…so sorry."

"I'm going with you." Felix stood, rolling back his shoulders, straightening his spine. Pretending he was not exhausted.

"No, I do this alone—"

"No, you don't."

"Gilbert. He goes with you," Edwin said.

Gilbert nodded.

I wanted to go, too. I did not want to leave Gilbert's side. But then Edwin asked me to make a small fire for heating water. For cleaning wounds. We made bandages from the hems of our tunics.

Ibrahim and Isabelle found us. Her dress was torn, and he had a bloody bandage around his arm in the same color fabric. The crow on his shoulders had ruffled feathers and a crooked wing, as if something had broken it. It snuggled close to his neck.

She saw me and ran. "Joan! Thank God!"

Somehow I knew I should stand and let her wrap me in a fierce, enveloping hug. I even let myself sink into her arms, and the muscles of my back unclenched, just a little. And I cried.

"Gilbert?" Ibrahim asked. Edwin explained, and Isabelle fussed over Ann.

As the sun sank west, we worried.

"How does he think we would get to Scotland?" I asked Edwin. I had stopped being able to speak French. I did not care.

"I do not know," he said. Ann and Isabelle slept. Ibrahim kept watch. Crows flew to him, and away, over and over, and he did not seem to like what they told him.

"Ibrahim?" Edwin asked.

"He is with the king. Still."

"We should have just left for Scotland. All of us," Edwin muttered.

We waited. A hawk came and perched in the tree overhead; it held a rabbit in its talons, which it let loose into Ibrahim's hands. He thanked it.

Far more useful than fire, to have birds bring you food. Edwin set to dressing and cooking it.

"Edwin. I don't want to go to Scotland," I said.

"It isn't nightfall yet."

But the sun was almost set.

Far overhead, a crow cried out—and Ibrahim looked up, listened a moment, and smiled.

Felix raced into our camp a moment later. He slid to a halt, breathless, and spoke too quickly for me to make out words. A blur of speech. He sounded annoyed. Ibrahim laughed.

Edwin raised a brow. "Felix always hopes to beat Ibrahim's crows with news. So far the crows are winning."

"What do they say?" I asked. The news can't have been bad, if Felix left Gilbert alone.

Felix grinned. "Gilbert comes. He will tell you himself."

Ann and Isabelle woke. Ann sat up and seemed in less pain, now that the arrow was removed. She scowled a lot, which Edwin took as a good sign. Ibrahim made Felix eat; he devoured a haunch of rabbit by himself.

We waited for Gilbert, who finally appeared as we were building up the fire to stand against the dark. We did not have to decide how to flee to Scotland.

Edwin stood to greet him. Took him by the shoulder, as he had done when Gilbert first brought me to them. But this time he almost seemed to be holding Gilbert up. Edwin guided him to the fire, and Gilbert looked around at each one of us, as if reassuring himself that we had survived.

"What happened?" Isabelle finally asked.

He asked for water; she handed him a flask and the last of the roast rabbit. He ate and drank in silence for a moment. Ann was even propped on her good elbow, watching. This small family. I felt safe here, and that was a wonder.

"William," he said finally. "William…" I did not have enough French to understand exactly what he said, and he spoke so low. The others did not seem entirely pleased.

What I thought he said was that he had given King William an ultimatum: either reward Gilbert as he ought, for so much service. Or dispose of him openly, without subterfuge, if he feared Gilbert's power. Gilbert had said that—or close to it—directly to the Conqueror. It was wondrous.

"And?" Edwin breathed.

Gilbert took a long drink and smiled. "I have been granted land in Wessex. With a great hall of our own." He looked at me and winked.

"No hundred servants, not yet. But we will be safe. For a time."

And so we came to live in Wessex. My hair grew long, and Isabelle taught me to braid it up. Gilbert still went out to fight for William. Often I went with him. With practice, I learned to light a candle from a hundred paces and destroy a timbered hall in a single burst of flame. William's enemies often laid down their arms, just knowing Gilbert and his company were present. My spark longed to be used, but I tamed it well enough.

Eventually, I learned French well enough to make myself a nuisance, but I mostly spoke English when I was angry, or sad, or willful. My new family gave me the freedom to be willful.

Brother Edwin is writing this down. He says that the chroniclers of the time are concerned with kings and battles, and they will say that Harold died with an arrow in his eye but not who made that happen. They will not write the name of a small Saxon girl with a spark under her skin, but that they should, and so he'll do it. I do not know that it matters. What matters to me is no longer being afraid that I am cursed. If being cursed means living this life, and not being locked up in the lonely cell at St. Edith's, then I will be cursed, and I will not mind it.

That is what Sir Gilbert gave to me, and I love him for it.

TO THE BEAUTIFUL SHINING TWILIGHT

Abby opened the till and found crumbled bits of dry leaves in the stack of five-dollar bills. Anyone else might have cleaned it out and not thought of it again, not even when they balanced receipts at the end of the day, discovered they were five or ten dollars short, and written it off as an honest mistake. But this was not a mistake and it was not honest, and so she was angry.

She had finished with all this thirty years before. That world had left her; she had coped with the loss. And now…now…

Judging by their position in the stack, the leaves disguised as money would have been used in the last hour or so. The drink that had been swindled with them might still be warm. She fished around in the pocket of her patchwork skirt and drew out a stone, gray and river-washed, with a hole in it that might have been drilled except it was as smoothed by elements as the rest of it. Her luck charm, sometimes good and sometimes bad, but if she kept it close, it couldn't sneak up on her. She held the hole to her eye.

Most of her patrons were just that, a couple of students plugged into tablets and earbuds, a couple of people passing through, reading books, sipping lattes. When Abby started her café, her hipster coffee shop, she hadn't really thought about what kind of image she was presenting to the world, only about the kind of space where she wanted to spend her days. Art covered the walls, potted plants overflowed their hangers and stands, and none of the tables and chairs matched; she'd picked them all up at yard sales. Besides coffee and pastries, she sold shelves of books rescued from library sales, and bins of used records and CDs. All of it thick with the smell of coffee and sandalwood. The neighborhood had gentrified around her, upscale restaurants, boutiques, and galleries filling in once-boarded-up storefronts on a street that had risen and fallen and risen again several times over. The place brought the tone of the street down these days. Still, not that anyone would admit it, but Bean and Back Again was the only reason the neighborhood had any bohemian cred left at all. For her, it was a retreat, an oasis, a small space that stayed just the way she liked it.

At the table directly across from the counter sat a white-haired old woman in a rose-colored skirt suit, sipping tea and reading a small cloth-bound hardcover. Only now, when Abby gazed through the hole in the stone, there was no old woman. In her place sat an impossibly handsome pale man, vaguely young but somehow weathered, with gray eyes, and lips turned up in a smile, looking back at her.

Her heart ached.

And now he was at the counter, the old-woman disguise shed, melted away like fog. He stood with hands behind his back, feet turned out like a courtier from another age, which he was, rather. He should have been wearing silk brocade, not the T-shirt, jeans, and suit jacket he had on now. But he did know how to blend in when he wanted to.

"Hello, Abby."

"Airen…what are you doing here?" She didn't mean to sound exasperated. Better than sounding angry, she supposed. Or hurt. Better for him to think she didn't care.

"I have come to summon you," said the Knight of Faerie.

Not again, she thought. He'd said this to her once before, and she'd been so excited. Thrilled and flattered, that here was the wardrobe, here was the Goblin King, just for her. Now, she didn't have time for it. She was trying to run a coffee shop, and he was throwing her till out of balance.

He must have noticed the hesitation, or maybe even annoyance, in her frown. "I thought you'd be happier to see me."

"You owe me five dollars. Or whatever." She scattered the bits of leaves on the counter.

His brow furrowed. "That's . . . unromantic."

"Airen. Why are you here?" Someone like him preferred chasing sweet and clueless young things. Like she'd been, back in the day. That was what she had convinced herself as the years passed and he didn't come back. You could only be that innocent once. And he never said he would come back; she'd merely hoped. So she didn't whine at him, why didn't you come back? To be fair, he *had* come back, eventually: here he was. To wish that it hadn't taken thirty years was a bit churlish, wasn't it?

Just then, Ian got up from his office in the corner—namely the table where he spent almost every day working, with his laptop and headphones, notepaper, and constantly refilled pot of tea. He was a musician, like Abby and the rest, and these days freelanced as a composer, making electronic themes and background tunes for various apps. Exactly the quiet, obsessive thing he liked. He was a mousy man in jeans and Keds and oversized flannel, same as he wore when they were in their twenties.

He leaned on the counter right next to Airen like he didn't see him. Maybe he didn't. The disguise was gone but the glamour remained.

"Abs," he said straight to her. "Are you okay? You look upset."

Airen narrowed his gaze at the composer. "Is that… That's not Ian, is it?"

"It is," Abby told him. "It's been a long time." Ian was thirty pounds heavier, half-bald, with a limp in his bad knee. She…she was mostly just tired.

"Why doesn't he see me?"

"Who are you talking to?" Ian said softly, nervously.

Abby handed the stone to Ian, who knew exactly what it was and glared like she'd handed him a scorpion. Lips pursed, he took it, looked through it, finally saw Airen, and might have groaned a little in annoyance.

"Oh. It's you."

"Hello, Ian," Airen said, amiably as he'd greeted her. Like he'd only been away for a month or two and nothing to get riled about.

"What are you doing here?" Ian asked, just as Abby had, and Airen, for all his inborn elegance, sighed a frustrated breath.

"I need a favor from Abby."

"She doesn't owe you anything."

This was sweet, Ian trying to defend her. They went for days without speaking to each other, sometimes. She'd hand him his first pot of tea; he'd nod and retreat to his table, always reserved for him. He didn't like talking to people, usually. But he'd stand here and face down Airen if he had to.

"It's really good to see you. Both of you. And where is Martine? Where's Kid?" Martine was their fiddler and Kid their drummer back in the day, when they'd been a band.

"Martine's around," Abby said, and probably wouldn't believe it when she learned Airen had been here. She lived in one of the apartments upstairs from the coffee shop and gave lessons to kids. Led the céilí in the shop on Sunday afternoons. Abby was surprised Airen hadn't known. Hadn't snuck in wearing some other guise to listen. What had he been *doing* all this time?

"Kid…" Ian's gaze went vacant, as it so often did when confronted with pain.

"He died about ten years ago. Hit by a car," Abby finished. She could say it without flinching these days. A terrible, mundane end for a vibrant man who should have been drumming armies into battle.

To his credit, Airen's features tightened, maybe with grief beyond the surprise. "I'm sorry. I didn't know." They were mortal, yes. His kind forgot, sometimes. They would all die, and Airen would lose track of time, leave, and return, and be baffled that they were not here to meet him.

"How could you?" Ian said. "You *left*."

"But *you're* still here," Airen said. Maybe trying to convince himself. "And you all still play—"

Abby shook her head, and Airen looked a bit lost.

"Abby," Ian said. "I don't know what this means."

"Neither do I," Abby answered. "It's okay. I'll figure it out, it'll be fine."

"Okay. Call if you need me."

"Of course."

Ian went away, glancing worriedly at her until he put his headphones back on and hunched over his table.

"He's changed," Airen said sadly, as if the change pained him.

"Thirty years, Airen," Abby said. How dare he feel pain over this?

"I didn't realize I had been away so long."

You should have, Abby thought. *You should have been paying attention.* "What favor?"

"Hm?"

"You said you needed a favor."

"Then you'll do it?"

"You haven't told me what it is."

"I have a quest."

She shook her head sharply. "I don't want a quest."

"It's an adventure—"

"I don't need an adventure!"

He tsked. "What's happened to you? Have you lost all your sense of wonder?"

"You left me." Not us, not everything. *Me.* That was why she was angry.

His gaze never wavered. "I've come back, haven't I?"

She grumbled.

"I need your help," he said.

He had said that once before, to her. He needed her help, he needed a band, a singer, and music, to secure the crumbling boundaries of his world. She had made the motions of disbelief at first, they all had—things like this just didn't happen. She had wanted so very badly for it to be true that she assumed it must not be, it was a trick, her fierce hopes were finally driving her mad, out of reality entirely. But the four of them, led by Airen, had gone into it together, fought past redcaps and ogres, somehow crossed the besieged boundary of shadows to the realm of the Queen herself to use their mortal magic in her defense. The border needed both sides, here and there, the mortal and the not, to rebuild itself, and so Abby and the others had played.

She would never sing that well again. He couldn't ask for that, not again. Stark despair must have shown in her expression. *I'm too old for this, I can't help you.*

"Please, Abby."

The Fae rarely asked. They never begged. They cajoled and tricked and obfuscated. But ask?

"What can I do?" She had meant it as a denial—what could she possibly do? He took it as acquiescence.

"It's simple. It's not like it was then. This is…I just need a few things, and I need them collected by mortal hands."

"What do I get in return?"

Last time, the Queen had given them a bag of gold. Real gold, not Faerie mischief. Abby used it to buy the building before the neighborhood gentrified. They would always have a home; they would never have to worry. If the place felt a little magical besides, well, that was what came of fairy gold. Reviews had called the café "a piece of a different world," which made her smirk. The business slipped into the red more often than not, but the rent on the couple of extra apartments upstairs made up for it. No one could ever call her impractical.

"My gratitude?"

And wasn't that open-ended?

In the studio space above the coffee shop, an eight-year-old boy was playing a passable "Turkey in the Straw" on a kid-sized violin. Martine, drawing on her vast wells of patience, didn't even flinch at the scratches. Abby lingered by the doorway, caught Martine's eye, and signaled that she could wait. The mother sitting on the bench in the hall outside glanced up from her knitting, smiled briefly, and went back to her Zen space.

Martine let the kid get to the end of the song, then praised him enthusiastically—"That was *so good*, kiddo! Great job getting all the way through this time!"—before adjusting his fingering and giving him suggestions on his bow technique. The kid played again, at least one verse, and his eyes lit up when he did, in fact, sound better. Only a scratch or two this time.

Abby could never do this, making her all the more grateful that people like Martine existed in the world.

The lesson ended, the kid packed up the violin and the mom packed up her knitting, and they were out the door.

"What's up?" Martine asked. She was tall, full of energy, brown skin and close-cropped hair, looking elegant in brightly patterned leggings and a flowing, embroidered tunic. Abby always felt a bit frumpy around her best friend, but Martine insisted they complemented each other perfectly. Two forces of nature.

"We had a visitor." She told him about Airen's sly approach and request.

Martine stared, caught up for a moment in the betwixt and between of memory as Ian had been. Then she shook her head. "Wow. Okay. I mean, he knows we're not a band anymore. We can't do what we did. Especially now." With Kid gone, yeah.

"He just wanted to talk to me. Ian and I didn't even see him at first, under his glamour."

"I could have walked right past him, then. So what's he hiding?"

That was a good question, wasn't it? "I don't know. He seemed… maybe not desperate. But he said please."

"Last time, he acted like he was doing us a favor, asking us to risk our lives for him. Like we should have been grateful for the chance."

And weren't they? For that little touch of magic? Even if it meant that afterward they were only ever comfortable holed up in their refurbished building that they lived and worked in and didn't need to leave, not if they didn't want to.

"That was different. This…sounds personal." If the Queen herself had needed a favor, Abby probably wouldn't be able to refuse, because no one could refuse her.

"So what are you going to do?"

"Try to help. And carry some iron in my pocket."

Airen listed the three items he needed—of course it was three—in the form of a riddle—of course it was a riddle. If he could just come out and tell her, he'd have done the job himself.

When her afternoon shift came on duty at the shop, she headed out. On a quest. Not much of one—this felt more like going for groceries or holiday presents. Or that one thing at the hardware store you needed to fix that one faucet, which you ended up going back and forth three times to find…

No, this was magical. This was riddles, and the riddles themselves did not appear to hold the clue of why Airen needed these specific things.

> A blossom that will not ripen.
> A corpse that will not rot.
> A song that will not end.

Simple enough, as riddles went, which made her suspicious.

Solving riddles and Fae quests shouldn't feel like grocery shopping. There was more to this; she ought to know what it was. He could have gone to any mortal, but he asked *her*.

And that same thrill was there; she *couldn't* trust this because she wanted so badly for it to be true. For the doorway to open, for the knight to hold out his hand to her. They'd had moments together, before the music summoned them, before they had to rise up and build a power that the mortals had never seen or felt or sensed, before they'd had to give themselves to the task and not to each other. Soft glades with leaves that chimed, foxgloves and roses that glowed, a sky that never darkened past twilight, so that all was blue and shadowed. Every moment, she felt like she might faint because the air itself made her drunk, but Airen was always right there to hold her.

She would never sing like that again, she would never make love like that again, and it was all right, because to do so even once was treasure. She had accepted the gold and tried to make something good with it, taken care of her friends, even as they moved through the weird haze of their lives after.

And now, here he was. The riddle wasn't the task he'd given her. It was *him*.

He returned in a week and a day, which was good. A year and a day would have tried her patience. Tried it even more, rather.

Now that she knew to look for him, his glamour didn't work, or he wasn't disguising himself, except that clearly no one else in the place could see him. If they could, they would stare in spite of themselves—he had the presence of a movie star, the confidence of a man who'd lived a thousand years.

Ian looked up and scowled, and that was it.

Airen approached the counter, stayed poised when anyone else would have leaned on it, managing to look both formal and casual at once. He could be everything he needed to be.

"Well?" he said by way of greeting.

"Hello," she said, in lieu of something more clever or formal. "Can I get you a drink? My treat." No more dead leaves in the till.

"I'll have the chamomile," he said. Because to ask for chamomile tea would be a lie—it wasn't made with tea leaves. He might obfuscate, but never lie.

Chamomile for him, a straight-up coffee for her, and they adjourned to a bistro table tucked in the corner, farthest from everyone else. She held a leather courier bag in her lap.

"What have you found for me?"

She brought out the items one by one.

"A blossom that will not ripen," she said, and set a silk rose on the table. "Rather obvious. But I think you'll like this one. A corpse that will not rot." She drew out a rock the size of her fist.

His brow furrowed. "What's that?"

"Trilobite." She ran her finger along the ridges of the stone creature's back. "A fossil. It didn't rot but turned to stone. Neat, huh?"

"And the song that will not end?"

For this, she pulled out her phone and played a song file, a hissing, ambient rumble that sounded both like a rocket and an ocean in a storm. You'd put this on in the background, forget about it, and in ten minutes wonder why your spine was vibrating with some force you didn't understand.

He lifted an eyebrow, silently asking the question she expected.

"Cosmic microwave background radiation. The sound of creation. Kind of relaxing, isn't it? It started when everything did, and it's still out there."

"I'm impressed," he said, but didn't sound it. The phrase was a placeholder. "It's not really what I would have chosen but I don't suppose I can argue."

"No, you can't. Now, what's it all for?" The real riddle. She thought she knew the answer.

"Can't you guess?"

"I can always guess, but it'd be faster if you just tell me." He gave her a wry look as if to say, *Indulge me.* Play this game, not because he wanted her to, but because it was fun. Often, it was. Fine, then. "This is a test. Isn't it?" She waved her hand over the trivial items. "This is make-work. Riddles and games. What do you really want? What's the real quest?"

He studied her with those otherworldly gray eyes, shining with the light not of actual stars, but how stars were supposed to shine in stories and poems. Now he would say something romantic and flattering about how she had inspired him, how enthralling mortal life was precisely because it was so fleeting, all the things he'd said when she was twenty that had sounded so important, so true. And why wasn't he off seducing some suggestible young thing? She couldn't have been the first, when he met her. Once, she thought she might be the last. He'd made it sound like he'd never need anyone else. But then…

"I wanted to see… No, that's not quite right. I wanted to learn…" He shook his head, his hands clenched around his mug. Airen, at a loss for words? He confessed, "I'm not really sure how to explain. But you're right."

She blinked, because yes, she'd gotten completely distracted by his Fae eyes. She ought to know better, but she didn't, not really. "What?"

"It's a test."

"Did I pass?" And what did *that* mean, when she should have been more focused on what the test was meant to measure, not if she won. She hadn't learned a thing, had she?

"You did."

"So now what?"

"I don't know. I thought I would know, but I don't. I can't tell what you want."

"Oh? You used to read me like a book."

"I think you didn't keep your cover so tightly shut then. But the test. First—you saw me. At least, you saw the leaves and knew what it meant. Knew what to look for. I wasn't sure you would. Ian didn't, until you showed him. Martine walked right past me, last week. Didn't even pause at the whiff of glamour. But you."

And Kid, she almost said. Kid would have recognized him straight off, if he were here.

Airen went on. "And the quest—for all your stated practicality, you accepted the challenge. You answered the riddles. You didn't even need to know why. You took up the call."

"You said please," she said.

"I wanted to ask you a question, but I wasn't sure you'd say yes. Now… I think you might say yes. And so I will ask: Will you come with me, Abby? I've come to bring you home."

To the beautiful shining twilight, where all music was sweet, every touch was silk, and every taste… She had only tasted him. They had not eaten or drunk anything, that time. They knew the stories, knew what would happen if they took the food and drink of the shadowed lands. Now he was asking. Offering. Eat me, drink me, all that you like, forever. A song that will not end.

Her voice caught, unsure what word to speak. Should have been an easy answer. He wouldn't have offered if he hadn't been absolutely sure of how she'd respond. Beings like him needed to *know*.

She said, "Why didn't you ask me this when I was twenty?"

He straightened, clearly taken aback. "I wasn't sure. And now I am."

What had happened in the ethereal Fae realm between that time and this, to make him sure? If she asked, would he tell her? Would he even know? If she asked, and he told, would the Fae answer even make sense to her?

Her coffee had gotten cold—the mug's warmth now came from her hands gripping it. Leaning back, she looked around the shop, her realm. Comfortably cluttered, more like the living room of someone with too many hobbies than a café. Plenty of clean, corporate coffee shops around if people wanted that. This…people came here to feel safe, and she was proud of that. The scuffed hardwood floor threw back blond-colored light from the tall windows. It was a nice day out, spring-like. There'd be lots of flowers. The Wailin' Jennys sang on the PA, folk with lots of harmony. Always some kind of music playing in the shop.

Ian was at his usual table, the usual level of chaos around him. His headphones were on tight, his eyes half-lidded, and he nodded along with whatever song was playing. Stopped abruptly and hit a key on the laptop, typed some commands, tried again. Abby looked over her shoulder just in time to see Martine duck in and wave before running up the stairs to the studio.

It should be enough, shouldn't it, for him to reach his hand out and for her to take it. Her gaze dropped.

He might have flinched. "You…you aren't going to say yes."

"It's not that I don't appreciate the gesture. It's not…" Not that she didn't still love him, weirdly and magically. "But I built this place from scratch and I have to take care of it. I want to take care of it." This maybe wasn't some enchanted realm that needed magic to keep its boundaries strong. It was all so little on that cosmic scale. But it was hers.

He bowed his head, looked back at her with his impossible gaze. "I think I understand."

"You can come visit. Anytime you like."

Abby did not tell the others what Airen offered her, or that she refused. They would have told her that she should have gone with him. Accepted the dream as it came to her. She didn't want to argue with them so she didn't mention it.

It was by chance, then, that they gathered that evening in the shop. Ian put away his work and retrieved his guitar. Martine was done teaching for the day and brought her fiddle. Abby took a bodhrán from its peg on the wall. Kid's. She wasn't nearly as good as he'd been, but she thought he wouldn't mind. Martine and Ian noted this, nodded.

"You going to sing?" Martine asked, kind of hopefully.

Abby shook her head. "Not tonight. Maybe another time."

Martine started them off with a jig on the fiddle, Abby picked up the beat quick enough, Ian added some rhythm, and soon they were smiling, jamming, throwing the tunes and beats back and forth between them, and it was almost like old times. Drawn by the sound, people came in and kept the kids behind the counter busy with their orders. The place got pretty packed.

Airen was there, sitting quietly at a table, a mug of his usual chamomile in hand. He wore a faint smile, an expression that was serious, for him. Abby pretended not to see him.

The music rolled on, and the deep blue of a twilight sky shone through the window.

Entanglement, or How I Failed to Knit a Sweater for My Boyfriend

This is a story about how you are not supposed to knit a sweater for your boyfriend.

The thinking goes like this: a sweater is some of the most complex knitting one can attempt. First is the expense: it takes a lot of yarn to knit a sweater, especially one for a well-built, broad-shouldered man who works out, and if you're being fancy about it you want the good yarn, the all-natural merino blend, the pretty, pettable yarn, and that stuff isn't cheap. Second is the sizing. Knitting a scarf requires no sizing at all, you just keep going until it's done. Hats are easy enough to estimate and stretchy besides. But a sweater? Has arms and armholes and necks and lengths and widths that all have to be *just right* if the finished product isn't going to be a laughable, lumpy mess, or just sad. Never mind if you decide to put in cables or some other pattern. A lot of anxiety goes into knitting a sweater, especially if you've never done it before. Not to mention time.

The thinking goes that putting all that effort into the gift will jinx the relationship. You will knit the sweater, which becomes symbolic of far more than a quaint handmade garment. You will give him the sweater, and he will gaze upon it not with love and admiration, but with dismay, because on a deep subconscious level he will understand the symbolic commitment involved in knitting a sweater for him and realize he does not reciprocate. The sweater, which you have so devotedly created in stolen hours on lunch breaks so you could surprise him, hurriedly shoving it into a bag and bringing out a decoy project if he comes home unexpectedly, putting love into every stitch, will come to mark the beginning of the end when he realizes he maybe isn't as into you as he thought.

The thinking goes, do not knit a sweater for your boyfriend until he is more than a boyfriend, until he has committed.

My thinking goes, even that's no guarantee that he'll regard your epic project with the same fraught love that you put into it. Making a commitment is no guarantee that he, or you, will keep it. So my question is this: when is it all right to knit your boyfriend a sweater?

And if your boyfriend has wings: how?

I've knitted sweaters before. I'm confident of my ability to knit sweaters that fit well, using the expensive yarn. That isn't my problem.

I've snuck a tape measure under the pillow so that once Alex has fallen asleep, I can size him up. He's half on his side, half on his stomach, hugging the pillow so it pooches up to cradle his head. His skin is between tan and brown, his hair dark and swept back, just long enough to delightfully tangle one's fingers in. He has an almost constant dusting of a near five-o-clock shadow. He's muscular, broad shoulders sweeping down to a trim waist, curving backside, strong legs. Sheets draped alluringly over his hips, his wings spread out behind him.

The wings have cream-colored feathers. The curve of them reaches up by his ears, the tips sweep down by his knees, and they smell of linen drying in sunshine.

Tape measure deployed: seven inches between the wings, six inches down from where his neck meets his shoulders. Where they attach to his back: six and three-quarters inches. Actually, the left is six and one-quarter, a whole half-inch smaller, and it makes me wonder if angels are left- or right-winged. I stare at him a moment, trying to work out the physiology of it, which makes no sense. As muscular as his shoulders are, they're not enough to support much less operate a pair of wings this size. He's too heavy to fly, one would think.

I try not to touch him—he's a light sleeper. I hold the tape measure hovering just above his skin. He feels it anyway and shifts, looking over his shoulder.

I quickly hide the tape behind my back.

"What're doing?" he mumbles, blinking sleepily at me, face still half-pressed to the pillow.

The thing about dating an angel, even a fallen angel, is they know when you're lying. I usually have no interest in lying to him. I wince a little and say, "It's a surprise." It isn't a lie.

He lifts a brow. Smiles a little. "Okay."

When he reaches for me, I drop the tape off the side of the bed and snuggle up to him. His arms wrap around me, and the nearer wing settles over me like a blanket.

I don't know where Alex gets his clothes. He might magic them from the ether. I've never seen him do this, but I've never really seen him do anything magical. He wears clothes, and they fit, somehow. I've never bought clothes for him—there are plenty of other gifts to bring him. He likes homemade food, craft beer, microdistilleries, and unusual soaps. His current soap is juniper and he smells faintly of a forest after he showers. I never seem to be looking right at him when he strips. Even when I'm the one peeling off his shirt, I somehow get distracted by the hair on his chest or the way his arms flex before I can really study how the shirt fits over the wings. I'd much rather look at him than his clothes, which is why he takes off the clothes, after all.

Which begs the question of why I want to knit him a sweater in the first place. It isn't like he's ever complained of the cold. He's one of those men who's a furnace, who I can stick my icy feet against and he doesn't complain.

It's not a sweater, it's a symbol, and the old knitters' warning rises up again.

It's just a sweater. I want to knit him a sweater because I can.

I think.

If I can figure out how to get it over the wings.

Not many people can see the wings.

I can see angels because I almost died once. I couldn't see angels and then I could. We met at the local farmer's market when I was looking at asparagus, and he brushed past me. I saw the wings and tried to get out of the way. He turned back to look, his brow furrowed.

"Did you just . . . you can see them?"

"Yeah," I said a little breathlessly. He was six inches taller than me and his T-shirt was just exactly tight enough. We moved a little closer— we were blocking traffic. "I drowned when I was eighteen. Well, almost drowned. I got better. Obviously."

His expression relaxed with understanding. "I'm sorry. That you almost drowned, not that you got better."

"I'm glad I can see you." I immediately blushed because it was such a silly forward thing to say.

"So, this is going to sound weird, but I work as a lifeguard sometimes and I'd be interested to hear how . . . professionally speaking, I mean. If it's not too traumatic."

"Oh, it's fine. There wasn't actually a lifeguard around and I honestly don't remember it very well, I don't know if that will be helpful at all." I'd been river rafting. It had been a very slow river, a very lazy trip, and somehow I still managed to fall overboard and get stuck. Next thing I knew I was staring up at sky with EMT's surrounding me and being told I'd stopped breathing. The next day I saw my first wings. That was how I knew I'd really been dead, just for a moment or two.

"Can I buy you a coffee?" he asked.

Yes. Yes he could.

I'm thinking buttons. Maybe a reverse cardigan, though that seems strange. Put a couple of holes in the back, or a flap that can button down between the wings. That might do it.

I work in a yarn shop, so I can tell myself this is a professional problem as well as a personal goal. It's a slow afternoon, only a couple of customers: a man pawing through sock yarn in the corner, and his long-suffering boyfriend, who clearly isn't a knitter, patiently waiting a couple of feet away and staring at his phone; and a determined gray-haired matron in a suit peering at a rack of needles through reading glasses.

I've got my base pattern laid out in front of me, the basic size and shape of the sweater I'll make. I've got my yarn picked out, a good, soft wool with a colorway in dark blues and grays, like a stormy twilight sky. I just have to figure out the back. I'm making notes.

Bette, who owns the shop, comes by and looks over my shoulder. "What're you planning?"

"A sweater."

She studies the pattern. Tilts her head, squints. "That . . . looks like it has too many pieces to be a sweater. "

I'm playing around with the idea of panels, or a gap with an i-cord binding for the wings to go through. "It's an experiment."

She's skeptical. So am I, to be honest. Well, if it starts to go wrong I can always frog it and try again. A big part of knitting that beginners don't always understand is you have to be ready to unravel anything, no matter how much work you've already put in.

I choose my needles: 24" circular, size 7, at least to start. I draw out a length of yarn from the first skein.

I cast on.

Now and then I see someone else with wings.

We're sitting in a park sharing lunch. These days, Alex is working as a bartender at a brewpub. I've learned that angels really are guardians, and they have their focus, their interests. Alex likes lifeguarding, as he said when I met him, but he really likes looking after makers. People who make things. He likes working for businesses that started out as someone making something, so he ends up at a lot of craft breweries. He's worked in wood shops and garden centers, and even a van conversion business once. His eyes lit up when I told him I work in a yarn shop. It was the first time a date ever had that reaction to my job.

"There. You know them?" I nod at a tall being with their hair cut very short, wearing a tank top to reveal ropy, powerful arms. Brown wings sweep behind, and I can't quite tell how the shirt fits over them. They're walking across the other side of the park. They glance over once, give Alex a little nod, and continue on.

"Yeah," he answers with an unenthusiastic sigh. "Don't worry about it."

I hadn't actually worried about seeing angels until he said not to.

Angels are veterans of the War in Heaven, and the War in Heaven created this debased world. People forget that angels fought on both sides. Lucifer was an angel.

You can't really tell which side any individual angel fought on, not just by looking. While you tell yourself of course you'd want to be with a soldier of Heaven, you actually need to think about that, because the soldiers of Heaven are, well, obedient. Perhaps unimaginative. I've never learned for certain which army Alex fought for. He says it doesn't matter, because the world that war was fought in doesn't exist anymore.

He likes helping people. Whatever he was then, that's what he is now.

We share an apartment within walking distance of downtown, which we picked together, mostly because the kitchen was big enough for him and his wings to turn around in.

When I get home he's already gone to work, and I'll have a couple of hours to work on the sweater before he gets back. First, I clean up a little, get the dishes out of the sink and the clothes from the bedroom floor. They've piled up and Alex kind of just doesn't notice messes, so I do it. I study his shirts, and they're just shirts, solid, no way to tell how he gets them over his head or how the wings fit through them. Some divine miracle.

I'm just knitting a sweater. It won't be miraculous but it will be fine.

The ribbing for the collar goes quickly. Next, the yoke, increasing the stitches to expand across the chest.

Knitting is binary. There are two basic stitches upon which every pattern is based: the knit and the purl. Needle up or needle down. The one and the zero. It's a language. You can combine the stitches a dozen different ways after that to make all sorts of shapes and patterns, but it starts with the binary. Experienced knitters can see what the finished pattern will look like just by glancing at the code, the Ks and Ps and ss1s and k2togs. I'm not quite that good, but I can read a pattern.

Once I start, the pattern knits up faster than I expect.

And then, suddenly, the thing on my needles doesn't look like a sweater.

That's okay, it doesn't need to look like a sweater yet. It doesn't have sleeves. It's just a length of soft wooly fabric. It'll come together in a later step.

"What're you making?"

Alex walks in the door. The surprise sweater is here in the open. I quickly hide it in my lap under a throw rug. "It's a surprise," I say.

226

He smiles, amused. "Well, all right then." He comes over to kiss my forehead and his touch is a shock, electric. I flinch, and he tilts his head quizzically. "You okay?"

"Yeah, I think so. I just need a break."

I've been knitting for six hours straight and haven't noticed. My hands aren't even stiff.

The shower starts running. I have a sudden urge to join Alex there and talk him into washing my back. My nerves are tingling. Sitting in one place for too long.

I strip my clothes and throw them with his, even though I've just straightened up, and tentatively push back the shower curtain. Wearing a big smile he draws me in under the hot water and puts his arms around me. His damp wings hovering nearby feel like shelter.

I knit in the park. Alex isn't meeting me for lunch today and I thought I would get out and get some sun while I add a few more rows to the surprise sweater, but the sky has gone cloudy with an unexpected storm. People mutter about it and glance up, shading their eyes. Parents gather up children and rush them away.

The fall of knitted fabric fills my lap, growing. Row after row.

The wind starts blowing and I can't keep the page with the pattern written on it flat, so I pack up. I'm late getting back to the store.

As I walk through the door, three displays fall over. Bette jumps and screams, and the couple of customers look over in a moment of terror and flee.

"Every time the door opens…" Bette mutters and starts picking up skeins of yarn and knitting magazines, wrestling the wire racks back upright.

"There's a storm." I head for the main desk and get out the surprise sweater. The rows curl back on themselves. Every time I try to straighten it out to see where I am, it curls back again.

"I don't suppose you could help me with this?" Bette says, a bit testily.

"What?"

She sighs, and I blush. I hadn't noticed the mess, shelves of yarn fallen over, bursting away from the front door like a bomb hit.

"Oh. Right." I rush to help clean up, even though the needles catch in my sleeve as I shove my project aside. As if they're trying to hold on to me.

"Something's in the air," Bette mutters and we finally get the space cleared up. "Mercury retrograde?"

Mercury always seems to be retrograde. Alex says that kind of thing doesn't matter, and he should know if it matters or not, shouldn't he? Seeing where he came from.

It's the panels in back, designed to fold around angel wings, that have made the garment look like it has six or seven extra edges, and I've added in a bit more ribbing to make it more stretchy. I'm sure the yarn is glaring back at me.

Soon, I suspect something has gone terribly wrong with the would-be sweater. There's a thing that happens when you knit in the round, but twist the stitches wrong on that first row, so you're not quite knitting a straight line. The thing you're knitting will become a Mobius strip.

I think I accidentally did that when I cast on the sweater.

I have asked this yarn, this pattern, to do something otherworldly. And bless it, it's trying. But it's going wrong.

I should frog it. Unravel the whole thing and start over.

But I kind of want to see what it looks like when I'm done.

Do you know what's a miracle? Knitting. Knitting is a miracle. Can you imagine? How did it start? Who sat down and figured out how to use a couple of sticks to make loops of yarn to make fabric that stretches? All the things you can do with fabric that stretches. Did it arise independently in multiple places? Or did an angel whisper in the ear of some woman spinning wool, *Let me show you a trick.* You could look at yarn wrapped around a spindle, maybe a couple of strands that got crossed and looped together by accident, and think, *a-ha.* Before you know it everyone in your family has socks and nice wooly mittens. A goddamn miracle.

I have an insight. How shirts fit over wings, how they seem to emerge seamlessly from jackets and tank tops: the clothing can't see the wings. The fabric has to pretend not to see the wings, and the problem with the surprise sweater is that it's covered with eyes.

I cannot knit the sweater because I can see the wings. I have seen a thing I should not and the sweater knows it.

On my walk home, I see three angels, and none of them are Alex. I try not to notice. It's not like they're together. Maybe it's just a coincidence.

I've ruined everything. And I mean everything.

My phone screams an alarm. A tornado siren blares.

Alex doesn't come home from work.

I call the bar, and it's closed. I leave a message, then another one because the first one wasn't clear, that I am Alex's girlfriend demanding to know where he is and not some crazy person. I probably sound like a crazy person. I tell myself I'm not worried because he's an angel and he's not going to get hit by a car or fall into a ditch. He *can't* get hurt, he just can't.

At least, I don't think he can. At least, he can't be hurt by the ordinary things that hurt humans. And there's no War in Heaven. At least not right now. I don't think.

In the morning, he still hasn't come home, and I've stayed up waiting for him, all night, working on the sweater that has veered far off the pattern I wrote in ways I'm having trouble understanding. The object on the needles definitely doesn't look like a sweater. It might look like a storm, with twisting, billowing clouds roiling in on themselves.

I will walk to the bar and look for Alex there, since no one's called back. I'm worried, and I'm not worried that he's gotten hurt because he's an angel, he can't get hurt. I'm worried that he's left. Because I got annoyed at cleaning up. Because I'm just a human and he finally got tired of me. Because I decided to knit him a sweater. That started it all. He's gone. He didn't even say goodbye. I suppose secretly I've always known this day would come, because the other big miracle is that someone like Alex would ever be with someone like me.

I head to the park, which has always felt safe to me. I find a bench and sit, just sit, and the needles are in my hand, and the pattern is in my head. The not-a-sweater surprise is pulsing in my hand.

A circle of quiet surrounds me, while a dozen yards away the wind howls, a wall of chaos.

I hug the needles and the knitted thing to my chest because I don't think I should leave it alone. It seems to be expanding by itself, the fibers and knots twining around my fingers, constricting. Clinging and comforting me. *It's all right, it's fine, you have peered into a cosmic truth and it's just fine.* I study the stitches to try to figure out what went wrong and I lose time, hours. Knitting is binary but this has stitches I don't recognize. Impossible stitches, neither up nor down. I have seen what I shouldn't.

In the street, people are running, screaming, like some overblown disaster movie and I wonder where the monster is. It's in my lap. It's not a sweater. I'm almost knocked over by someone fleeing nothing in particular. Angels arrive, dozens of them, walking, gliding, flying. Wings broad and powerful, barely moving. I've never seen Alex fly. The angels are stabs of light against the storm. I look for Alex among them. Even if he's there I'm not sure I would recognize him.

The angels converge. Here. The not-a-sweater cringes away from them. It hisses a little.

There are eyes and wings and wrath in the storm bearing down on me.

The angels have their own language. No one can speak it but them, and no one can hear it without going mad.

I start to scream, but suddenly there are words in the wind.

Be not afraid.

And there is Alex.

He is cosmic, the sun and moon, and he is armed for battle, wearing a cuirass made of quicksilver and carrying a spear forged from comets. He seems to draw in light and throw it out again. And his wings—they're spread wide, flecked with iron, a weapon themselves, tensed and ready to launch. They're moving, a nervous flutter, like the tapping of a foot. They whisper.

I should be blinded, I should look away. If I hadn't already been crying I would have started.

The host is arrayed around him, ready to fight a war. But Alex stands in front of me, and we regard each other with no small amount of confusion.

I'm in a bit of a panic. My gaze is pleading. "Help?"

He says, "What are you doing?"

"I'm knitting you a sweater. It's a surprise."

This seems to make perfect sense to him. He sets his jaw. "Sweetie, I love you dearly, but you need to stop."

I look at the mess of celestial knots draped around me, whose shapes I can't even see anymore, though if I studied them I might, *might* be able to replicate the pattern or go mad trying. I'm not entirely sure what I've done, but I'm at the center of the storm that rages, and Alex is only one of the angels standing here, weapon in hand, wondering what the hell it is they're supposed to be fighting.

It's only a sweater.

I yank the needles out of the live stitches, leaving a row of dozens of angry little lost loops behind. They're like empty eyes. When I tug on the yarn, the staring loops vanish.

Then the next row vanishes.

And the next.

Frogged.

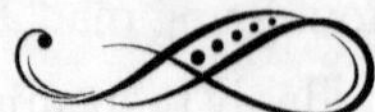

Right there in the park, he sits cross-legged in front of me and helps, holding the remains of the work taut while I pull the yarn loose and wind it into a ball. All partners of knitters know this ritual, holding a skein in outstretched hands, maintaining tension so the strands don't become tangled.

The would-be sweater is unmade.

The wind stops, the storm vanishes, and the angels disperse. Many of them look sidelong at me and come to speak to Alex in a language I can't hear. The armor and swords and spears are gone and they all look like people again. Except for the wings.

I just concentrate on winding the yarn into a ball, so that it's nothing more than potential again.

"Maybe we should get rid of it? Burn it or bury it or something?" There's still a charge in the air, the sense of rocks sliding down a hill into an avalanche. The pattern was cursed, certainly, but what about the yarn?

"No, it's good yarn," he says. "It's okay now."

"The sweater. I thought I could make it work with your wings."

He smiles. "I think it's amazing that you tried. Maybe knit me something else?"

And maybe trust that an angel understands something about symbols.

"Tell me about God," I ask.

We are naked in bed after performing several acts that certain reactionary religious sects insist will damn us.

"You don't want to hear about God," he says.

232

He's right, mostly. "I'm just curious."

"Unsatisfied curiosity is the essence of the divine. You must feel without knowing."

But there must be a God somewhere. "You can't have angels without God, right? So where is He?"

"After the War, that question isn't as pressing as you think it is."

"But you all are ready to go to war again. You're just ready for it."

He wraps his arms around me, pulls me close, and doesn't answer.

The problem with knitting a sweater for a boyfriend is you go through all the effort of making it, and what happens if he doesn't wear it? It might be a perfectly good sweater. Him not wearing it might have nothing to do with you or it. He might be allergic to wool. He might never have worn a sweater in his life—which is something you should have noticed, before knitting a sweater for him. You will be quietly, subtly hurt, if he doesn't wear it. You'll try not to be but you will, and you'll realize you should have noticed that he's allergic to wool or doesn't wear sweaters. The flaws in the fabric have been revealed. It was never about giving him a sweater, but about the need for a symbol that will bind him to you.

Not knitting a sweater for your boyfriend doesn't mean you don't love him. That's the kicker. The absence of a symbol is not its opposite. It's not binary. Neither is knitting, really, whatever the pattern says.

I knit Alex a scarf in a simple garter stitch, which is only a knit stitch over and over again. The first pattern anybody learns to knit. Not even a clever border or ribbing. I use a different yarn, chunky and undyed, that came from sheep raised in the Navajo Nation.

It's a nice scarf, and Alex wears it. It fits neatly around his neck and over his wings. He puts it on during the first driving snow at the end of autumn, and smiles at me, and that's the miracle.

THE LADY OF SHALOTT

As far as she could remember, the Lady had never been outside the tower. She might have been born here. She assumed she had been born, but maybe not. Maybe she just appeared, her complete adult self, flowing red hair and porcelain skin, dressed in a gown of blue trimmed with gold, with no memory of anything outside these rounded walls.

All day, every day, she wove a tapestry set on a loom against the wall. She might have been weaving forever, and she didn't know if she would ever finish. The cloth was filled with pictures: ivy climbing up an old stone wall, willows dripping into rivers, tangled rose vines, flocks of birds soaring in a blue sky. At least, she thought that was what she was making. She could only shape what her mind told her, not what she saw.

She knew one thing for certain, as firmly as she knew she had bones inside her skin and flesh: She must not look out the window set in the wall of her tower. She must never look outside, because that was her curse.

And what would happen if she looked out? She didn't know that either.

A knight must do good.

Make a name for himself by doing good, by going on quests and such. Succoring the weak. Slaying monsters. Or all of them at once, if the opportunity presented itself.

Sir Lancelot found a task that might encompass all the fame and virtue he could wish for. If only he could be clear as to what this was actually about.

"A curse, you say?"

"On the tower," the lowly swineherd replied, pointing.

"That tower there?" Lancelot asked, also pointing.

"Aye, that's the one."

Across the vale, past a river, down a glen, and nestled in the middle of a dense copse, the tall stone edifice stretched straight up. The top was crenellated, and a single window gazed out. The space was black, nothing visible within. He hoped there might be a maiden looking out, brushing her hair while humming with a sweet voice.

He had seen the tower from the road. It looked promising, so he asked around. Nobody seemed to know anything about the storm-gray tower, except that it was cursed.

"Does anyone go there?" Lancelot asked.

The swineherd scowled. "No. It's *cursed.*" The grubby man looked the knight up and down, squinting, appraising. Encased in shining armor, Lancelot sat mounted on a powerful white steed, great sword secured to the saddle, all bedecked in bright colors and heraldry, but the fellow didn't seem very impressed. Well, after all, this was the road to Camelot. Knights passed this way all the time.

"How long has that tower stood there? And who built it? What banner does it fly? What manner of folk travel to and from it? Are they armed?"

Clearly overwhelmed, the swineherd gaped at him.

"Then simply tell me this: How many men guard the tower?"

"None, sir!" the swineherd declared. "There's just a maiden lives there, but she's cursed!"

The knight brightened. "A maiden? Then she is a prisoner. I must rescue her and lift the curse!"

The swineherd gaped at him again and said, "I need to be going, sir."

"Right then! I thank you!"

The grubby man trundled off, walking stick digging into the dirt along the side of the road. There were no pigs in sight.

Lancelot could not find anyone who knew the manner of this curse, so he assumed it was the usual: a witch, envious of her beauty, had locked the maiden away until some true knight might rescue her. *This* was going to be a good day, he decided.

The silk thread she wove with had always been there, piled in a basket by the loom. Sometimes in the evening, when the sun no longer came into her chamber, and her eyes grew too weary for weaving, she'd light her lanterns and sort the thread into colors and thicknesses, imagining what pictures she might make of them, what scenes they'd be best for. Then she'd gather them all up and sort them again, seeing different scenes and shapes this time. She'd stroke the fibers, brush the skeins along her cheek. They felt so rich.

Only rarely did she wonder where the thread came from and why she never seemed to run out, no matter how much she used or how long and ornate the tapestry became. She had never taken the whole thing down to measure it—the finished length of it was rolled up on the loom's cloth beam, waiting. The rolled cloth seemed quite thick. Surely she'd woven enough and could finish—bind off the edge, pull it down, consider the whole of what she'd made.

But she never did. She kept weaving because it was all she had. She might throw all her thread out the window just to see what happened, but she never did that either, because doing so would require going to the window, and she did not dare look out. As long as there was always thread in her basket, she would keep on. She hummed to herself sometimes, but apart from that, all she ever heard were sounds that came in through the window. A breeze, maybe. Distant thunder. The music that she knew came from birds. She had seen a bird once—it flew in through the window and perched at the top of her loom. The drab little thing had brown streaked feathers and a black eye. But it made such beautiful sounds, warbling and trilling through its tiny beak. It only stayed for a minute or two, hopping back and forth, fluttering its wings, obviously distressed. When it finally took off and swooped out the window, she almost watched it go, almost looked out to see the sky that must be there. But she did not.

One morning, a new sound came from outside the window, something she had never heard before, and she could call up no image in her mind to match it. It was like the sound when she dropped a bobbin on the floor, wood and stone crashing together, but much louder. Like pigeons clambering on the roof. Like banging on a rug to clean it. Rhythmic, loud, like thunder but going on and on. And there was shouting. There were voices. Other voices, not hers. Outside the window.

She couldn't ignore it, and she couldn't look out.

It was the curse coming to life, and she curled up on her pallet with her arms around her ears, trying to block out the noise, wondering what she'd done wrong—she hadn't looked out, not even once, not even to see the sky.

Once, she tried to cover the window to curb her fear that she might accidentally steal a glimpse. It was difficult, attempting to peg a blanket from her bed to the stone, while also not, again and always, looking out the window. She managed it somehow, but the air in the room grew quickly stuffy and smoky. With the sunlight blocked, she only had lanterns, and they filled her chamber with fumes. She had to leave the window open or suffocate.

Truly, she was cursed to be trapped here without knowing why. She wondered if she had angered someone, but she couldn't remember who. She couldn't remember how it had begun.

The noise stopped at dusk, but started again in the morning. When she tried to weave, her hands shook with every beat and banging. She left the loom to wash her face and brush her hair, to distract herself.

She had a mirror stored in the same little box where she kept her brush and knife and other essentials. The circle of polished bronze on a filigree handle showed her pink lips and blue eyes, locks of red hair framing her face. She did not know if she was pretty or not, because she had nothing to compare to. Moreover, she wasn't entirely sure why being pretty was so important, but she thought it must be, or she would not have a mirror.

The mirror reflected back *anything*, which was how she got the idea that maybe she could hold it up to the window, then look at the mirror and not out the window.

Hunkering down, keeping her face and eyes well below the sill, she held the mirror up. Angling it back and forth, she tried to alight on some discernible image. Blinded herself for a moment by flashing a bit of sun into her eyes. But then, finally, she resolved a picture of blue sky and clouds. They must be clouds, the white smears and shapes. She angled the mirror again, panning it down, and saw trees. She *knew* all this, as if she must have spent some time outside the tower at some point. A great green carpet standing on tall posts of living wood. Trees, yes.

And then she saw men cutting down the trees. That was the noise, sawing and chopping with axes, the crashing as a tree fell through its fellows, ripping branches as it went. She couldn't hear the words they shouted. Instructions, maybe. Warnings.

There were so many people, she was afraid. Who were they, what did they want, what were they doing to her tower, and did they know she was cursed? They were clearing a wide space and using the fallen lumber to build—ladders, maybe? Scaffolding? Whatever it was, a latticework of wood was taking shape below her.

She moved the mirror again, and the reflection showed her a new picture: a figure standing apart from the others, mounted on a pure white horse, observing. He was silver, his hair blond and gleaming gold in the sun. His jaw was square, his bearing noble.

A knight in armor she thought he must be, and he was beautiful. He was the moon and sun. Someone nearby spoke; he turned to the voice and smiled. She fell in love with him, just like that, without warning, without choice, without hope.

Now she truly saw the depth of her curse.

When Lancelot first went to the tower, he left his steed behind and crept forward carefully, sword in hand, waiting for the demons or ogres who must be guarding it. Nothing opposed him. The place might have been abandoned.

He shouted a hail up to the single window, but his voice fell flat, absorbed by the forest, and a chill went up his spine. Of course someone lived in the tower, how could they not? An abandoned tower would have been crumbling and covered in ivy. There would be ghosts and creatures nesting amid the broken stones. This was a perfectly serviceable tower. Only it was not attached to any castle, and he had no way of getting inside.

He must reach that window and rescue the maiden. And so he went to Camelot, to the chief castle builder, who suggested constructing a scaffold to reach that height.

It didn't make quite as good a story, a knight seeking help from a castle builder, but he only had to think of that maiden trapped in the tower. He would do anything to help her, and so he did. Hired the castle builder, brought in all the workers and tools required, and got to work. The scaffold would be finished in a week, and then he could simply climb to the top and look within.

"But sir, my lord," the chief castle builder said to him on the first day. "What of the curse?"

"Ah yes, the curse," Lancelot agreed. "What of it?"

"The locals have been telling the men stories of the maiden in the tower, and of the curse laid upon her."

"Do they say what the curse is? What will happen because of it?"

"Well, no…"

"Then that is why I must go up there." He smiled at the window in the tower with great anticipation. "To rescue the maiden. That is her curse, that she is trapped in the tower."

The chief castle builder furrowed his brow. "Sir, my lord—it is my impression that there is more to it, that she is perhaps trapped in the tower because she *is* the curse."

Lancelot frowned. "How so?"

"Well, no one seems to know. My lord."

"I'm sure this has all been blown entirely out of proportion."

"You're probably right, my lord." The man went away to supervise the clearing of the forest and the raising of the next level of scaffold.

The Lady went into a panic. According to her mirror, the workmen below had built a third level on the scaffold. They were getting closer, and she wasn't entirely sure what would happen when they reached her. She knew, absolutely, that she should not look outside the window. But what happened if the outside came in?

"No no *no!*" she muttered, putting the mirror away and pacing around her little room, tugging at her hair. Maybe they didn't know about the curse. Maybe they didn't realize the danger of what they were doing.

She ought to send a message. Maybe scrawled on a scrap of paper secured to the leg of a pigeon. A flaming arrow. However, any message she sent would require looking out the window to deliver it. This was terrible.

Her tapestry hung on its loom, showing mountains and forests blending into a scene of ducks flying above a silver lake, or how she imagined such things might look if she could remember seeing them. For the first time ever her heart ached, thinking she might never get to complete the tapestry, that she might never see it finished. Even though she still couldn't imagine what she might do with it when it was finished. If it ever was.

She *could* send them a message. Find some way to tell that beautiful knight with his silver armor to stop building, to save them all. Maybe she could even find a way to tell him how much she loved him. Such a thing was absurd—he'd never even seen her. He would think she was mad, and maybe she was. But she had to try, and if she was going to send a message anyway, she ought to tell him.

Choosing several skeins of yarn and thread, she set up a makeshift loom, tying down the threads of her warp, stretching the warp and securing it to a weighted basket. This would be a band, like a girdle, with words crafted upon it: *Stop, I am cursed, you must stop or we are all doomed. (I love you I love you I love you!)*

She had to weave faster than she ever had, but the weaving also had to be clean and neat, so they could read the words she stitched. She had to do it before the scaffold grew any higher.

By the third day the scaffold was more than halfway up the tower, and Lancelot knew that very soon he'd be looking through the window. The anticipation was almost more than he could bear. Who was this maiden, and what had she suffered?

To pass the time, he rode to various settlements in the area, searching for more news about the tower and its curse. No one knew the details. But everyone was sure there *was* a curse, and that it was no doubt terrible.

This lack of information was frustrating.

In the middle of the fourth day, an object sailed out of the window.

He'd left his horse picketed some ways off and was walking a circuit of the tower once again, searching for any detail he might have missed, when the thing fluttered down like a wounded bird. He was in just the right spot to catch it.

It was a woven band made of silk, slippery in his hand. The kind of favor a lady might tie around his arm before he rode in a tournament. It was black and red with hints of gold, a swirling pattern running through it, odd swoops and curls that drew the eye but that he could not follow. It might have been runes, it might have been some spell woven in arcane patterns. Between the colors and strange shapes, the thing hurt his eyes. The pattern seemed to writhe of its own accord.

It might have been a plea for help.

This must have been the meaning, surely. The maiden was there in the tower, she was real, and he would see her soon. This token she'd sent him was an omen, a sign of hope. Lancelot's heart soared. Only one more day, perhaps less.

They did not stop building the scaffold, and the knight gazed up at her window—as she saw in her mirror—with such an expression of longing and assurance that her heart nearly gave out. She swooned, falling back upon her pallet. Oh, how she loved him! He must be the noblest knight in all the world!

And she wept, because she did not know what would happen next, and she was terribly afraid.

Her unfinished tapestry looked down on her, bright colors mixed with pale, swirls and patterns that she once thought made a picture, even a blurred one, of the world she could never see—what she thought she might see if she ever looked out the window. Now she saw that the picture she had woven was chaos, all abstraction: shapes and shadows, meaningless splashes of clashing color. The cloth now seemed to expand, mocking her, filling the room with the beautiful and terrible truth of her life, of her curse: None of it was real, and none of it mattered.

Only *he* mattered. The knight. He was *perfect*.

If she was cursed anyway, if the workmen and the scaffold came relentlessly closer, if they were so determined to ruin her by disrupting that boundary that encapsulated her life—why then, she would look out. She would see the knight with her own eyes and know the truth before the curse—whatever it was, whatever doom it held for her— came to pass.

First, though, she tore the tapestry from the loom, ripped apart every careful knot she'd made, sliced through it with her knife until the chamber was covered with a flurry of wool and silk. Fiber flew everywhere, a choking mess of it that made her laugh. The true worth of all her work, all this time, however much time it was. Colored bits of thread flashed as they floated through the air, catching bits of sunlight.

Then she fell to the floor and crawled. Her goal: the stone ledge of the window. The space within its arcing frame shone blindingly, the sun coming directly at her. She reached up, put her hands on the ledge. Gripped hard, pulled herself up, and looked out.

Where the images in the bronze mirror were blurry, wavering, uncertain, what she saw directly with her eyes was clear and sharp. The pale naked wood of the scaffolding, the brown and green tunics of the men working, passing to and fro across the newly made clearing around the tower. The brilliant blue of the sky—the blue thread she had been using to make skies was dull in comparison.

She passed over all this quickly, wanting only to see one thing, one solitary image: the knight in armor. He was tall; he was handsome. He stood with hands on hips, gazing upward. His smile was uplifting; his eyes shone with depth. She could see rivets and fluting in the steel across his chest and shoulders that she couldn't see before.

Leaning on the window ledge, she gazed her fill of him.

She had a hope, for just a moment, that nothing was going to happen. The curse wasn't real, and she wouldn't be punished in any way for looking, as she always believed she would be. She leaned out the window to feel the sun on her face, a fresh breeze on her skin. She smiled, and then she laughed, because the world was beautiful and she was free.

The knight saw her and raised a hand in salute. She started to wave back.

That was when the skin of her hands split and red flesh spilled out in a ropey mass, dripping blood.

An earthquake rocked the land, shaking the tower, rattling stones from the walls above her. Clouds gathered, blocking the sun, turning day to night. And she thought—ah, so this is the curse. So this is what happens if I look out the window.

And the monster that burst out of her swallowed the trappings of her mortal self.

He saw her, and she was lovely. Because of course she was, being a maiden in a tower in need of rescue.

She waved at him, laughing, and his heart sang. This was a worthy maiden. Perhaps this was fate, and they were meant to be together. He cupped his hands and started to shout at her, to ask how she fared and assure her that all would be well—

And then things got very confusing very quickly.

The maiden vanished. Or something. She was, apparently, instantly replaced by a spray of blood and a glabrous mass of dripping tentacles, writhing out from the window as if reaching for the sky itself. They curled and gripped like fingers around the edge of the window and ripped, tossing the stones away. The tower cracked like a snail's shell, and a massive, pulsing body oozed out. The thing was far larger than ought to have been contained by the tower that had until recently stood there.

It smelled of swamp and despair.

The chief castle builder came up to Lancelot, shoulders slumped, a defeated look in his eye. His men were running, screaming in terror. One of the tentacles grabbed one of the workers and thrust the poor screaming soul into what was presumably a mouth. It wasn't entirely clear.

"I told you," the chief castle builder said tiredly. "Cursed."

"Huh," Lancelot replied.

Well, he was here to either rescue maidens or slay monsters. He could no longer attempt the former, but at least he still had the latter. He drew his sword, which would have glinted nobly in the sun, but undulating black clouds had roiled in from every horizon and now covered the sun utterly. An unbreakable darkness fell upon the land.

Lancelot wanted to drop his weapon and weep uncontrollably, but that just wouldn't do. He was a *knight*. Of *Camelot*. And he was here to slay monsters. This encounter would be *legendary*.

He gave his sword a swing, and it whistled as it sliced the air. He squared his shoulders, set his jaw, and knew that this was what he'd been born for.

One of the dozen—three dozen? three hundred?—gray and veined tentacles came for him, cracking like a whip, curling as if weightless, ready to snatch him and squeeze until he popped. But Lancelot was ready. With a quick lateral cut and a slash down, he separated the tip of the offending limb from the rest of it, and stabbed it where it lay writhing on the ground. The monster groaned, a bone-leeching noise that rattled the very earth. Thunder and lightning rocked the air continuously.

The next awful limb attacked before he could catch his breath, and he dispatched this one as well. His heart was proud, his arm strong, and his sword true. He turned to the panic that had erupted throughout the clearing.

"Men! Draw weapons! To me, to me!"

But these were workmen, not knights and warriors. Not a trained soldier among them. These were men who might pick up a pitchfork to defend a homestead from marauders, but they were not his vassals to call to some greater need of war.

Still, at his voice they paused at the edge of incipient madness.

They looked at their hands and saw their tools, looked at Lancelot and saw his sword. And they saw what might be possible. They raised a cheer and turned to face the monster that was now sprawling over a great swath of countryside.

For a while they rallied. Axes, saws, awls, and hammers in hand, the workmen formed a line, slashing and stabbing until the thing's fetid blood soaked the ground. The shattered stone of the tower seemed to melt in the acid ooze of it. More tentacles grew to replace the old, but for a time they seemed to keep ahead of the onslaught, and drove back the creature from whence it came. They learned to brace against its howls and screams. They somehow grew accustomed to the stink of its slime.

But the thing had an eye. A great, muddy, golden eye. And when it opened and turned its gimlet gaze upon him with all the power of its unholy origin—that was when Lancelot finally dropped his sword and screamed.

And then it was over. All of it.

SIDEKICK

I was not sick before I came here.

The room is quiet except for the soft buzz of electronics—a ticking clock, a beeping monitor. The bed is soft, the linens comfortable, if thin. The opposite wall has a chart on a whiteboard that I can't quite read from where I lie. I wake up and instantly know this is a hospital room, but I don't remember how I got here. I try to be calm. Someone will explain all this.

Sure enough, a nurse comes in and bustles around the bed, checking monitors just outside my line of sight. I don't have any tubes or wires connected to me. No needles, no sensors. I brush both my arms and feel all around my head to be sure. None of this has anything to do with me.

I ask her why I'm here.

The nurse is a short woman, auburn hair primly tied back in a bun. Her scrubs have tiny cartoon rabbits on them. "You fell, don't you remember?"

Of course I don't. She knows I don't.

"You don't remember anything about the accident? Falling off the horse?"

I don't even remember going riding.

"You weren't wearing your helmet," she adds. "Why weren't you wearing your helmet?"

"But I always wear my helmet." I wouldn't ride without wearing my helmet; I never don't wear my helmet.

"Well, never mind, loss of memory is common with head injuries," she says and bustles back out of the room without explaining anything.

I don't even have a headache. I feel *fine*.

A doctor comes in next, a man in a white lab coat wearing a serious expression. I must have fallen asleep because I wake up when the door opens. I don't remember falling asleep.

"How are we doing?" he says, wearing a condescending smile. We? He's on his feet, I'm in bed, apparently with a head injury. There isn't any *we* here.

"I'm fine. I think I feel fine. Can I get up, walk around a little bit?"

"Not so fast," he says. "We're still making sure you're stable. For now I'd like to ask you a few questions."

"Okay." My voice sounds small. I'm not sure I can sound anything but small, lying in this bed.

"What do you remember about the accident?"

"I don't remember anything," I say, even though I know that's the wrong answer, an answer that will keep me here, in bed.

He tsks, shaking his head. Consults a clipboard sitting on a side table. "What's the first thing you remember, then?"

"I woke up when the nurse came in. I…was that a few hours ago? This morning? I'm not sure."

"So you're having trouble keeping track of time."

"Maybe if you could put a clock in here—"

"Has your boss been in to see you yet?"

My boss? "I'm not even sure he knows I'm in the hospital."

"Oh, he's been alerted. His information was listed as your emergency contact."

That doesn't sound right—my mother is my emergency contact, and why hasn't she been in to see me yet? I really want to see her. To see any familiar face.

"Do you have my phone?" I ask. "I'd like my phone. I could call him. And my mother. I'd really like to talk to my mom."

His smile is a kind mask. "We don't want you to get too excited, not yet."

"But I'm not—"

"Never mind that for now. With a head injury like yours, we don't like you to read anything or strain your eyes too much."

It sort of makes sense. Sort of.

He takes out a light pen and shines it in each of my eyes, clicking his tongue as if he's found something there he doesn't like.

"What's wrong?"

"How are you feeling?"

I'm starting to get a headache. "I'm okay. I think I'm okay."

"But you weren't wearing your helmet."

I hadn't been riding, I know I hadn't. My horse died ten years ago. I still miss her.

The doctor holds my wrist, taking my pulse. I assume he's taking my pulse. "What do you remember from before the accident? What was the last thing you remember doing before you woke up?"

"I think I was going to work…"

"What kind of work is it you do?" he asks conversationally, that fake smile still in place.

"I'm an administrative assistant."

"Oh? For what kind of business?"

"An accounting firm."

"You must get a lot of questions at tax time."

"Not really. I'm not an accountant myself, I just run the office."

"So you pass folks along to your boss?"

"He isn't really that kind of accountant," I say. Darren is an auditor and forensic accountant. Tax time isn't really a thing—he goes out on jobs year-round. "It's all pretty dull."

"Oh, I imagine not. If you're his assistant—"

"I just answer phones, stuff like that. Keep the office running."

"It would all fall apart without you, hmm?" He makes it sound like a joke but also sort of not.

The blandness of the questions and intensity of his stare make me nervous. I don't want to talk anymore.

"Your pulse is a little elevated," the doctor says seriously.

I look for a name tag. I don't find one. I don't know what to call him. "I might be a little nervous," I admit.

"I think we'd better keep you sedated for the next few days."

"But I'm feeling better." In fact, my new headache is getting worse.

The doctor pushes a button, and a nurse comes in with an IV stand and bag. I don't argue, because what if they're right?

The next time I wake up, the doctor is waiting for me, asking more questions.

He checks the IV bag, brushes his finger on the tape holding down the needle in my arm, and pretends to take my pulse again.

"Where did you say you worked again?"

"An accounting firm," I say wearily. "It's not very interesting."

"Can you tell me who your boss is?"

"He's Darren Bane. He's an accountant. An auditor."

"I mean who he really is?"

I shake my head, confused. "That's it, that's all he is, I told you."

"And who are you, Miss Smith?"

"I'm nobody. I just run his office."

"What do you mean, 'run his office'?"

"He's good at his job but he's not very practical, you know? I have to remind him to pay bills, I make sure there's coffee for the coffee maker—"

"Are you sure?"

"What do you mean, am I sure? Of course I'm sure."

"There's nothing else?"

I wince. "He also never remembers the network login. I have to reset his password a couple times a week."

"An administrative assistant," the doctor says flatly.

"Yes."

"Your pulse is elevated again," the doctor says, as if disappointed. "Do you know where Darren Bane is now?"

"No. But if you gave me my phone I could call him—"

"Get some rest for now. I think your injury may be a little worse than we thought. You really should have worn your helmet."

"But I didn't… I don't think…"

"You definitely seem agitated, Miss Smith. Maybe we ought to increase the dosage."

"No, I'm fine. I'm really fine."

The doctor leaves.

This time when I wake up, I'm strapped to the bed by my wrists and ankles, nearly immobilized. I don't panic. It seems a natural progression. The room is the same, smelling of antiseptic cleaner and exhaustion. The IV needle is still in my arm, a clear liquid dripping into it.

"Miss Smith, how are you today?"

I flinch because I hadn't heard the doctor come in. "I'm not feeling too good," I say honestly. I want to get up and walk around. I want to know how long I've been here.

"Well then. We just need to find out a few things, then we'll get you fixed right up."

"I don't think you ever told me your name," I say. "I don't even know what hospital I'm at."

He looms over me, smiling. "Now, don't worry about that. Just worry about getting well."

"Are you the doctor?"

A beat, and then, "I'm wearing the white coat, aren't I?"

That doesn't seem like a good answer. "I don't know what's wrong with me."

"You fell. Don't you remember?"

I still don't remember. I've fallen off lots of horses lots of times, but that was years ago, when I was a kid. When I still had a horse. And I would have worn my helmet.

"Miss Smith, tell me about Darren Bane."

"He's my boss," I say plaintively. "You know that. I don't know what else you need to know."

"He's out of the office a lot."

"He travels," I say. "He's an auditor. He does on-site audits."

"And you handle the office while he's gone."

"Well, sort of. It's not that big a deal. I get the mail and answer the phones and stuff. I'm his administrative assistant."

"Now, Miss Smith. Tell me the truth. What are you *really*? Just what is it you do for Darren Bane?"

I pull my wrists, kick my legs, but caught up in thick nylon and Velcro straps, they only move an inch. "He's an accountant. I'm the administrative assistant—"

"No. What are you really?"

"That's it, an administrative—"

"You're lying."

"I'm not—"

"What are you?"

I start crying, embarrassed and ashamed to be crying, sniffing hard as my nose clogs up.

"This doesn't have to be hard," the nameless doctor says. "Just tell me who you really are, and what you really do."

I've always been so sure that I could be strong if I needed to be. The kind of heroine I've read about. And here I am, crying wet, messy, painful tears.

"Miss Smith, I need to know—"

"All right, fine, fine! I'm a secretary! Just a secretary. A glorified secretary! I have a master's degree in literature and mostly I just make coffee and go out for dry cleaning. That's it. I mean—I've read *Finnegans Wake* but this is the only job I could get! I'm sorry!"

The doctor frowns. I sniff, catch my breath. Think maybe I've stopped crying but I can't feel my face anymore. The clicking of some monitor fills the silence.

"You're lying," he says finally.

"I know, I should have said it right off, I'm a secretary, just a secretary."

"I don't believe you," the doctor says curtly.

"But—"

"No one's read *Finnegans Wake.*"

"But I did, I wrote a paper on it, on anticipatory postmodernism, it even got published, and now I'm just a secretary—"

The doctor turns and leaves. The door shuts firmly behind him.

Being scared is probably normal when you're stuck in a hospital bed. But I'm not really sick. At least, I didn't start out sick. This time I'm woken by a bright light, and the expressions on their faces are no longer kind. The questions continue, and what I learn: these people, whoever they are, are on a deadline.

"Where is Darren Bane?"

"How am I supposed to know—"

"You work for him, don't you? You must know what he really is—"

The doctor—the man in the white coat, rather—and nurse are both in on it.

"Is he nice to work for?" the nurse asks conversationally as she changes out the IV bag. Like this is normal.

"I guess. He gives out Christmas bonuses and things."

"Do you ever travel with him?"

"No, I take care of the office." I've said this a dozen times already. "So are you a neurosurgeon or what?"

The doctor seems taken aback. "Why do you say that?"

"You keep saying I have a head injury, that I fell off a horse. So I figure you must be a neurosurgeon, if there's something wrong with my head, you must know what—"

"Miss Smith, I need to you tell me everything you know about Darren Bane."

"He drives a BMW," I say. "And even if he asked me I wouldn't date him."

He blinks. "Why not?"

"Because he's never around. And when he is he's irritable. I don't think he gets enough sleep."

The doctor leaves, and even the nurse looks after him, surprised. But he returns just a moment later carrying what looks like a phone, and I think, finally. I can call my mom, I can call Darren and tell him these people really want to talk to him—

The nurse's eyes widen. "Are you sure?"

"We're running out of options."

He holds the device—which is not a phone, it doesn't have a screen—flat in his hand and presses a button. A light comes on in the center and projects up. Within the light blurry shapes appear, then resolve into a clear image. A movie plays in full color and three dimensions.

"What is that?" I say, gaping. "It's…it's a hologram, isn't it? I've never…is that even possible?" Clearly it's possible—it's right in front of me.

The holographic movie shows a fight. A group of maybe six men wearing leather jackets and balaclavas are gathered on a dark, damp street. At night, the details are obscure, but their reactions to a powerful figure dropping into the middle of them are plain. They try to overpower the man, but he's too fast, delivering a roundhouse kick even as he smacks two heads together, and those movements flow into a smooth pivot, another kick, and a clean punch that flattens its recipient.

The man, the amazing fighter, wears a formfitting suit of black tinged with silver. It might be made of leather, sleek and supple, with some armored plating. He has on a mask that covers his head. He's like a shadow given form, and in short order all his opponents lie writhing on the ground.

"Is this a movie?" I ask. It's probably a movie.

"No, Miss Smith, it isn't."

He's right. The angle's all wrong, taken from too high up, as if from a security camera mounted on a building, and the frame never moves.

"Who are you people?" I demand. "How are you even doing this?"

"Can you tell me who that is?" the doctor asks.

"How am I supposed to know?"

"The man in the mask is Darren Bane. Now can you tell me where he is?"

I blink at him, then stare at the image, which has started over again, the masked figure punching and kicking his way through the mob of thugs again. That my boss, the accountant Darren Bane, is some kind of masked crime-fighting vigilante is the least surprising thing about all this. All the business trips, his apparent lack of social life and yet also lack of free time, the occasional days he comes to the office with bruises and stiff joints and blames it on racquetball—

"I don't know anything," I say. Maybe I should have seen it. Maybe I should have known. But really, what makes more sense, crime-fighting vigilante or racquetball? "He told me he was playing racquetball."

"The problem," says the man who I'm pretty sure isn't really a doctor, "is that crime-fighting vigilantes usually have sidekicks. And you know Darren Bane's business better than anyone. No one is closer to him than you."

But I'm just a secretary. No, that isn't right… I'm the administrative assistant. I manage the office. Does that make me a sidekick?

"But I'm not—"

There's an explosion just then. But I don't remember it, not at first. Head injury. They tell me about it later.

"What's the last thing you remember?"

I don't actually remember the last thing I remember, not anymore. I woke up in a hospital bed, and before that I woke up in a hospital bed.

"I think I got kidnapped," I say groggily. My head hurts, for real this time. It's not my imagination. "These guys, I have no idea who they are but they made me think I was in the hospital, and they kept asking about my boss, and they showed me this video only it wasn't really a video, it was a hologram. They kept asking questions but I swore I didn't know anything."

A man in a white coat is standing by my hospital bed. A different man than the last time, ten years older and thirty pounds heavier, and maybe this one really is a doctor. The tight set to his jaw suggests he is frustrated. "Do you remember the explosion?"

"Explosion?"

I have to think for a moment, and realize that yes I do remember. I remember the explosion that blew the side wall of the hospital room inward. A man appeared. I couldn't see his face, he wore a form-fitting armored suit, his face obscured behind a mask. He came straight to the bed and unfastened the restraints. I was free, I was finally free. And I was sick. Really sick. "I don't think I can stand up," I'd told him, and he seemed prepared for this, carefully sliding out the IV needle, taping over the wound, pulling out other wires and monitors. The medical devices were all screaming, shouting came from down the corridor, and the masked vigilante scooped me up into his arms and there was no place I more wanted to be.

Maybe I will say yes if Darren Bane ever asks me out on a date.

"Hold on," he said, but I was already clinging to him, arms around his neck. He was close enough that I could smell him, some kind of spicy aftershave blended with the sweat of heroism. A gun fired. I grit my teeth and hid my face. Which meant I didn't see what happened, but I felt flames, heard more gunfire and a muffled voice shouting, "This way!" Then we were in sunlight, I was outside, in fresh air, away from the hospital stink. But all my limbs felt like butter and I couldn't move. The masked vigilante, who sheltered me all this time, whispered that everything was going to be all right, that I was safe now, and I believed him, and we were moving away and away—

And I passed out again. I hadn't had anything to eat in days and I hadn't even noticed. Now I'm here. In a hospital bed. Again.

"Do you have a phone?" I ask. "I really need to call my boss. I really need to talk to him." I have so many questions.

"Your boss knows you're here. That's what I'm trying to get you to remember. There was an explosion at the office."

What?

"A gas line," the doctor continues. "You were working late. You were able to call 911, but you have a very bad concussion—"

But that would mean—" I really need to call my boss. Can I have a phone?"

"With a head injury like yours we really don't like you to strain your eyes too much."

"But. Maybe. I could just tell you the number, and you can call—"

"All in good time. For now, I'd like to ask you a few questions. What can you tell me about Darren Bane?"

"He's my boss," I say. "He's an accountant, a forensic accountant. At least I thought he was." My brow furrows.

The doctor takes my wrist with chilled fingers and frowns. "Your pulse is slightly elevated."

"Of course it is!" I'm groggy this time, really groggy. And maybe it was all true, maybe I really was sick, and I should just lie back, let it all fade. But I get out of bed anyway because I don't really have a choice.

"Wait a minute, Miss Smith!"

I walk right past him. Or rather I kind of sway and stumble, with a hand on the bed, then a wall, then the doorknob. A cloth hospital gown hangs loosely on me, flapping around my legs, open in the back, and I don't care. The doctor reaches for me but doesn't actually take hold, which makes me think he really is a doctor. He really is worried.

I open the door and walk out, and I don't know what I'm expecting. A sound stage. A warehouse. A wall held up with two-by-four struts, proving that this is all a fake, a sham. But I'm in a hospital hallway. A normal, institutional hospital hallway with a tile floor and fluorescent lights and cheerful signs on the wall ordering people to wash their hands. And in a chair shoved up against the wall, reading a magazine, is Darren Bane. He looks like what he is, what I always thought he was, a slick hotshot businessman filling out his perfectly tailored suit. He looks up at me and raises an eyebrow.

"He told me you weren't here," I exclaim.

"He thought you weren't strong enough yet for visitors."

I start to say something angry, close my mouth. Glare.

"Out with it," he says.

"This is a stunt." I try to yell, but I'm too tired for that. "You brought me here to try to make me think this was all a hallucination so that you can convince me you aren't really a masked vigilante, that I somehow imagined the whole thing, when it's not true. I mean it is true. And you have enemies, and you were probably keeping all this secret because of some idea that if I knew, I would be in danger, but, well, look what happened, I'm in danger anyway! And here I've been keeping up your front this whole time and…and… I want a raise. And a better job title. I want to be office manager. I mean, you don't even know the office email login, you need me to do that. And I'm sorry, I'm getting dizzy, I need to sit down."

He deftly stands and guides me to sit in the chair. I put my head between my knees for a minute and when the floor stops shimmering, I straighten and look at him. He smells like aftershave and heroism.

"Office manager, hmm?"

"Yes," I say.

"All right."

This seems easier than I was expecting. "And the raise?"

"Of course." He names a number that makes two hospital stays, even if one of them was fake, seem worthwhile. "Okay then. I'll see you at work, when you're back on your feet."

"Okay."

He brushes his jacket off, smooths back a strand of hair that wasn't out of place, and walks away to the elevators.

The doctor is standing at the doorway. "What did you say your job was?"

Both of us are still watching Darren Bane's departure, the suave poise of him. When I open my mouth to answer, to state my relationship to my boss, I realize the terrible truth. My *actual* new job title.

I say instead, "It's complicated."

ORIGIN STORY

Living in Commerce City, odds are you're going to get caught up in something someday—pinned down in the crossfire of some epic battle between heroes who can fly and villains with ray guns, held captive in a hostage crisis involving an entire football stadium, or even trapped by a simple jewelry heist or bus hijacking.

When my turn came, I got stuck in a bank robbery.

I was waiting in line to make a deposit when a hole opened up in the ceiling. A glowing green laser light traced a perfect circle, and that section of ceiling dropped to the floor, scattering the line of people underneath in a cloud of dust and noise. I was too far back to really see what was happening, just that there was debris and screaming, some of which might have been mine. Then Techhunter rappelled through the hole, wielding a laser pistol and shouting at everyone to get down and lie still. We did.

He was just one guy. No henchmen, no partners. That was Techhunter's M.O. in the news stories I'd read. He worked alone, with only his machines as backup. This time, he had a swarm of hovering metallic balls zooming down the hole in the ceiling with him. They fanned out around the room and trained tiny cannons on everyone. They probably shot lasers or tranquilizer darts. Surely in a place like Commerce City, with so many vigilantes and criminal gangs battling each other, bank tellers would be trained how to handle situations like this, but the ones here all stepped back from their counters, arms in the air, staring at Techhunter with trembling gazes. As if they didn't live in Commerce City, where this kind of thing happened on a monthly basis at least.

Techhunter didn't ask for the manager to open any safes; he just drilled through the locks with his laser pistol, collected cash and emptied a pair of safety deposit boxes into a hard-sided case. He wore wide goggles that hid most of his face, and a headset with all kinds of wires and antennae sticking from it, probably what he used to control all his devices. His suit was made of some slick material, supple as leather but appearing to be much stronger, probably armored. Pants, tall boots, padded shirt, and a fitted trench coat, all in a midnight blue so dark it looked black, except when the light caught it right.

Everyone cowered. Except me. I couldn't help it, because by that time I'd had a chance to really look at him. The superhero stalker website Rooftop Watch had posted a half dozen or so pictures of Techhunter over the last couple of years, blurry action shots in semi-darkness, and I hadn't paid much attention because he was just another guy in a mask. Now, seeing him in person, the way he moved, smoothly and urgently; the way he studied the room and pursed his thin, slightly chapped lips—it was all familiar. I should have thought it was just a coincidence, but I was sure. Even under those face-obscuring goggles, I knew him.

Then he looked across the room at the one person not cowering in his presence. Through the goggles, he caught my gaze. His lips parted and he froze, just for a second. *He* knew *me*.

Before I could call his name—or think that maybe I shouldn't call his name, or find any way at all to ask what the hell he was doing here, a masked villain with a super-high-tech armory—the guy next to me reached out. While I'd been staring at Techhunter, this unassuming young businessman with a goatee and a red tie had very slowly and carefully drawn a gun out from inside his jacket. Was he an undercover cop or just paranoid? Didn't know, didn't care, because he proceeded to take aim at my old boyfriend.

I grabbed the gun out of his hand and threw it across the room. He wasn't expecting that, and he stared at me in consternation, stammering out, "What—"

And I was kneeling there, shocked at what I had done, wondering if this made me a bad guy now. Again, Techhunter and I looked at each other, and I started to call out, "Jas—"

But he shouted me down. "You—get up!"

I knew that voice. It was definitely Jason. I stood, and then it all happened very fast. Police sirens blared—the whole incident had only started a couple of minutes ago—and some guy on a megaphone shouted at him to stand down and lower his weapons, and someone else yelled that Techhunter had a hostage. Remote gun spheres altered course to zoom toward the front of the bank and aim their weapons outward.

Techhunter—Jason?—went into action, hauling the case's strap over his shoulder as he wrapped his arm around my waist and pulled me close. He clipped himself to the rope, then clipped me, and at some command the thing wound up on a winch and carried us to the roof of the bank and then into his stealth hovercraft. The floating gun spheres swarmed back up with him. A dozen police cars surrounded the bank now, and cops poured out of them with weapons drawn, ready to fire until they saw me, the hostage. The hatch at the bottom of the ship closed, Jason went to the cockpit, pulled back on a control stick, and I fell over as the thing tipped back and zoomed away.

Techhunter was not known for kidnapping, but I must have been special.

I wasn't hurt, wasn't even scared. I was just waiting for him to stop being busy so I could ask what the hell was going on. The ship was small. The cargo area, which held the rope winch and a few equipment cases, wasn't any bigger than the back of an SUV. The cockpit was one bucket seat surrounded by control panels, looking out through panels of a wraparound windshield.

We flew for what felt like a long time.

The last time I saw Jason Trumble was the week before high school graduation, right after he found out he wouldn't be allowed to graduate because he had too many unexcused absences from gym class. He punched his hand through the window between the principal's office and reception, shattering the glass with the sound of ringing bells, and marched out, right past where I was waiting for him, dripping blood along the way and not caring. I called after him, and he turned around to look at me. My heart fluttered a bit, thinking, *he really does care, he really does like me.* But then he scowled and kept going out the front doors, never to return. I got a birthday card from him a few months later. He said he was joining the army, which sounded like a bad idea to me, but he didn't give me a return address, and he hadn't answered his email since he left, so I had no way to tell him that.

I decided maybe he didn't care after all, and I moved on.

That was eight years ago. Sometime between then and now, he'd become a supervillain. On reflection, I wasn't surprised, not exactly.

I waited for Jason to say something.

The ship finally came to rest on something solid, street or helipad or garage or something. I was able to sit up and arrange myself more comfortably. The engine whined to silence, the hum of electricity ceased, and in the cockpit Jason flipped a last few switches before turning around. He seemed to take a deep breath, as if steeling himself, before crouching to enter the cargo hold.

He took off the goggles and headset, and it really was him, his sharp nose and thin eyebrows, spiky brown hair and scowling expression.

"Sorry about that," he said. "You okay?"

"Jason, I—" For just a second, I teared up, but the moment passed. "I thought you died or something. What happened to you?"

He looked at me for a long time, his expression distant, thoughtful, before saying, "It's good to see you, Mary."

And just like that we fell against each other, hugging, like none of the time since high school had passed. After that long, impossible hug, we sat side by side, knees pulled up, and he explained.

"I tried to join the army. Washed out of basic. I guess I should have known that wasn't going to work out. I…kicked around for a while. Here and there, this and that. Picked up some things." He glanced around the ship, regarding his gear with a pleased, proud smile.

"Why didn't you write? Why didn't you tell me what happened to you?"

"I didn't want you to worry," he said, deadpan.

"*Jason.*"

"Do you…um…want a drink or something? I only have water and coffee and a couple of energy drinks. Can't really *drink* drink while I'm out in the ship. You know."

"Coffee, I guess."

We drank coffee he poured from a thermos into Styrofoam cups. I had another flashback of us in high school, at the diner after an all-ages show or late movie, sucking on coffee and planning to take over the world.

It had been a joke, I thought.

"Um. I never expected to run into you like that," he said. "I thought I was seeing things, but you just kept staring at me."

"I'd recognize you anywhere."

"Yeah, but what were you *doing* there?"

"Making a deposit. Going to the bank, like a normal person."

A bit of the light went out of his eyes. "So that's what you are, now? Normal?"

He said it like I was the one who'd been committing crimes.

I'd been doing really well with my own tailoring and dressmaking business. I was designing, making custom evening gowns and wedding dresses. A couple more high-end gigs like that, and I'd be on my way. I was proud of myself, but I couldn't read Jason's expression, which seemed blank, uncomprehending. Old high-school Jason would have accused me of selling out, making cocktail dresses for society bitches, hustling for their dime like some peasant. But old high-school Jason had left me behind. I spent a lot of months—years, maybe even— missing him and wondering where he'd gone. Then I just couldn't, anymore. Would new Jason, with his unreal gear and flashy persona, understand that?

"Well," I said. "And look at you. You're famous. Techhunter, one of the archvillains of Commerce City."

"Yeah. Who'd have thought?"

I always figured he'd either take over the world or die in a gutter, and since I never heard what happened, I figured it was the latter. I should know better than to make assumptions.

For the next minute or so, we drank coffee in silence. We never had a problem coming up with things to say in the old days. The old days— as if we were really that old, as if it really had been so long. It hadn't, on the scale of things, but it sure felt like it.

"I'm sorry," he said finally, abruptly. I stared at him, not sure what to say. "For not letting you know what happened to me. For not telling you where I was. I figured…I just figured you were better off without me. That it'd be better if I left you alone."

I wanted to punch him. I had to think about it, but then I did it, slamming my fist into his shoulder. My knuckles banged against the armor plate protecting his bicep.

"Ow," he muttered, rubbing his arm, just as I hissed and studied my skinned knuckles.

"Jerk," I said. I looked around his ship, gray and sleek, like something from outer space, with levers and monitors, winches and crates holding who knew what, hatch covers and control panels. The hovering gun spheres nested in a rack on one wall, lurking ominously. Had he built all this? Found it and co-opted it for himself? And why did he rob banks, when he could use all this to be a hero?

"I didn't do it for the money," he said, when he caught me staring at the case of loot he'd taken from the bank. "I don't need money, it's just to confuse them. But the safety deposit boxes—"

"I don't think you should tell me," I said, gesturing for him to stop, closing my eyes, as if I could unsee it. I should have waited until tomorrow to drop off that deposit. But no. I wouldn't have missed this for anything.

"Right. You're right."

More silence. Too much to say, rather than too little, maybe.

"And I'm not really trying to take over the world," he said, as if he had to explain himself. "I'm not that ambitious. Not yet, anyway." He showed that sly grin again.

A beeping alarm drew him back to the cockpit, where he checked a monitor. "Police band," he explained. "They'll sweep the area soon. I have to get moving." He swallowed, licked his lips. Just like he had when he asked me to prom. "Would you—do you want to come with me?"

He'd said later that asking me to prom was the most difficult, bravest thing he'd ever done, not because he was afraid I'd say no, but because he was afraid to go to prom at all. He was sure he wouldn't be welcome. He didn't think it would even be fun. No matter what he did, he'd be made fun of, pushed to the fringes, like he always was. But he wanted to show that they couldn't keep him out, either. So just for once, he did the normal thing and asked a girl to prom, and of course I said yes because I'd been waiting for him to ask, and we hatched a plan together. I made our outfits, his tuxedo and my knee-length cocktail dress, out of leather scavenged from thrift store handbags and biker jackets. We looked wicked, in patched-together leather in a dozen different shades of brown and black. He found a black lily for my corsage, and I made a boutonniere from old resistors and wires. God, did people stare at us, but once we got to the hotel ballroom we behaved ourselves so no one could kick us out. We even had a good time.

I thought—I'd thought back then that things could only get better, but then came that meeting in the principal's office, and that was the last straw for Jason, who must have decided that not only were the rules not fair, they weren't worth dealing with at all.

I wished I'd known what to say to him, then. Or that he might have thought then of asking me to run away with him. I'd said yes to prom, hadn't I?

Shaking my head was hard. My neck felt stiff, and I wondered if I pulled a muscle when he winched me up on the rope. Or if this was just hard.

"I can't," I said. "My business is taking off. I've worked too hard. I can't leave all that. Even if it is *normal.*"

He nodded as if he really did understand, as if he hadn't really expected me to say yes. "Yeah, okay. So…you must have a boyfriend."

That was his problem. He made too many assumptions.

That anxious-sounding beeping from the police monitor sounded again. All serious, he went to check, flipped a couple of switches and held a hand to his ear—listening to a signal coming in through an earbud.

"They're getting close. I'll let you out, but I should probably tie you up. They'll treat you like a victim then, and not an accomplice—"

"No," I said, the word just bursting out of me like a gunshot.

He stopped, his expression neutral. "No, what?"

"No, I don't have a boyfriend." I had never really wanted one, after he left.

He had this look in his eyes, hungry and angry, and I didn't know if I'd given him the right answer, or the wrong one. He moved back to the cargo compartment, was just a few inches away from me, a length of rope in hand. He smiled apologetically. "Then can I maybe see you again?"

I nodded, and by some mutual signal that I didn't recognize, we came together. His hand pressed around my waist, the length of our torsos fit together, my hands on his shoulders, our lips, kissing. A slow, careful, melting kiss. Both his arms wrapped around my back, me clinging to the slippery fabric of his trenchcoat. Then we came up for air.

Just like the old days, except so much sadder, because we knew now what we'd lost.

We had to let go when we heard the police sirens through the hull of his hovercraft.

In addition to tying nylon cord around my wrists and ankles, he blindfolded me, explaining carefully what he was doing as he did it, tying the cloth over my eyes, securing me to the rope and winch, gently setting me on what felt like a concrete sidewalk. Giving my hand a squeeze as he released me.

The hatch hissed as it slid shut, the engine whined as the ship climbed away, and I listened until I couldn't.

The police arrived just a minute later.

They were very nice to me, because I was the victim. Jason had been right about that. I sat in an empty conference room at the police station, a blanket over my shoulders and a paper cup of bitter coffee in my hands, waiting for someone to arrive to take a statement. I was assured it wouldn't take long, that it wouldn't be difficult. They asked if I wanted a social worker or victim rights advocate with me. I said no.

A pair of detectives arrived, a man and a woman, both in their thirties and looking haggard, like they'd been working for a long time without sleep. They sat across from me, and the woman set down a manila folder stuffed to bursting with records.

They asked the standard questions. My name, why I was at the bank, what happened there, why Techhunter had picked me, and what had happened after. Did I know where he'd taken me? Did he say anything about where he was going? About what he stole from the bank and why? And so on, and I didn't know anything, and I said so. The detectives nodded, resigned.

"Did he tell you his name? Who he really is under the costume?" the man asked, and I knew I was in trouble. I could feel my face blush and my stomach turn over. They must have heard my stomach turn over.

"No," I answered truthfully, because Jason hadn't told me. I'd just known.

"Can you tell us anything about him? Anything that might lead to identifying him?" he asked, and again I didn't really feel like I was lying when I said no.

Then the woman pulled a photo from the file folder and slid it across the table to me. "Do you remember this, Mary?"

It was our formal picture from prom, the two of us side by side in the patchwork leather outfits I'd made, only Jason was snarling and flipping off the camera with both hands, and I was hanging on his arm and laughing. The photographer didn't bother trying to get us to stand still and be nice, just snapped the picture and took our ten bucks for copies. Mine was in my scrapbook back home, which meant this was Jason's copy, and I wondered how they got it. Or maybe the photographer had saved an extra proof or something. I wasn't going to ask.

We looked so young. So bony and new, and I wouldn't say we looked particularly happy, but we were something, and it was good.

"Yes, I remember that," I answered, and the catch in my voice made me sound vulnerable and worthy of sympathy, I hoped.

The woman spoke kindly. "Mary, what would you say if I told you that we suspect that Techhunter may be Jason Trumble? That he may have taken you hostage because he knew you?"

"I would say that makes a lot of sense." I hoped my watering eyes made my story sound more true.

"Did he reveal himself to you? Give you any sign that he was Jason and that he knew you? Did he say anything that made you suspect?"

Everything, I didn't say. I shook my head and touched the edge of the picture, like I was mourning him. I could have told them anything, that he didn't look anything like that skinny kid in the picture anymore, that he used a machine to disguise his voice, that I couldn't recognize anything under his goggles. But they assumed all that, so I didn't have to say anything. And that's how I became a bad guy. Henchwoman to a supervillain, and weirdly that was okay.

"If Techhunter contacts you again, you'll let us know?" the woman said, and I nodded. The man handed over a tissue, and I scrubbed my eyes.

They let me go. But I assume they're watching me, and that my phones are tapped and my computer hacked and all that. I'm not really even angry about it, because of course, and if it were any other former girlfriend of any other supervillain I'd think it was the right thing to do. But I also can't stand the idea that they'll use me to catch Jason. So I mostly don't talk about him at all, and I hope he doesn't contact me. At the same time, I hope he does. I constantly watch for little flying drones, buzzing as they follow me, and wait for him to make his move.

But he's too smart for that, so he hasn't.

Yet.

WHERE WOULD YOU BE NOW

K ath sat on the roof of the beat-up Tesla S, legs draped down the back window, shotgun in both hands, looking out into the dark for whatever might hurt them. They'd come forty miles or so to an encampment in what had once been a park with a picnic area and duck pond. A playground with a plastic slide and jungle gym was still intact, though weeds came up through the bark mulch footing. A collection of trucks and campers clustered here, circled together with space for a campfire in the middle. The fire was banked now. Some tents and lean-tos had been set up a little further out, along with a couple of rickety sheds. In summer, people didn't need much more shelter than that. Winter, the camp would pick up and move south, if they could get the gas for it. Getting hard to find gas, though. The place was starting to look permanent. One of the trailers had a chicken coop built next to it, and a couple of roosting chickens were visible, feathers plumped out. The camp probably housed about thirty, but this late, everyone had gone to bed.

The packed-dirt mounds of four graves were lined up outside the circle of campers. The doctors didn't ask about them, the ones they couldn't help.

Turned away from the light, Kath kept watch. Nothing around the area moved. No one seemed inclined to charge in and grab such a valuable commodity as a doctor.

They'd parked the Tesla next to a medium-sized RV, from which came the groans of a woman in labor. Only this box of a room was lit up with candles and lanterns. The waiting and noise of effort made the air thick. The tenor of the groans had changed over the last twenty minutes, becoming more urgent, and also more exhausted. Kath could try to peek in the door, at the woman tucked up on her cot, straining. But she just listened.

"You've got this. One more push."

That was Melanie's voice. Did Dr. Dennis have her handling this delivery? She usually assisted him.

One more loud groan, then came silence. Kath held her breath until a tiny wail sounded, the new baby successfully announcing itself. A ruckus followed, the handful of people in the RV talking over each other, making admiring noises.

Unless something went wrong in the next little while, which could involve anything from the mother bleeding out to the baby showing some kind of illness or injury, Dennis and Melanie would wrap up and they could be on their way. Might be smarter to wait until dawn to make the trip back to the clinic. But the road between here and there was still passable, and Kath wanted to get home.

The light from the open door changed as figures stood in front of it. Dr. Dennis was standing with the thirty-something bearded man who'd summoned them here that morning. Dennis was giving him instructions.

"We've still got vaccines lying around. Bring her to the clinic in a couple months, we can give her a good start." The man, presumably the father, nodded with a distracted air. Leaning forward a bit, Kath could peer through the doorway and catch a glimpse of the camper's interior. The new mother was there, nested on a narrow couch, sweat matting her hair to her face, sheets tumbled around her. Melanie was helping her bundle the new baby against her skin, probably explaining everything she could about nursing in a handful of minutes. The mother didn't look up at what Dennis was saying.

They might or might not bring their baby to get her shots. They might decide they had bigger problems than worrying about measles or whooping cough.

Dr. Dennis came down the aluminum steps and paced a moment, hands on hips, looking into the night air. "Everything okay?"

"Yeah. No trouble," Kath said.

"Good. I want to get out of here as soon as we can."

So he was on edge, too. The unfamiliar settlement, the warm thick night, might draw out people they didn't want to talk to.

"You okay, Doctor?"

"Six months. I give that baby six months, based on the condition of the rest of the camp. It's so goddamn pointless."

Dennis and the other doctors at the clinic went over the statistics all the time. Without proper nutrition, clean water, medicine, without so many little necessities, infant mortality spiked. And there didn't seem to be anything they could do about it. If they were in the area, maybe one of the doctors could come out to vaccinate. Or maybe the parents really would bring the baby to the clinic.

The man returned to the door and handed over a threadbare pillowcase, half-filled. "Here. It's what we can spare. Thank you. Thank you for coming."

Grimly, Dr. Dennis took the makeshift sack by its bunched-up neck. "You're welcome. Just keep her as safe and healthy as you can, right?"

Dennis took a quick look in the sack, which Kath knew would be filled with canned goods, maybe some wire or screws, some glue. Odds and ends. Whatever salvage the parents thought worth the doctor's attention. Barter. Dennis used to get paid thousands of dollars for delivering a baby.

He looked up. "Kind of a weird question. Do you have any golf balls?"

The man pursed his lips and shook his head. "No, I don't think so."

"Well if you find any, maybe save them for me?"

"Yeah. Yeah, sure."

Two other women came to the doorway to look out. One of them was pregnant, maybe five months. She seemed worried, brow creased, lips tight, hands laced over belly. As if she could use her fingers to cage her unborn child to keep it safe. The other woman looked tired.

Dennis frowned at them. "You all aren't using any birth control at all around here, are you?"

Both women cringed, and the man crossed his arms. "Not like we can pop into Walgreens for condoms."

"It's just…never mind."

The man added, "I mean, so many people have died—don't we need to think about repopulating—"

"Oh Jesus fuck, *no*! Look, repopulating the planet or whatever can take care of itself. You—you just worry about keeping the people you already have safe and healthy. *Fed.* Grow some fucking potatoes!"

For just a moment the man's glowering gaze hardened. He was thinking of trouble, of taking the doctor down a notch for the outburst. Kath straightened, shifting the shotgun on her lap. To show she was watching.

He backed off. "We're trying, here. We're *trying.*"

Dennis sighed and came around to the other side of the car to wait for Melanie.

She emerged a moment later, shrugging the strap of an equipment bag over her shoulder and pushing a strand of black hair out of her eyes. She looked the most tired of all, even more than the mother, who at least was smiling when Kath glimpsed her.

Kath hopped off the car and opened the back door. "You okay?" she asked.

"I think so," she said, sighing. "Doc made me handle the delivery on this one."

"How was it?"

Melanie shook her head, her eyes widening in a look of half-panicked disbelief. "It's a lot different when the baby is falling into your own hands. I just kept thinking, God, don't drop it." She closed her eyes and sucked in a breath. "I hope everything stays okay."

Kath touched her shoulder. "Let's get out of here."

Melanie practically fell into the back seat, and Dennis started the motor and pulled away. Kath rode in the front passenger seat. Literally shotgun. That had stopped being clever a while back. She kept the window rolled halfway down and listened for the sound of approaching engines.

"You did great," Dennis said, glancing at his assistant in the rearview mirror. "You should have asked them to name the baby after you."

"No, that's okay. What'd they give you?" She went through the bag, to the sound of cans knocking together. "Eh, not bad. A couple boxes of nails. We can always trade that back out. Canned peaches." She paused, looked quizzical, and drew out a glass jar. "Capers. There's a jar of capers in here. They're organic."

"Organic capers," Dennis snorted. "We're saved."

Dennis kept the headlights dimmed to save the battery. If there'd been enough moonlight, he'd have shut off the lights entirely. But the roads had gotten too hazardous, full of potholes and debris, to risk going entirely dark. Still, the doctor didn't see the three kids standing in their path.

"Stop!" Kath screamed when she realized those shapes weren't odd shadows but children, one older gripping the hands of two little ones, there in the middle of the road, unmoving. Like they intended to get run over.

The car lurched to a stop, skidded a few feet. The bag of loot fell clattering to the floor, and Melanie braced herself on the seat. Kath was already out the door, with Dennis calling after her.

The kids stared back at her quietly. Their eyes were sunken, their cheeks hollow. It could have just been odd shadows cast by the dim headlights, but Kath didn't think so. They were hungry, starving. She scanned around for an adult, maybe a caravan they might have wandered off from. But they seemed so purposeful, the way they looked back at her, their eyes round and shining. They didn't seem lost.

"Hey, what're you guys doing here? Are you okay?" She tucked the shotgun under her arm, muzzle down, and approached them.

The older child looked like a girl, stringy brown hair in a loose braid, her eyes big and unblinking. Kath thought she was around eight, then revised up—ten, and malnourished. The other two might have been anywhere from two to five. Upright, but still uncertain in their movements. They clung to the older girl, gripping each hand and hugging her legs. All three wore T-shirts and loose pants. Only the oldest had shoes, dirty sneakers, toes poking through holes.

Kath inched closer, trying to look friendly and harmless even with a gun under her arm, but she stopped short of reaching out. Both Dennis and Melanie had left the car as well.

"It's okay," Kath said softly. "We're not going to hurt you, I just want to find out what's wrong."

The oldest child licked her lips. "She told us to stand here. She told us to wait for the doctor to come and then go with him to the clinic. She said you'd take care of us."

"Who? Who said?"

Her lips pursed, the girl didn't answer. Kath thought she was about to cry, but she just kept staring, any kind of emotion, any response, locked up.

Kath tried again. "Where'd you come from? From the camp back there? From somewhere else?" It had to be the camp, to know that they'd be driving back this way.

"She just said to wait here. She said you'd take care of us."

How did they know that? How could they be sure? Could have been anyone that came along the road here, and the girl seemed to know it. She was trying to be firm, to be confident. But her lip trembled, and her grip on the little kids' hands was white-knuckled. She might have known just how dangerous this was, trusting in the good will of strangers.

Dennis had gotten out a flashlight and panned it around, scanning broken-down buildings and debris-strewn streets in all directions. No movement, nobody watching, nothing. Whoever had abandoned the kids here had fled.

"We need to get moving," Kath said. She was the guard on this run, but Dennis was in charge. It was his call.

"Jesus Christ. Okay, fine. Everybody in the car."

The littlest one started crying. At what in particular, Kath couldn't say. Maybe it was just general exhaustion. She could understand that.

"What's your name?" Kath asked.

"Chloë. These are Tom and Dakota." She sounded relieved. Her shoulders had lowered a notch.

"I'm Kath. Let's go."

The two little ones fell asleep as soon as the car doors closed, and Kath marveled. How trusting, to climb into a car with strangers and somehow feel safer. This was a different set of rules than what she grew up with. The girl, Chloë, sat in the middle of the back seat, arms draped over both little ones, staring straight ahead.

Dennis drove with both hands on the wheel, clenched. Melanie also fell asleep, not looking at all peaceful. She was going to have a good cry later, Kath was sure.

"Where would you be now?" Dennis asked after a long stretch of silence. His profile was shadow.

"Hm," Kath said. "College. Maybe I'd be at a party. Getting drunk? I dunno."

His smile brightened his voice. "Getting in trouble. Sounds good. I approve."

"Maybe I'd be studying for a test. Would it be exam time right about now?"

"Naw, you should go to the party. Have some fun."

"Where would you be?" she asked in turn.

"Palm Springs. The back nine at Indian Wells. With a Corona in the cup holder of my cart."

"Golfing in the middle of the night?"

"Well, no, not golfing right this minute. But I guess that's where I'd rather be. I suppose that's cliché, the doctor who'd rather be golfing."

"You think it's still there? The golf course?"

He shook his head, a scrap of movement in the otherwise still night. "Even if the grass hasn't all died it wouldn't be getting groomed."

They drove on a little while, tires crunching on pitted asphalt.

"I wish you'd had the chance to go to college," he said. "Even just a year or two. I'm sorry."

"It's okay," she said, because it was what she always said. The entire concept of college was becoming abstract.

Her older brother Eddie had gone to college. He'd gone back east, and that's where he'd been when it all fell apart. She wondered what happened to him. Would always wonder, and it was maddening, not having any way to find out. Maybe even now, five years after his last call, before the power went out, he was still trying to make his way across the country like he said he would. Maybe he'd made it as far as, say, Colorado. Gotten caught in the mountains in winter. Maybe he was just resting. Maybe he'd found a safe place to stay, like the clinic here. Maybe they needed him, so he stayed. How long did it take someone to walk three thousand miles, anyway? She didn't have any idea.

She left a note for him back at the house. Stuck it to the door, covered it with packing tape so it would survive wind and weather. Maybe he'd find it someday. Maybe he'd find her.

They rolled back to the clinic at dawn, when the sky was gray and chilled. Jim was keeping watch on the north side this shift, rifle tucked under his arm, perched on one of the derelict trucks that made up the barricade around the compound. Kath sat up on the edge of the open window and waved an arm high, giving him plenty of time to spot and ID her and the Tesla. She could see him shade his eyes to look out. He waved back and started to open the gate.

The car's charge was just about finished. Eighty miles round trip was at the far end of its range these days; its battery didn't hold as much as it used to. They might need to start rethinking trips like this. Or figure out how to bring solar panels along for a recharge.

A couple of others had come out to help Jim move aside the flatbed trailer stacked with twisted wreckage that served as the north gate. They could move it in and out easy enough, and then use chains and locks to anchor it to rebar loops sunk into concrete pits in the ground. As soon as the Tesla was inside, they shifted and locked the trailer back into place. Dennis rolled the car to a stop in its spot in the back of the clinic, where its charging station was, hooked up to a roof full of solar panels. That had been an epic bit of engineering, to get that all situated. The clinic was the only spot for twenty miles around that still had electricity.

Maggie must have been waiting for them; she came out the front door as soon as the car stopped. "How did it go? Everyone okay?"

"Bouncing baby girl," Dennis said, climbing from the car and stretching his back. "They gave us capers. We can resurrect fine dining."

The other doors opened; Melanie herded out the children. Chloë was carrying the youngest propped on her hip, asleep.

Maggie was a middle-aged woman, tanned, brown hair growing gray, tied up in a bun. She wore a wrinkled blouse, jeans, and workboots. Kath looked at Maggie and saw her own mother, who'd been dead for five years now. Maggie and her mom had been friends; hard not to see her as some kind of stand-in. Kath hadn't wanted to leave home. She'd been waiting, as if her parents might come back. As if Eddie might find her there, and if she left, maybe he never would. Likely, she'd be dead now if Maggie hadn't made her come to the clinic.

Maggie stopped and gaped, looking among the adults for explanation. "What's this? Who're they?"

"Found 'em on the road," Dennis said, casually, like this sort of thing happened all the time.

The older doctor's mouth opened, horrified. "We can't… we don't… we don't have enough food! We can't take care of any more people!"

"Were we supposed to just leave them there?" Kath asked.

Maggie put her hand to her forehead. Her mouth had sunk into a deep frown. "No, of course not. It's just… God." She turned and walked off, scratching her hair.

"Come on," Kath said to Chloë. "We'll get you set up inside."

Kath had them wash faces and hands while she heated up a can of beans to feed them, and made them each drink a glass of water and take a few chewable vitamins. They still had a couple bottles left, and this seemed like a good use for them. After that, the kids curled up on a cot in one of the exam rooms, all three of them together, snuggled under the blanket Kath had tucked them in with despite the heat. Maggie watched from the doorway, arms crossed, clearly unhappy. But she hadn't really been happy ever, the last couple years.

"We couldn't just leave them," Kath insisted.

"And we can't keep taking in strays. We had to throw out those potato plants on the east side of the building. Rot got them."

They weren't strays, Kath thought. They'd been dropped off. People were going to start leaving babies on their doorstep. And the clinic didn't have enough food. "We'll try again," Kath said, because what else could she say? "We'll figure it out."

"Yeah, I know, I know. You should get some rest, okay?" Maggie ran a hand over Kath's hair, something she'd been doing since Kath was five.

Kath smiled grimly, double checked that the shotgun and its spare shells were locked up, and went out to the row of tents lined up along the clinic building. She hadn't really thought about being tired until Maggie mentioned rest.

Kids and doctors slept in the clinic building. Everyone else used the row of tents, some old-fashioned canvas jobs, a few nylon domes, everything in between. Kath used one of the canvas ones, with the flaps tied up during the day to let in air, mosquito netting in place to try to keep out bugs.

Melanie was already inside, stripped to tank top and panties, sprawled face down on the sheet-covered mattress. If Kath was tired, Melanie was probably flattened after the night she had. But Kath paused a moment anyway, to see if she was really asleep. Admired the curve of her shoulder, the slope of her back where it arced to her hip. Melanie had the most amazing, artful shape to her.

Quietly, moving slowly, Kath pulled off her own dusty, rank clothes, then sat with her journal, squinting in the dark to write a handful of words about the image of those kids in the road, the nerve-wracking groans of the woman, the sticky-hot night air. These days, she mostly kept the diary out of habit, and her handwriting had turned tiny, scrunched—trying to conserve space, since she didn't know when she'd ever find another blank book. She figured she'd keep writing until she ran out of space.

Kath tried to be quiet, but Melanie woke up anyway. "Hmm?"

"Sorry, didn't mean to wake you," she said.

"Hm, s'okay, c'mere."

Kath set aside the book, collapsed onto the mattress, and Melanie gathered her into her arms. They clung to each other, body to body, and Kath's near-constant, watchful tension from the night melted a couple of degrees. The scent of Melanie, the soap-and-sweat of her, the warmth of her skin, made Kath feel a little drunk. Melanie shifted, brought her mouth to Kath's, and they kissed, a little desperately. Melanie sighed, like her own tension was finally fading.

"You okay?" Kath asked.

She squeezed her eyes shut. "We're going to be back there in two years helping that same woman deliver another baby, there'll be twenty babies running around that camp and they'll all be starving—"

Kath hugged her. Melanie shuddered a moment. Trying not to cry, unable not to cry. Kath didn't know what to tell her.

"That's optimistic," she said finally.

"What?"

"That any of us are still going to be around in two years."

Melanie pulled away and stared at her a moment, then busted out laughing. They fell together in another tight hug, conveying powerful comfort. Anchoring each other.

"Where would you be now?" Kath whispered.

"Med school. I wanted to go to med school." She laughed, but the laughter turned to crying, like it often did. She didn't try to hide it this time, and Kath held her till she fell back asleep.

Just a year or so into their time camping out at the clinic, a fire flattened the strip mall on the other side of the street. Could have been anything that started it, from a leaking gas line and static build up to lightning. Some traveler tossing a lit cigarette. With no one to fight the fire, it burned walls to the ground, collapsed roofs, and kept going. The few shade trees spaced out on the sidewalk went up like torches, and folk at the clinic stayed up all night stomping on ashes and dumping water on hot spots to keep the fire from jumping the road and claiming their home. The barricade of derelict cars, trucks, and trailers had already been put in place by then, but after the fire died down they hauled, towed, and wrangled the barricade another fifty feet out, and added on to it, to increase their buffer zone. To increase the perception of safety. They also spent six months demolishing buildings up and down their own street. Took a long time, clearing all that space with sledgehammers and controlled burns, but it gave them great line of sight after. And more space for gardening. After security, gardening was their biggest preoccupation.

It had only taken a few years for the entire character of that street, the neighborhood surrounding the clinic, to change. When they sat around at night, drinking whatever bottle of booze turned up, and asked how this could happen, they only had to look around.

The next day, after stopping by the kitchen tent for a cup of water and an apple, Kath went on her daily walk around the barricade. She usually did this in the morning, but after the long night she slept past noon. Melanie had already gotten up and was probably at the clinic helping with the work of the day. Kath would check in in a little while, see how the new arrivals were getting on.

The air was sticky, humid, and the sun was roasting. Calendar said it was April, but this felt like July. She was dripping sweat in moments. She wiped her face and pulled the brim of her baseball cap down to better block the glare.

The clinic housed thirty-two people these days. Thirty-five, she revised. Most of the clinic residents were up and about, working in garden patches, tinkering with the couple of cars they still had, cleaning and maintaining the camp. A half dozen stood at the barricade with weapons, watching. Kath waved when people waved at her, said hello. The day felt ordinary.

On the west side of the compound, Dr. Dennis stood outside the barricade and hit golf balls with a driver. Flung them up the road, one after the other. When it was safe enough he'd go collect them, and for some of the kids it was a game, to see how many golf balls they could recover for him. A few always stayed lost, but Dennis kept hitting them anyway. Swing, a whoosh of air, *thwack*. He'd shade his eyes to follow the arc of the ball until it hit the ground a hundred yards or so on. Kath didn't know enough about golf to tell if he was any good. Didn't seem to bother him, that he might never play a real round of golf ever again. He just seemed to enjoy hitting balls to nowhere.

Kath sat on the edge of the barricade and watched for a little while.

"Morning," Dennis said finally.

"What happens when you run out?"

He shrugged. "Maybe I'll start hitting rocks. But, maybe I won't run out. Maybe I'll get back to Palm Springs, when everything gets back to normal."

This is normal, she thought. She was thinking that more and more, but never said it out loud.

"You want to try it?" Dennis asked.

"No thanks. I'm just taking a walk."

"Enjoy."

"You, too."

He took another ball from the nylon bag at his feet, set it on a bare patch of ground, and lined up for the next swing.

Kath finished her circle around the compound and headed to the squat, concrete building in the middle.

The front room was crowded. The compound's handful of resident kids swarmed. They were supposed to be settling down for the impromptu class one of the nurses taught every other day or so, but something had set them off. A giant spider, Kath gathered from the shouting. The room was loud. Anita, one of the clinic nurses, was trying to settle them down, yelling in both English and Spanish, but nothing worked.

Kath's three refugees cringed away from it all, huddled at the side of the room, watching cautiously. She grabbed a couple of picture books from the basket under one of the chairs and called to Chloë. "Let's go get some air, okay?"

The girl considered a moment, lips pressed in a suspicious frown. She was looking marginally better today, Kath thought. Some color in her cheeks. But then, she couldn't look much worse than she had last night, standing in the dark, bleakly washed out by headlights. The two little ones were hunched up next to her, staring at the proceedings with round, glazed eyes. Maybe trying to decide if this was dangerous. Chloë picked up their hands and tugged them toward the door.

Kath found a shady spot around the side of the building where the clinic's pots of lettuce plants lived. Wasn't exactly a garden, but it was kind of a nice place to spend a few quiet moments.

"Want to do the honors?" Kath asked, opening to the first page of one of the books. The little ones scooted closer, drawn by the colors and pictures of round friendly animals, putting their hands on the paper.

Chloë winced, drawing her limbs in to hug herself. "I can't. I know I should… but…"

Kath thought that might be the case. "No worries. We'll work on it now." She read to them, following with her fingers, showing Chloë the words. She wasn't going to teach the girl to read in one sitting. But they had to start somewhere. The little ones were rapt.

They went through the books she'd brought, went through them all again at the little ones' insistence, and Kath asked them which were their favorites and why. They finally seemed normal. Acted normal, engaged and talking. Then they lost interest in the books and ran off to chase a grasshopper. Kath let them; they couldn't get into too much trouble around here.

Chloë was still suspicious.

"They your siblings? Brother and sister?"

"Yeah."

"Where are your parents?"

She shrugged, shuffling through the books, brushing fingers on the covers. "What's the point? I mean, does anybody still read?"

"We still have books. We have a whole library inside. It's still a good way to learn things."

"I guess."

Kath wanted to draw her out. "Do you remember anything from before?" She was old enough; she might, unlike her siblings. Or depending on how bad things had been for her, she might have blocked it all out. "I remember a lot. I definitely don't want to forget how to read."

Chloë stared out at the barricade of junked cars. Kath didn't think she was going to talk and was going to let it go. Suggest they go in and find some lunch. But then the girl said, "I remember Disneyland. We went when I was really small. Got my picture with Ariel. She's my favorite. Wish I still had the picture but it got lost somewhere. I guess it's still there? Disneyland? What's going to happen to it?"

Honestly, Kath couldn't remember the last time she'd even thought of Disneyland. But the question suddenly filled her. What had happened to Disneyland? Another stab of grief followed. Another thing to mourn, or lock away and forget.

She said, "It must still be there. Some of it, at least. But the lights have probably gone out."

"I wish I was there. Even with the lights out."

"Yeah."

Kath looked up; Maggie stood at the corner of the building, arms crossed. Her face was screwed up in the way it usually got when she was thinking of crying. Holding it in so hard she seemed to be in pain. Then, the look was gone.

Maggie said, "Hey there! Anita's got soup cooking. Chloë, why don't you take the others around and get yourselves fed."

The girl nodded, clambering to her feet and going to fetch the others, who'd been playing some kind of tag. She didn't call out to them, and Kath wondered about that. That she didn't feel safe, raising her voice.

Kath stood and watched them go, and Maggie watched Kath.

"You're good with the kids. They're comfortable with you."

"Yeah, I like them too." She didn't worry so much with the kids. She didn't think about the future so much. Kids were easy: keep them fed, keep them clean, do everything to keep them safe. Simple. If she could teach them to read, then she'll really have accomplished something.

Maggie seemed to draw even tighter to herself. Her shoulders were rigid, her hands in fists.

Kath's brow furrowed. "What's the matter?"

"It's just… you looked like… you don't want to have your own kids, do you?"

She hadn't thought about it at all. Food and security, that was what she thought about these days. The question startled her, and she had to think a moment, but that moment was too long for Maggie.

"Oh God, you're already pregnant, aren't you? That's why you like the kids, you're practicing—"

"What? No! What gave you that idea?"

This didn't seem to help. "But you're having sex. Tell me, are you having sex?"

Kath glared. "I'm twenty years old, of course I'm having sex!"

"And you're pregnant."

"No, God no!"

"But have you been using protection? How do you know?" Maggie seemed desperate.

Kath paused, then shot back, "Because I'm sleeping with Melanie!"

Maggie drew back, and Kath wondered what she was going to rant about next. It wasn't that she and Melanie had been hiding anything. It just made sense to double up on tents to save space, and they hadn't actually announced anything when they became more than friends. It wasn't being gay that Kath thought would upset people. It was being… adult. She wasn't growing up. She was *grown*.

Now, Maggie did cry. Or laugh. Something that came from tension releasing, and causing whatever was holding her together to collapse. She slumped against the wall, both hands covering her face. "I'm sorry, Kathy. I'm sorry. It's just… we can't feed everyone, and people keep having babies and we can't do anything, we can't feed them—"

Kath put her arms around the woman and just held her.

"God, look at me," Maggie said around sobs. "I'm supposed to be taking care of you and just look at me."

"You don't have to take care of me," Kath said. "You have enough to worry about, just let me… be me."

They stayed like that awhile, hidden in the shelter of the building where Maggie could lose it in private, and Kath stayed to make sure she was okay. The older woman had been right at the edge for such a long time.

Maggie finally pulled away, scrubbing tears off her face and chuckling at herself, a strained and painful sound.

"So, you and Melanie, huh? I think I knew that. Yeah. Oh God, I'm so messed up I can't see what's right in front of my face. I promised your mom I'd look out for you and if you turned up pregnant in this mess—" She took a shuddering breath, rubbed her face one more time. And like that she had put on a new mask and was smiling. "I'm sorry. I forget sometimes that you're grown up."

Kath offered words, a gesture of comfort, though it might hurt as much as it helped. Kath wanted to say it. "I never got to come out to Mom," she said softly. "I mean, I sort of knew, I was starting to figure it out. Figuring out that I didn't just put those pictures on my wall because I liked beach volleyball so much, you know? But I never told Mom."

"Oh, hon. You know she'd be okay with it, right?"

"Yeah, I know. But I wish…" She shook her head. They all wished.

"You should be in college," Maggie murmured, running a hand over Kath's hair.

All the adults said that to her in their most maudlin moments. She should be in college. Not staying up half the night with a gun under her arm. Kath herself had stopped believing anything would ever change. This was just what life was now. There'd never be somewhere else.

"Where would you be now?" she asked Maggie.

She looked around at the wide-open compound that used to be part of a pleasant street, the modest building now crammed with solar panels it didn't used to have. "I'd be here, I think. But it'd be a lot different. Can you do a watch shift tonight? Mike's come down with something."

"Bad?"

"No, just a cold."

"Yeah, no problem."

"Thanks. Just… thank you."

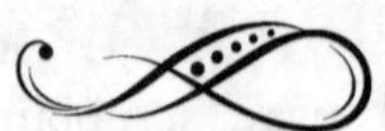

Kath's watch shift started late afternoon and went into the evening. She covered about half the perimeter, walking on top of the barricade, stepping from car roof to truck hood to trailer and on. They'd bolted on sheets of metal and spikes, fencing, and other odds and ends to the basic framework over the years. Occasionally she'd come upon a loose bit, a piece of sheeting that moved under her feet, a car roof that was rusting out, and the next day someone would come to repair it. Used to be, they'd have four or five people covering the barricade, especially during the night watch. But since the fire and clearing the line of sight, they needed fewer people watching and could save the effort for other chores. The long approach gave the watchers plenty of time to spot trouble and raise an alarm.

This evening, trouble came right around dusk. The worst time, with the light fading. Her first hint came as movement on the horizon. Could have been anything, so she waited for the movement to resolve into shapes, or fade into nothing. Shadows appearing in wavering heat lines in the distance could be deceptive. She brought binoculars to her eyes, spent a moment focusing with one hand, the other clenched on the shotgun.

The shadows gained definition. Not a mirage, not deer or something else wandering in the distance. Now that she saw them, she heard the noise, a rumbling sound that was becoming rare. Gas-powered engines, beating against the air. Three cars, a couple of motorcycles, more than a dozen people, and those were just the ones she could see from this distance. Who knew how many were hiding inside the vehicles?

The convoy was racing straight for them.

She let the binoculars hang off their strap and cupped a hand to her mouth. "Incoming! Incoming!"

Someone at the clinic heard her and clanged the brass bell hanging off the front overhang.

They didn't need it very often, but they had a routine for this, when strangers came barreling at the clinic compound in a way that didn't suggest friendship. Those standing watch at the barricade stayed put, in case the invaders came on multiple fronts. A dozen others, whoever was on hand, grabbed weapons from the locker and came out to where the alarm had sounded.

Kath waited for her backup, shotgun in both hands, watching her targets come into range. The cars bounced and jutted over broken asphalt, while the motorcycles curved and weaved.

"Where the hell are they getting gas from?" Dennis asked. He'd climbed up on the barricade next to Kath.

Maggie was right behind him. "Don't know, don't care. What do they want?"

Kath said, "Better get down, in case they come in firing."

The barricade had places to shelter: inside cabs, on shielded truck beds. All the invaders would see was their shotguns and rifles bristling out.

The caravan stopped at the edge of firing range. If one of the rifles fired at them now, it might or might not hit. A big man, white, wearing a leather jacket and cowboy hat, scrambled out of the driver's side of one of the cars and marched forward a few paces. He didn't seem to be armed.

Kath stood tall and shouted at him across the barrel of her shotgun. "Stop! Stop and show your hands!"

The man's thick beard worked, as if he was biting his lip under it. He raised his hands. "Is this the clinic?" he shouted. "The one people talk about, that has doctors and medicine? Is that you?"

"What do you want!"

He gestured back. "We have wounded! We need help! We can trade for it! We have gas, guns, bullets—"

"Food?"

He paused a moment. "Yes!"

Kath looked at Maggie and Dennis.

"What kind of wounded?" Dennis shouted back. He stayed behind his shelter.

"Gunshot! Two men. God, please, help them!"

It could be a trick. Or the man could be honest. In the end, half the people here were doctors and nurses, and they recognized that kind of desperate plea.

290

The clinic had a process for this kind of situation, too.

Maggie and Dennis both emerged on top of the barricade, and Maggie called out. "Okay, here's how it's going to work. You bring the injured men inside, the vehicles stay out. Just the injured and two people each to carry them, no one else gets in, and you leave all your weapons outside. Got it?"

"Yes, okay, fine!"

And they checked, too. While the caravan pulled their injured out of the backs of the vehicles, Maggie and the clinic folk hauled open the gate, but only a couple of feet, just wide enough for two people to walk through. Two of the clinic's biggest guys, Jim and Jorge, patted down everybody at the opening, even the injured. But they didn't have anything, which gave these people an incremental point of trust.

The injured men were being carried chair style, one by two men, one by the man who'd greeted them and a woman. One of the injured seemed to be unconscious, but the other was making the guttural, deep-belly groans of someone moaning through clenched teeth. Every shadow on them looked like stains of blood.

"Okay, get 'em inside!" Maggie, Dennis, and a trail of clinic folk escorted them to the door of the clinic.

Jim stayed at the barrier. "Kath, go with them, stand watch inside, we'll keep an eye out here."

An odd quiet had fallen—the vehicles in the convoy had shut off their engines, turned off their headlights; those left behind waited quietly. Evening light had all but gone, so figures moved as shapes in the dark. Shotgun in hand, extra shells jangling in the pocket of her windbreaker, she trotted after the others.

Unlike the quiet at the barricade, inside the clinic was loud and brightly lit. Someone was herding the kids outside, to sleep in tents. Kath spotted Chloë and spared her a smile. She and her siblings looked like they might bolt at the sign of the injured men. Kath hurriedly told her, "It'll be fine," and hoped that was enough. Chloë nodded and might even have been convinced.

Past the waiting room, the first exam room was noisy with shouted orders. Dennis and Melanie had taken the first of the injured men here, the one grunting with fierce pain. Maggie and Anita took the unconscious man to the second exam room. Both doors stayed open and Kath was able to keep an eye on them all. Dennis was shouting orders. Melanie was talking to the first patient in Spanish, telling him to lie back, to breathe, *respire, respire, bien, bien.* The man started crying, *ayudame, ayudame!* Help me, help me.

In the second room, Maggie and the gang's spokesman were talking.

"We can barter," he was explaining. "We have a whole warehouse, whatever you need. We have food. Just save them. Can you save them?"

The man laid out on the table had a great stain of blood covering his chest. It seemed centered on his right shoulder. A gunshot wound, not necessarily fatal. Likely he was in shock and needed support, fluid and oxygen, while the doctors cleaned the wound. But they'd need to get started on him right away. Anita and one of the nurses had cut away his shirt, inserted an IV and were peeling away cloth that had been stuffed into the wound.

After a deep breath, Maggie seemed to come to a decision. She explained, "We don't need food as much as we need protection." She looked him straight in the eye, unwavering. "We help you, you help keep us safe. You get the word out to your people, to anyone else—this is neutral ground. We stay safe, no matter what. No one attacks us, no one hurts us, no one hurts anyone while they're here. Got it?"

"We protect you. And you help us and no one else. Just us."

"No. We help everyone or it doesn't work. We're not a commodity. We're here for everyone."

"Can't promise that."

Maggie bit her lip in a moment of thought. Then she put up her hands and stepped back from the table. After glancing at her and each other in a moment of hesitation, Anita and the other nurse stepped from the table, hands up like hers, blood on latex gloves.

The guy and the woman with him started forward, fists raised as if they could beat her into saving the man's life. Kath stepped in front of him, shotgun raised, warding them off. The standoff persisted for a handful of heartbeats.

The lead thug grinned. "You ever even shot anyone, kid?"

"Yes, I have." No hesitation, no hint of bluffing. She didn't need to bluff. Her tone convinced him; his smile fell, and he backed off.

Everyone watched him now, the one who would decide. His gang would listen to him. But Maggie and the other doctors were the ones who could fix things.

"Okay. Fine. This whole place is off limits. I'll spread the word."

"And you'll make sure we stay safe."

"As much as anyone can stay safe."

Maggie and the others closed back to the table in a flurry of action. Low-voiced commands and bits of information passed back and forth. In moments an impromptu surgery was underway.

Maggie said, "You all should probably wait outside."

A spike of tension followed, both strangers poised to lunge forward again. As if the doctors would really do something nefarious if they weren't supervised. Kath reasserted herself and the shotgun.

The clinic director made a calming gesture. "My people need room and quiet to work, it's better if you wait." She added, "One of you can stay to watch. Her—"

She nodded to the woman with the leather jacket and wary gaze looking past too much eye makeup. And where had she found a stash of useable eyeliner? "Why her?" the man asked.

"Because she's quiet."

"Cynthia?"

She nodded. "Yeah, okay."

"There are chairs in the waiting room," Kath said, trying to sound neutral, if not friendly. Nodding, he went out.

Dennis had managed to kick out both of the gang members in his room. His patient was sedated now, finally quiet. The medical team was busy with gauze, alcohol, forceps, removing bullets from legs. Melanie glanced up once and gave Kath a thin smile. Kath smiled back, unsure who was comforting whom.

She stayed in the corridor, keeping watch over both rooms and the waiting room. There, the gang members had settled down. Too tired to argue anymore, maybe. One of them had even fallen asleep.

The clinic treatment rooms were made for routine outpatient care, not trauma. But Maggie, Dennis, and the others made do. By morning the two injured men were bandaged, sedated, and recovering quietly. Splashes of blood and red-stained gauze littered the floors, and a whole tray of scalpels and forceps and other instruments lay piled on a tray by the autoclave in the back supply room. The medicals were trying to clean up, wiping down surfaces, peeling off latex gloves. Wiping faces on sleeves and looking out, shell-shocked.

Maggie made a trip to the back supply room. When the woman, Cynthia, followed, Kath quietly moved in behind her. Just to keep an eye on her.

Cynthia glared a moment. "Can you close the door? Just for a minute."

Kath looked at Maggie. Confused, Maggie nodded. Kath shut the door and waited, hands ready on her weapon.

Then Cynthia said, whispering, "Can you help me not get pregnant?"

Maggie froze a moment, processing. The woman pursed her lips and seemed to be holding her breath. When Maggie didn't answer right away, Cynthia tried again. "I mean if I wanted an IUD or something, could you do that?"

"Yes, we can do that. We'll have to do a pregnancy test first—are you pregnant?"

Cynthia's eyes widened. She looked terrified. "Oh God I hope not, I don't want to be, that's why I was asking—"

"But you might be," Maggie asked, and Cynthia ducked her face to hide spilling tears. Maggie touched her shoulder. "Come on, let's check.

Not a big deal. Kath, come in back and help me clear off that table."

They went to the back exam room where they'd been stockpiling canned food. Kath had to shift boxes so Cynthia had somewhere to sit, while Maggie dug around one of the cupboards. Cynthia talked. Rambled.

"Adam, the big guy who does all the talking… he's taking care of me. He's promised to take care of me."

"You could take care of yourself," Maggie muttered.

"Don't judge me," Cynthia said through gritted teeth. "Fucking that man is keeping me alive right now. I can't not do it, I can't force him to wear condoms, and I do not want to have a baby in this mess."

Maggie looked away.

Cynthia continued. "My… my sister got pregnant. I'd managed to keep her with me all this time, I'd promised to take care of her. But seven months in she got sick. Massive headache, vomiting, cramping. Then seizures."

"Sounds like eclampsia," Maggie said. "It's a thing that happens sometimes. We might have been able to help her, but maybe not."

"I couldn't save her. The baby killed her, and it isn't supposed to be like that, I don't want to go through that. There'd be no one to help me."

The whole thing took maybe half an hour. Maggie had Cynthia go back to the bathroom to pee in a cup. The test came back negative, and Cynthia started crying again. Maggie coaxed her to undress and pulled out the stirrups on the table. "Kath, why don't you see how they're doing up front?"

Kath ducked out.

Both injured men were stable. Dennis was in the waiting room, talking to the gang's leader, Adam.

"They shouldn't be moved for at least a couple of days. Especially not if you're going to shove them in a car and bounce them around—"

"Hey!"

Dennis put up a calming hand and tried again. "You can leave them here, no problem. And yes, any food you want to give us will be appreciated."

"And protection," he said, his curled lip almost making it a sneer.

"We're the only medical help for a hundred miles around. Maybe more. Your people would be dead now. You tell me whether or not we deserve protecting."

Adam didn't have anything to say to that.

Cynthia and Maggie emerged a little while later. Cynthia looked tired, shadows under her eyes, a slump in her shoulders. But she also seemed determined. An edge of that ever-present anxiety was gone. Kath was close enough to hear Maggie say to her, almost under her breath, "We've got a cupboard full of IUDs. I think we even have a few diaphragms stashed away somewhere. Tell your friends. We'll help anyone with birth control, no barter needed. Spread the word."

Cynthia nodded. "Yeah. Okay."

In what Kath thought was a gesture of supreme goodwill, Maggie invited Adam and his gang to stay for the day, to get some sleep, and to share breakfast. Kath realized later the underlying motive: make the clinic compound feel like home. Make it feel safe, and give them a stake in keeping it that way. They declined, however. Adam muttered something about not wanting to feel even more indebted. Cynthia took hold of his arm, whispered something, and the man settled.

They agreed to leave their injured and return for them in two days. That gave the clinic a couple more days to get them as strong as possible, and make sure infection didn't set in. They had a pretty good track record with this sort of thing so far, but it would only take one death from sepsis to undo everything.

The stakes seemed so high, for everything they did.

"We're running out," Dennis said, as they stood on the barricade, watching the caravan drive away, tires kicking up chips of broken asphalt.

"Of what?" Maggie said tiredly.

"Everything, really. But specifically—I think we should try to start growing some penicillin."

She stared. "Can we do that?"

"I think we can. I think we have to."

Maggie bowed her head. "What you're saying is you don't think this is ever going to end. It's never going to go back to the way it was."

"No," he said, folding her into his arms when she started to cry.

Technically, Kath's watch shift ended hours ago. A second night on her feet, she ought to be exhausted. But her nerves were wired, her skin itched. She set off for a circuit around the barricade. Still had the shotgun slung over her shoulder, shells hanging in her pocket.

She hadn't gotten a quarter of the way around when she spotted Melanie standing at the barricade, looking out at the sun-baked plain.

"You okay?" Kath asked cautiously.

"Would it sound weird if I said that was kind of fun? Good trauma practice, you know? Nice, thinking I actually helped save someone."

Kath stepped forward, well into her space, and kissed her. Jangling nerves stilled. Melanie pulled back, surprised, glancing around to see if anyone was watching.

"We're not being discreet anymore?"

Kath shook her head. "I told Maggie. She was freaked out that I was going to get knocked up."

She laughed, hugging Kath close. "That woman needs to chill the hell out."

"Yeah. But I don't know. She's the one holding all this together."

They walked on for a while, arms around each other. The sun felt warm this morning instead of scorching. Kath finally felt ready to lie down for a nap.

Looking ahead, along the junkyard edge of the barricade, Melanie asked, "Where would you be now? If none of this had happened?"

She wouldn't be in Melanie's arms, for one. That was a weird thought, that if none of this had happened she wouldn't have Melanie. And that would be a shame. She rested her head on her shoulder and sighed.

"It doesn't matter. This is where I am."

SINEW AND STEEL AND WHAT THEY TOLD

I am cut nearly in half by the accident. The surviving fibers of my suit hold me together. I am not dead.

And this is a problem. I expected to die in this job, in my little scout runner, blasted apart, incinerated, torn to pieces with nothing to recover. All that would follow would be a sad memorial service with a picture and an old set of boots on a table. That is how scout pilots usually die. But I am just cut almost in half. And the doctor on my ship, *Visigoth,* is very good.

My biologics are mostly shut down with shock, though I'm dutifully trying to monitor the pain. It's all-enveloping, a fist squeezing my brain. My mechanics are in full self-repair mode, overheating because there's so much to knit back together. Because of them, I have survived long enough that I will probably not die. This is going to be awkward.

From my own internal processor I send out an emergency signal to piggyback on ship comms, so that maybe someone can come and explain.

On autorecovery, my half-exploded runner manages to slam into its berth on the *Visigoth* and rescue crews are standing by. Once they seal all the locks, I try to help them peel me out of the cockpit but it's not really working. There are many pairs of hands and shouting voices.

"Graff, stop, lie back, you'll be fine, it's fine, it's going to be fine—"

I might laugh at this.

The dock crew and medics are full of panic and repressed horror at what they must be looking at. Then I am horizontal, fully supported, no strain at all on my body, which feels wet and wobbly, and the pain is lead weight on every nerve. Fingers pry at my eyelids, a light flashes, and I see him, Doctor Ell, who is also my lover. He has a pale face and a shock of blond hair and intense eyes, and his whole expression is screwed up and serious. I want to pat his shoulder and say everything will be fine but nothing is working. So I look at him.

"I'm sorry," I murmur.

"Graff, no, what are you talking about?"

"You're about to find out I faked my medical scans." I try to smile.

He stares. "What?"

A medic's voice interrupts. "Doctor! God, look at this—"

Finally, happily, I pass out.

Five other people are in the room when I wake up. Ell and Captain Ransom. A support medic, standing by. Two guards at a door that has never had guards at it before.

"When will he wake up?" Ransom asks.

"He's awake now," Ell says. He must be watching a monitor.

I'm listening hard—I can hear heartbeats, if I focus. I think I can open my eyes. But I can't move anything else. There's a fog; I battle past it.

"Am I paralyzed or on medical restraints?" My voice scratches.

Some rustling as the guards flinch, like they didn't believe I was awake. The medic perks up.

"Drug-induced paralysis," Ell says.

"So both."

"Yes."

"Because of the injuries or because of everything else?"

Nothing for a long pause, then, "It would be better if you lie still for now."

"Okay." I sigh. My lungs still work but feel like they've been scrubbed out with pumice.

Ransom curses and begins to pace. He doesn't have a lot of room and his steps fall hard. His presence always seems to expand to fill whatever space he's in. It's actually a comfort right now. Ransom is here, he'll fix everything.

My processor seems to be fine. Ell didn't mess with it when he had a chance to look inside me. The self-repair has settled down; I'm still recording. I check the time; it's been two days since they pulled me out of the runner. Diagnostics say I'm…mending. Mechanics repaired. Biologics will need more time. I took a beating. But Ell didn't try to dig in or disconnect anything important. He could have, if he'd wanted to.

I have a lot of questions. I imagine they do, too. We try to wait one another out. My eyes open to a dimly lit ceiling in Medical. I want to see Ell but he's standing back.

Ransom and Ell finally break at the same time.

Ell says, "How did you fake the scans—"

The captain says, "You sent a signal—"

I chuckle. I can't help it. This would be funny if it weren't me. Ransom curses again.

"This isn't funny," Ell says.

"No, I know that," I reply. "I'm sorry." I would laugh outright except it hurts too much, because if I had thought about it before the accident, what Ransom would do if he ever found out about me, this is about how I'd have expected it to go. My ongoing chuckle comes out like a cough.

Ransom is losing his temper. "Graff—"

"Let it go. You know how he is," Ell says.

"I thought I did."

I stop chuckling. "Ask me. Ask me everything."

Ransom starts. "Are you dangerous?"

"Yes. I mean no. Not to any of you."

"Graff, you're not helping," the doctor says.

"What do you want me to say?" I murmur.

"What are you?" the doctor asks.

"Human."

"No, you're not—"

"I didn't fake the DNA records, just the physiological. Look at the DNA." I'm tired. But I need to get through this. I need to know what they're going to do with me.

Ell has touched every inch of me. He must have thought he knew me.

"When was all this work done? How…" Now Ell is pacing. "I've seen cybernetic implants, but this… this is extensive. This is part of your nervous system. Work this extensive should kill anyone… but you don't even have any scarring from it. It's all perfectly integrated. How?"

They think I'm dangerous. They think I'm going to go off like a bomb. "Can you send the kids out, please?"

The two guards, the medic. They're not kids, of course they're not. I know them all; I trained with them. But I outrank them. Another long, taut silence follows.

"I'm not going to hurt anyone," I insist. My head is throbbing. "There are more secrets than mine here. I'll tell you and the captain but no one else."

Ell comes to my shoulder, a syringe in hand. I can't flinch, I can't resist. He pumps the liquid into a tube already connected to my body somewhere that I can't see.

"For the pain," he says gently. "Your vitals are spiking."

He touches my shoulder, naked under a thin sheet. I almost start crying. My blood stops pounding quite as hard. Nerves fray a little less. Ell steps away. I want to reach for him.

"Drugs work on him at least," he says to the captain.

"Do you trust him?" Ransom asks. A question that cuts. He's always trusted me before.

"I don't know," Ell says.

I think I might start crying. I wait. We all wait, in air thick with anxiety, like trying to wade through gelatin.

"Marcel, Xun, Brown. You're dismissed," Ransom says finally.

"But sir—" He must give them a look, because no one complains further.

They leave reluctantly. Ell murmurs reassurances at them. They all take second, third looks at me. I wonder what the ship's rumor mill is saying. It will never be the same.

"All right, Graff," Ransom says. "How… what…" He waves his hand at me, shakes his head.

I've never explained this; I've never needed to. I don't regret having to do so now. It's how I'm going to survive. Assuming they believe me and trust me at the end of it.

"It's done in utero," I say. "It's grown. Artificial gestation, of course, but that's—"

"Oh starry fuck," Ell curses.

I've never heard him say 'fuck' in all the years I've known him. This is probably going to go badly for me.

"Is that even legal?" Ransom asks.

"I'm not sure. It's certainly not ethical," he says.

Except it is. It is for us.

"Why didn't you say anything?" Ransom asks calmly. I recognize the tone, the resolve, that he now knows what the problem is and is closer to figuring out what to do about it. "Why not tell us what… about this? Why bother hiding it with fake scans?"

"Because we don't tell anyone." This drops even harder than the first confession.

"We," Ransom says.

"I hope you understand what I'm trusting you with, telling you this. I'm trusting you." This is a plea. I am vulnerable. I trust them. Not that I have much choice. Or I could shut myself off. Burn out my processor, keep all the secrets. But I don't want to.

"We," the captain repeats. "You sent a signal. At least, the signal originated from your position. It tried to sneak out on ship comms."

"But you blocked it before it got out," I say. And start chuckling again. "I thought that might happen but I had to try. I… I wanted someone to come and download my processor in case I didn't make it."

"How many of you are there?" he asks.

"Not as many as you're afraid of," I say.

"Fuck, Graff, what am I supposed to do with you?" Captain Ransom asks.

"I don't know, sir. Right now I think I would like to sleep. But I'm a little wound up." I need to know I'll wake back up again, if I go to sleep. I'm not sure right now.

"You should be dead," he said. "If you were anyone else in a runner that blew up like that you'd be dead."

"Yeah, I was sort of thinking if I ever blew up in a runner there wouldn't be enough left for anyone to learn about any of this."

"Bad luck there," Ransom says, deadpan.

"Yeah."

"I'm about to kill you myself," Ell says. Then to Ransom: "We should let him sleep."

"Does he really need to sleep? All those wires…"

"Yes, I need to sleep. And eat. And everything else." Sex. I need that, too. Just maybe not right now. Where did Ell go? They're conferencing in the back of the room. Like they can't bear to look at me. I try to stay awake, so I can explain some more, but the painkiller is also a sedative and it pulls me under.

The very best thing I ever ate was ice cream with pieces of dark chocolate and brandied cherries mixed into it. Decadent and comforting at once, served at a too-fancy café with real wood furniture and paneled walls. They made everything themselves with dairy from real goats. I remember thinking, *this,* this is what it's all about.

I got that memory out on a previous download, at least.

I try to send out another message, masking it as a trojan and slipping it in with another signal before the comms operator notices it. But they've got the whole room jammed. I can't access anything, not even the medical computers.

This is bad. I'm not Graff anymore; I'm a thing on a table. Explaining hasn't helped.

I can't explain it, that's the problem.

The memories are pristine. I've got them all stored away, and with them the emotions that goes along with them. The flush on my skin when Ell asked if he could buy me a drink like he was making a dare. The flush on *his* skin when I said yes, because he hadn't thought I would. This was right after he'd come on board as ship's doctor; we'd been in a station-side tavern that was too dark and loud with lots of people dancing. Two days of leave and better make the most of it, right? Ransom had been there, rolling his eyes at the both of us flirting like it was a contest. And only a couple hours later, out in a quiet corridor, I put my hand on Ell's neck, gently pushed him against the wall, and kissed him.

That was a good night.

I write the best after-action reports because I remember. No one ever questions it. I just have a good memory, right? I can still feel the exact sensation when the reactor on the runner blew out, my gut parting like taffy as shrapnel went through it.

Leave that memory and go back to that first night with Ell. That's better. Close my eyes, slow my breathing.

Checking my processor, I know exactly when I've slept and when I haven't. I fall in and out of sleep all day. The door opens, waking me. There are footsteps. I try to look and still can't.

"Doctor?" I ask, rasping. I'm getting hydrated through a tube in a vein, but my mouth is bone dry.

Ell appears next to me. I sigh, relieved. I shouldn't be relieved.

"What's happening?" I ask. I'd meant to ask for water.

He turns away, and my heart lurches. But he's back a moment later with a bottle and straw. "Drink," he orders, and I do. "Better?"

"Yeah. What's happening?"

"Are you a spy?"

"What? No." I mean, I don't think so? Would they think I was, if I told them everything?

"Because Ransom thinks you're a spy."

"For who?"

"I don't know. For whatever you are."

"How bad am I hurt?"

"You should be dead. Your spine was severed. At least I thought it was, but then…it fixed itself."

"Yeah, it does that."

"You'll be on your feet in another week, and I've hardly done anything but hook you to a feeding tube." He's offended that he can't take credit for saving my life.

"I'd be dead without the feeding tube. That stuff needs calories."

Flustered, he sighs. "What are you?"

"I'm me." That will never be a good enough answer. "What is Ransom saying?"

"He suggested dissection. I think he was joking."

I chuckle.

"It's not funny," Ell says.

"No, I guess not." I look at him because I don't know how much longer I'll get to. My smile feels a bit ridiculous.

He doesn't smile. He's pursed and worried and hurt.

I can move enough to breathe. This takes a deep breath to get it all out. "I would like to be able to move, if you think I might be ready to stop with the nerve block."

"I'll have to ask the captain."

"So it isn't for medical reasons."

"No."

Yeah, this may not go well. "I'm not a spy, I'm not a danger to you or anyone, I would never hurt this ship or anyone on it. Where is Ransom, let me talk to him—"

"He doesn't trust you. Not after this. You *lied*—"

"I didn't!"

"The medical scans? You hacked into the ship's computers and hijacked my diagnostics systems! You always scanned out as an ideal textbook human and now I know why!"

"Yeah, okay, I guess that was sort of like lying."

"Graff." He says it as a reprimand. He's wondering if everything was a lie.

"I was raised by the ones who provided my genetic material. I have parents. Does that help?"

"It might." He gets up, puts the bottle of water on a table.

It's infuriating, not being able to see anything, except that I'm too drugged to be really furious about anything. "Captain's listening right now, isn't he? On a monitor? Is he outside the door or what? Or does he have marines ready to storm in if I do something screwy?"

"You can't do anything, you're immobilized. Unless the drugs really don't work on you and you've been faking it." He raises a brow, as if this is a question.

"Well, fuck." I seriously can't move. He knows this. I roll my eyes at the ceiling, as if I could get Ransom's attention that way. "Okay. Captain? Remember the time you had me sit in a runner out on that asteroid for two weeks waiting for those pirates to show up? And remember how you *didn't tell me* why you wanted me to sit on that rock, or for how long, or anything?"

"Graff—"

The door to Medical slides open, slides shut. Footsteps. And Ransom says, "So you wouldn't anticipate and launch your burn too soon and spoil the trap."

"Right!" I exclaim, excited, probably too excited, because Ell appears in my peripheral vision, looking at a monitor and frowning.

Ransom continues, "It's not that I didn't trust you—"

"No, see, that's the thing. It was a good plan, and it wasn't about you trusting me. I trusted *you*. I'd have sat on that rock for a year if you told me to."

"Now you're just trying to guilt me into listening to you."

"Yes. Yes, I am. Also, I want to keep on following your crazy plans. They're kind of fun. You know what I was thinking, when I was stuck on that rock?"

"How you were going to kill me for not telling you?"

"No. That I couldn't wait to see what you had planned. I knew it'd be good." And it had been. Lots of explosions. "And I was thinking of how many drinks you were going to owe me when I got back." Those had been my first words when I got back to *Visigoth,* sweaty and stinking from being cooped up for so long: "You owe me a drink, sir." He'd laughed. I'd known Ransom since flight school, almost right after I left home. I can't imagine what this looks like from his end. I'll never make it up to him.

The captain's voice is taut. "This might have been easier if a switch flipped and turned him into some killer robot." He's talking to Ell, who grumbles.

I ask, "Why didn't you burn out my processor when you had me open, right after the accident?"

The doctor says, "I didn't want to hurt you."

"Doctor, can we have a word?" Ransom says. I can picture him jabbing a thumb over his shoulder, but he never enters my line of sight.

Ell nods, looks at me one more time. "Do you need anything? Anything critical to your current state of health, I mean."

"You?" I ask hopefully.

He looks away. The door shuts, and I close my eyes.

I spend the next two days trying to think of exactly the right thing to tell Ell and Ransom that will make everything all right and get everything back to the way it was. Or at least have them not look at me like I'm a villain in a bad drama. And I think I've got it. I stay awake by sheer force of will. Assuming I ever get to download again, whoever gets the package is going to know every inch of this ceiling. It's got just the littlest bit of texture, like a partially worn pebble. The gray is rather pleasant once you get used to it.

The door opens. Many footsteps enter. My heart rate increases. The pain is so much less than what it was but that makes it harder to lie still. I want to sit up. I want to use my hands when I speak.

Ell appears at the side of the table. I get it all out in one go before he can say anything.

"It's the stories. The stories, the experiences. Everything. A computer could do it, but then we wouldn't get the… the experience. The hormones. The dopamine. The endorphins. The meat and nerves of it all, right? *That's* the important bit. We go out into the galaxy and collect stories, and then we bring them home. It's who we are, it's what we do. And love, we go out to find all the love we can and try to keep it…" This ship is full of love and I'm afraid I've broken it. "I've never had to explain it before and I know it doesn't make sense—"

Ell studies me for a long time. He seems calm. Some decision has been made.

"Love?" he says, his tone even.

"Yeah. Just like that."

He lowers his gaze, raises a syringe full of some ominous liquid.

Well. I tried. I set my jaw in what I hope is a picture of fortitude. "This is it, then."

"This is what?" he asks.

"You induce a coma and ship me off to some military R&D facility. Or is this… I mean, you wouldn't."

He gets this very familiar—delightfully familiar—frustrated look on his face. Like he's about to snarl. "I wouldn't *what*?"

"Just finish me off."

"God, Graff. No." He injects the syringe into the line. "This is probably going to hurt. At least, I think it'll hurt."

"It already hurts."

"I wasn't sure you could hurt, after I saw all that metal. Until I looked at your readings."

"You know me, Ell. You do." I finally catch his gaze. His familiar, shining gaze. He sort of looks like he's about to cry, too.

Then there's a warm rush though my veins that hits my heart and all my muscles seem to melt into a dull throb. I groan, but it's kind of a relieved groan because I can wiggle my fingers and toes now and that feels pretty good. My processor's diagnostics hum away; I'm still not optimal but stress levels are decreasing.

"Warned you," Ell says, leaning in. "Now don't move. You're still not entirely in one piece yet."

"Okay."

I reach out, touch his hand. Just brush it, then let him go because I don't want to scare him. He jumps a little. His breath catches. But he stays near.

Finally, I can turn my head to look at the rest of the room. Captain Ransom is standing there, arms crossed. And someone new is with him. She appears female, fine boned, with short-cropped red hair and a wry frown. A smirk. A judgment. I've never seen her before, but I know who she is. Tez, her name is Tez. My circuits hum in proximity to hers.

I look at Captain Ransom. "You let the signal get out after all."

"I did."

"Why?"

"To see what would happen. She showed up a day later. Do you people just hang around in deep space waiting for edge-of-death signals?"

"Yes," Tez says calmly.

"I'm not dying actually, it turns out," I say awkwardly.

"You had a close call," she says.

"Very."

"Is it a good story?"

"I'm not sure."

She comes to the table, holds out her hand. I take it. The spark of a circuit completing pinches my palm, and hers.

The download takes a few minutes. I get all of her memories as well. It's like meeting an old friend from home. We're all old friends from home. It's kind of nice. I'm not sure I can explain that part of it to Ell and Ransom.

Tez holds my gaze, and in hers is forgiveness and understanding, along with the mildest of reprimands.

You convinced them, I tell her.

No, you did or I'd never have gotten your signal. They wanted to be convinced. You know you should meet up with someone to download a little more often, don't you?

Yeah, I just get distracted.

But is it a good story?

It is. I'm sorry I told them about us.

No, you're not.

The connection breaks. She takes a breath, resettling herself into her skin. Looks around. Sees Ell with new understanding. He ducks his gaze, self-conscious.

"So. They know," she says, just to get it out in the open.

Tez can take me back home for this. If I can't keep the secret, then I can't be allowed to travel. But . . . I'm valuable. I almost start whining like a child, telling her how valuable I am, out in the universe, collecting stories.

"I trust them," I say.

"They may not want you to stay." She looks up, around. "He's afraid you won't want him to stay."

"It's a lot to take in," Ransom says flatly. "I confess, I'm not sure what to do next. I was hoping you might tell me."

But she doesn't. She asks, "Graff does a lot of good where he is?"

"He does," Ransom says. I wasn't sure he would.

"Thank you, sir," I murmur. But it's Ell's decision that matters most, and I look at him next.

He says, "I can purge all the files from the accident and recovery. Go back to the faked scans. Keep that secret. With the captain's permission." Ell looks; Ransom shrugs. I want to laugh at the back and forth but that would probably be bad so I don't.

"You want him to stay?" Tez asks Ell.

"I do. I think I do."

She looks at me. "Graff?"

"Is it going to be weird? It's going to be weird, isn't it? Me staying."

"Yes," Ell says. "But I think you should stay anyway."

We both look at Ransom. He's like a rock, his chiseled expression unmoving. He says, "Yeah, it'll be weird. For a while."

She smiles, her brow crinkling. "I like them."

"Yeah, me, too," I say.

Tez brushes off her jumpsuit. "Captain, if you can spare the time, I wondered if someone on your crew might take a look at my ship? Just a routine once-over."

It's not very subtle. He looks at her, then at me, then at Ell. He raises his brow. "All right. This way."

He actually flashes a little bit of a wry smile over his shoulder as they leave. Then Ell sits by the table and gives me the most exhausted, long-suffering, and sad look I've ever seen.

I'm also exhausted, which is frustrating. I've slept enough. "I was never going to tell you because I couldn't tell you and it didn't make a difference anyway and I'm sorry."

After a hesitation, he touches my forehead. He ruffles my short hair, looks me up and down like he's studying me. Studying his handiwork, or maybe he's really looking at *me*.

"I have a lot more questions," he says.

"Yeah, I know."

I open my hand. Wait for him to make the move. And he puts his hand in mine.

STORY NOTES

This collection came to life with help from the 272 backers of my Kickstarter campaign. Thank you, Backers, for your support and validation at a time when I needed it.

I owe thanks to so many others. To the short fiction editors and publications I've worked with, all of whom have asked for my work and offered creative and professional support. Thank you to Elizabeth Leggett for the use of her artwork, "Illuminate," for the cover. To Max Campanella for graphic design. Wendy Neathery-Wise and Tobias Buckell for Kickstarter coaching. Leanne Neathery-Wise and Yaz Campanella for cheerleading. The Rio Hondo Writers Workshop members, who critiqued a number of the stories here. My family— Mom, Dad, Rob, Deb, Emery, and Grandma, who've always been there for me.

Now, the age-old question: Where do I get my ideas? Everywhere. I get them everywhere.

That Game We Played During the War

This was my second story to be a finalist for the Hugo Award for best short story, so I'm fond of it for that reason alone. I'm also fond of it because I talk about this story a lot when I teach writing workshops. It's a perfect example of how I move between short stories and novels, and the differences between them. (I'm a bit unusual in that I write both—many authors prefer shorts, many prefer novels. I like both. I need both, and this story is an example of why.) When I first got the core idea for the story—a war between a country of people who are telepaths and a county of people who aren't—I thought it was going to be epic. The sweep of history, battles, the sheer logistics of these very different cultures dealing with each other. I wrote out pages of notes, possible scenes, had my two main characters, Calla and Valk, all drawn up—and I closed the file. Didn't look at it again for maybe six years. For whatever reason, my brain didn't want to work on it. Years later, I opened the file, looked it over—and immediately wrote this story. It turns out I wasn't interested in the epic sweep of history; I was interested in these two people. I could tell the story in a scene about Calla and Valk meeting again after the war is over. This story was never meant to be a novel, but I do think that part of what makes it work is the epic scope implied in the backstory. No work is ever wasted in this gig.

The Girl Who Loved Shonen Knife

So, editor Nick Mamatas came to me and said, "Hey, we're doing an anthology of Japanese crime stories, you want in?" I had to think about it because "Japanese crime stories" is so far outside my wheelhouse I really had no idea what I would write about. But then I thought about it. Step one, I made a list of things I *didn't* want to write about, because the ideas were too obvious, too cliché—everyone else would be writing about them, right? I did *not* want to write about samurai, ninja, yakuza, geisha, or kitsune. Okay. So what about "Japan" and "crime" *could* I write about? I came up with three things. 1) The way Tokyo is portrayed in 1980's cyberpunk as a high-tech utopia/dystopia. 2) High-school themed anime of the 1990's. (I watched a lot of Ranma ½ in college. I mean *a lot*.) 3) The amazing all-girl punk-pop band Shonen Knife.

Right. What happens when I smoosh those things together? Well. When people say reading this story feels like binge-watching a million hours of anime, that makes me really happy.

The Mind is Its Own Place

I wrote the first draft of this story something like fifteen years before it saw print. I submitted it, it made the rounds, got rejected a dozen times, and I put it away as a failure. Trunked it.

Years later, I looked at it again. Turns out I'm a better writer than I was back then. I knew how to fix it. I stripped out pages of extraneous exposition and description, focused more on the character, cleaned it all up. And it sold—it appeared in *Asimov's Science Fiction*.

Even though it took a long time for this story to come into its own, I've never stopped thinking about it and the world, a space-faring system in which interstellar navigation runs the risk of injuring navigators in strange, literally mind-bending ways. I'd been reading about neuroplasticity—the ability of the mind to change, to physically alter its own pathways in response to damage, or sometimes just by thinking about it. The way some mental illnesses (like obsessive-compulsive disorder) are caused by literal breakdowns in the physical pathways of the brain. Also, conditions which affect perception (like synesthesia) or conditions in which communication between the mind and body breaks down. Heady stuff. It's been pointed out that the structure of the universe resembles a collection of neurons. Throw in some fractal geometry. What if, what if… Mind you, this isn't hard science so much as a philosophical meditation on the way that so many of the scientific concepts I read about seem to connect to each other and fold back in on themselves in ways that reveal patterns to me. This is a thought experiment.

This is also the back story for a novel I'm working on right now. More on that in a bit.

Dead Poets

Another anthology assignment, from Jonathan Strahan this time: time travel romance. I had recently stumbled on the poetry of Frank O'Hara for the first time and became obsessed. While O'Hara doesn't appear in the story, the idea—of falling madly in love with a long-dead writer just because his work was the thing I needed to read at the right time (seriously, go read "Why I Am Not a Painter." Knocked me to the floor)—was something I thought about a lot. The poet who does appear in the story, sixteenth-century English poet Sir Thomas Wyatt, was another obsession of mine, when I was eyebrow deep in Renaissance studies in college. So yeah, the story is about that, and a lot of other things besides. I've written a number of stories now with main characters who are English professors (see my novel *Questland*). Paying tribute, I think, to the alternate timeline where I took that route. This is a pretty personal story. I majored in English, and I did it for love, for the actual physical emotional rush I get when I read good words, especially good words that were written hundreds or thousands of years ago. I love feeling those connections across time—and that's how I hooked into the anthology's theme.

We Take Care of Everything

This was originally published in three parts, in three different connected anthologies about the rise of a dystopia, life in a dystopia, and how the dystopia is overcome. (*The Dystopia Triptych*, edited by John Joseph Adams, Christie Yant, and Hugh Howey.) My favorite thing about this is it's barely science fiction.

After spending of a lot of time on game apps and Duolingo, I became a bit hypersensitive to the mechanics of "gamification." It's how these apps keep your attention with reward levels, points, competitions, and literal bells and whistles that spur dopamine rushes. "Just one more level," I think, and then suddenly two hours go by. It's insidious— and it's engineered this way on purpose. It goes beyond phone apps. I've heard news stories and eyewitness accounts from friends about programs some corporations have adopted wherein employees get rewarded with points they can then cash in for stuff. Again, it's about the dopamine rush, like little mice clicking the button for pellets. Then came news about a certain large monopolistic corporation suggesting that it wants to provide housing for employees, build company towns, and here we go. We're being programmed and we hardly notice. We keep pushing those buttons for the little pellets, and…it's not great, y'all. Corporations are using technology to mold our behavior and lock us into systems that benefit them and not us. This isn't the future—this is already happening. It's been happening for years.

The first part of this story got my single greatest editorial comment of my career so far: "Holy fuck kill me now."

The Outlaws of Barnsdale

You ever see *The Adventures of Robin Hood*? The one with Errol Flynn? The classic Robin Hood story that still, eighty years on, ends up at the top of every "best Robin Hood" list? The last scene is Robin and Marian joyfully running off into the sunset after Bad Prince John has been slapped down and exiled for his misdeeds— Except in the actual history, just a couple of years after this, King Richard dies and Bad Prince John becomes Bad King John and Robin of Locksley, as one of the barons of England, will need to swear fealty to him for real. Huh. How do these sworn enemies get along? Answer: they don't, and Robin is one of the barons who forces John to sign the Magna Carta in 1215. Gosh, sometimes history just works out so nicely for the stories we want to tell! Even better, John's heir, who will be Henry III, is just a bit younger than I imagine Robin and Marian's children would be.

I've wanted to write about Robin and Marian's children ever since.

This idea sat in my files for twenty years before I found my way into an actual story. (Ideas and stories are not the same thing. Stories need characters, plot, tension, meaning, and so on.) Watching a couple of truly wretched recent Robin Hood movies also served as motivation. In 2020, I published two novellas, *The Ghosts of Sherwood* and *The*

Heirs of Locksley. My elevator pitch: They're Robin Hood's kids! He's underage Henry III! Together, they solve crimes! Anyway, I had this whole potential mystery series on my hands, with these kids running around solving murders in medieval England, Brother Cadfael style.

The publisher decided not to continue with the series, so I haven't gotten around to writing the murder mysteries, but I'm not quite ready to leave these characters behind. At the end of *The Heirs of Locksley*, Robin and Marian's eldest daughter Mary marries the man she was betrothed to. What happens next? I sent her to Barnsdale because that's the location of the original Robin Hood stories. Really, this is just a nice little side quest for her. I wanted to see a bit of her married life, and how she carries her legacy with her.

Historical note: I found Mary's husband by searching through the list of rebel barons mentioned in the Magna Carta—these would have been Robin's friends. One of them, Robert de Ros, had a son around the right age, William. So I borrowed him. William's mother, Isabelle mentioned in the story, was the illegitimate daughter of King William the Lion of Scotland. I've possibly done her a great disservice by portraying her being so mean, but I have to think she was just a tad frustrated, getting married off to some minor Yorkshire lord

This collection is the first time this story has been published.

The Huntsman and the Beast

Genderflipped Beauty and the Beast. I was frankly shocked it hadn't been done before, or often, really. I'm pretty sure I wrote this fairly soon after seeing the live-action version of Disney's *Beauty and the Beast* with Emma Watson and Dan Stevens. I'm a little bit obsessed with Dan Stevens and you can safely cast him as Jack in the story in your head.

The challenge on this one is the gender politics of it all, and I shook those up quite a bit. This isn't really the same story, because in the original, the Beast deserves his punishment for his cruelty, and his challenge is to learn humanity from one that he loves. Like in a lot of fairy tales, the gender roles are traditional—the woman represents civilization, domesticity. It's women who must temper the aggression of men, to reinforce the domestic sphere. Yeah, whatever.

The idea of a man taming a woman in that way…it seems less about taming and more about subjugation, doesn't it? It's *Taming of the Shrew*, isn't it? That wasn't a story I wanted to tell.

In my story, the Beast doesn't deserve her punishment. She's not punished for cruelty, but for not submitting. For not being domestic. She's trapped by the expectations of her society. She needs to fall in love, yes, but what does that mean here? Her challenge isn't to submit, but to recognize when someone comes along whom she can trust. Jack's the right one because he recognizes what she's been through and supports her. In breaking the wizard's spell, they also subvert it, and that's a better story for me.

I admit Jack is a very ideal hero, exactly who the Beast needs. But what else is fiction for?

The Burning Girl

The Norman Invasion of 1066, but with superheroes. That's it, that's the story.

Well, I mean, of course there's more than that. I was doing a ton of reading on English history from the Norman Invasion through the reign of King John, in preparation for writing my stories about Robin Hood's children. The thing about the Norman Invasion: on paper, it shouldn't have happened. William the Conqueror should not have been able to make it happen. He was a bastard son and whatever resources he had he seemed to gather through sheer charisma…and changed the entire course of European history for the next thousand years as a result. But…what if he had superheroes? What if he was the guy who decided to use people with superpowers instead of burning them as witches? Boom, alternate history. Actually, it's a secret history— the history happens the way it does in our world, but for different, fantastical, reasons. It just seems too convenient that the arrow went right into King Harold's eye at the Battle of Hastings. What if it had help?

This was another idea that I had to mess with for a while before the story arrived. I started a couple of different versions that fizzled. I kept trying to make Gilbert the main character. (Pronounce it the French way, Jil-BEAR.) Then I figured out I needed to use a superhero story structure, not just the idea of superheroes. It's basically The X-Men, right? Joan thinks she's alone, and outcast—and then discovers her found family. Her voice came through, then, and held the whole thing together.

I had so much fun with this and want to write more with these characters.

To the Beautiful Shining Twilight

This is very much a story about being the age I am rather than the age I was. About being in my forties, looking back at the me in my twenties who worked at the Colorado Renaissance Festival, and just feeling tired.

That came after the initial idea, though.

So this one time my friends and I were in downtown Denver and stumbled on a funky coffee shop none of us had ever seen before (and we haven't been back since), that wasn't just a coffee shop, it was also a used bookstore and comics shop and had vintage records and mismatched furniture and was basically like five of our favorite things mashed together. Clearly, it belonged in one of those early 90's rock-n-roll elf novels so many of us were obsessed with. So I got an idea for a rock-n-roll elf story.

But of course mine isn't anything like those stories. My friend, writer James Van Pelt, calls this a "Carrie Vaughn story." Take a trope, and then…just kind of keep asking questions about it until you've gone way past what anyone really wants to know. Take the trope and wonder…what about twenty years later?

I'm constantly asking that about epic fantasy stories, in which the characters tend to be young, in their twenties, going out and saving the world and all that crap. What do they do next? What does retirement look like? And do they have PTSD? Oh, probably. I have some ideas.

Entanglement: Or How I Failed to Knit a Sweater for My Boyfriend

This one's another good example of how things get smooshed up in my head and turn into something unexpected.

I knit. I'm a competent knitter, not a great one, and that's fine. (I'm competent enough that I offered gloves as one of the rewards on the Kickstarter campaign for this book and had a lot of fun with that. It was also an excuse to buy new yarn. Not that I need an excuse…) I like to knit. It activates a different part of my brain than writing does, I like using my hands, and I like making something solid and concrete that I definitely know when it's finished. Unlike writing, which takes a long time and is, as has been said, often abandoned rather than finished. There's a lot to love about knitting and I put a lot of that in the story. Textile arts in general are just great. They're one of the oldest technologies we have, and some of it hasn't changed much in that time. I also spin wool on a drop spindle, which people have been doing for twenty thousand years. The symbolism of knitting is powerful. Remember those pink hats at the Women's March? Remember Madame Defarge in Dickens' *A Tale of Two Cities*? Anyway. It was inevitable I'd eventually write about knitting.

And then I read this one fanfiction where it took all the characters from that show I love and put them in the modern world and made one of them an angel and made them fight demons and— That story lived in my brain for a long, long time (during the pandemic, my coping mechanisms were fanfiction and hyper-fixation), and I started writing about angels as a result. But, you know, my version.

My version of angels is heavily influenced by Milton's *Paradise Lost*. After the fall and all that. Angels are veterans and they're tired, you know? Oh, and also Lovecraft? Yeah, let's add in some cosmic horror. Sounds good.

The Lady of Shalott

The traditional version of "The Lady of Shalott" is a terrible story and a terrible poem and I fixed it. Once again, with cosmic horror. Cosmic horror fixes everything. Or unfixes it maybe?

Okay, backing up, this is the Arthurian story of the lady locked in a tower, cursed that she may never look upon the outside world or something bad will happen. But lo, one day, she looks, and sees the most handsome knight ever, Sir Lancelot, riding by, and woe betide! She leaves the tower, gets in a boat, and dies. That's it.

I hate this story. It makes no sense. So I made the curse a real actual curse. If she looks out the tower window something really, really bad will happen. Cosmic horror bad. It makes the story so much more interesting. You want a curse? I'll give you a curse. Fortunately, the story was a good fit for the anthology, *Swords V. Cthulhu*, edited by Molly Tanzer and Jesse Bullington. This story has both.

Fact: the more I worked on this the more Sir Lancelot sounded like John Cleese and I decided that was okay.

Sidekick

This is a superhero story, but I don't think it started out that way. It's my take on a classic trope, waking up in a hospital with no memory of what happened, with nefarious goings-on that follow. But I wanted it to be funny. (In putting this collection together, I realized I use that trope a lot. I should probably think about why that is.)

I don't suppose this story *needed* to be a superhero story. When I put a character in a confusing situation where she has to try to figure out what's happening, I suppose the answer could have been something other than *superhero*. But would that have been as much fun? I think not.

I spent eight years as the administrative assistant in a small accounting firm, and many of my stories draw on that. Both accounting, and the weird little quirks of working in an office. (The heroine of my superhero novels *After the Golden Age* and *Dreams of the Golden Age* is, in fact, an accountant, which according to her superhero father is actually worse than her not having powers.) One of the quirks of working in an office is how frequently the high-powered executive who is nominally in charge doesn't actually know how the day-to-day routine of their own business runs. They might be extremely skilled and knowledgeable about their area of expertise. But holy cow, don't ask them to change the toner cartridge in the copy machine. Superheroes probably need secretaries but no one talks about that, do they?

In fact, this heroine draws on a lot of my personal experience because she's both administrative assistant *and* an English major! But I have not read *Finnegans Wake*.

Origin Story

I really do love writing about superheroes. I particularly like trying to replicate cinematic action in prose and making it epic. I think I did a pretty good job with the opening scene in this one. I also like the interiority of writing about superheroes, which we don't get in the movies or TV. What the characters are thinking, how they feel, their general outlook.

I tend to write more about average people who live in superhero worlds than the heroes themselves. I like reading them too—one of my favorite comics is *Marvels* by Kurt Busiek and Alex Ross, which tells the story of the whole Marvel Comics timeline, but from the point of view of an ordinary photojournalist. It's great. It's also what I think about when writing yet another set of superhero stories, my work for *Wild Cards*, the shared world series edited by George R.R. Martin and Melinda Snodgrass. What does reality TV look like with superheroes? What's it like being a kid in this world? What's it like buying groceries? What are the gossip magazines like?

This situation in this story—running into an old boyfriend who is now a supervillain— just seemed obvious, something that's bound to happen in a world full of superheroes. Having the boyfriend be the villain rather than the hero seemed more interesting—more surprising.

And yes, I do think Mary and Jason find a way to be together after their chance meeting.

Techhunter appears in the written but as-yet unpublished third novel in my superhero series that starts with *After the Golden Age*. I'm working on getting it out there. Stay tuned.

Bonus Note

If you're starting to think that a lot of my writing is connected, you're right. Once an idea or a world gets into my brain, it often stays there and spins out more stories and characters. On top of this, I'm really lazy about worldbuilding. Why come up with multiple space worlds or superhero worlds when I can just set all the stories in the same one? Also, I often have questions that don't get answered in a novel I'm writing because there isn't room or it isn't relevant. Short stories are *great* for that. It's part of why I write so many of them. And on that note…

Where Would You Be Now

This is a prequel to my novel *Bannerless*. That novel has a character named Auntie Kath, who is very old, blind, and the very last person in the community to remember what the world was like before a catastrophic economic and environmental collapse.

This story is about Kath as a young woman, in the early years of that collapse. Her parents have died. She's been taken in by friends of her parents, doctors at a women's clinic in a town that has otherwise burned down. *Bannerless* doesn't really describe the apocalypse—I figure we've all seen and read enough about that. I wanted to get past that story to dig into the community that has rebuilt after. But this story gave me a chance to show what that transition might have looked like, and the decisions the community made early on that determined the makeup of the world decades later.

Here's my whole take on apocalypses: They don't wipe the slate clean. It's not going to be a Mad Max bondage gear free for all. Those folks stockpiling guns are going to be so surprised when they end up dying of staph and cholera, which guns can't do anything about. I was on a panel once where it was pointed out that the people who survive an apocalypse are going to be the ones who wash their hands.

Communities will survive. Communities will save what they can. What those communities decide to save will determine what their world looks like after. This community is trying to save medicine and cooperation. If you want to see how it turns out, read *Bannerless*.

Sinew and Steel and What They Told

I'm just going to say it, even though writers aren't supposed to have favorites, even though we like to talk about how our stories are our children and we can't possibly have a favorite—this story is my favorite.

I love Graff.

What else can I say... Writers sometimes talk about characters taking over the story and having lives of their own. For as much as I've written, I've only had that happen a few times. Kitty, my werewolf talk-radio host, was very alive to me. I often couldn't predict what she was going to say, I'd be writing and this crazy stuff would just come out of her mouth. Enid from *Bannerless* was alive to me. The minute she showed up I knew I was going to write novels about her, she just had so much to say.

Graff is a whole other level of that. Kitty and Enid, I can see parts of myself in them, I can work out where they came from, and I usually have pretty good control over their stories—I know where they're going and can craft their arcs, even as they feel alive in those stories.

Graff is a gay hedonistic cyborg and I have no clue where he came from. I don't know what of me is in him. He really did just show up, and I've been writing about him ever since. I know a lot about him, but he feels like his own person in a way no other character has for me. Writing those stories—it's his voice, not mine. I talk to him, and he talks back.

This isn't entirely true—I do have some idea of where he came from, and the ideas that went into the mix had been percolating for a long time. But I never would have predicted what came out of that brew. I wrote the first draft of this story in one sitting. I hardly ever do that, but Graff was ready to speak and all I had to do was let him.

I owe quite a bit of inspiration to Martha Wells' Murderbot series, which I love. I love the voice—we almost don't care what happens, as long as we get to stick with Murderbot for the ride, because it's just that distinctive. Murderbot got me thinking about cyborgs and various cyborg tropes. But it also made me appreciate what a strong voice can do for a story.

Usually, we meet cyborgs and androids who aren't human but want to be, or have difficulty interacting with humans. (Commander Data, hello.) Well…what if we met a cyborg who was indistinguishable from human beings? Who really likes people and gets along great with them? Who rather than struggling to be human is actually kind of a hedonist? Who's all about emotion and feeling even more than unaugmented people? And then what if his reason for being a cyborg is about all that—emotion, experience, physicality, connection? Science fiction has had this idea that we can upload brains, that minds and bodies are somehow separate. Well, science is figuring out that we're not. We're as much our hormones and neurotransmitters and gut biome and the experience written into our bodies as we are what's in our brains. You can't separate them.

And that's Graff.

A bit more about what Graff means to me: This story was published on Tor.com in February 2020. The pandemic was crashing on us, and my grandfather went into hospice care after a cancer diagnosis. It was just me and my dog Lily in lockdown. Grandpa died at the end of March. Then Lily died in August. Things got hard and weird and stayed that way for years. I put my head down and kept going because what else could I do? I sewed masks. Read a couple million words of fanfiction. I wrote.

Graff kept me company through it all. Between 2020 and the first half 2023 I wrote five more short stories and a novel about him. I'll probably write a lot more about him before I'm finished. Remember a few paragraphs up when I said I was expanding the ideas in "The Mind Is Its Own Place?" I like smooshing ideas together. It's lots of fun, so I'm smooshing that background into Graff's novel. You heard it here first.

One More Note

Thank you for reading. Writing brings me joy, and finding an audience expands that joy, so thank you.

Carrie

About the Author

Carrie Vaughn's work includes the Philip K. Dick Award winning novel *Bannerless*, the New York Times Bestselling Kitty Norville urban fantasy series, over twenty novels and upwards of 100 short stories, two of which have been finalists for the Hugo Award. Her most recent novel, *Questland*, is about a high-tech LARP that goes horribly wrong and the literature professor who has to save the day. She's a contributor to the Wild Cards series of shared world superhero books edited by George R. R. Martin and a graduate of the Odyssey Fantasy Writing Workshop. An Air Force brat, she survived her nomadic childhood and managed to put down roots in Boulder, Colorado. Visit her at www.carrievaughn.com.

For writing advice and a behind-the-scenes look at Carrie's writing process, subscribe to her Patreon.
www.patreon.com/carrievaughn